TRIBAL

KEVIN WALSH

outskirtspress
DENVER, COLORADO

Tribal Bonds

v3.0

Outskirts Press, Inc.
http://www.outskirtspress.com

Paperback ISBN: 978-1-9772-0756-2

Editing by Edward Schnur.
Interior image design by Ron Haley.

PRINTED IN THE UNITED STATES OF AMERICA

To my Irish friends and relatives, both here and gone:

Thank you for your humor, the gift of gab, and the love of language. Thank you for your steadfast support and loyalty. We're not perfect, but as tribes go, you have to admit, we know how to have a good time.

Thank you JoAnn for your encouragement to start writing. I will be forever grateful.

I am dedicating this book to Patrick and Michelle, who could not have made their father prouder.

TABLE OF CONTENTS

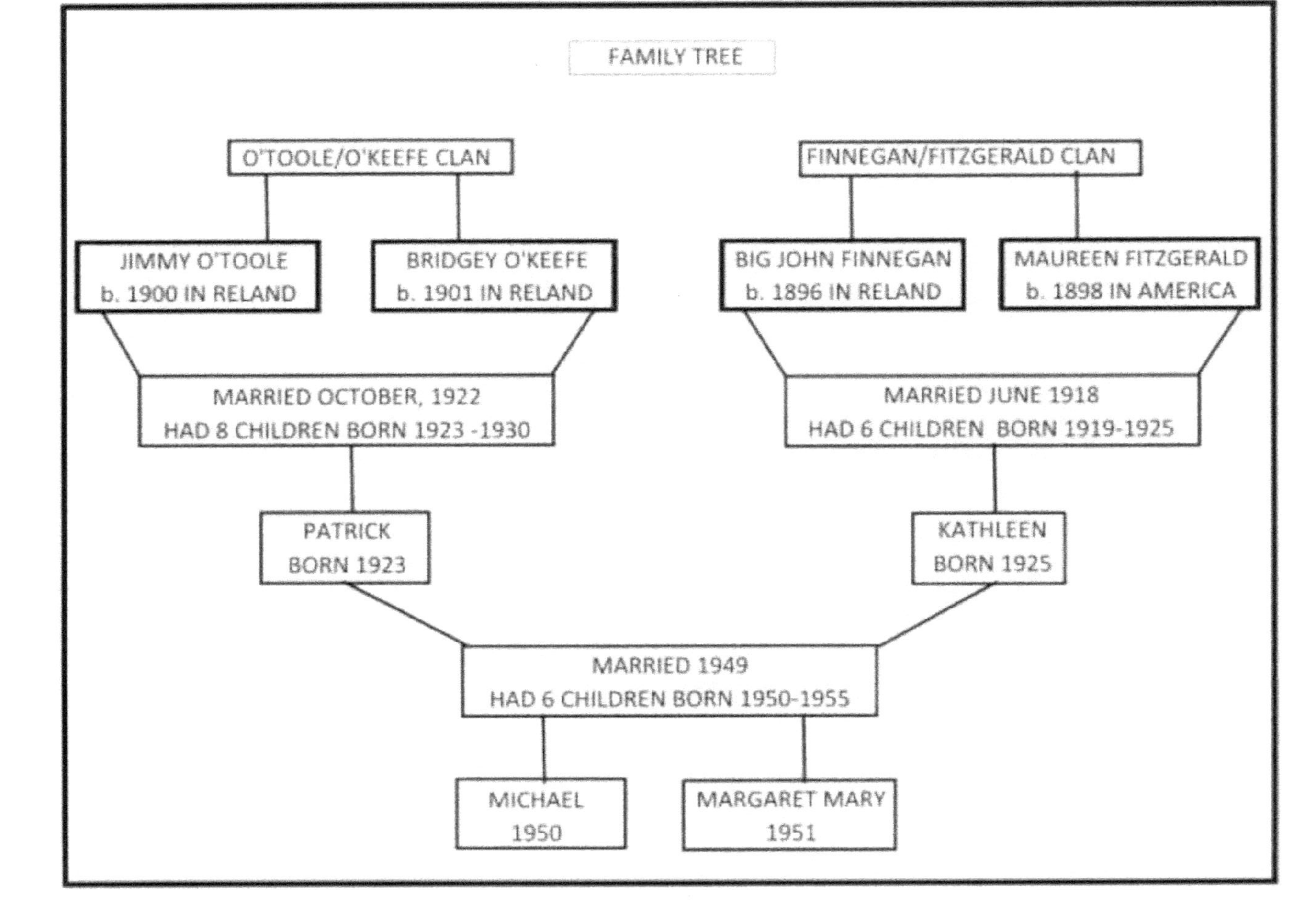
FAMILY TREE
O'TOOLE/O'KEEFE CLAN
FINNEGAN/FITZGERALD CLAN
JIMMY O'TOOLE
b. 1900 IN RELAND
BRIDGEY O'KEEFE
b. 1901 IN RELAND
BIG JOHN FINNEGAN
b. 1896 IN RELAND
MAUREEN FITZGERALD
b. 1898 IN AMERICA
MARRIED OCTOBER, 1922
HAD 8 CHILDREN BORN 1923 -1930
MARRIED JUNE 1918
HAD 6 CHILDREN BORN 1919-1925
PATRICK
BORN 1923
KATHLEEN
BORN 1925
MARRIED 1949
HAD 6 CHILDREN BORN 1950-1955
MICHAEL
1950
MARGARET MARY
1951

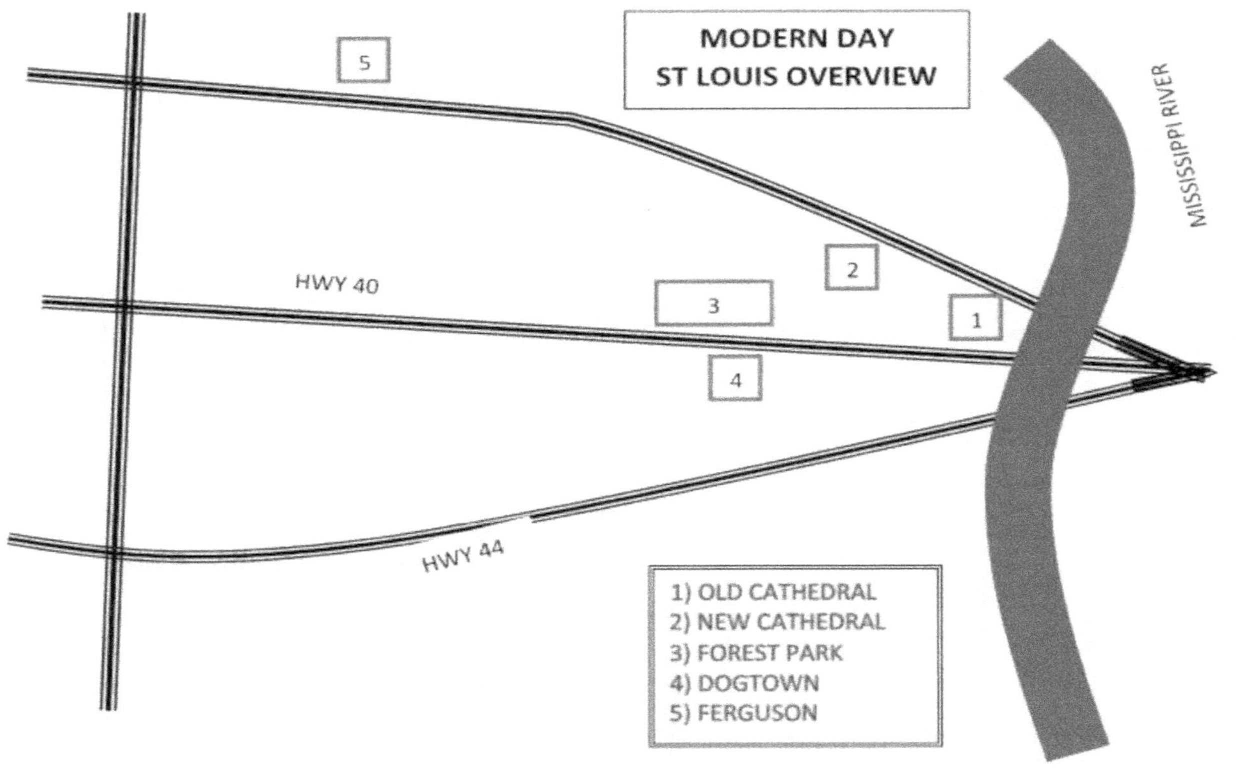
MODERN DAY
ST LOUIS OVERVIEW
MISSISSIPPI RIVER
5
2
3
1
4
HWY 40
HWY 44
1) OLD CATHEDRAL
2) NEW CATHEDRAL
3) FOREST PARK
4) DOGTOWN
5) FERGUSON

ST LOUIS CENTRAL CORRIDOR

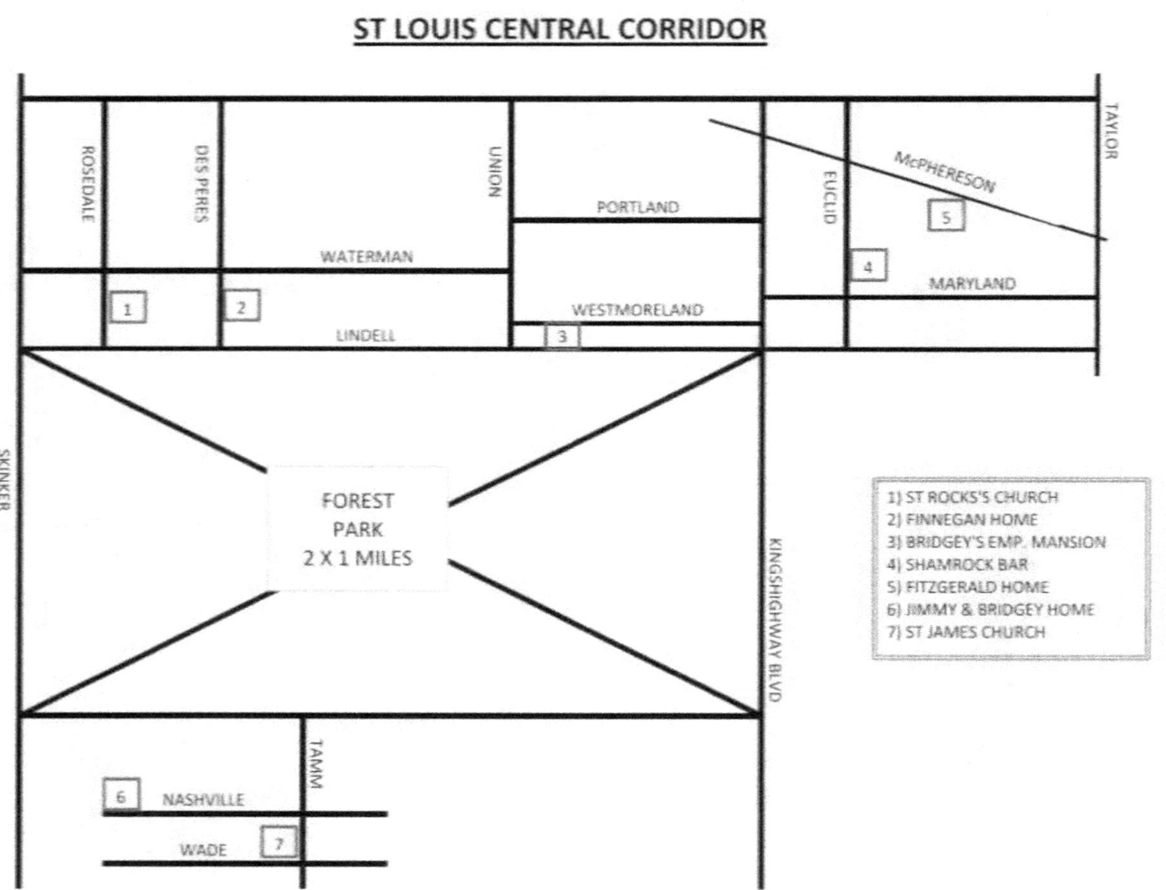

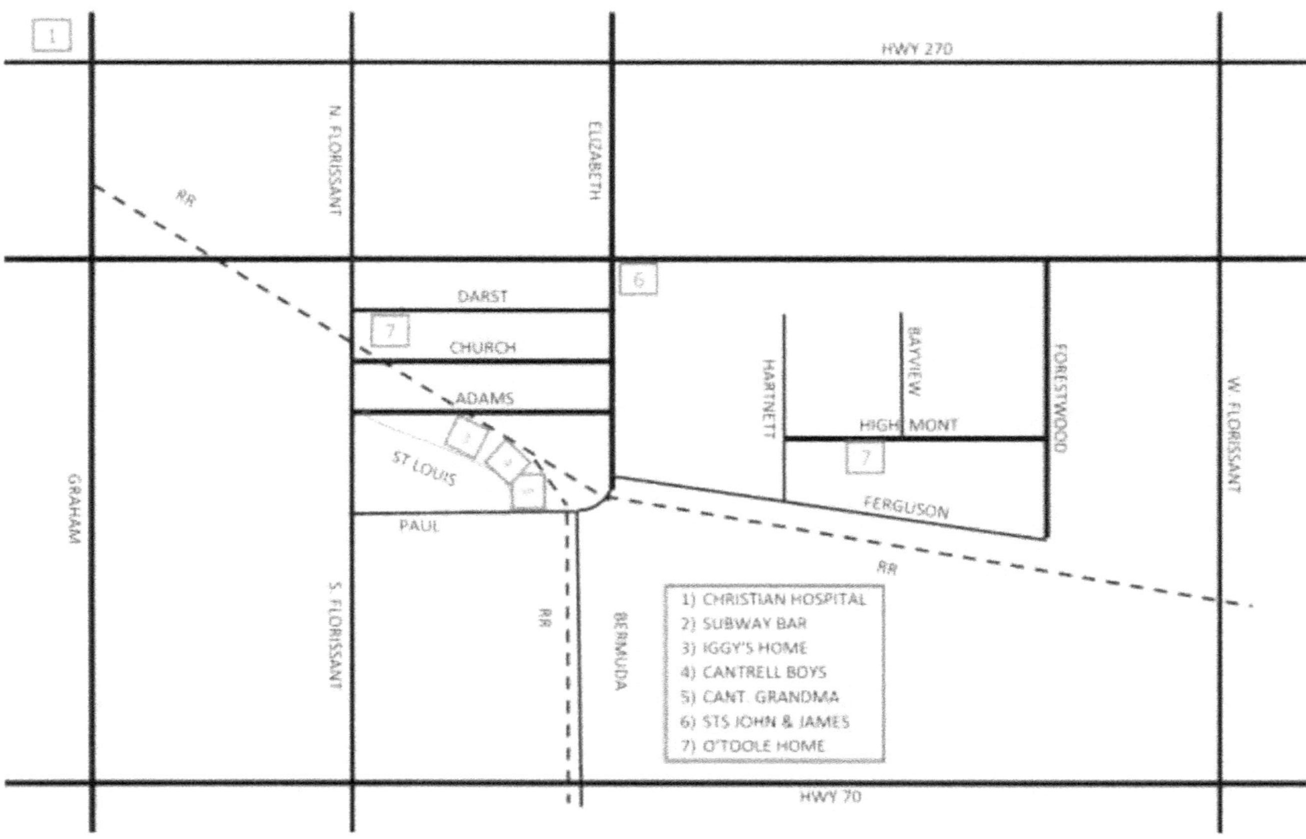
FERGUSON
HWY 270
N. FLORISSANT
ELIZABETH
RR
DARST
CHURCH
ADAMS
ST LOUIS
PAUL
HARTNETT
BAYVIEW
HIGHMONT
FORESTWOOD
W. FLORISSANT
FERGUSON
RR
GRAHAM
S. FLORISSANT
RR
BERMUDA
1) CHRISTIAN HOSPITAL
2) SUBWAY BAR
3) IGGY'S HOME
4) CANTRELL BOYS
5) CANT. GRANDMA
6) STS JOHN & JAMES
7) O'TOOLE HOME
HWY 70

Prologue

The End of the Road

OCTOBER 18, 1994; 3:00 PM

Margaret Mary O'Toole was walking across the grounds of the institution that her brother, Michael Patrick O'Toole, called home. The grounds were always meticulously cared for and gave visitors a definite sense of order. It made her feel so peaceful and serene looking at all the trees that had been planted on the front grounds. There was a straight line of hundred-year old trees on each side of the wide concrete walk, stretching one hundred yards or so from the entrance of the main building to the visitor parking lot. In addition, there were dozens more scattered about the huge front lawn. Sycamores, maples, oaks, hickories and many other varieties had been planted to put on a brilliant, festive autumn show.

Margaret Mary was strolling slowly, enjoying the fall colors and kicking at small piles of leaves. She wondered how many people over the years had walked this same path, looking up at the trees when they were feeling happy and carefree. She also wondered how many had taken that same walk, staring only at the aged, pocked concrete when they felt life's burdens weighing on their shoulders. It was definitely 'Boo Radley' weather, she smiled to herself, remembering how much she and Michael had loved reading *To Kill A Mockingbird* in grade school. The telltale cool breeze picked up occasionally, scattering the leaves as the sun dipped in the clear blue afternoon sky.

It was one of those perfect, Midwestern fall days that brought back lots of pleasant memories. "Sweater weather's here!" her mom used to say before they left the house for school this time of year. The vibrant palette of color in the trees jumped out at you against their cobalt canvas. Someone with a creative, careful vision had arranged this gorgeous setting. Someone had taken extraordinary effort and time to plant this scene she was enjoying today. She marveled that a hundred years before, armed with dozens and dozens of saplings, the anonymous landscape artist had started to align, dig and plant, knowing he would never get to see his mature masterpiece.

So many people go unheralded for their efforts thought Margaret Mary. They sacrifice and work hard for the benefit of those sometimes not even born yet. Her thoughts turned to her own parents and grandparents who had toiled, persevered and deferred their own gratification so that their children and grandchildren would have an easier road to travel; the proverbial 'better life'. They wanted us to be able to look up at the trees, rather than having to always look down at the sidewalk, she mused.

As if tapped on the shoulder by a hidden force, Margaret Mary whirled around to look back at the four-story stone edifice of the building she just left. Over to the right on the third floor she saw Michael waving. Smiling, she waved back. She sensed him watching before turning. Twins are like that, having a sixth sense about each other. They were so close as kids that this ability developed between them, even though they were only Irish twins as the saying goes, having been born just ten months apart. Michael was forty-four now and she was forty-three.

They may as well have been twins, she thought to herself, as close as they had always been. She could still make out Michael's smile through the old wavy leaded glass. It was the same smile that always made her feel safe, warm and loved growing up. It was the same smile that had made the girls swoon at the Saturday night Catholic Youth dances. It was the same smile that had sadly disappeared for a long time. Turning slowly back towards the parking lot she felt a wave of melancholy at the unpleasant memory.

Melancholy...the unwanted by-product of being an Irish Catholic she thought to herself as she opened her car door and got in behind the wheel. She wondered if it had formed in their DNA as a result of their ancestors living for centuries in isolation on a cold, rainy island. Layer in the virulent strain of Catholicism practiced in Ireland, and you have a perfect recipe for "the melancholy".

Like so many others of her generation, Margaret Mary had a love/hate relationship with the Catholic Church. She loved the beauty and pageantry of its sacramental and liturgical celebrations. She loved the stained glass, the statues, the smell of candles and incense, and the sounds of its uplifting hymns, especially the Gregorian chants. She felt closer to God in a Catholic church than anywhere else on earth. Most of all she loved being a part of the Church's loving, compassionate presence with the sick and the poor.

The flip side of their Irish Catholic upbringing placed the heavy burden of sin on their shoulders, forcing far too many of them to walk through life with their eyes on the pavement. Sadly, so many could only find the joy of gazing up at the trees and sky with the liquid assistance of their precious distilleries and breweries.

Sitting in the front seat, she could feel these thoughts starting to bring her mood down. Margaret Mary said aloud for no one to hear, "You are doing it again! You're going to ruin a great day! Just start the goddam car and head home!"

Part I

Dirt Roads...and Floors

CHAPTER ONE

On a cool, cloudy Saturday in late October of 1922, James Michael O'Toole, age 22, married Bridget Maureen O'Keefe, age 21. Margaret Mary's paternal grandparents were wed at St. James the Greater parish by their pastor, Father William Kelly. All three of them had been born and raised in Ireland. The parish was located in an area of St. Louis, Missouri called Dogtown, on the near south side of the city. It butted up to the massive St Louis jewel called Forest Park, where the 1904 World's Fair had been held. Dogtown was a poor rough neighborhood inhabited mainly by the Irish, with a few Germans and Italians in the mix as well.

There were more than just a few tongues wagging at the news that Bridgey, as she was known, had actually married Jimmy O'Toole. The older women of the parish, who often acted as surrogate mothers to the young immigrant girls, had hoped she would catch the eye of an educated Irish gentleman. Jimmy O'Toole was anything but that for which they had hoped. He was a hard-drinking bricklayer's laborer, a hod carrier, who was prone to fighting.

There was a deep divide between the "lace curtain" Irish and the "shanty" or "dirt floor" Irish in America. The "lace curtain" Irish were accused of putting on the airs of the wealthy Prots, short for Protestants, because of some education, fashionable attire and a well-maintained home. The "shanty" Irish by and large were laborers and maids, dressed as such, and usually rented their living space. Nonetheless, in times of strife with a perceived enemy, they could be counted on to unify under their common religion and ethnicity. An educated Irish Catholic shopkeeper could be counted on to side with an Irish Catholic laborer over a German Lutheran lawyer every time. Irish Catholics had a psychological bond that unified them against all comers.

Bridgey had come to America at age seventeen, as a smart, quick-witted girl, who turned more than a few of the young men's heads on Sunday mornings, when she made her way up the center aisle to receive Holy Communion. She was sweet, well-mannered and educated through the eighth grade in Ireland. She was fair skinned and had the bluest eyes this side of Dublin, as the saying goes, and her brown hair showed a tinge of red when hit with sunlight. She was tall for a girl, maybe five feet seven, with long slender legs that carried her quickly with bounce and purpose. She loved to talk, laugh and tell jokes, having the gift of gab ready at her disposal. Had she been a man she would have been an excellent candidate for politics.

Bridgey and her sisters worked as maids and lived in mansions on Westmoreland, a gorgeous boulevard just north of Forest Park where St. Louis' wealthiest citizens lived, along with their Irish maids, cooks and nannies. On Sunday mornings, the three of them would walk a little over a mile across Forest Park to St James the Greater for Mass. It was their only day off, and the girls loved wearing their good dresses and shoes while catching up on all the week's events and gossip. Not having eaten anything since before midnight, so they could receive Holy Communion, they always stopped at McGuire's Bakery after church, for a piece of breakfast cake, to stop their stomachs from rumbling on the long walk home. They also liked to complain and giggle about the long-winded fire and brimstone sermons from the old pastor, Father Kelly.

The sisters were very close and cherished their brief time together. The oldest, Maeve, who worked for the Schultz family, had sponsored Bridgey to come to America after securing her a job with the Teasdales, five mansions down. Bridgey had done the same in turn for their youngest sister, Mary Margaret, at the Stogsdill mansion just two more doors away.

The wealthy families preferred the Irish girls as servants, rather than say, Italian or Polish girls, for a variety of reasons. First, they already spoke English, which made training and communication much easier. Also, unlike most of the young female immigrants, they had been educated usually through the eighth grade, by the nuns in Ireland. The fact that they could read and write, made them even more valuable to the family, because they could tutor the children in the evening after the cooking, cleaning and laundry were finished for the day.

America for the girls was even better than they had hoped. They left wretched poverty, to live in opulent surroundings with central heat in the winter, and cool breezes blowing through their sleeping quarters on the third floor in the summer. It was said you could tell how long an Irish girl had lived in America by the width of her hips. They could not believe how much food was available to them after the family ate their meals. For the first time in their lives they could eat as much as they wanted. Life was good.

In addition, the girls were in awe of the soft comfy beds in which they slept, with clean white linens and soft pillows to boot. But even this paled in comparison to the nearly sinful pleasure of soaking in one of the beautiful bath tubs. It was all a far cry from their lives in Ireland, where one slept on a thatch mat on the floor and cleaned with a wet towel while standing in a large wash tin. It seemed that in America, the servants lived better than anyone they knew in Ireland. They never mentioned it to their employers, but the fourteen to sixteen-hour days as a maid or cook, was a walk in the park compared to squeezing out a living on a potato farm.

Unfortunately for the young Irish men in America, it was a nearly impossible task to woo these young women from their palatial surroundings, with clean linens, soft beds, limitless food, and Sunday off. Most of the men were laborers who could barely pay rent and feed themselves. Truth be told, it wasn't only the paltry wages that kept them broke, but an overzealous penchant for beer and whiskey on payday. Many of these young women turned their noses up at these raucous suitors. Unlike the girls, many of the young men had little or no education upon their arrival in America. Often, they had been put to work in the fields as boys both at home, and for neighboring families, for wages that were given to their fathers. School was a "lace curtain" luxury for most boys.

Jimmy O'Toole fit the mold. He was a brash, tough talking hod carrier who could barely write his name on the back of his paychecks. Every other word out of his mouth was "fook this" and "fook that" and he was completely unconcerned who his language offended. In addition, it was rumored that Jimmy had left Ireland with the law at his heels. No one seemed to know the exact nature of his purported crimes, but he did like to sing ballads praising the heroics of the IRA late at night in his favorite drinking establishments. If one was to stay even later at the bar, Jimmy was likely to share his theory that Jesus' admonishment to "turn the other cheek" was actually a lie made up by the rich Prots to keep the Irish Catholics as docile as possible so they could steal the island's riches. Finally, he was adamant that Jesus was Catholic himself and would have never instructed his people to lie down and take a beating at the hands of the "fookin' Prots".

Jimmy was what they called a black Irishman in those days, because of his dark hair and swarthy appearance. If he didn't speak with such a heavy Irish brogue, making him almost unintelligible in non-Irish circles, a passer-by may have taken him to be Greek or Italian. They would have been well advised to keep such an appraisal to themselves, as Jimmy would have considered either reference an insult. Depending on the level of whiskey or stout consumed that evening, he might answer the insult with his fists.

Jimmy carried an eighty-pound hod full of mortar up and down ladders for a living. Consequently, his huge arms, shoulders, chest and neck looked almost cartoonish on his five-foot five-inch bowlegged frame. Buying clothes to fit was almost impossible. Shirts that would fit his chest had arms six inches too long, and his pant legs always needed to be rolled up at the bottom, leaving him looking disheveled. No one who knew Jimmy ever made fun of his appearance though. They had all witnessed the poor, broken and bleeding souls who had made that mistake being carried out of the neighborhood taverns. He was short tempered, tough and seemingly oblivious to pain. It was always a wiser choice to call Jimmy O'Toole your friend than to call him anything else.

CHAPTER TWO

Like many of the Irish parishes in those days, St. James the Greater held socials, or dances, as some called them, once a month in the parish hall which doubled as the school cafeteria. The socials were held on Sunday afternoons after twelve o'clock Mass. It was a chance for the young men and women of the parish to meet in a chaperoned setting. Sunday worked best because the bars were closed, and the men had little else to do. For most of the women it was their only day off.

Usually one of the younger assistant pastors was there to chaperone along with a couple of the school nuns. The nuns used a ruler to keep a respectable distance between the dancers, since only their hands were allowed to touch. The young priest stood guard at the door to send any young man who showed up drunk on his way. The gatherings were rather subdued under the ever-watchful eye of the priest. Whatever he told them to do or stop doing was the law. The Irish held such reverence for the beloved priests, it was no different than if Jesus himself was giving them direction.

On a cold, snowy and windy Sunday in February of 1922, Jimmy O'Toole sauntered in to the social looking nervous, angry and out of place. The angry look was brought on not only by a throbbing headache left from the revelry of the night before, but also the fact that he had drank every last drop of his whiskey and had no "medicine" left to heal his head. Within a minute of arriving, under the hard stare of young Father Timothy Kerrigan, Jimmy was already regretting his decision to accompany his boarding house roommate, Liam Dugan, to the hall. The priest had reluctantly let the two disheveled men in, cautioning them first that he would be keeping his eye on them.

Jimmy and Liam shared a ten by ten room furnished with a bed, a chair and a small table. The house was owned and operated by a rotund, crabby widow by the name of Katherine O'Hare. For the most forlorn looking arrivals from the old country, she allowed two of them to share a room, and rent a fold up cot for the outrageous sum of twenty-five cents a week extra. There was no meal-sharing though, as every man had to pay for his own before the week started, or he didn't get to eat. Liam and Jimmy had become fast friends while talking to pass the time at the labor pool. They were both working as hod carriers, trying to save enough money to rent a real apartment. They were failing miserably because of their fondness for spirits of the unholy variety.

It wasn't long before Jimmy spotted the O'Keefe sisters laughing at a table across the hall. What he didn't know was that he and Liam were the subject of their laughter. They had their dirty flat caps pulled down low, and their work dungarees rolled up high to keep them out of the snow. They had their hands tucked deep in the pockets of their heavily patched work coats and were rocking back and forth to try and get warm after the long walk to the church. The girls were laughing because they noticed that the men were inadvertently rocking in unison, in time to the music. Jimmy and Liam watched as the sisters took turns dancing with each other, feeling even more miserable now that they realized they had absolutely no idea how to dance.

The tallest of the three women caught Jimmy's eye though. He liked the way she tossed her head back when she laughed and liked the sound of her laugh even more. More than a couple of times, he happened to notice the curve of her hips under her flowered dress, as they swayed back and forth to the music. He always averted his eyes quickly though, remembering the priest's admonitions in Sunday school that to stare was a serious sin of lust.

Jimmy was extremely thirsty due to his monumental hangover, and on the first of his many trips to the punch bowl, he passed the sisters' table. The tall one had the bluest eyes he'd ever seen. They seemed to sparkle. He made sure to slow down as he passed their table on each trip, so that he could take in the scent of the lavender soap around them. On each trip to the punch, he made up his mind to say something to the tall one, only to pass by silently each time.

Finally, after Father Kerrigan announced the last dance, Jimmy told himself he would time his next trip to meet the tall one as she was leaving the dance floor. He had settled on just saying 'hello'. He timed it perfectly, but not a sound passed his lips. After filling his glass for the fourth time, he strode back toward Liam across the hall, mad at himself for not speaking, and relieved that he had not spoken and made a fool of himself.

A few feet past the O'Keefe girls table, he heard a female voice say, "Hey you! You with the punch!"

Jimmy turned and realized it was the tall one with the blue eyes calling to him. Jimmy O'Toole, a man who feared no man, felt his hands shaking and perspiration break out on his forehead.

"You must have been feeling no pain last night, if you need four big glasses of punch to get through an hour here," Bridget called out loudly with a smile.

"I...I...I..." stuttered Jimmy.

"Aye...Aye...Aye...so you're a sailor, are you?" she chided, as her sisters giggled.

Jimmy hated that he became so tongue-tied when he became nervous, which was basically any time a young woman began talking to him. Now he had three of them staring at him, grinning and waiting to see what he would say or do. The sisters could be a formidable bunch when they were together, and they knew it. Jimmy knew that if he did speak he would be the butt of more jokes from these uppity girls, because of his unusually thick Gaelic brogue. The isolation of growing up on a farm far from any city, where the adults only spoke Gaelic, left some immigrants like Jimmy struggling to communicate clearly in English.

Bridgey's rarely exposed soft heart, for some reason, allowed her to feel sorry for this bow-legged creature in front of her. Feeling his obvious discomfort, she turned quickly and told her sisters to go on ahead, that she would catch up. Seizing the moment, Jimmy turned and started walking back towards Liam, when she called out again and walked towards him.

"Don't run off punch boy, we were just having a bit of fun," she said noticing the first time the shaking and the sweat. Liam watched wide-eyed.

Turning, he haltingly replied "I...I...know." Jimmy felt he had never seen a girl as beautiful as this one. He even felt a bit light-headed as she neared and the scent of that lavender soap clouded his brain.

"So, you're a man of few words, are you?" Bridgey asked, quieter now, not needing to impress her sisters anymore.

"I...I...could ah...could I...would you like an escort home?" Jimmy blurted, surprising himself with the sudden burst of chivalry.

"Now you know, Father Kerrigan has an eye on us now, and old Father Kelly will be out on the sidewalk when we leave. He gave a sermon recently about the sinful possibilities when a man and woman spend unchaperoned time together," she added.

"Fook them," Jimmy blurted, his natural response to being told what to do, overriding the decorum needed at the moment. And then immediately, "Sorry, sorry girl...it slipped...I don't usually..."

"Well I don't believe I could walk around in public with a man who talks that way, and about the priests to boot!" she said crossing her arms in front of her. At the same time, the surge of manhood in his voice and demeanor intrigued her. In that moment, the flash in his eye and the set of his jaw quickened her heart beat.

For a few seconds, they just looked at each other. "I am truly sorry," said Jimmy noticing a sudden twinkling in those gorgeous blue eyes.

Then suddenly she whispered, "We can't leave together. Meet me at McGuire's bakery in a little while." Then she turned quickly, walked to her table, got her coat and left.

Jimmy stood motionless for a moment, not believing his ears. As he looked around the hall, it was nearly empty. Father Kerrigan, from across the room, was watching, as always, and Liam was fidgeting against the wall where they had spent the dance. He couldn't wait to hear what Jimmy and the tall girl had said to each other.

"What did she say?" asked Liam, followed by, "What did you say?"

"Not now Liam," Jimmy replied tersely. "I've got somewhere to go now so you're on your own." With that he was gone, leaving poor Liam standing there with his mouth open.

The conversation was taking a dramatically different tone two blocks way with the O'Keefe sisters.

"You have got to be kidding Bridgey!" exclaimed her oldest sister, Maeve, "he looks like a bum!"

Mary Margaret chimed in, "Bridgey, you said we were not going to get involved with these drunken laborers. You said we deserved better!"

"He is just walking me home girls. Jesus, Mary, and Joseph, you would think he proposed!" shot back Bridget.

"He can't propose if he can't even talk!" Maeve said through clenched teeth.

"Please don't Bridgey," added Mary Margaret.

The three of them were still huddled in front of McGuire's' when Bridget spotted Jimmy coming towards them. "He does talk, and he's coming now. Go on now the both of you," Bridget pleaded.

With eyes rolling, and short glances over their shoulders at Jimmy, they walked away. Bridgey looked again at the bow-legged, shabbily dressed Jimmy O'Toole walking towards her, and secretly wondered if her sisters had been right.

"What is your name girl?" asked Jimmy as he approached.

"Bridget O'Keefe, but everyone calls me Bridgey," she answered.

"Would you like a cinnamon roll Bridgey?" he asked.

"That would be grand. Thank you. And what is your name?" she added.

"Jimmy O'Toole," he answered. A minute later, handing her the roll, he asked gruffly, "Where are we going?"

"This way," she said pointing north up Tamm Ave. towards the park.

With that, they started walking about two feet apart, with her eating and Jimmy staring at the ground. He never said a word unless there was a question directed to him. By the time they crossed the park a half hour later, Bridgey was laughing to herself that Jimmy's less than sparkling personality was definitely going to keep him out of politics.

This same scenario played out every Sunday over the next couple of months. Jimmy never danced, he delivered punch to the sisters and answered all questions with one-word answers. Bridgey would leave with her sisters, and he would stack chairs for a while before meeting her at McGuire's. Then Jimmy would walk in silence as Bridgey chattered about her week and her sisters.

The meeting at McGuire's had to stop after one Sunday when Bridgey arrived to find Father Kelly, their pastor, in the bakery. She nervously ducked around the side of the building until he left. When she peeked around the corner a few minutes later, Jimmy was standing out front looking worried. When she walked up he asked where she had been, and she explained about the unexpected appearance of their pastor.

"We've got to meet farther down Tamm. We can't afford to have Father Kelly catch us together. I couldn't stand it. He'd never look at me the same again. I'd have to confess our meetings to him in confession. Let's go," said Bridget.

"Don't you want a cinnamon roll, girl?" asked Jimmy.

"Not today. This upset my stomach," Bridgey replied as she turned to start walking.

During these same months, Jimmy told Liam and anyone else who would listen, except Bridgey, that he felt like the luckiest man on earth. He couldn't wait for Sunday afternoons, for those long walks with this beautiful blue-eyed woman chatting to him and smelling of lavender. It was like a special dream come true.

Neither of them realized that something would happen very soon that would seal their bond forever.

CHAPTER THREE

It was the Sunday before Easter, with warmer air, sunshine and flowers starting to replace the months of winter doldrums. As usual, Bridgey left the dance first, and headed down Tamm a couple of blocks past the bakery to wait for Jimmy. What she did not know was that Jimmy had been grabbed by Father Kerrigan, along with a couple of other men, to move some desks around upstairs in the school. About the time he thought he was free, the priest then ordered them to move a couple dozen boxes from the school to the church basement for storage.

Saying no to a priest certainly meant more years in Purgatory, and Jimmy quietly mused that he definitely did not need more years heaped on at this point. He was literally running up and down the stairs, sweating profusely, but there seemed to be no end to the boxes. He had never been late with the cinnamon roll for his beloved Bridgey, but he knew she would understand, as he sprinted down Tamm. He hoped she wouldn't be mad at him, but mainly he hoped she had not left for home. As he glanced at the clock in McGuire's, though, he realized he was an hour later than usual.

As usual, Bridgey sent her sisters on their way, becoming more and more impatient as her usual ten-minute wait morphed into thirty and then forty-five minutes. Impatience turned to anger as she stared down Tamm. If he stopped at a friend's or didn't feel well and went home, wouldn't he first come and tell her? She too had started to look forward eagerly to their Sunday walks. Sure, Jimmy was not a slick talker or dresser, as her sisters constantly reminded her, but she had begun to really admire the fact that he was so kind and reliable. But, reliability seemed to be a fading trait at the moment. He always listened attentively to her stories of life in a mansion and laughed out loud when she did her pompous imitations of her wealthy employers. Most importantly, he looked at her with adoring eyes. She loved how his stare made her feel. She had even been thinking of taking his hand as they walked through the park today.

Hurt and angry, she started north on Tamm towards the park. The dances usually ended around three-thirty, and it was nearly four thirty now. In addition, the skies had become overcast, and thunder in the distance hinted at a coming storm, making it look even later. Now she was going to have to walk through the park alone, which she had never done before. Forest Park, for all its expansive beauty, was home to any number of transients and low lifes who lived in the woods and under bridges. Walking around the park instead of through it, would add about four miles to her trip, and with her church shoes on she would certainly be crippled by the time she got home. In addition, she needed to hurry home, because it was her Sunday to be on evening call, in case the Teasdales needed anything from the kitchen that night. Walking around the park would make her late, and that was unacceptable not only to her employer but to the other women who expected to have the night off.

"He better have a damn good excuse!" she muttered to herself as she quickened her pace.

As she entered the park, there were lots of couples and families leaving, not only because it was nearing the dinner hour, but by now there was no denying the storm building in the west. Bridgey could feel her palms sweating and her heart beating faster as she walked quickly, with her head down. Deep breaths were not helping. She knew what was causing her anxiety, no matter how hard she tried to forget. Situations like this, where she felt vulnerable, always brought the memory back.

That terrible day in Ireland, Bridgey stayed late at school to help the sisters. She loved school, and she loved the nuns who taught her the last eight years. She knew this was her last year of school, so she spent as much time helping them as she possibly could. This particular day she had lost track of time and stayed longer than normal. With the sun dipping, she knew she would have to hurry to escape her father's temper for being late to supper. Jogging now, she thought she might save some time by taking the alleys behind the shops in her village. Their family farm was on the opposite side of town from school.

Suddenly, a form lunged at her from the right from behind some piles of trash, slamming her against a brick wall. She had the wind knocked out of her and hit the back of her head on the wall, before falling in a heap to the ground.

She was gasping and trying to see but her vision was blurred. She was being dragged across the alley by her arms behind the trash pile. The attacker raised her uniform skirt, then roughly pushed her legs open and began raping her. Dazed, breathless and unable to see, she never moved, never cried out, never really saw him. It was over almost as quickly as it started. Finally, he stood, zipped up and walked away, leaving her there with the trash. As her senses began to return, she slowly made it to a seated position trying to make sense of what had just happened. She touched the back of her head and felt blood. She felt terrible pain between her legs. Her head hurt and throbbed.

She had struggled to her feet with wobbling legs and started home. She was really going to be late now and that meant answering to her father. What was she going to say? Sobbing, she remembered poor Molly, her friend three doors down who had come home dazed, with her dress torn, the year before. Molly told her father that she had been raped. Like most Irish fathers at the time, he could not bear to have a daughter at home who was no longer a virgin. He had screamed at her that she must have brought it on herself and that it was her fault. He even slapped her. He had screamed that no decent man would marry her now.

Like other girls before her, Molly disappeared a few days later. Their parish priest, Father Brannigan, had come in the middle of the night for her, at her father's request. He took her to the Sacred Heart sisters who ran a large industrial laundry in the next county. The Sisters did laundry in Ireland for state institutions like prisons and orphanages, and had agreed to take Molly, and girls like her who had been labeled temptresses. Some girls were sent there for the crime of being pregnant and unmarried, and some for being mentally "unsound".

At the time, being locked behind the walls of the laundry was deemed a much better life for these girls than their only alternative, which was to work as a prostitute in larger cities like Dublin. They were often incarcerated for life in the laundry for the sin of lust. Ireland's beloved Catholic Church, had determined that this was surely the most humane way to keep these sinful girls off the streets, so they could not tempt more boys and men to commit adultery. It was felt that the girls and society were both better off.

With the memory of Molly foremost in her mind, she had begun to straighten and brush off her clothes and arranged her hair over the wound in the back of her head. She had also begun to construct a tale to explain being late. In the coming weeks and months, she tried to push the incident from her mind. She never even asked for help or guidance in the confessional every Saturday, being terrified that the priest would recognize her voice. She did not want to disappear like Molly. She begged for God's forgiveness also, wondering if somehow, she may have been at fault. Why else would the priest have taken Molly away?

Back in the park, Bridgey struggled to keep these memories at bay, but it was no use. She walked quickly, head down, on the well-worn path she and Jimmy had used every Sunday. The path wound around a large hill to the left and then bent around a wooded glen.

As she rounded the bend, she heard male voices talking and laughing in some sort of Slavic language she did not understand. When the three of them spotted her, they got quiet and started smiling and spreading apart from each other. Their clothes were dirty and they each held a bottle of liquor.

Immediately, Bridgey knew she was in trouble and started shaking and sweating while walking forward more quickly. They started calling to her and making kissing noises. Quickly, one man moved behind her, one moved to her left, and one jogged up in front of her on the path.

"Get out of my way you filthy bastards!" she cried out and started to run to her right.

Right away, the man behind her grabbed her hair and yanked her off her feet. The one in front picked her up legs and the three of them carried her towards the woods. When she screamed, one of them slapped her so hard she went into shock. Not again, not again, God help me, she thought. Dazed, and feeling everything was in slow motion, she felt one pull her arms over her head and kneel on them. The other two were raising her coat and dress and pulling at her underclothes. She closed her eyes and began to silently pray the "Hail Mary".

Suddenly Bridgey heard a sickening thud followed by another, and then the hands of the men came off her. When she opened her eyes, the one kneeling above her had blood streaming down his face and he was falling slowly towards her. She rolled quickly to her right just as he fell where she had just laid. It was then she heard the unmistakable voice of Jimmy O'Toole screaming, "Run, Bridgey, run!"

Scrambling to her feet, she began to run barefoot as fast as she could. When she glanced over her shoulder, she saw Jimmy struggling with the two much larger men.

Again, she heard him scream, "Run, girl, run!".

Bridgey didn't stop until she was all the way to the north border of the park along Lindell Blvd. It was nearly dark now and all she could do was sob and cry, while crouching behind a row of bushes.

"Hail Mary, full of grace, the Lord is with thee..." she started, followed by "Our Father who are in heaven, hallowed be thy Name...". "Jesus, Mary and Joseph help us..." she sobbed.

What to do? What to do? Her mind was racing with worry about Jimmy. She hoped no one would spot her from the boulevard, crouching there crying, barefoot, and dirty. She was staring back into the gathering dusk of the park from the bushes. Then after what seemed like an eternity, she spotted Jimmy limping towards her down the path.

As she ran towards him, she realized how badly beaten he was. One eye was closed and bleeding and blood was running from his nose. He was holding an obviously broken arm against his chest and trying to not put any weight on his right leg.

"Dear God Jimmy!" she exclaimed.

"We've got to go somewhere Bridgey...somewhere we won't be seen...right now girl!" Jimmy said through clenched teeth.

"I can take you into the garage behind where I stay," she answered, "come along I'll help you."

"Hurry now," Jimmy grimaced, "there is going to be trouble."

CHAPTER FOUR

The two of them stayed in the shadows after crossing Lindell. They turned into the alley behind the mansions on Portland Place, moving as quickly as Jimmy could in his condition. To anyone who noticed, it looked like a poor woman helping another drunken servant home.

Bridgey used her key to get in the rear gate. She knocked at the door leading up to the living quarters above the garage. Hurry, hurry she thought, before one of the Teasdales spots us. A few seconds later, the round, kind old face of the groundskeeper, Seamus Donnelly, appeared. Seamus didn't say a word when Bridgey asked him to help. Between the three of them, they got Jimmy upstairs and on to Seamus' bed. Turning to her, Seamus said quietly, "Bridgey, get me some old towels or rags and a sewing kit. I'll get some water."

When she returned, Seamus was already holding a bottle of whiskey to Jimmy's lips, in anticipation of the pain he knew was coming when he stitched the wounds and set the bone. Seamus had seen plenty of young men in this condition in his youth after riots in Belfast. He set to work, patching Jimmy up the best he knew how. "Bite down on this boy," he ordered Jimmy as he handed him a rolled up wet towel. "We don't want the Teadsdales to hear us now do we?" he grinned. "Bridgey, you go on now before they miss you."

Jimmy nodded and took a long drink from the bottle before biting down on the rag. By midnight, Jimmy's patching was over, and he was thankfully asleep when Bridgey came up the stairs. Seamus agreed to let Jimmy stay until he could get around, as long as Bridgey told no one he was there. "I can't afford to lose this job, girl. I'm too old to go back to construction, and I'm still sending money home to my wife and kids," he told her.

"I won't tell a soul, Seamus," she answered. "You have been so kind. Thank you so much! You never even asked what happened," she added."

"I don't need or want to know, girl," he replied.

On the following Tuesday afternoon, Seamus walked west on Portland to the market on Union Blvd to get another bottle of whiskey for Jimmy and pick up a newspaper. When he got back home and opened the paper, his eyes immediately went to a headline on the front page. It seemed two mounted police officers were making their way around the park at eight o'clock Monday morning, when they heard a moan from the woods next to the north/south path. Upon investigation, they found three Russian seamen, two of whom were dead, and one clinging to life.

The article went on to describe how the first man had the back of his head bashed in, probably with a stone, and was clearly dead. The second dead man had his windpipe crushed, and an ear bitten off. The third was clinging to life but would be unable to identify his attackers since his eyes had been gouged from their sockets. He told police they had been the victims of an unprovoked attack by a group of drunken Irishmen. Within forty-eight hours, he was dead too, having lost too much blood from his various wounds.

A week later Seamus and Jimmy made their way down the garage steps and into the alley, well before dawn, so as to not be noticed by the Teasdales. Seamus helped him walk, as they made their way east to Kingshighway, to catch the bus south to Dogtown. Jimmy thanked the kind, older man and Seamus wished him well. Fifteen minutes later Jimmy was on the bus heading south. Two blocks later a forty-year old uniformed beat cop by the name of Donovan got on the bus at Lindell, as he sometimes did to cut down on walking. With the park bordering the street on the right, he only needed to walk back on the east side of Kingshighway to satisfy his duties, on this part of his beat.

After pleasantries with the driver, Donovan walked back in the bus to check on who was out and about at this early hour. Jimmy, sitting on the right side of the bus, caught his eye, and peaked his interest. The cop could see Jimmy was hunched down, with a hat pulled low, trying not to be noticed.

"Good morning!" Donovan called at Jimmy.

As Jimmy raised his head to address the cop, he showed the bandage covering his left eye. The cop noticed as he got closer, that Jimmy's right arm was not in its sleeve and there was a makeshift cane leaning on the seat.

"What does the other guy look like?" Donovan asked, now at Jimmy's seat.

"Nothing like that officer. I'm a hod carrier. I took a bad fall a while back," said Jimmy.

"My cousin Tim Donovan is a hod carrier. Hard work to be sure. Do you know Tim?" asked the cop.

"I don't believe so," answered Jimmy, quickly adding, "I'm getting off here," as they came up to Oakland Ave. As Jimmy limped off the bus, he thought to himself that a cop getting on the bus was the worst of luck. Donovan hopped off the bus right behind him. He didn't let on, but he knew Jimmy from the taverns of Dogtown.

"Good luck to you, boy!" offered Donovan.

"Thanks, I'll be fine," answered Jimmy.

As Donovan turned to walk across Kingshighway, all his cop instincts were alerted. First, Jimmy clearly did not want to be noticed or make small talk. Second, every cop in the precinct was on alert for any suspects in the killing of the Russians. Third, not a single man had sought treatment at the hospitals nearby, and certainly after a battle like that, they could not have been unscathed. Fourth, not a single bartender had heard anyone bragging of the fight after drinking too much. Many crimes like this were solved in just such a manner. A drunkard could not help boasting.

CHAPTER FIVE

Later that afternoon, as officer Donovan was filling out his paperwork for the day, he motioned to his boss, forty-five-year-old Lieutenant Tommy Fitzgerald, to come by for a chat away from prying ears. In a confidential manner, he relayed the details of his encounter with Jimmy on the early morning Kingshighway bus. Donovan, who was bucking for sergeant, knew Fitzgerald was just as ambitious as he was, and would appreciate quietly getting exclusive knowledge of the event. Fitzgerald was a tall, nearly six-foot, broad-shouldered cop, who had worked his way off the street with a no-nonsense approach to both arresting and interrogating criminals.

"Do you think he was telling the truth about having an accident at work?" Fitzgerald asked Donovan.

"No way Lieutenant," he answered briskly. "He was trying to hide his face when I first got on the bus. As I got closer you could tell he had been in a fight by the way his face was scratched and banged up. He had an ear stitched up, his knuckles were raw, his right arm was in a sling and he was using a cane. The wounds were old and it looked like an alley doc worked on him."

"You say you've seen him around?" asked Fitzgerald.

"Yeah, he's a mick named Jimmy something or another. Got a reputation as a brawler. He sounds like he just got off the boat last week," answered Donovan.

"Half the population of Dogtown fits that description for Chrissake. What's your gut feeling? Could this guy be our mystery park killer? We need to clear this case to get those three dead bohunks off the front page."

"Well if he was there he wasn't alone. This character is just a little shit. No way he killed those three Russians himself."

"Truthfully, I don't give a damn about these Russians," Fitzgerald said quietly so no one could hear them. "Its just that it would be a big feather in our cap, the way the papers are tooting their horns about the lawlessness in the city ever since this thing broke. I wish they wouldn't even let these smelly bastards off their ships. They're godless heathens on their way to hell anyway as far as I'm concerned. A little sooner rather than later doesn't bother me a bit," he finished, grinning.

"I'm with you a hundred percent on that note Lieutenant," Donovan grinned back.

The police had not released the information yet about finding a pair of women's shoes at the crime scene. Remembering them, Fitzgerald went on, "Why don't you nose around Dogtown tomorrow in your street clothes and see if you can get a last name and an address on this Jimmy character. Then see if anybody knows if he has a wife or girlfriend somewhere. No matter what we think of the Russians, if this Jimmy was involved we need to find out. We can't have some little drunken mick from Dogtown thinking he can just kill anybody he wants to. Why we'd have chaos over there," he laughed, "as if it isn't bad enough already when they get paid on Fridays."

"I'm on it Lieutenant," Donovan answered crisply. He knew that getting to do a little detective work on the side was the boss's way of saying thanks for bringing him the information, rather than taking it upstairs. Besides, anything to get away from being a beat cop for a day was always a good thing.

The next day, Donovan didn't have to work too hard to get his answers. The barkeepers on Tamm Ave all knew Jimmy once he was described to them and gave Donovan his last name and address. Donovan had been acting like he wanted to hire Jimmy to do some work for him, and since his beat kept him out of Dogtown, they were unaware he was a cop.

He gave the same song and dance to a couple of old ladies who worked at McGuire's bakery. They had disapproved of Bridgey meeting up with Jimmy out in front of the bakery and filled Donovan in on their relationship. They knew both of them from St. James. Their own distant memories of clandestine meetings with boys, that their families would never have approved of, kept them from reporting Jimmy and Bridgey to the old pastor, Father Kelly. It didn't take Donovan much longer to find out that Bridgey worked as a maid over on Portland Place. These two knew as much about the women in Dogtown as the barkeeps knew about the men.

When Donovan got back to the precinct house, he looked carefully at the precinct map on the wall. Sure enough, if you drew a line from the intersection of Tamm and Oakland to the address where the girl lived on Portland Place, it crossed directly over the spot where the dead Russians were found. Upon receiving this information, Lieutenant Fitzgerald congratulated Officer Donovan on his fine police work, and then immediately began pondering his next move.

Could this little mick be that tough or did he have help? Should he talk to this Jimmy O'Toole first, or try to shake up the girl? At some point, he was going to have to pay Jimmy a visit to let him know he KNEW. He needed to put the fear of God in him, or at least the fear of Fitzgerald, he chuckled to himself. A guy who can fight like this is not going to be easily scared to give up any information. IF this is the guy, he mused.

Even though Lieutenant Tommy Fitzgerald was an Irish Catholic born in Ireland, his parents came to America not long after his birth in 1874, to escape the hunger and poverty still tormenting the island since the Famine in the 1840's. He didn't speak with a heavy brogue like the current wave of immigrants and prided himself on using perfect English. He had gone through the tenth grade in

Catholic school, whereas most of the Jimmy O'Toole types showing up in St Louis were illiterate. Tommy was embarrassed by these new immigrants, and felt he had to work extra hard to not be lumped in with them by those in positions of power. He called them by the derogatory term "mick" even though he was Irish. He stopped short of using the term "paddy", which for an Irishman was the same as calling a black man a "nigger". In earlier times the Irish were stereotyped as drunken, illiterate brawlers. Therefore, the police vehicle used to carry them off to the police station would forever be called a "paddy wagon".

Tommy would not have been caught dead living in Dogtown, with all of its rowdy bars. He, and his wife, Colleen, lived in a neat two-story brick home on McPherson, in the Central West End of the city, just northeast of Forest Park. It was a little pricey on a police lieutenant's salary, but Tommy was not above taking an "anonymous" gift here and there, to spring a few of the wealthy elite's black sheep from jail. In the process, he had also made some important and powerful friends.

Forest Park itself was a rectangle about two miles long and a mile wide, bordered by Kingshighway Blvd. on the east, Skinker Ave. on the west, Lindell Blvd. on the north, and Oakland Ave. on the south. Where you lived in relation to the Park said everything about your socioeconomic status in St Louis. To the immediate north were the stately mansions where Bridgey and her sisters worked. To the immediate south, was the rough and tumble streets of Dogtown where Jimmy lived. To the west, the park was lined with a variety of houses of worship and stately homes fronting an affluent neighborhood. To the east there were apartment buildings, hotels, hospitals and less affluent neighborhoods.

There was a definite class order among the Irish. Tommy was "lace curtain", and Jimmy was "shanty" Irish. The latter group was a constant embarrassment to all the Irish who had worked so hard to earn a respectable place in society. The fact that Tommy's parents were in exactly the same position as Jimmy at one time was completely lost on him.

A couple of days later, Lieutenant Fitzgerald, the newly promoted Sergeant Donovan and a young beat cop, paid a visit to the boardinghouse where Jimmy lived. The beat cop was left on the front porch to block any visitors from coming upstairs. The lieutenant wanted to let this low life know, that he knew about everything that went on in his precinct. After a few gruff pleasantries, the lieutenant told Jimmy that he knew he had a girlfriend named Bridgey working on Portland Place. He asked him, if the old pastor at St James, Father Kelly, knew that he and Bridgey were parading about town without an escort. He told him that he had called the other precincts, and none had heard of any construction accidents around town. Finally, he dropped the bomb, by saying that the three dead Russians were found along the path that Jimmy and Bridgey took every Sunday from Dogtown to Portland place.

Even though Jimmy's brain was spinning wondering how this pompous cop knew so much about his life, he didn't so much as flinch or blink. Tommy didn't know it, but Jimmy had taken his share of beatings by cops in the old country, and never gave up a bit of information. Also, Tommy didn't show it, but so far, he was impressed by this little man's lack of fear. It was time to ratchet up the intimidation. Donovan had positioned himself standing behind Jimmy who was seated in the only chair in the room. Tommy was standing in front of him.

"We have witnesses that saw you on that path two Sundays ago," stated Tommy, leaning in towards Jimmy, "what did those Russians do anyway; insult your precious Bridgey?"

"I've never met a Russian in me life."

"Don't get cute asshole! And how 'bout you explain looking like you got run over by a train. How did those knuckles get raw from a fall? How did those four perfect nail scratches get across your cheeks?" Tommy asked, getting louder and closer.

"How is it you cops are so smart? Is it something you eat? I'd love to get some if you could spare a bit," taunted Jimmy.

Slowly, Tommy started to take a billy club from Donovan. "Okay tough guy, before I leave you are going to tell me what happened."

Once again Jimmy just grinned.

"First who was with you? Who helped you beat these Russians to death?"

"Just my guardian angel and a couple leprechauns, lieutenant."

With that the club came down on top of Jimmy's head, making him dizzy enough to start to fall out of the chair. Donovan straightened him up for Tommy and held him in place. It was obvious that he was already so weak that any more pounding would just make him pass out. The pain in Jimmy's head was excruciating but he once again managed a rueful smile, angering Tommy even more.

"Alright tough guy. When you wake up the next few days with that head pounding, I want you to remember this face," Tommy hissed, almost touching Jimmy's nose with his own. "I am not a guy you want to fuck with, you dumb mick!"

Neither of them would forget that day. They didn't know it, but their paths would cross in little and big ways in the future. For his part, Tommy Fitzgerald found himself actually admiring Jimmy O'Toole's toughness. He never begged for mercy or cried out when Tommy hit him. He was the type that just might have killed those bohunks all by himself.

As for Jimmy, his basic hatred for anybody in a uniform just got reinforced. He would always tell anybody who would listen that cops were always tough when they outnumbered you and had weapons. At least this Fitzgerald character had not beat him half to death like the Prot police did in the old country. Fitzgerald is going to find out this is one Irishman you don't want to "fook" with, he thought to himself, smiling.

Bridgey continued to nurse Jimmy back to health, along with his roommate Liam, by bringing him food, fresh bandages, and doing his laundry on the sly. No one would ever understand, and she would never reveal, how she came to fall so deeply in love with Jimmy O'Toole. It happened the minute she saw him dragging himself out of the park that night to see if SHE was alright. Jimmy had saved her from getting raped, and who knows what else, while almost getting himself killed in the process. Every time she held his face in her hands she got teary-eyed. She had even taken to kissing him good bye once his lips were not so swollen and sore.

Bridgey knew that she would always be safe with Jimmy at her side. Later, she would learn the reason men had quit smiling at her, and averted their eyes from her, even when Jimmy wasn't around. It was his reputation. Men either respected or feared Jimmy, or both. He was never the least bit violent around her, and in fact was so smitten, that he never even raised his voice to her.

And so, it came to pass, on that Saturday afternoon in October of 1922, that James Michael O'Toole married Bridget Maureen O'Keefe in St. James the Greater Church in the Dogtown neighborhood of St Louis, Missouri. Bridget's older sister Maeve was her maid of honor, and Jimmy's best friend Liam was the best man. Bridgey lit a candle on the side altar in front of the statue of the Blessed Virgin Mary, which was the custom for young Irish newlyweds. They knelt together and held hands as they prayed to the Virgin Mother to bless them with children. Many have mused over the years that in the case of Irish Catholics, they could dispense with this custom, due to their legendary propensity to procreate. But old habits and customs are hard to break.

The few dozens of their friends and family that were able to get off work, followed the couple into the church basement hall, where they had met just six months before. In keeping with the rules set by the old pastor Father Kelly, there was no longer any alcohol served, only punch and cake. He had sworn there would be no more alcohol on church grounds, due to the poor parish's inability to repeatedly repair the damage done by the drunken brawls at such affairs. After an hour or so, the wedding party and guests, with the exception of Jimmy and Bridget, made their way to a succession of taverns in the neighborhood to celebrate well into the night.

Jimmy and Bridget went straight back to their new flat on West Park, a few blocks away, and proceeded to conceive their first-born child, who they named Patrick James O'Toole. Patrick arrived exactly nine months after the wedding, in July of 1923. He would grow up to be a fine young man, who would eventually become the father of Michael and Margaret Mary O'Toole. Eventually, seven more bundles of joy would follow. Clearly the Blessed Virgin heard their prayers.

Part II

Mystical Roads

CHAPTER SIX

Years later, when Grandpa Jimmy O'Toole told Michael, Margaret Mary and their siblings and cousins grand tales of Irish history, they would sit in a hushed wide-eyed circle of wonder. Their paternal grandfather was uneducated in documented history but loved telling his grandchildren the stories he had been told as a child. His audience never questioned his credentials or the facts of his stories. When your grandfather is telling you Irish history at six or seven years old, it is accepted unconditionally as true. It didn't hurt that Grandma Bridgey was often nearby nodding in agreement.

The Irish love stories and revere the art of storytelling. A well told story can take your mind, if not your body, to magical, mystical places of long ago. It was at Grandpa Jimmy's feet that they heard the stories of fairies and leprechauns who lived just out of sight in the forest, and pots of gold that awaited them at the end of rainbows. It was from him they learned of mighty, fearless Irish heroes who slew their enemies and protected the Irish people from harm.

Cynics have made the case that their belief in this sort of folklore made the Irish perfect fodder for their patron St. Patrick and the promises of Christianity, or more correctly, Catholicism. In other words, their willingness and ability to believe in things they could not see made St Patrick's job of conversion much easier. In religious terms, this willingness and ability is called faith.

As the children sat and listened to their beloved Grandpa Jimmy O'Toole, they were captivated by his tales of Irish heroes and heroines and grew up wanting to emulate them. The following is just one of many stories Grandpa told them in his flamboyant manner, acting out some parts and changing his voice to enhance its believability.

'Long before St. Patrick arrived in Ireland, the ancient people who lived there, were proud, fearless warriors who refused to let any seafaring invaders set foot on the island. They guarded their families and their land with a ferocity that went unmatched by any of the great armies in history. Even the Irish women and children fought alongside the men because it was necessary to do whatever it took to defeat the invaders. The key then and now, was to always stick together. Seafaring captains from around the globe have written in their journals, about their unsuccessful attempts to land in Ireland and conquer its people.

One such journal of a Viking sea captain had been found hundreds of years before in a frozen cave in Norway. Irish monks came in to possession of the journal during one of their missionary trips to the European mainland. The Viking captain wrote that as his ship approached the coastline of Ireland, he looked through his eyeglass beyond the sand beach dunes, trees and brush, to see if he could spot any native inhabitants. What he saw startled both him and his officers. In clearings beyond the beach vegetation, there were groups of large, muscled, nearly naked men, who were smearing a dark brown grease all over their bodies. The grease was being scooped from large cauldrons suspended over open wood fires. They were putting the same grease into their disheveled hair, which was hanging past their shoulders to the middle of their backs. Then, they were molding each other's hair into clumps around their faces to resemble something like a lion's mane. The result, gave them the appearance of wild ferocious beasts of the forests and jungles.

When they were done with their bodies they began to swing their spears and clubs wildly at each other in some sort of a frenzied ritual, drawing blood. They seemed unfazed by the pain they were inflicting on each other, as the intensity and screaming built to a maniacal fervor.

The women, who were scantily, yet modestly clad, were much larger and muscled than any women that the captain and his men had ever seen. They had an equally frightening appearance as well, having covered themselves, and their wild unkempt hair, in the same hot grease. Afterwards, the women went about the camp, laying out an assortment of carved, ghoulish weaponry in the shapes of spears, axes and clubs. The most unsettling thing that the captain saw as he watched, was the fact that all the savages, as he called them, appeared to be smiling and laughing as if they were actually relishing the upcoming battle. There seemed to be about a hundred men and women combined.

He wrote that he felt sorry for the poor bastards, since his men would be going ashore covered in body armor and brandishing far superior weapons made of hardened steel. He felt certain that all the savages who did not run in fear, would be quickly and mercilessly killed. After all, his men had been battle tested all over the world by this time and had always been victorious against the native populations. He gave the order to begin dropping the four landing craft, two from each side of his ship. Each of the four boats would carry twenty-five men. An hour later he watched without apprehension, as the four boats landed on the beach, and his men made their way across the open hundred yards of sand toward the brush covered dunes.

He could hardly believe his eyes as that brushy vegetation came alive with what seemed to be hundreds of children, both male and female, firing a torrential wave of small arrows at his men with their smallish bows. Dozens of the razor-sharp arrows found their way between pieces of the warrior's armor, causing both small and lethal wounds. The captain could hear his men crying out in pain and cursing loudly at having been surprised by such an unlikely and unusual foe. As each of the children fired their arrows, they turned and disappeared into the vegetation once again. With rapid precision, the ninety or so remaining warriors from the ship formed three lines of defense, and upon the order of their commander, began to walk in military precision towards the dunes.

The captain raised his spyglass to find none of the natives left in the clearings. They had all disappeared either into the trees or amongst the dunes. As his men trudged up and down the dunes, and towards the thick tree line and vegetation, he and the others on the ship began to hear a wild blood-curdling din from the natives getting louder and louder. The viciousness of the screaming from the male and female voices raised all the hair on the captain's arms and the back of his neck. The sound lasted for the better part of an hour, and then there was silence. Finally, the only the sound remaining was the waves hitting the shore. As darkness began to fall, all that could be seen from the ship was the four landing boats.

Before dawn, fires began to glow on the beach. Certainly, they were being built by his men, the captain thought, signaling that all was well. Instead, the sight that awaited him at dawn was more horrifying than anything he had ever seen in all his days as a seafaring man. The fires were actually being fueled by the four boats his men had used to go ashore, and dozens of spears had been stuck into the sand in a long straight row at the edge of the surf. The spears were adorned with the wide-eyed, bloody heads of his men.

Looking through his eyeglass, the captain watched as men, women and children began emerging from the dune vegetation, covered in dried blood. Some were carrying more heads and began dropping them into a huge pile near the water. Suddenly there was the sound of drums beating and some flute-like instruments being played, as the natives began dancing, singing and beckoning to those who remained on the great ship to come ashore.

The captains last journal entry, was that not a single man in his crew complained when he gave the order to turn the ship back out to sea.'

As Grandpa Jimmy surveyed the wide-eyed stares of his grandchildren, he chuckled to himself that their parents would have a good time getting them to sleep tonight. He remembered how his children had the same trouble when they first heard the tale. Nevertheless, Jimmy felt that learning how any enemy could be defeated as long as they stuck together, was more important than sleep. Truthfully, as far as he was concerned, the lesson from the story was more important than any math or reading lessons the children had in school.

Part III

Paving Roads

CHAPTER SEVEN

John Patrick Finnegan, age twenty-two, married Maureen Beatrice Fitzgerald, age twenty, on a cloudless day in June 1918 in the St Louis Cathedral. The Cathedral was located on a gorgeous mound overlooking the Mississippi River in downtown St Louis Missouri. They were married by Bishop Robert J. O'Connell in grand style before an overflow crowd. The groom, the bride's parents and the bishop were all born in Ireland. The father of the bride was a well-connected St Louis police Lieutenant by the name of Tommy Fitzgerald. He was the same Tommy Fitzgerald who would have that serious conversation with Jimmy O'Toole. He had pulled strings and called in a host of favors to arrange the Cathedral wedding officiated by Bishop O'Connell. John and Maureen eventually were to become the maternal grandparents of Michael and Margaret Mary O'Toole.

John Patrick Finnegan, forever referred to as Big John, was born in Dublin, in 1896. His father owned a dilapidated pub called of course, The Shamrock, in a run-down section of Dublin. He had won the pub in a card game. Big John grew up literally in a boisterous, smoke-filled environment, listening and learning from thousands of saints and sinners. He liked to say that both groups had their share of well-appointed and shabby members.

He came by his nick-name naturally being six feet two, but eventually the name would also have been rightfully dispensed as a reference to his girth. He had a huge head, covered in a thick mass of red hair, which sat directly on a pair of broad shoulders. He liked to tell a gathered inebriated audience that although the Good Lord had not seen to provide him with a neck, he was more than generous in granting extra length in other body parts that proved to be far more valuable, even if not readily visible. Big John was gregarious, with a large booming voice, and an infectious laugh.

His mother was a quiet woman who only set foot in the pub once each day in the morning to extricate enough money from the register to run their home and see that they had tuition for private Catholic school for her only child. The early visit was necessary to beat John Sr. to the register, before he arose, and began his daily schedule of drinking and gambling.

It was a tearful day when Big John, at age eighteen, announced to his parents that he was leaving for America. He had a distant uncle, his father's half-brother, who was going to sponsor him in St. Louis, Missouri. His parents were devastated that he was leaving, but he assured them he would own a dozen pubs in no time at all. His parents, both having experienced hunger as children after the Famine, were quite fearful for their only child's well-being, but they needn't have worried.

Big John arrived in America, and then St Louis, with a perfect blend of personality and life-skills that would serve him very well. In addition, he had a classic education, compliments of the Christian Brothers and his mother, to go along with impeccable array of street smarts learned at the feet of his father's patrons. He was able to top off these fore-mentioned qualities with what the Irish call the "gift of gab", which means he excelled at the art of conversation. His smile and laugh endeared him to most everyone he met.

Big John was eventually known by everyone who was even remotely connected to St Louis politics. He became a classic power broker in the city, yet always managed to stay out of the public eye, meaning the newspapers. Privately he was often urged to run for mayor, but always jokingly replied that he wasn't about to take a demotion. Truth be told, most people would have agreed that he was more powerful than the mayor, and certainly the title would have put constraints on his drinking, gambling, cursing and other enjoyable activities, both legal and otherwise.

The older Big John got, the larger his influence and girth became. Nevertheless, he was always impeccably dressed in tailored suits, looking just as stylish and affluent as any of the moneyed class in town. He eventually opened a tavern which of course he named, The Shamrock. It was said that there was more city business conducted in the rear booth at The Shamrock in a day than at City Hall in a month.

If you needed a job for a sister or brother, so that they could come over from Ireland, Big John could make it happen. The law stated that an immigrant needed a guarantee of a job and a place to stay before he or she could come to America. Needless to say, there were not many Germans or Italians mopping floors, changing light bulbs, cutting grass or picking up trash in the St Louis parks or at City Hall.

Maureen Beatrice Fitzgerald, named for her father's mother, was the only daughter of Tommy and Beatrice Fitzgerald. Beatrice loved being the wife of a well- known police lieutenant, and the respect it brought her. She looked after the family's beautiful home on McPherson in the city's fashionable Central West End neighborhood and raised her five children almost alone. Tommy's job on the police force kept him away a great deal, even as a patrolman, since he had always been ambitious and willing to put in the extra hours to get promoted. Beatrice felt lucky to have such a hard-working husband and never complained of his absence. They had both been born in Ireland to parents who escaped abject poverty to come to America and seek a better life. The Fitzgerald's had two sons who were beat cops and two who were firemen.

Maureen had gone to twelve years of private Catholic girl's schools, followed by a year as a novice with the Sisters of St. Joseph at Fontbonne College. Her father wanted her to be a nun, thereby ensuring that no man but him would ever lay a hand on his only daughter. He should have known that getting a red headed daughter to do anything you ask was a waste of time. So, after she left the safety of the Sisters, Tommy made inquiries and landed her a civil service job in the tax department at St. Louis City Hall. It was here that she met a young, ambitious floor mopper by the name of John Patrick Finnegan.

A couple of years after arriving in America, Big John was still mopping floors by day and tending bar at Rafferty's pub, until closing time, six days a week. He was getting discouraged about ever saving enough money to open a bar of his own. His day job barely kept him in food and rent money. Compounding his dire financial straits, was the fact that Rafferty made him pay half price for his drinks, which only led to his drinking twice as much to take advantage of the discount. It was certainly cheaper to drink when Rafferty was gone from the pub, but those times were far too infrequent. To complicate matters, he was hungover and late nearly every morning for his day job at City Hall, which greatly limited his chances for career advancement.

Big John had noticed the new gorgeous young woman who had begun working in the tax department on his mopping rounds. He thought that he might be able to charm her into looking up which bars in the city were in arears in paying their taxes. This, he felt, would give him a leg up approaching the delinquent owners about a cheap sale price, if he were ever able to save any money. His plan was to slowly but surely win her affection by taking apples and pieces of cake from the City Hall cafeteria and leaving them on her desk every couple of days or so.

Maureen enjoyed the extra attention in her otherwise desperately boring job and began to be quite fond of the unusually tall red-headed custodian. Over the next couple months, Big John had noticed that at first one button, and then weeks later two buttons, had come 'accidentally' undone on her blouse, just under her chin, whenever he came around with his gifts. Occasionally, there was an envelope on top of the last file cabinet, which held a piece of paper with the names of a couple taverns in arears on their taxes. These he casually slid into his pants pocket while cleaning. Both of the young Irish City Hall employees were becoming smitten with one another.

For his part, young Mr. Finnegan could always make her laugh with a never-ending litany of crazy stories about the lives of the patrons in his father's pub. He had also splurged on a small bottle of scented water, which he would judiciously dab on his neck just before entering the tax department. As time went on, passers-by noticed the two of them speaking to each other in hushed tones, with their heads almost touching. In those times, his voice was low and rich, and she could feel herself starting to quiver. For his part, Big John was finding it harder and harder to fall asleep at night, thinking about her face and her scent and what lay beneath those remaining closed buttons.

The Sisters of St Joseph, and the Christian Brothers, had made it perfectly clear to these two that they were committing the sin of lust on a regular basis, even though they had never touched each other as of yet. Without ever speaking of it, they both knew that if they were not careful, this situation could lead them to commit a mortal sin. They had been taught that the devil himself had set his sights on them, and they could feel his pull. So, after a tortuous year of huddling to talk in the tax department and an occasional walk at lunch on the City Hall grounds, young Mr. Finnegan asked young Miss Fitzgerald if she might like to marry him. Little did he know that his proposal was to bring him a whole host of issues before it brought him happiness.

CHAPTER EIGHT

Maureen's father, Lieutenant Tommy Fitzgerald, did not rise through the police ranks by being a kind and demure sort of fellow. He had a red Irish face atop his 6-foot frame, a quick temper and lack of patience to go along with it. He had repeatedly threatened his daughter with being put out on the street if she went out with a man behind his back. He also let her know that he continued to pray daily for her to return to the convent. It is a tremendous honor in Irish families to have a child, or better yet children, enter the religious life. Surely, only a faithful, pious family could raise such devout children. God's grace for the parents would surely follow, along with an abbreviated stay in Purgatory.

Tommy also let his daughter know that with hundreds of beat cops out there watching her every move, the chances of her not getting caught sneaking around was very slim, indeed. Maureen, her eyes welling up with tears, had to tell Big John that their flirtation was never going to be able to go any further.

"John, I am so sorry, but there is no way my father will allow me to go out with you formally. Understand, it doesn't matter to me, but with you being a custodian...oh dear Lord..." she whispered, as she turned away from him in embarrassment at even saying such an unkind thing.

"But he hasn't even met me girl. Wouldn't he at least respect that I work two jobs...or is tending bar also on the list of banned professions," he asked sarcastically.

"I am so sorry," she repeated without turning back towards him. "I should never have flirted with you. It's my fault. I was hoping that you would buy a bar and then at least you would be a business owner."

"It's harder than you think, girl," Big John said in a sullen voice.

"I know, I know," she answered, "but my father won't even like the fact that you have a brogue. I've grown up hearing over and over how, 'no daughter of mine is going to marry some poor Irish mick,'" she whimpered softly.

"Maureen, maybe if I spoke to him...if he got to know me...this last year you have been on my mind constantly..."

"John, it makes me nervous to even take these walks with you at lunch. If word got back to him...I don't know what...he still wants me to become a nun for God's sake." With that she darted past him and walked quickly back to the building, as if the mere thought of them being discovered had spooked her.

For his part, Big John felt as though someone had just handed him his heart on a platter. He had always been able to use his wits and humor to win over just about anyone he had ever met. This was a predicament for which he had no answer. The thought of being turned down simply for who he was, was inconceivable. What kind of man would make such harsh demands on his only daughter anyway?

Over the course of the next couple months, the two of them purposely stayed away from each other as much as possible. Gone were the little treats from the cafeteria, and certainly there were no more "accidental" button mishaps. Making matters even worse, was the fact that they could not commiserate with friends or family, for fear that word of their dalliance would get back to Tommy. Hence, they were left to deal with their sadness separately and alone. Nevertheless, both secretly prayed to their patron saints and to Jesus himself for some sort of Divine intervention. It was a bit slow in coming, but the intervention eventually did come in a most unorthodox fashion.

As Maureen was quite aware, Big John had become friendly

with, and even admired, a regular late-night patron at Rafferty's by the name of Brian Reilly. Brian was at least five years older than Big John and was always impeccably dressed in the finest suits and ties. He was a thin, quiet-spoken, private sort of a guy who liked to sit at the very end of the bar while nursing his shots. He carried a large, black businessman's briefcase everywhere he went. It was from this case that he sold a variety of watches, rings and other assorted jewelry pieces for both men and women. Any of the bar's patrons who wished to make a purchase, made an appointment through Big John, to see Brian's wares in the men's room. Big John then made sure to direct any unsuspecting patrons who needed to use the facilities, to the ladies' room for the duration of the sales presentation.

So, Big John was in effect vouching for the character of any potential jewelry customers and providing security for the jewelry owner. Finally, since Brian was not always present at the tavern, Big John took care of what may be called Brian's lay-a-way payment plan. For instance, if a customer picked out a ring for his fiancée, but could only pay a few bucks a week, Big John collected the weekly payments and kept a precise book on the details for Brian. Brian had become quite fond of the big gregarious bartender, noticing his professional, low-key discretion concerning the jewelry business. Also, his honesty handling the bar's money and affairs, let Brian know that he was trustworthy.

Brian had only alluded to his "business interests" in conversation with Big John, and for his part, because of his experience in his father's pub, Big John knew better than to ask questions about the patrons' personal affairs. In truth, Brian had started a little empire for himself by paying Irish maids, gardeners and chauffeurs for information regarding the travel habits of their wealthy Protestant employers. His rationalization during the recruitment process was that stealing from a wealthy Protestant would be easily overlooked by Jesus, who was of course the first Catholic.

Any remaining qualms of conscience were usually removed by Brian, using the memory of their parents and grandparents being forced to denounce their Catholicism, by the wealthy Protestant landlords for whom they worked in Ireland, so that they could get food during the Great Famine. Brian, would also quote a famous Oxford professor named Nassau Senior who said that the Famine, 'would not kill off more than a million of the Irish, and that would scarcely be enough to do any good'.

Unfortunately for Brian, the landlady in his boardinghouse had a drunken bum of a son who was in jail for the umpteenth time and the word was he might not be getting out anytime soon. She was always looking for some leverage in the form of information to give to the police, to get the hapless lad out of jail. With the help of a few well-placed small holes in the tenant's walls, she could listen in on some of their conversations. Recently she had been able to listen to Brian and one of his "business associates" describe the date, time and place of their next excursion into the home of a wealthy family on Westmoreland, who were going to be in Europe. The usual routine was for their in-house accomplice to leave a door or window open on a certain date, and then one of Brian's men would slip in to the house after the help had retired to the servant's quarters on the third floor.

Desk Sargent Raymond Doyle took the landlady's statement privately in the late afternoon on the day of an upcoming burglary. He immediately left and made his way to the home of his boss, Lieutenant Tommy Fitzgerald. It was Sunday and he knew Tommy would be home. He knew better than to share the information with just anyone on the force, because one could not know where the loyalties of all the men would lie in such a case as this. After all, eighty percent of the force was Irish, and according to his source, so were the thieves. In other words, he couldn't take the chance that someone would tip them off.

Doyle and Fitzgerald shared a zealous contempt for the shanty Irish who came to America and then broke the law. They felt that this criminal element gave all the Irish a black eye in terms of their standing in the community. They had worked hard to get where they were, and these lazy criminals were the reason why so many of the city's population looked at all the Irish with disdain.

There had been a number of these thefts in recent months, from some of St. Louis's wealthiest families, and those families were clamoring for the mayor to do something. He, of course, publicly berated the police department for their inability to catch those responsible. Doyle and Fitzgerald could hardly contain themselves in their excitement over their good fortune, and immediately began to see themselves in their next promoted position with the police force. They were seated on Tommy's front porch quietly planning a strategy to catch the thieves.

"I can't thank you enough for coming straight to me with this Doyle," Tommy smiled as he shook his hand. "This would have been another field day for the Prot newspapers running down the low-life Irish."

"No problem sir," replied Doyle.

"So, we are dealing with a couple micks and you have the address that they are going to hit?" asked Tommy.

"That's right sir. The one in charge is named Brian Reilly. No name for the other one, but she said they both have a brogue. The house is just a block off Kingshighway. How do you want to handle this?" asked Doyle.

"Well for starters, go back to the precinct house and hand pick five men you can trust, but I still don't want them to know where they are going or why. We can't take any chances on these guys getting tipped off. Have them all change into dark street clothes. I will meet you all on Union a block from Lindell in the Park," Tommy said as his brain whirled through all the details.

"What time sir?" asked Doyle.

"It's four o'clock now. It gets dark around six-thirty. We can meet at seven. We think they have been getting in the houses after midnight when all the help is asleep because no one ever hears a thing," mused Tommy, thinking aloud. "I'll get a warrant from judge Callahan up the street, and we'll plan on setting up in the house around eight or so. Remember that none of the servants can leave after we get there. They might have inside help, and again I don't want anybody tipping these bastards off."

"Alright sir. See you then," Doyle said as he stood to leave.

CHAPTER NINE

Unknown to her father, during his conversation with Sargent Doyle on the porch, Maureen had been reading in a wing-back chair next to the porch window. It was a warm spring day and the window was open a foot or so. She heard every word, and now her heart was beating faster and faster. She heard Big John speak about his friend Brian Reilly many times during their walks at lunch, and how he was a jewelry salesman. She hadn't thought anything of it at the time but selling jewelry in a bar was certainly not a reputable way of doing business. Dear God, she thought, what if this was Big John's friend? Her next thought made her stomach flip and her head hurt almost instantly. What if the other man they spoke of with a brogue was her beloved John?

As her father quickly gathered his things, and kissed her mother good bye, Maureen began to panic. She could not stand the thought of Big John going to jail. Then she thought that there was no way he could possibly be a thief! Could he? He worked two jobs for goodness sake, didn't he? He was hard working and honest, right? But oh, dear God, what if the pressure to open a business so he could marry her had driven him to a life of crime? It would be her fault if he went to jail! Oh, dear Lord help me, she prayed. I could not bear it!

After calling to her mother that she was going for a walk, Maureen ran out the front door and began walking as quickly as possible west on McPherson towards Euclid. She knew Big John cleaned Rafferty's on Sunday afternoons, and she was praying that he was there, because she had never been to his boardinghouse, and wasn't sure of its exact location. She released a huge sigh of relief, when she saw Big John locking up and begin to walk towards her. Quickly she caught his eye and motioned for him to follow her into a small walkway between two buildings, where they could talk unnoticed by passers-by. He knew by the look on her face that something was terribly wrong.

"What is it darlin'?" he asked right away.

"I overheard one of my father's sergeants tell him that they had a lead on a burglary tonight on Westmoreland. He said they were after a man by the name of Brian Reilly," she gasped, barely noticing a slight rise in Big John's eyebrows at the mention of his friend's name. "They said his accomplice spoke with a brogue. Dear God Johnny, tell me you're not involved. I could never believe you are, but I could not take the chance."

"Of course not, darlin' now slow down. My goodness you're talking so fast I can barely keep up!" he told her as he touched her arm lightly.

"This is a terrible sin that I'm committing going behind my father's back like this! Jesus, Mary and Joseph Johnny!" she exclaimed while crossing herself. "Tell me again you aren't part of this thing! I was so afraid that my turning you down in marriage could have led you to a life of crime to make more money!"

"Dear Lord, Maureen calm down! I am no thief for God's sake! And I don't think for a minute that my Brian is either. Thank you for your concern, but I assure you it was unnecessary worry."

She searched his face for any sign he wasn't telling the truth, but nothing showed. Wiping her eyes with the backs of her hands she said, "I am so sorry Johnny. I got so scared. I guess my imagination got away from me."

"It's alright darlin', really. You have nothing to worry about here," he grinned, "but you better get back home, before your father's henchmen find you here with a lowly bartender."

"Stop that now," she grinned, "I will see you tomorrow."

"Now that's my girl. Tomorrow won't come soon enough then," he laughed.

While he was settling Maureen's fears, there were more than a few of his own developing. He had told a white lie to her when he said he did not suspect his Brian. It was entirely possible that the police were after the man he knew as Brian Reilly. Big John knew that he had to at least try to contact his friend, just in case. Brian was the secretive type and therefore he had never shared where he lived. Big John was racking his brain trying to think of anywhere he might be able to find Brian and tip him off, just in case. He finally remembered, that Brian had mentioned on more than one occasion, how he had a thing for the evening waitress at the Jewish deli down the street, where he often ate dinner.

Glancing at his watch, Big John noticed it was almost five o'clock, the supper hour, and so he began lumbering down Euclid as fast as he could. At least the waitress could say if Brian had been in yet or not. Please, please be there he whispered in his head. Three long blocks later he entered a nearly empty deli out of breath and with a redder face than usual. No Brian in sight. Damn! Quickly he walked straight over to the only waitress in sight, where she stood behind the counter.

"Miss," he started, "Can you tell me if you know of a regular customer here by the name of Brian Reilly?"

"I do indeed big man," she answered, smiling.

"Well, have you seen him this evening?" he asked hurriedly.

"No but I am expecting him any minute," she grinned, "Can I help you?"

"No, no. I will just sit and wait," he said anxiously, while trying desperately to think of anywhere else he might find his friend.

After much pacing, three glasses of water, and two trips to the bathroom, Big John saw Brian crossing the street towards the deli. Out the door he went waving and motioning to Brian to come with him down the block in front of a closed barber shop. Big John was wiping his brow and looking at Brian with all the concern he felt.

"What brings you here my friend," said Brian, trying to smile but noticing the big man's discomfort.

"There is only one way I know to be Brian, so I am going to give it to you straight. The police have a tip that a couple Irishmen, one by the name of Brian Reilly, are going to break into a house on Westmoreland tonight. They are going to be waiting. That is all I know and all I want to know. I apologize if I am putting you in this scenario because of another man with the same name. I certainly am not saying I have any reason to believe it is you. But I could not forgive myself if in the interest of not hurting your feelings, you wound up in jail," Big John finished, speaking as quickly as he could, and studying Brian's face for clues.

Brian was sharp enough to deduce that this information had probably come from Big John's girl Maureen but knew better than to ask. He knew the big man had just saved him from a prison term but wanted to honor his wishes about not knowing the details. As casually as possible, he said, "You are a good man John. Thank you for your concern and your effort on my behalf. Now if you don't mind I have another appointment to keep this evening, so I will have to say good bye for now."

Brian made a quick retreat to the boardinghouse where he stayed, to let his accomplice know of the situation. One of them always stayed with the black case. He gathered up his belongings in his suitcase, headed down the stairs and disappeared into the gathering dusk. Dropping everything with another friend, he got into some old, dark clothing, and made his way to the alley behind the houses across the street from the house they were going to break into. He hid in some large bushes next to the house and waited just long enough to watch seven men walk down the street and enter the house around eight o'clock. Well, well, well Big John. I owe you a steak dinner or two or three he thought to himself, as he quietly made his way back to the alley and eventually to his friend's apartment. Along the way, he came to the realization that it might be time to change professions.

A month later, Brian took Big John out for a steak dinner, and during the meal, slipped into the conversation that he wanted the two of them to go into business together. When he noticed Big John stopped chewing, he laughed and told him that there was nothing to worry about. This was to be a legal proposition.

"I know you want to open your own tavern, my friend, so that you can show your girl's father how respectable you are. Am I right? Well I think we can make that happen. I have some money saved up, and if you can find one with tax problems like you are always talking about, maybe we can buy it," said Brian, in a low business-like voice.

Big John was staring at Brian's face without chewing and holding a forkful of steak dangling in thin air, waiting for the punch line or laughter to break out. Seeing neither, he slowly lowered his fork and started to chew again. "Don't fool with me now, Brian. You know how much I want this."

"Look," replied Brian, "I don't want to operate the bar myself or be tied down with a bunch of paperwork. I just want to be able to invest in a legitimate business as a silent partner. You can pay me fifty per cent of the profits until you pay off your half. How does that sound?"

Big John could hardly believe his ears or his good fortune. A silent partner who fronts all the money and won't get in the way of the operations. This was a dream come true. Within seconds the two relatively new immigrants were shaking hands and grinning wildly at their upcoming joint venture. "Thank you, Brian," said Big John more than once.

"My pleasure, Big Man."

Neither of them ever spoke again of the night of the burglary, and they never would. Brian liked the fact that Big John never asked a lot of questions, and Big John liked that Brian stayed completely out of the bar business. The bar was going to give them both the respectability that they needed. Brian needed a genuine business for tax purposes, and Big John needed the same thing so that he could ask Lieutenant Tommy Fitzgerald for his daughter's hand.

A month later a big red headed barkeep by the name of John Patrick Finnegan signed the final papers on a well-worn drinking establishment on Euclid near Maryland. It was in the heart of the central west end business district, and just a few blocks from Forest Park. Others may have used different adjectives to describe the place, but Big John preferred that particular description when speaking of it to friends. As mentioned before, he named it, The Shamrock, of course, after his father's pub in Dublin. He wished his dad and his mom were there to see the grand opening. It brought tears to his eyes when he wrote to them of his good fortune in having opened a bar of his own after just over a year in America. He knew there would be tears on the page on the other side of the ocean as well, when they read the letter.

The bar came with a couple of offices upstairs on the second floor. They were quickly rented to a small business by the name of Acme Enterprises. The only way to access those offices was from a locked and enclosed stairwell. The only way to access the stairwell was from the alley. The result was that no one in or around the bar ever saw anyone come and go from those offices or heard footsteps overhead. But most importantly, the rent was always on time in the bar's mail slot. The check was always signed by a certain Robert Reilly, who was Brian's brother.

Big John proved to be a perfect fit for the neighborhood, and his robust personality drew people of all persuasions to him, and the bar. He had an endless supply of clean and bawdy jokes at the ready, depending on the hour and the nature of the clientele. He had a beautiful Irish tenor voice as well, that many said they would pay to hear, even if they weren't there to just drink. Ballads were his specialty, but a rousing song of marching into battle could be coerced from his lips, as long as everyone promised not to start swinging at each other when the spirit moved.

Business was always booming during the baseball season, since everyone with a game ticket got a free beer. On these days, they were usually four deep at the bar. Big John also had a policy of never charging the beat cops who came in both on and off duty. Cops were a bar owners best friend. Having them around meant that he didn't need bouncers in the event a fight broke out. Also, any fool that tried to rob the place was generally going to have to get past three or more cops on his way out the door. Most importantly, the news that Big John Finnegan was taking care of cops got back to Lieutenant Tommy Fitzgerald.

Big John let any reputable charity that asked, put a donation jar on the bar. When he emptied the jars in front of the charity's representative, he would tally the cash, put it in the register, then write a check, signed by him with a big donation added. Word got around the city that this young businessman was kind and generous with his time and money.

After about six months, the bar business was doing so well, he decided to give up the City Hall job for good. He told Maureen that it was time for him to talk to her father and ask for her hand in marriage. Nervously she agreed, and Big John bought himself a new suit and shoes and marched over to the Fitzgerald's on a Sunday afternoon in the spring of 1917.

Maureen had been coyly dropping the name of John Finnegan at the dinner table for a few months. While casually relaying some of his fine attributes to her parents, she never mentioned that he was a custodian, but merely that he worked at City Hall. Truth be told, she needn't have bothered, since Tommy's "eyes" all over the city had made him aware of his daughter's eye for one John Patrick

Finnegan. As more of his beat cops spoke so highly of Big John's generosity and good nature, the Lieutenant had to admit, that he was looking forward to their eventual meeting. Grudgingly, he was giving up his dream of Maureen becoming a nun. After all, at least this barkeep/custodian had a decent work ethic, and he wasn't a 'daygo' or a 'pollock' or from some other God-forsaken ethnicity. Last year one of Lieutenant Brennan's daughters had run off with a fuckin' 'kraut'. At least Brennan had three more daughters, he thought, shaking his head. I only have one!

Big John knocked on the Fitzgerald front door at precisely one o'clock as Maureen had instructed him. It was an hour after they got home from Mass and an hour before Sunday dinner. He was nervous but steady, with a bouquet of flowers in one hand, and a church bulletin he had grabbed from a guy sleeping on the streetcar in the other. He had wanted to make a good impression on Maureen's deeply religious parents, but suddenly realized he had not looked close enough to know if it was a Catholic church and stuffed it in his pocket. Wouldn't that be the perfect start he thought, standing there with a Baptist church bulletin.

The door swung open and for a couple of seconds the two big men sized each other up before they both smiled and roughly shook hands. Tommy hated a limp handshake and was pleasantly satisfied with the young man's first test results.

"So, you are Big John Finnegan, are you?" he said, revealing by using the nickname that he had already done some checking.

"It is sir, unless me mother lied on the birth certificate," Big John cracked with his ever ready, disarming humor.

"Now, young man, have you ever heard of an Irish mother who lied?" shot back Tommy.

"Not to another Catholic sir," grinned Big John.

The two men began laughing simultaneously, as Tommy invited the younger man in, and as Maureen and her mother sighed and crossed themselves in the kitchen. Dinner and small talk went equally as well, with the ladies of course taking a back seat in all the conversations. Eventually the two men went out on the front porch, lit their cigars and let a minute or so of quiet settle in around them. When they finally exhausted all the male topics of baseball, boxing and horse-racing, Big John knew it was time to bring up the topic he had come to discuss.

"Lieutenant Fitzgerald, your lovely daughter Maureen and I have both worked at City Hall for well over a year now, and I must say I have grown quite fond of her. Unfortunately, we will not be seeing each other in the near future, because I have recently opened a small tavern in the Central West End called, "The Shamrock". Are you familiar with it sir?" John asked.

"I am indeed. I've heard from the men at the precinct that you are a generous businessman where they are concerned. Policing is a thirsty business as I'm sure you are aware," replied Tommy.

"I am aware, and I have the utmost respect for the men in blue. You have a very difficult job keeping us all safe. Also, I appreciate the fine compliment sir," he added as he started to slowly rise to a standing position. "But I have a more important topic to discuss with you. With all the respect I can muster, I have come here today to let you know that I have fallen in love with your daughter Maureen. I have come here to ask you for her hand in marriage."

Slowly, Tommy rose from his chair until the two men were standing toe to toe and eye to eye. "You seem like a fine young man Mr. Finnegan, and I have to say I would be happy to have you for a son-in-law."

"Thank you, sir, thank you," Big John beamed as he vigorously shook the older man's hand.

"I just want you to always remember one thing," Tommy said quietly, his countenance quickly changing from joyful to very serious. At the same time, he had tightened his grip on the younger man's hand, and pulled him closer, so that if the ladies inside were listening, as he was sure they were, only Big John could hear what he had to say.

"What is that sir?" Big John asked just as quietly and seriously, while bending forward.

"Maureen is the love of my life and my only daughter. If you ever lay a hand on her in anger, only Jesus Christ himself will know where all the pieces of your body are buried. Do you understand me boy?" Tommy whispered as he stared directly into the eyes of his future son-in-law.

Squeezing the older man's hand just a little bit harder, Big John whispered back, "I do."

Then in a louder, upbeat voice for the ladies' benefit, Tommy bellowed, "Well then let's go and deliver the good news and see if we can't find a decent bottle of Irish whiskey to help us celebrate!"

About a year later, as was previously mentioned, the young couple were wed in a regal affair at the St Louis Cathedral. Many of the St Louis hierarchy both in and out of the police department attended the service. The newspapers' social columns estimated a crowd of five to six hundred present for the event. Many made sure to attend because they guessed, correctly, that within the very near future, the headstrong and ambitious father of the bride would soon become a captain on the St. Louis police force. Then, since the Irish had no problems with the practice of nepotism, two of Maureen's older brothers were quickly promoted to the rank of Lieutenant.

Big John could hardly take his eyes off his bride, in her lavish white gown, auburn hair, and the bluest of blue eyes. It seemed like an eternity since he first laid eyes on Maureen, and the open buttons on her blouse.

After the ceremony, the young couple made their way to the side altar of the Blessed Virgin. They lit a candle together, bowed their heads and prayed to be blessed with children. Their prayers were answered exactly nine months later, when the first of their six children were born. The youngest of their brood, Kathleen Beatrice Finnegan was born in 1925. She would eventually marry Patrick, the oldest child of Jimmy and Bridget O'Toole. Patrick and Kathleen were to become the parents of Michael and Margaret Mary O'Toole.

Part IV

Historical Roads

CHAPTER TEN

Years later, the Irish history that Michael and Margaret Mary O'Toole, and their siblings and cousins, learned from their Grandpa Finnegan, was decidedly different from the history they learned from their Grandpa O'Toole. Grandpa Finnegan went to school in Ireland through the tenth grade, whereas Grandpa O'Toole could not read and write.

After a few caramel colored drinks served in a tall water glass by his grandchildren at family gatherings, Grandpa Finnegan's oratory usually began with some reference to his beloved St. Patrick. He would lean forward in his solid metal lawn chair, the only style that would safely carry his three hundred plus pounds and enlist his ten or twelve grandchildren's attention by using an unnaturally subdued, conspiratorial tone.

"It is a lie that St Patrick drove the snakes from Ireland," he would whisper hoarsely, his eyes darting from one wide-eyed round face to another. "The snakes just hid or swam back to become the ancestors of the English bastards that are in Ireland to this very day! The thieving, murderous Prots are the mortal enemies of the Irish, and don't you ever forget it," he would say while spitting the words out, with his voice getting louder, and his eyes getting wider. Goose bumps would always rise on the arms of his precious grandchildren as he began his tale.

The history lessons could last for an hour or more, interrupted only by the request for one of the favored group to refill his glass. Have no doubt that this lifelong patron of Irish pubs and American bars, had a very specific set of instructions for the designated urchin sent to make his next Manhattan. He didn't call them Manhattans to the children, not wanting them to think he was pretentious, instead asking for certain levels within the glass of bourbon and vermouth. As the day wore on, the line on the glass where he would point for the bourbon to be filled got progressively higher, leaving less room for the vermouth.

Along with history, the art of making mixed drinks is imparted to Irish children at an early age so that the adults do not have to interrupt their high-level discussions of politics, religion and current events. The children were deemed to be ready for this very important mark of maturity when they could do two separate functions correctly. One was intellectual and one was physical. You might say it was sort of an Irish Bar Mitzvah. The first was being able to read the bottles, and the second was being tall and steady enough to pour from a fifth or quart into a glass without spilling a single precious drop. This important milestone, while not receiving the same sort of public celebration as say a First Communion or a Confirmation, was nonetheless both courted and well rewarded by cash tips, instead of a card with an enclosed check.

As the day or evening wore on, an extensive list of horrific crimes perpetrated by the English against the Irish, was relayed by Grandpa Finnegan to his rapt audience. In addition, some of the children's parents, aunts and uncles, would stop by to add their own favorite examples of English debauchery, and sinful behavior. The genocide of the Great Famine was never excluded. By the time they were eleven or twelve, Big John Finnegan's grandchildren had a long list of events in Irish history etched into their young brains by hearing them over and over. Decades later, if put on the spot as adults, any one of them could recite a litany of sins committed by the English against the Irish, because the history lesson always took a familiar path. It went something like this:

"Alright now children, let's quiet down," Grandpa John began, "it's time for you to hear the truth about your ancestors," he told them with a serious look upon his face, to make sure they realized the gravity of what they were about to hear. "By the time St Patrick died at the end of the fifth century, Ireland was one hundred percent Catholic. By the end of the sixth century, St Brendan set sail from Ireland as its first missionary. He discovered America a thousand years before the lying 'daygo' named Christopher Columbus claimed this feat for himself."

"Why isn't St Brendan in our history books?" one of the younger kids who had not heard Irish history from their grandfather before asked.

"It's because the English were the first to write down America's history before 1776, and they would never have given the Irish credit," he answered quickly. "Now then, to continue," Grandpa John said as he cleared his throat. "The heroic Catholic Irish fought off the godless heathen Vikings in the ninth century, then did the same to the sub-human Norman hordes in the twelfth century. By then, it was clear to everyone in the civilized world that the Irish were the fiercest warriors on earth, supported as always by their Catholic God.

"It wasn't until the sixteenth century that Ireland's fortunes began to turn. The Irish had been fighting heathens for centuries to protect the one true religion called Catholicism that Jesus gave to his people. Now the devil sent a man named Martin Luther, who in 1517 formed his own army of sinners called 'Protestants'."

At this point, Grandpa John took a gulp from his glass and then spit it on the ground to wash his mouth clean after just saying the word 'Protestant'. A few of the older kids glanced at each other, having been taught in school that Luther had good reason for his actions. Instinctively they knew that this was not the time to bring up the discrepancy. After wiping his sleeve across his mouth, Grandpa began again.

"In 1533 King Henry VIII defied his holiness the Pope and divorced his first wife to marry his floozy girlfriend."

"What's a floozy Grandpa?" asked seven-year-old Elizabeth.

"It's a woman with poor morals," he replied.

"What's morals?" asked eight-year-old Sean.

"Ask your parents when you get home," Grandpa told him gruffly before continuing. "Being excommunicated, and in a state of mortal sin, King Henry became a Protestant and declared that all of England was Protestant as well. This enabled the devil to take control of an entire country and all its people. Allowing divorce led to rampant fornication, and a complete moral breakdown of the English, from which they have never recovered."

"What's fornication?" inquired seven-year-old Liam.

"Ask your uncle Robert," Grandpa relied, "he's an expert on the subject." Then after a big swallow he began again. "King Henry proclaimed himself King of Ireland and sent thousands of armed soldiers and settlers to invade Ireland and convert the devout Irish. Their advanced weaponry killed thousands of the Irish who refused to be subjugated. Unfortunately, the Irish were no match for the invading Prots, being outnumbered ten to one. Eventually they stole all the Irish land and put the remaining Irish Catholics to work as slaves, forcing them to hand over all that they produced to the English landlords."

"Did they give up Grandpa?" asked nine-year old Joan.

"Absolutely NOT child!" he bellowed back, clearly angry at the thought of such a thing. "Let me tell you what the devious bastards did to our people. By the end of the seventeenth century, England enacted what was known as the Penal Laws in Ireland. Even though ninety percent of the population was Catholic, they could not own land or live within five miles of a city. Also, Catholics could not vote, hold public office or go to school. They were only allowed to be slave farmers, giving up all they produced to the English landlords. If that wasn't bad enough, ANY laws that were broken were punishable by death!"

As his rapt audience digested what a horrible life this must have been, Grandpa John sensed it was a good time to hand his glass to twelve-year-old Mickey for a refill. He knew Mickey was old enough not to need instructions, which might break the somber mood he had set for his grandchildren.

"But even that wasn't the worst children," Grandpa John continued, "the Penal Laws made it illegal to attend Mass or practice Catholicism in any way! The poor people began to harbor and protect their beloved priests so that they could continue to receive the Blessed Sacrament. Only Catholic priests, with their God-given powers, could transform the bread and wine into the sacred Body and Blood of Christ. They had to be protected at all costs. The best and brightest young men were chosen to secretly study to become priests. Having a child chosen for the priesthood or the convent, was the highest honor that could be bestowed on any Irish Catholic family both then and now!" he told them, while emphatically jabbing his finger at each child, one by one. Then he paused to allow his grandchildren a few moments for reflection on the possibility of their own religious vocations.

CHAPTER ELEVEN

At this point, bolstered by another well-prepared caramel colored drink, and gazing into the innocent faces of his grandchildren, Grandpa Finnegan took out his handkerchief and dabbed at his eyes, before he began the story of the Great Famine. Normally he was not given to such emotional displays, but there was something about looking into these little round faces that pulled at his heartstrings. Later on, he told their parents that his tears came from a feeling of pure joy, that all of them had good solid homes, warm clothes and plenty to eat every day of their lives. Not overtly religious by nature, he nevertheless thanked the Almighty every single day for these children's safety and security. Truth be told, there was no sin he would not commit to keep it that way.

"Why are you crying Grandpa?" six-year-old Maeve whispered quietly as she climbed onto his lap, then stood on his knees and put her little arms around his neck.

"I'm just so happy that none of you have to endure such things here in America," he whispered in her ear loud enough so all the kids could hear. He then settled his precious granddaughter on his left knee with his arm around her, while his right hand held his precious glass.

Twelve-year-old Mary Ellen stood up and put her head on his right shoulder while using her left hand to rub her Grandpa's back. "It's okay Grandpa. Don't worry."

"Well now I would dare to say there isn't a man alive with a finer group of grandchildren," he grinned. His grin seemed to take some of the seriousness out of the air and the kids began chatting a bit as they resettled themselves on the grass.

"Okay Grandpa, start the story again," Mary Ellen told him as she returned to her place on the lawn.

"Well now if things weren't already bad enough," he started, "the Great Famine struck in 1845. The Irish peasants were only allowed to keep and eat potatoes from their farms. That year, for no apparent reason, all the potatoes came up out of the ground black and rotten instead of white. This continued for over five years while the English landlords shipped all the grain and livestock back to England, so that the English could stay fat and happy. Thousands of the weakest started to die in their beds, and in the fields, from starvation. If the Irish peasants agreed to convert to be a Protestant, the landlords would give them a slimy soup for their families. Sadly, some converted for the purpose of keeping their poor starving children alive, although in truth they remained Catholic in their souls."

"How could anyone be so mean Grandpa?" asked seven-year-old Barbara.

"It was the devil himself who took over the souls of the Prot landlords to be sure," he answered. "There were still thousands dying of starvation because the filthy kettles of soup would not sustain them. Disease of all sorts began to kill thousands more who were too weak to fight off sickness. When the men died, the landlords burned their homes, took all their possessions, and drove the women and children out into the elements, where most succumbed to a tortuous death from exposure and starvation. Eventually over a million poor souls passed away, and half of the remaining four million tried to come to America. They were packed into what were called English coffin ships, with the hulls holding twice as many people as they were designed to carry. Over one third of all the immigrants died on their journey because of disease, starvation and even drowning, due to the ships not being seaworthy."

"Grandpa, I don't know if I can keep listening. This is making me too sad," whimpered little Angela, as a few other heads nodded in agreement.

"I know it's difficult to listen child, but not nearly as difficult as what these poor souls were forced to endure," he reminded them, "so stay with me for a while longer, will you?"

After she nodded bravely, he continued, "During the height of the Famine in 1847, four hundred thousand people died of starvation in Ireland, while in that same year, four thousand ships left Irish ports for England, loaded with grain and livestock. The food they were producing was kept from them purposely. Then when ships full of grain from America headed towards Irish ports, the English blocked them and made them return to America. The self-righteous English government officials were quoted as saying things like, 'If we start feeding the Irish now, we will wind up feeding them forever' and 'the Famine is a direct stroke of a wise and merciful God'."

"Surely, they went to Hell for this didn't they?" asked eleven-year-old Jack, who, like some of the other kids, was visibly angry. "I mean every time I hear this part of the history it makes me so mad."

"Just remember this when you hear of other people in the world who are being starved and mistreated young man. It's our job to stand up for them," Grandpa John told him, in an attempt to let the children see that there is a strong lesson in this story for them to carry throughout their lives. "It's hard to hear all of this, but don't ever forget it."

After another refill, he told them that at first it was not a whole lot better for the Irish who made it to America. "Children, there were so many Irish landing in America's cities that the devilish Prots were afraid of becoming out-numbered and out-voted by what they called the Catholic papists."

"What is a papist Grandpa?" asked nine-year-old Margaret.

"It's a nasty term for Catholics because we believe the Pope is our spiritual leader young lady," he told her solemnly. "In addition, people called nativists were trying to pass laws that said you could only vote if you were born in America. If that wasn't bad enough, the penal laws in Ireland had outlawed education for the Irish, so many of the immigrants to America could not read and write. The nativists wanted laws that would make it illegal to vote if you could not read a ballot on your own."

"What is a nativist Grandpa?" asked eight-year-old James.

"A nativist is someone who was born in America and feels no one else has a right to live, work or vote in America," he replied. "What fed a lot of this hatred and anger directed at the Irish was wealthy Prot families who owned the newspapers and factories. They drew the Irish in cartoons to look like chimpanzees, or other animals, with long ears and tails. They wrote stories on how the Irish were lazy drunken bums who did nothing but drink and brawl. Irish women were depicted in the cartoons as having litters of children and feeding them with multiple teats like dogs and cats. Up and down the east coast, they hung signs outside their factories that read 'no niggers nor Irish need apply'."

"Why did they hate us so much Grandpa?" Mickey wanted to know. A half-dozen little heads nodded to show they were wondering the same thing.

"The Prots hated Catholics because deep down they knew they had abandoned the one true religion. The people who were already in America were afraid that with so many Irish immigrants landing every year, that eventually we would outnumber them. Then we could vote them out of office, and vote for Irishmen instead," he told them. "Listen, it was so hard for an Irishman to find work that during the Civil War, that tens of thousands of them signed up with both the Union and the Confederacy to try and feed themselves and their families. Then even after serving in the military, the only jobs they could get, was working with freed black slaves and the Chinese, to build America's canals and railroads for low wages.

"Finally, in the late 1800's, many of the Irish who remained in the big cities, found that they could get work as policemen and firemen, because the work was so dangerous, nobody else wanted these jobs. From this base, they got their own people elected as aldermen and other city officials. By the early 1900's Irish mayors were being elected, and powerful political machines in the big cities were being run by the Irish. Finally, we had a way of controlling not only the police and fire departments, but all of the civil service jobs that were handed out at city hall."

"That's what you do isn't it Grandpa? I heard Daddy saying nobody works in St Louis until you say so!" eleven-year-old Michael happily added.

"Your father should learn to keep his thoughts to himself, Michael. Some things are better left unsaid," he added, looking over his shoulder for a moment. "Anyway, children, things did start to look up for us starting in the 1920's and 1930's. Irish laborers and craftsmen began bonding together to form labor unions, to try to get their bosses to pay them decent wages. The wealthy Prot businessmen tried to get the cops to beat up on men who were on strike, and pass laws against unions. Irish politicians fought to get the laws changed in their favor and Irish cops, who were also trying to form unions, often looked the other way when the men went on strike."

Grandpa Finnegan told his grandchildren that the Irish were the toughest and smartest people on earth. They had survived an attempted genocide and landed on America's shores without a penny in their pockets. He told them how Irish politicians ran a lot of the biggest cities in the country. He told them how Irish laborers and craftsmen built the roads and buildings in America with decent wages, because of their labor unions. He told them their families and homes were safe because of Irish policemen and firemen. He told them how Irish priests had built countless churches and parishes in America so that they could worship freely. He told them how Irish nuns were responsible for millions of Irish kids finishing grade school and high school for the first time in history.

Finally, Grandpa leaned forward, and once again using that low, conspiratorial tone he asked them, "What are the two most important things to remember after hearing all of this?"

Hesitating, he would slowly look from one adoring, and adorable, round face to the next. The older kids who remembered the answer remained silent so that Grandpa could deliver the answer to the younger ones. With the hand not holding his drink, he would point deliberately at each one of them as he said, "First, always remember that our Catholic faith has sustained us for centuries through the best and worst of times. Second, always remember that the Irish take care of and protect our own. As long as you stick together there isn't a thing in this world you can't accomplish."

While their little heads were nodding up and down, each of them now felt that they belonged to something wonderful and magical. For the coming days, weeks, months and years they walked around feeling happy, confident and full of pride because they were Irish Catholics.

Part V

Yellow Brick Road

CHAPTER TWELVE

On a crisp, sunny afternoon in October of 1949, Patrick James O'Toole, age 26, married Kathleen Beatrice Finnegan, age 24, at St. Roch's Catholic church on Waterman Ave. in the central west end of St. Louis, MO. St. Roch's was the bride's lifelong parish, as the Finnegan's lived just a block away on Waterman. The long-time pastor at St. Roch's, Monsignor John McMullen, who had also baptized the bride, married the young couple in a beautiful service. The bride and groom were born in America. The bride's father, the groom's father and mother and the monsignor were born in Ireland.

Patrick O'Toole was the eldest child of Jimmy and Bridgey O'Toole. He was born and raised in a bungalow on Nashville Ave. in St James the Greater parish with his seven younger siblings. Jimmy had built two additions on their eight hundred square foot home as the family grew, so that it was now just over a thousand square feet. He was quite proud of the dimensions of their home and worked that figure into the conversation as often as possible.

Patrick spent eight years under the tutelage of the Dominican sisters at St. James, in Dogtown. By the time he reached the eighth grade, there was an O'Toole in each of the grades at the school, which was an enormous source of pride for both Jimmy and Bridgey. Patrick was an excellent student, and after graduating near the top of his class, he received a scholarship to St Louis University High School in 1938, where he studied under the demanding eyes of the Jesuits.

During high school, Patrick worked at any number of part-time jobs, to help the family make ends meet. He also became sort of a father-figure to some of his younger siblings, consisting of three boys and four girls, since their father was often absent. Due to the Depression, construction work had been slow, and Jimmy was frequently forced to work out of town. In addition, while in St. Louis, Jimmy was heavily involved in "union activities" which kept him out late many nights. Occasionally, the "union activities" got him arrested or hospitalized, and Patrick would have to watch the rest of the kids while Bridgey went to the emergency room or bail Jimmy out of jail.

Bridgey never complained or spoke poorly about Jimmy at these times to Patrick or the other children. Rather, she explained that he was working hard and fighting for decent wages so that they could all have a roof over their heads and food to eat every day. The fact that their father was jailed once in a while was nothing to be ashamed of, but at the same time, she told the children that they needn't share that information with neighbors or schoolmates. It was a personal family matter. The children also took notice that their mother was not above lying to the police about Jimmy's whereabouts, when they knocked on the front door.

Halfway through Patrick's senior year in high school, the Japanese bombed Pearl Harbor, and ended any hopes that he may have had about going to college. The Jesuits granted an early graduation for him, and many other young men, so that they could enlist in the service of their country. Patrick enlisted in the Marine Corps, where his smarts, self-discipline and leadership skills, due in no small part to his Jesuit training, were quickly recognized. Before he shipped overseas, he had been promoted to sergeant and was made a platoon leader. He liked to quip in later years that Uncle Sam gave him a paid European tour. "You were on your own though when it came to dodging bullets and land mines," he'd laugh.

While Patrick was away, Jimmy made a number of influential friends while conducting "union activities". One of them was a well-dressed, affable fellow who, like Jimmy, had grown up in Belfast. His name was Brian Reilly, the same Brian Reilly who had befriended Big John some years earlier. If Brian overheard the union men at the Shamrock plotting and planning their next move, he would offer the use of his brother Robert's private office above the bar. During those meetings, he was able to gain their friendship and trust. Eventually, he would casually mention that during their youth in Ireland, Robert had acquired the skills to make things blow up. During the war, the Reilly brothers' reputation as reliable friends of the unions grew. Eventually, they were appointed "special" business agents for the Pipefitters Union in St. Louis. By the time the war was over, Brian's political savvy and ambition, got him elected to the number one job at the union, that of Business Manager.

When Patrick came home from the war, Jimmy approached Brian about getting him into the Pipefitters Union, and Brian gladly made it happen, since Jimmy had done a lot of late night "union activities" for him. If a contractor was putting up a commercial building using some non-union labor, the union workers would walk off the job and put up a picket line. Before too long, it would become nearly impossible to get materials delivered to the site. After a week or two it was entirely possible that the contractor would start missing some building materials that had already been delivered. After another week or two, the building would often catch fire at night. There were never daytime fires.

Jimmy wanted his son to have a skilled trade instead of being just a hod carrier like himself. Hod carriers, who were members of the Laborers Union in St. Louis, mixed mortar, shoveled it into their long-handled hods, and then walked the eighty pounds up ladders and across scaffolding to the bricklayers. Since the Irish were running the Bricklayers Union, Jimmy had gotten two of Bridgey's brothers on as bricklayers but felt that Patrick could work steadier as a fitter because they usually had a roof over their heads. The bricklayers and hod carriers missed a lot of work due to the rain, snow and cold. The bottom line in the building trades, was that the more hours per year you worked, the more money you made, meaning less need for side work or a second job.

Patrick was six feet tall and barrel chested, with a ruddy complexion and a thick head of wavy brown hair, that held a red tint in the sun. He had caught the eye of more than a few young women from the neighborhood, who waited all those years for the men to return home from the war and hopefully, start families of their own. He seemed in no hurry for such things though, and fell into a regular pattern of working on construction sites by day, and working on barstools at night.

Physically, he was able to hold his own with the notoriously rough pipefitters. They had acquired more than their share of ex-cons and rounders due to Brian's belief that every man deserved a second chance, since he had done time himself. He also liked to have men close at hand who had a variety of "useful" talents, and who were not too overburdened with matters of conscience. Men who grow up without enough to eat or a place to live, often fit that very description.

Kathleen was the youngest of Big John and Maureen Finnegan's six children, consisting of three boys and three girls. She despised being pushed around by anyone, including her older siblings, and therefore never forgot to place an incredibly large chip squarely upon each shoulder even before getting out of bed every morning. When she got angry, which was not an unusual occurrence, hundreds of loose strands of her reddish orange hair tended to stand at attention from her head, her green eyes threw sparks and her jaw set out from her face a couple of extra inches. She had very white skin which made her freckles stand out even more. The angrier she became, the redder her face would get, until it looked like all the freckles ran together. To top it off she was short, barely five foot, and therefore had to endure the trifecta of red head, freckle and short jokes at school.

All this tickled Big John so much that he would often have to leave the room, holding his hand over his face, to try and suppress his laughter while she was reading some poor soul the riot act. Maureen, having been raised in a much more genteel home, was mortified at her youngest child's tough demeanor, always coaxing her to take on more lady-like qualities.

By the age of eight or so, bolstered with a couple years of religion classes at St. Roch's, Kathleen would defiantly tell her mother, "I am who I am mother! After all God made me this way, didn't He?"

Big John would be doubled over with laughter in the next room, much to Maureen's displeasure. He had to admit, only to himself of course, that this little terror was his favorite.

Kathleen went to school for eight years at St. Roch's, then to the Archdiocesan all girls Catholic high school on Lindell Blvd. called Rosati-Kain. After graduation, her mother desperately wanted her to go to college, especially since her intelligence tests at school were through the roof. But it was not in Kathleen's nature to do as directed or expected. Big John loved to tell the patrons about the battles at home between his wife and daughter while holding court at the bar. They loved his animated descriptions, and responded with tales of their own unruly progeny at home. Big John liked to end his stories about Kathleen, by holding his flat cap over his heart and feigning a silent prayer for the poor bastard that married his beloved daughter.

Two years after the war in the summer of 1947, a tall, red faced, blue-eyed workman by the name of Patrick O'Toole walked into the Shamrock Bar on his way from work on a new building a few blocks away. He was wet from sweat from head to toe, and his clothes and face were black from welding, and crawling along pipes all day. He had walked down to have a couple beers in the tavern before he headed back to Dogtown on the bus. When the door closed behind him, blocking the bright sun, he was standing at the front door squinting to see in the darkened bar. It was his first visit to the Shamrock.

"What will you have young man?" boomed the bartender.

A female voice to the left of the bar cracked, "How about a bath and some clean clothes?"

A split second later, Patrick heard a group of men in a corner booth farther to the left roar with laughter.

As his eyes started to adjust, Patrick spotted a short red head in pants and a shirt with a broom in her hand. "Well now darlin' are you just making an observation, or are you offering your services to bathe and change me?"

With that, he could see one hand of the woman raise the broom slowly like a club, while her face got beet-red and she stuck her jaw out. At this point, the four men in the booth roared even louder sensing it was to be a fair fight after all. The largest of the four, wearing a stylish suit, was facing out of the booth because his stomach would not fit in it. He was pounding the table top with his right hand and laughing heartily with his head tilted way back.

"The only way I would bathe you would be with a good dousing of gasoline followed by a lit match," barked Kathleen.

"You better learn to be nice now little red. I don't want to have to take you over my knee," grinned Patrick.

"You and who else coal miner?" she shot back.

"Since when do taverns look down on poor coal miners?" he asked, with a look of innocence on his face.

"The minute you walked in!" Kathleen replied loudly.

"Would it be alright if I have a cold beer before you give me that bath?" Patrick asked, feigning his best straight face now.

"Just stay far enough downwind so I can't smell you," she commanded, while making a sweeping motion at him with the broom.

As the bartender sat a cold glass of draft beer in front of him, Patrick asked him loud enough for all to hear, "Since you have rules on appropriate attire and make fun of the dirt on a workingman's face, I would imagine that you're not allowed to fart in this fine establishment either?"

"You are a disgusting pig, sir!" Kathleen growled at Patrick, not yet willing to concede.

"I believe it is your winning personality, little red. You've brought out the best in me, as all here can surely see," Patrick answered formally with a courtly bow.

"That's enough out of you coal miner. Let's have more drinking and less talking," Kathleen howled as she turned towards the back room to deposit the broom.

By now Big John was laughing so hard, that he was wiping the tears from his eyes with one hand and holding his huge stomach with the other. He loved watching his youngest do battle with her sharp wit and quick mind, but for once she seemed to have met her match. Patrick was making her head look like it might explode, which was the reason for the men laughing themselves to tears. All of them had watched her successfully take on all comers since she was just a little thing.

Kathleen thought to herself that it had been a long time since she had done battle with such a formidable opponent. She had to admit to herself, while maintaining her scowl of course, that she had enjoyed herself a bit as well. He had guts saying some of those things with her father right there in the booth. Unless he didn't know who Big John Finnegan was, if that was even possible in St Louis. Regardless, most men were sheepish around her. She knew she intimidated them and she enjoyed it. This one walked into a strange bar with an air that said he didn't fear much of anything. Mr. blue eyes and wavy hair was full of himself, dirt and all, she mused.

By this time Big John was making his way down the bar to where Patrick was sipping his beer. "Young man, you've accomplished something her mother and I could never do!" he bellowed over the new song on the jukebox.

"What might that be sir?" Patrick asked weakly, standing up straight as he realized he had been sparring with the big man's daughter.

"Why you put her in her place for a moment or two anyway," he laughed.

"Dad PLEASE!" Kathleen shouted from the backroom.

Sticking his hand out he said, "I'm Big John Finnegan, owner of this fine establishment. Can I buy you another beer?" he asked, putting the younger man at ease.

"Absolutely sir. I meant no disrespect. But I've got a couple red headed sisters at home. It comes natural," Patrick grinned while shaking hands.

"That was very clear my friend. What is your name if I may ask?"

"Patrick O'Toole, sir," he answered.

"A good Irish boy to boot!" Big John smiled, embellishing his brogue a bit.

"Both parents are from the old country," Patrick added.

"That's grand Patrick. Are you Catholic?" he asked in a straightforward manner.

"I am, sir," he replied quickly.

"Well Patrick, tomorrow being Saturday, we will have a fine band playing here starting at seven. We do some singing and dancing and drinking. If you clean up a bit, I might just let you dance with my Kathleen!" he grinned, as he took a swig of his Manhattan.

"Dad STOP!" she yelled from the other end of the bar, still listening in as her father knew she would be.

"I was beginning to think that the man who was going to finally stand up to her would never walk through that door," he added amicably.

"I just might take you up on that sir," Patrick answered, glancing at the red head again as she pretended to wipe tables nearer to them now so she could hear better. He had to admit to himself that she had stirred something in him.

"Alright then, we will be looking for you Patrick, and I just may give my daughter the night off," he grinned.

Kathleen had once again been let go from a clerical job for telling a supervisor off and was earning her keep working at the bar. Patrick stole a quick glance at her while Big John ambled back over to the corner booth, otherwise known as the throne, where his cronies were waiting.

What is it about red hair and freckles, Patrick mused. They did him in every time. Plus, this one had been more fun than the girls who just bat their eyes and act like you're just the smartest man they ever met. This girl reminded him a lot of his mother, both tough, and with the sharp wit to boot. Another glance showed that she was still frowning. He wondered if he could get her to smile. Surely, she smiles once in a while, he hoped. But it was best not to get too interested, as she might not even show up tomorrow. Oh well, I'll be here, he thought to himself, and with one quick move, downed the beer Big John had bought him, and made his way to the door.

Kathleen kept her head down, while scrubbing tables, silently hoping he would be back the next night.

Saturday night at the Shamrock, the band started precisely at seven. They played Irish folk ballads and encouraged the patrons to join in the singing. Later they played more upbeat Irish tunes that encouraged the patrons to show off their dancing skills. After an hour or so, Kathleen was still standing in the doorway to the back room, becoming thoroughly dejected, after letting herself get her hopes up that the "coal miner" would return.

Patrick had forgotten that the buses didn't run north as often on Saturday, since he usually stayed in Dogtown. While waiting for connecting buses, he kept hoping that she would still be there when he finally arrived. Even worse, what if some other guy had gotten her to smile and dance?

At ten after eight, he walked through the door to the Shamrock and immediately started scanning the room for that red hair. It was crowded, and with everyone dancing, he could not see her, and began to fear she wasn't there. Slowly he started to make his way to the rear of the tavern so he could inspect the place a little better.

When Kathleen spotted Patrick coming towards her, she could hardly believe it was the same man. He looked so handsome with that unmistakable wavy head of hair neatly combed. My Lord, he's even wearing a coat and tie, she thought, as her heart began to beat faster. Gently she closed her eyes and said a quick prayer, asking that this not be some kind of dream.

When Patrick spotted Kathleen, he just stopped, about fifteen feet from her, mouth open, taking in her newfound beauty. She had that long red hair pulled up on top of her head, exposing her neck. She was wearing an emerald green dress that matched her eyes and perfectly hugged her previously undisclosed curves. The high heels made her a few inches taller. When his eyes met hers, he felt something new and indescribable stir inside.

The two of them walked slowly towards each other, instinctively knowing that words were unnecessary at the moment. The band had just stopped for a break, announcing they would return in fifteen minutes. Someone quickly plugged the jukebox back in, which began playing a trilogy of romantic songs from Sinatra. Looking into each other's eyes, they gently came within inches of each other, joined hands and began to rock back and forth. Halfway through that first song, still not having spoken a word, Kathleen laid her right cheek against Patrick's chest. He followed by placing his left hand in the small of her back, and ever so gently, pulled her to him as they continued to sway. No one else was dancing. They were all ordering drinks and talking loudly. Only a few of the older patrons watched, as Patrick and Kathleen continued slowly moving back and forth as one, all alone, in the middle of a crowd.

Big John was one of those older folks who was watching the whole scenario unfold from behind the bar. He continued to watch intently as his baby girl and his future son-in-law came together. Not long after Kathleen laid her head against Patrick's chest, he excused himself and made a quick retreat to his small rear office, where he closed and locked the door. If only the walls in that office had eyes, they would have seen Big John Finnegan...at six foot two and three hundred pounds...one of the most powerful men in the city of St. Louis...a man who could make and break political careers...a man responsible for thousands of immigrants having a roof over their heads, and food in their bellies...they would have seen him break down and cry like a baby. They were tears of joy. Only a daughter could make that happen to a man like Big John Finnegan.

CHAPTER THIRTEEN

Patrick and Kathleen were married two years later, after Patrick finished his apprenticeship with the pipefitters. The O'Toole/O'Keefe clan had wed the Finnegan/Fitzgerald clan. The shanty Irish and the lace curtain Irish were officially joined for all eternity.

Jimmy O'Toole had invited an uneasy alliance of nefarious characters with whom he had "worked" with over the years helping the building trade unions gain respect and power. He could never hold a union position himself because he couldn't read, but no one except Bridgey knew that. Regardless of his academic shortcomings, in some circles, Jimmy O'Toole was one of the best known and most feared men in St Louis.

On the groom's side of the church, in addition to the cadre of union organizers and officers, there were a group of twenty or so of Jimmy's hod carrier buddies. They were all seated near the back of the church with their wives, looking as uncomfortable in their suits as they felt wearing them. In addition, there were a wide range of different tradesmen and their sons, who Jimmy had helped get jobs over the years. Jimmy's old roommate and best friend, Liam, was there at his side attending to whatever Jimmy asked of him all day.

On the bride's side of the church, some of Kathleen's brothers, uncles and cousins made up a large contingent from the St. Louis Police Force. Jimmy, now almost fifty years old, had never been a huge fan of the men in blue, having been arrested a dozen or more times. So, it did not exactly sit well with him when he found out that his new daughter-in-law, Kathleen, was actually the granddaughter of the late Captain Tommy Fitzgerald. This was the same

Tommy Fitzgerald, who as a lieutenant, had come to Jimmy's room at the boardinghouse to question him about those dead Russians in Forest Park, many years before. Jimmy still had a knot on his head to remind him of that visit.

No one except Bridgey ever knew for sure what happened to those Russians, and she would certainly never tell a soul. But the fact was, that Tommy Fitzgerald and Jimmy O'Toole had formed an uneasy alliance after that meeting in the boardinghouse, that benefitted both of their causes, so to speak. Neither of them ever told any of their own associates about their relationship either. They helped each other with certain "activities" that only could be performed by someone who operated on the other side of a fine line.

Many of the older men from Ireland were more apt to trust each other, than anyone who was not Irish, regardless of their station in life. For instance, Jimmy always made sure to get word to Tommy if he heard of any impending illegal activity being planned by the Italian gangsters in town. Tommy Fitzgerald made a career out of busting Italian gangsters. In return, when non-union building sites burned to the ground, the police department was rarely able to find the necessary evidence to make an arrest or prove arson. There had been a bond and mutual respect born out of necessity between the two men that ended the day Tommy passed away a few years before.

Bridgey's sisters, Maeve and Mary Margaret, were there for the wedding with their husbands, who along with Bridgey's two brothers, were all bricklayers. Jimmy had gotten all of them jobs when they first came to America. Her brother Tommy O'Keefe was in fact now a business agent for the Bricklayers Union. The bricklayers in the church were easy to spot because their faces and necks looked like red leather, due in part to working outdoors, and due in part to being able to drink throughout the work day. They were a raucous bunch, but each of them swore to Jimmy that they would be on their best behavior on the wedding day.

The bride's side of the church at first glance had the look of a police academy graduation. Sitting up front were her mother Maureen's two brothers, Martin and Sean Fitzgerald, who had both risen to the rank of captain in the St Louis Police Department.

They were Tommy's sons, and Kathleen's uncles, but they knew nothing of their father's relationship with Jimmy O'Toole. Many of the men in the Fitzgerald/Finnegan clan had become either policemen or firemen over the years, giving this Irish wedding a much better chance than most of avoiding a brawl at the reception. Their fear of bad publicity in the papers about the police force or the fire department, worked to ensure a relatively calm reception.

The bride's mother, Maureen, had hired Maguire's Bakery to make the cake, and Shaughnessy's Florist to do the flower arrangements. Donnelly's Catering supplied the food for the reception, and O'Gorman's Dress Shop made the bride's gown and the bride's maids' dresses. The musicians who were playing at the Shamrock the night that Patrick and Kathleen had their first dance, were hired to play at the reception. They were of course, named The Irish Rovers.

Big John, who was fifty-three now, was making his third and final trip down the aisle to give a daughter away. He did not have any blood relations at the church, but virtually every politician in St. Louis had gotten an invitation and knew better than to miss the service. Without even holding a political office, Big John had built a small empire of political influence that would keep the Democratic Party in charge of St. Louis for generations.

In addition to getting politicians elected, he had helped hundreds of Irish immigrants get good civil service jobs. Also, hundreds of cops drank free at the Shamrock every year. This made Big John the first stop if you needed to get a traffic ticket, a drunk and disorderly charge, or even a minor felony disappear from a court docket. As the years went by, and some of those cops' kids made it through law school, his influence in the city became even greater.

He also was a major source of knowledge in backroom dealing, when it came to putting up a new building or opening a new business. Labor leaders, contractors and business owners knew no one who could get permits and licenses through city hall faster than Big John. After all, many of the City Hall employees owed their livelihood to him. He was the master at making red tape disappear.

Seated discreetly at the back of the church on the groom's side, was the always impeccably dressed, Brian Reilly. He had become one of the most influential men not only in St. Louis, but statewide. The Pipefitters Union, which he headed, were getting some of their members elected to state offices, thereby increasing their influence in Jefferson City, the state capital. That's where legislation was written that was crucial to the life of labor unions. His relationship with Brian widened Big John's influence as well.

Brian and Big John would go through this day without ever saying a word to each other, preferring to keep their decades-long relationship private. Part of the problem was that Brian was rumored to have ties to criminal elements, and he had a criminal record of his own. Big John had married into a well-known police family, did business with a lot of politicians at City Hall, and therefore needed to be seen as squeaky clean, at all costs, to remain effective. They would be considered strange bedfellows indeed, if some ambitious newspaper reporter wanted to start digging. Sitting in the back, Brian was just another one of the labor leaders in attendance at Jimmy O'Toole's request, as far as anyone knew. But Acme Enterprises still had its offices above the Shamrock, and Robert Reilly still paid the rent with a check every month.

After the wedding Mass ended, the bride and groom, made their way to the side altar of the Blessed Virgin Mary. They lit a candle together, then knelt to say a prayer asking her to be blessed with children. Their mothers, Bridget O'Toole, and Maureen Finnegan, who both felt a special bond with the Mother of God, and prayed their rosaries every week to her, bowed their heads and dabbed at their eyes.

Everyone's prayers were answered nine months later, in July of 1950 when Kathleen gave birth to a bouncing baby boy. They named him Michael Patrick after the warrior archangel, and Ireland's patron saint. Ten months after that glorious event, Kathleen gave birth to a beautiful baby girl they named Margaret Mary. After all, nearly every Irish family has to have a Margaret Mary or a Mary Margaret, or both.

The Irish are known for their facility in the use of the English language, especially in creative vehicles like storytelling and poetry. Yet for some reason, they keep a very short list of names that they consider suitable for their offspring. This provides one more example of a confounding duality in the culture of this mystical and religious, yet practical and irreverent tribe.

CHAPTER FOURTEEN

In the years immediately following World War II, the returning servicemen bought their first homes on the GI Bill. This meant they could secure low interest home loans, and the government would guarantee payment on them. This produced a huge housing boom in the suburban areas around all the major cities, including St. Louis.

In late 1951, after the birth of Margaret Mary, Patrick and Kathleen definitely needed more space. The one bedroom flat in Dogtown had them bumping into each other all the time, so they began to look for a home of their own. The best deal that they found was in a huge development called Forestwood in a north county suburb called Ferguson. Ferguson was originally built on a rail line coming out of St. Louis and had prospered for over fifty years as a place where some of the affluent city dwellers built their summer homes.

Surrounding this original enclave of two and three-story homes, was an ever-growing number of these post-war subdivisions, full of two and three-bedroom bungalows as far as the eye could see. Forestwood was one of the largest of its kind, with hundreds of houses all looking pretty much the same and having the same floor plan. The more "affluent" buyers had the option to add an attached one car garage. The two-bedroom model had 750 square feet, and the three-bedroom model had a luxurious 850 square feet. The homes were selling for around ten thousand dollars. The name Forestwood was merely a marketing ploy, since by the time the developer's bulldozers were done, there wasn't a tree in sight.

The O'Tooles picked out a lot on Highmont Drive, and like the majority of new home owners, decided to pass on the luxury of a garage. They did pay extra for the three-bedroom model though, which came with hardwood floors and gravity heat but no air conditioning. For a brief time, Michael and Margaret Mary had their own rooms, until one by one their four siblings began to arrive. Eventually, the family had to invest in the favorite invention of many large families of the day, which was bunkbeds.

Patrick built the other two-family staples in the neighborhood, which was a swing set and a chain link fence. He was of course able to do it much cheaper than most, since he got the pipe to make both of them free off job sites. Kathleen stayed busy trying to keep up with an endless stream of bottles, diapers, dishes, laundry and meals. It was a thankless job but as she liked to say with her dry wit, 'At least the pay is good'. In general life was good, or at least as good as any of the other families surrounding them. There was a little more money coming in now, since Patrick had made foreman and was starting to run some small jobs.

Like most Irish girls, Kathleen was used to the men in her life drinking on a daily basis, often to excess. Her own father had stumbled home from the Shamrock every night after midnight as far back as she could remember, usually making a lot of noise singing or cooking in the kitchen. Her three older brothers never missed an opportunity to tip a glass or two or twenty, either. Her mother's two brothers, who were both police captains, were notorious for having squad cars take them home a couple nights a week from their favorite watering holes. The men laughingly referred to their drinking by a variety of phrases like: unwinding the clock; whetting their whistles; making a package; filling the tank; greasing the gears; and so forth.

This cultural phenomenon displayed by Irish men, had a series of subsequent effects on Irish women. First, it meant that Irish girls were often a lot tougher than say their French or Polish counterparts. They were forced to hold their own with their boozy fathers, brothers and ultimately their husbands. They were schooled in how to survive by watching their gritty Irish mothers. It meant they often had to shoulder a lot more of the household duties than they should have had to. Also, they were never willing to back down from a verbal battle with any man, and if need be, could curse and swear with the proficiency of any dockhand or sailor.

Oftentimes they smoked, drank, and told bawdy jokes just like the men. A husband who got out of line the night before, might get to work the next day with a lunchbox full of potato peels and garbage instead of a sandwich and chips. It was often said that you never got an Irish girl china or crystal for a wedding gift, because within a year it would all be broken in vain attempts to hit their inebriated husbands.

There were two lines the men knew not to cross under any circumstances. Hitting a woman was an unforgiveable sin, which brought ten times the blows from the girl's father and brothers. As little boys, growing up in Catholic school, they were supposed to emulate the saints, and as such, were asked if they could even imagine St. Joseph striking the Blessed Virgin Mary. The model was clear, and there were of course some who fell short of this goal, but St. Joseph almost assuredly never drank a case of Budweiser in a day either.

The second line the men knew not to cross was to let the drinking affect your ability to get up and go to work every day. Being too hungover to make it into work, and therefore letting drinking get in the way of feeding your family, was inexcusable. To the Irish who survived The Great Famine, then came to America with nothing, a job was the difference between life and death. These were people who had worked night and day for decades to gain some power through politics and labor unions, for the purpose of getting control of jobs, so their children would never experience hunger.

Nevertheless, it seemed that most families wound up with one shit-bum, as they were so lovingly called. The Irish refer to this male family member as the one having "The Gene". They would never say that this member of the family was an alcoholic, because the definition of that word would have encompassed most of them. The shit-bum, on the other hand, could not hold a job or feed his family. Those men saddled with "The Gene" could not stop drinking under any circumstances and were usually shunned by the family. So, to recap, drinking too much every day was alright, as long as you did not hit women or fail to show up for work the next day.

There is an old Irish anecdote, handed down from father to son for as far back as anyone can remember. The father is proudly telling the boy how many city halls, police departments, fire departments and labor unions that the Irish control. After letting the enormity of this revelation set in for a few moments, the father asks the son, "Do you know why God created whiskey, boy?"

Whereupon the attentive young man answers dutifully, "No I don't."

The father replies, "He created it to keep the Irish from taking over the whole fucking world!"

About four years into their marriage, Kathleen woke up around seven on a very warm Saturday morning in July and realized Patrick had not come to bed the night before. This was not so unusual, and she preferred he stay on the couch in the living room when he had been out drinking anyway. The panic started when she saw he wasn't on the couch either. He usually stopped at the Shamrock, or one of a dozen other drinking holes after work on Friday, but he always made it home. Frantically she began looking in the kid's rooms, then the basement, to no avail. Finally, she threw open the drapes over the living room picture window and saw their station wagon parked at an angle, with the two front tires on the lawn and the two rear tires on the driveway. The driver's door was wide open, and Patrick was passed out face down on the lawn, about six feet from the sidewalk and six feet from the car on the passenger side.

For a moment, she stood there blinking in disbelief at the scene in her front yard. Then her jaw started to protrude, and her face went from white to red to purple, and all the freckles disappeared. She began to feel anger start to raise its ugly head inside her, before she caught herself. A screaming scene in front of the neighborhood would not do anyone any good she thought. But, she whispered through clenched teeth, "I am not going to live my life like this."

Quickly she turned around, went to her room, dressed, brushed her angry hair, and got the kids up. By this time, Michael was three, Margaret Mary was two and little Sean was a toddling one year old. Number four was still a few months away from his or her arrival. Kathleen was six months pregnant, and hormonal surges were playing a significant role in this morning's decision-making process. She told the kids they were going to have a picnic breakfast out on the front lawn, which of course, was a first for the young troop.

In a matter of minutes, she had a card table, an adult folding chair and three little seats for the kids set up next to the still comatose Patrick. The next time she came outside, she had little Sean on one arm, and a shopping bag filled with a box of cereal, half gallon of milk, spoons and bowls on the other arm. All three kids were still in their summer pajamas and barefoot, and Sean needed a diaper change. Anyone who has ever raised little ones, and attempted to change their morning routine, knows the children had a few questions for their Mommy.

"Why is Daddy laying in the grass Mommy?" asked Michael.

"Is Daddy alright, Mommy?" asked a concerned Margaret Mary.

"Daddy," Sean added as he pointed toward Patrick.

"He's alright. Your Daddy got drunk and passed out," Kathleen answered in a surprisingly calm voice, so as not to upset the kids.

True to her word, each of the kids now had a bowl full of cereal and milk, except Sean who only had cereal, as he had not mastered the spoon yet.

"What's passed out Mommy?" asked the ever-curious Margaret Mary.

"Passoot, passoot, passoot," laughed little Sean as some of his Cheerios fell out of his mouth.

"When will he wake up Mommy?" asked Michael, now standing over his father.

"I really don't know, Michael. Soon I hope," answered Kathleen, once again in an uncharacteristicly calm voice.

The neighborhood was beginning to stir, and clearly the O'Tooles were going to be the center of attention for the start of the weekend in Forestwood. "Is everything okay Kathleen?" hollered the kind senior, Mr. Siegfried, from across the street.

"Just fine, thanks!" waved Kathleen cheerfully.

"Kathleen, do you need an ambulance?" yelled Roberta DeNatalli. She was cupping her hands next to her mouth to make sure she was heard from her next-door porch to the right of the O'Tooles' house, as you looked from the street.

"Oh, no thanks Roberta!" yelled back a smiling Kathleen.

The children were now starting to roam around the yard a bit in their pajamas, doing what little kids do with freedom. Sean decided he would use his Daddy as a sort of a jungle gym and began crawling all over him, mumbling, "Dadadada".

"Look Mommy," shrieked Margaret Mary as she held up a new found shiny rock.

An older couple in their late fifties, the Hanfelds, who were out walking their little toy poodle, made a point to cross the street before reaching the O'Tooles. They wanted absolutely no part of whatever was happening in their yard.

"Good morning!" called Kathleen warmly, while waving to them.

Eyes down, the Hanfeld's hurried on down the sidewalk as Karl Hanfeld whispered to his wife Gertrude, "I told you the Irish were animals."

Bob and Harriet Wilson, were the O'Tooles' neighbors on the left. They were a little older, in their forties, and had two kids in high school. They had come out together to go grocery shopping and were standing next to their car with their mouths open, taking in the scene of their neighbor's breakfast table. Slowly they walked past the O'Toole family car and stopped next to Kathleen. Patrick stirred just enough to assure them that he was, in fact, still alive.

"Sorry I can't offer you coffee this morning," Kathleen smiled from her chair, "just haven't gotten around to it yet."

Slowly Harriet leaned down, put her hand on her younger neighbor's shoulder, and whispered, "Kathleen, why don't we all go inside? What do you say? Bob can get Pete DeNatalli to help get Patrick up."

"No, no, the family that eats together stays together," cracked Kathleen while waving her finger from side to side.

"I gotta go poo poo, Mommy!" shrieked Margaret Mary.

"Poopoo, poopoo, poopoo!" added Sean.

"Can we watch cartoons now Mommy?" asked Michael, getting his three-year-old face within a few inches of Kathleen's.

"Not yet honey. Go over and kick your father and see if he wakes up," she answered.

"Honey please, let's all go inside," pleaded Harriet.

"I'm going to get a couple guys to help," said Bob as he backed away.

"Don't you dare!" Kathleen ordered as she stood up. "I know you mean well, but this is a private family matter," she asserted through clenched teeth, clearly missing the irony in that statement.

"Alright, alright then," said Harriet softly while raising her hands to show her palms, "we'll just go on to the grocery store. But at some point, one of these old busy bodies is going to call the police, you know."

Kathleen let her head fall back as she laughed heartily. "I'm afraid that is one thing this family need never fear!" she grinned.

As the Wilson's retreated, Harriet thought how lucky she had been marrying old boring Bob, as her mother had referred to him years ago. Bob, who rarely ever drank, was a junior accountant at McDonnell Douglas Aircraft, and got home from work every day between 4:55 and 5:00. Twenty some odd years before, she had almost fallen for a good looking, fast talking Irish boy by the name of Brendan Flanagan, who her mother thought was just wonderful. He was always the life of the party until he passed out. As they drove up Highmont, Harriet reached over and gently stroked boring Bob's arm. He had no idea why.

A half hour later, after a few more kicks from Michael, and Margaret Mary using his back for a trampoline, Patrick began to stir, and opened his eyes. It was nearly nine o'clock now, and almost eighty degrees. He had grass in his hair, and his mouth, and a few wayward horseflies were landing intermittently on his arms and biting him. His head felt like someone was pounding on it with a ten-pound sledge hammer. The pain was unbearable, but he couldn't seem to move yet.

All he could see was two familiar female feet in plastic thongs, and the tubular metal legs of a lawn chair. He closed his eyes again to keep the world out a little longer, and realized he had a toddler crawling on him. All he could hear was the chattering of the other two kids. Slowly he began to roll over, catching Sean and spitting out grass as he came to a seated position.

"Hi Daddy!" cried Michael cheerfully.

"Why did you sleep on the grass outside?" asked the ever-curious Margaret Mary.

"Dadadadadada," Sean babbled as he made his way onto Patrick's lap.

When his eyes met Kathleen's, it was readily apparent, that she would not be giving as cheerful a reception as he had gotten from the children.

"Well, well, well," she chirped, feigning an Irish brogue, "Will

you look at Himself now. The man of the house. Our protector and provider, in the flesh."

"Kath..." he started.

"Don't you say a goddam word," she shot back.

"Goddam, goddam, goddam," bubbled little Sean, trying to get his dad to pay attention to him. The other two kids started to back away, sensing the mood change.

Lowering her voice, she literally spit out her prepared speech. "Listen to me Patrick. I want you to know that the whole goddam neighborhood saw us out here this morning. They are in their houses right now, talking about the shanty Irish on their street, and how we are exactly what they thought we were. To them we're nothing but a drunken Mick laborer and his nutty red-headed baby machine, who is getting ready to drop another mouth to feed in their litter. I can't live like this," she cried, with her voice shaking.

"Kath..." he tried to start again.

"Shut the fuck up Patrick," she hissed as she leaned close enough for him to smell her breath. It was then he saw something he had never seen before. Kathleen had tears in her eyes. "If you want to keep this up, behave like our fathers, that's fine. Just go inside and pack your shit and get the hell out of here. But I want to remind you, that you promised we would have a normal quiet life, like all the other normal quiet people in this world. You just broke that promise for the last time."

With that she grabbed Sean off his lap, hoisted him on her hip and yelled at the other two to get inside. Patrick watched as his beautiful pregnant wife climbed the three steps of the porch, held the screen door for Michael and Margaret Mary, and slammed it behind her. Slowly he got to his feet, sweating profusely now in the hot sun, and walked over to the wagon and repositioned it properly in the driveway. He could feel the eyes of a dozen of neighbors on him as he did.

From that day forward, Patrick never drank another drop of alcohol. Clearly, he had been born a proud recipient of "The Gene". His friends said he was no fun anymore, and a lot of them stayed away. Guys at work called him pussy-whipped when he went straight home from work. Even his own father, Jimmy, said he did not think he could ever trust a man completely that did not drink. Other family members thought he surely was sick in some way, as this was such a rare occurrence in Irish families.

To his credit, Patrick never wavered regardless of the occasion. To her credit, Kathleen never again brought that Saturday morning up to him, and she never told a soul why he quit drinking.

CHAPTER FIFTEEN

Michael Patrick O'Toole was born in July of 1950 to Patrick and Kathleen O'Toole at St. Mary's Hospital in Clayton, MO. Clayton is the nearest suburb west of St. Louis city, and is also just west of Forest Park. The hospital was only a five-minute drive from their flat in Dogtown. They felt very blessed and thanked the Blessed Virgin every night for their good fortune at having such a beautiful, healthy baby boy.

Patrick could tell early on that Michael was going to be a good athlete. Even as a little guy he would effortlessly catch, kick, throw or hit any ball that came his way. Patrick also relished the boy's confidence as he grew, and how he seemed to be a natural leader among his friends. Wrestling and roughhousing in the living room were a regular event as long as mom wasn't home.

For her part, Kathleen was determined that her oldest be a kind and compassionate soul, with a good heart. She felt they had enough hard drinking, hard fighting Irish laborers in the family already. She wanted her son to have impeccable manners, never curse, go to college and make something of himself, that did not include construction work or police work. When the opportunity presented itself, in a quiet one-on-one moment, she would whisper her expectations and dreams to him.

Both of his parents felt Michael was the most handsome little boy in his first-grade class photo. He had a full head of wavy brown hair, twinkling blue eyes like his father, and big wide smile like his mother, that made everybody in the room smile right back. Grandma Maureen said it was a Kennedy smile.

He started first grade in 1956 at Sts. John and James Catholic grade school in Ferguson. It was a fifteen-minute walk to school from their home on Highmont Dr. Seven minutes if you ran the whole way, which was sometimes necessary if you were late. The Sisters of St. Joseph of Carondelet ran the school in an orderly fashion. The girls wore navy blue jumper dresses with a white blouse and a blue tie. The boys wore Navy pants and tie with a white shirt. When the kids lined up for anything like lunch or to exit the playground, the boys and girls were in separate lines. The parish school eventually had over nine hundred kids in eight grades, by the mid-sixties.

Michael's first grade class had forty-seven students ruled by single five-foot one-inch nun by the name of Sister Alicia. Even with Sister being severely outnumbered, you could hear a pin drop in her classroom most of the day, just like every other classroom in the school for that matter. If Sister's disciplinary rules did not make you behave properly, a call home from her, would ensure proper behavior from that day on. Sister was always right and the child always wrong when those calls were made. There were four Michaels, four Kevins, three Patricks, three James, two Johns and two Seans in Michaels class alone at Sts. John and James. Once again this illustrated the lack of creativity in Irish families when naming their progeny.

Michael was smart and kind to his classmates, and his quick smile just enhanced his popularity with both his teachers and the other kids. To his father's delight he played a sport in every season from third grade on, in the Catholic Youth Council leagues, or CYC for short. He played soccer in the fall, basketball in the winter and baseball in the spring, excelling at all three. His teammates regularly elected him the team captain.

To his mother's delight he got all E's on every single report card, no matter what the subject, and always received a glowing character review from the Sisters as well. The nuns liked to give Michael extra books to read to keep him challenged, and he devoured them. He never bragged or gloated about his academic or athletic prowess, and even displayed patience and empathy towards other students who were struggling. The Sisters even asked him to tutor sometimes, because of the large class sizes, and he gladly helped.

The children were all required to go to Mass every morning before school, and Michael never had to be scolded for pushing or shoving in line or talking in church. Michael knew that he would have to confess any of that kind of behavior as a sin, when the family went to Confession every Saturday afternoon at four o'clock sharp. The Sisters told them it was better to do as you are told, because then you were in and out of the confessional in no time at all, with a short penance of just a couple Hail Marys and a couple Our Fathers. Clearly, you didn't want to be in the confessional very long because then everyone assumed you had a long list of sins. In short, Michael was a good Irish Catholic boy.

In sixth grade Michael petitioned, and trained, to be an altar boy, which was a great honor. His father, uncles and grandfathers had all been altar boys, so it was a time-honored family tradition. Not all of the boys were chosen, especially if they displayed any poor behavior or lack of reverence around the altar while training. After all, as an altar boy, you were entrusted with very important responsibilities, and there could be no mistakes during the Holy Mass.

First, there was the lighting of the candles without any mishaps, like knocking one over. Second, you had to pay close attention, and ring the bells at precisely the moment that the priest changed the bread and wine into the Body and Blood of Jesus. Most importantly you held the gold dish under the communicants' chins as the priest put the Body of the Lord on their tongue, making sure that they had it safely in their mouth before moving on. Letting the Body of Jesus fall on the ground was an unacceptable mistake and could lead to being dismissed from the server's corps.

By the time he was thirteen, Michael was nearly a head taller than most of his classmates. During eighth grade, he began to fill out and shave and notice that some of the girls at school smiled at him for no reason. At fourteen, after eighth grade, you could join your parish CYC teen group and go to their monthly dances.

He was particularly conflicted by the girls' attention at these dances, because he had been asked by the Sisters, the pastor, and even his grandmother, to consider the priesthood as a vocation. There was, of course, no greater honor that a boy could bring to his family, especially an Irish family, than to become a priest. Unfortunately, the vow of celibacy was nearly incomprehensible to most fourteen-year-olds.

Girls had become a pleasant distraction though. Michael loved the way they smelled and the way they tossed their hair when they were talking to him. He tried as hard as he could not to look at their breasts or their legs, because then he would have to confess the sin of having impure thoughts. No matter how much he prayed, sometimes he just couldn't make those thoughts go away.

Their old pastor, Father Donovan, had warned the boys about this when they split from the girls for health class in eighth grade. He told them that kissing a girl was alright if it was only for a few seconds. Kissing any longer would lead to the sin of lust. Open-mouth, or French kissing, was a form of intercourse, and therefore considered a sin as well. Father Donovan also told them that it was a sin to touch themselves "down there" unless they were going to the bathroom or bathing. All other touching "down there" was a sin called masturbation.

They all knew that a mortal sin was a heavy black mark on your soul which would keep you out of heaven for all eternity if you were to die before confessing it to a priest. You received a mortal sin for serious offenses like murder or adultery. A venial sin was a smaller mark on your soul, for things like talking back to your parents or lying. If you died with venial sins on your soul, you would have to spend time in Purgatory, before you could get into heaven. Depending on the amount and seriousness of these venial sins that time in Purgatory could be years.

There wasn't much talk amongst the boys after these sessions. They were left to contemplate the hurdles that their pastor had just given to them on their quest to get into heaven. Unfortunately, their bodies and minds were urging them to act in a completely opposite manner, about twenty-three hours a day. When Sister Mary Joseph, their old principal, returned the girls to the classroom after a very similar lecture, they were unnaturally quiet as well. Father Donovan told the boys, and Sister Mary Joseph told the girls, that keeping busy with schoolwork, sports and prayer would save them from having these impure thoughts. Like everyone else, Michael did not see how soccer or algebra was going to help. The only hope, maybe, was prayer.

Michael started high school in 1964 at St Thomas Aquinas Catholic High School in Florissant, Missouri, which was the next suburban municipality north of Ferguson. It was a ten-minute drive from the house if there wasn't too much traffic. Aquinas was a coed school run by the Archdiocese of St. Louis. It was a burdensome expense for Catholic families especially those with a lot of kids, but it was still cheaper than the all-girls or all-boys Catholic schools run by religious orders like the Jesuits.

At orientation, a couple weeks before school started, the freshman football coach, Bob Ahearn, came over to talk and shake hands with Michael, Patrick and Kathleen. The six-foot two-inch, one hundred and seventy-pound Michael naturally caught his eye.

"Have you thought about going out for football, Michael?" he asked.

"I've never played so I'm not sure, sir," Michael answered.

"We don't really know much about the sport, Mr. Ahearn. He only played CYC baseball, basketball and soccer," Patrick added.

"That's usually the case. We can teach you the rules and basics pretty quick. With your size, you could be a big asset to our team, Michael," he smiled, "So we would love to have you. You need a fall sport anyway because we play soccer in the winter as you probably know. Think it over. All the info you need is over at the athletics table in the corner."

After the coach walked off, Michael asked his dad, "Well what do you think?"

"We'll see. Books and class sign up first," Patrick answered.

"Amen," added Kathleen.

Little did they know that Michael and football would turn out to be a match made in heaven. After a couple games as a freshman the coaches moved him to the sophomore squad. In his sophomore year, they moved him up right away to the varsity squad. He started as a sophomore on the varsity playing both ways, at defensive end and running back. By his junior year, anyone who followed high school sports in the papers, knew the name of Michael O'Toole, for his multi-sport abilities in soccer and baseball, but mostly for his prowess on the football field. He was setting all sorts of local records in football, especially in rushing yards and touchdowns, which led to his being voted to the All-State team. He had single handedly put little St. Thomas Aquinas on the statewide sports map.

In his senior year, now at six-foot three-inches and two hundred and twenty pounds, he was declared Aquinas' scholar athlete of the year. He had been in the National Honor Society for four straight years, and became a National Merit scholar his senior year, virtually guaranteeing him a scholarship to the university of his choice.

When the acceptance letter from Notre Dame, complete with a combined academic/football scholarship, was pulled from the mailbox on Highmont one Saturday morning halfway through his senior year, every O'Toole, O'Keefe, Finnegan and Fitzgerald in St Louis knew about it within an hour. The entire extended family was delirious at the thought of Michael becoming part of The Fighting Irish. For the next few hours there was an unending stream of friends, neighbors and relatives knocking at the door, or just walking in the house, or congregating on the lawn, or even in the street, in various stages of inebriation as the word spread and the party grew.

At one point, about two hours after they opened the envelope, Michael realized he had not hugged and kissed his mom yet, and in fact, had not even spoken to her. Not seeing her anywhere else, Michael walked down the short hall to his parent's bedroom, where he heard some undeniable sniffling and nose blowing from behind the closed door.

"Mom, can I come in?" he asked at the door, like he had done hundreds of times over the years.

"Yes, of course Michael," she answered. When he poked his head in, he saw Kathleen with two red eyes and a red nose and a box of Kleenex and a photo album. It was a rare occasion indeed to see Kathleen O'Toole in tears. In fact, she was not above pontificating on the uselessness of the practice when the occasion arose. "Sit down Michael," she ordered gruffly, while dabbing her eyes with one hand and patting the bed with the other. "I hate crying. It makes women look weak," she declared.

"What's wrong mom?" her hulking soft-hearted son asked, while staring at her profile, since she still had not looked directly at him.

Still staring ahead, she blew her nose one more time before turning to look directly into those beautiful, cobalt blue eyes she had brought into the world. These were the same soulful eyes of his father and grandfather, but without their surrounding weathered and lined skin. His face was still the smooth and innocent face of a boy as far as she was concerned. She reached up slowly and laid her palm against his cheek. All her thoughts were running to the hopes and dreams she had secretly held onto all these years for Michael's future.

"My sweet boy, you are going to be the first member of this family on either side to go to college. And of all places, Notre Dame. My God Michael, I am so very, very proud of you," she told him quietly, tearing up again.

"Thank you, mom," he smiled, "so these are happy tears?"

"Of course, of course. Now move along, I have to fix my face. Your Grandpa is throwing a big bash in your honor at the Shamrock tonight. Put on some decent clothes so we can show 'em that the shanty Irish can clean up occasionally," she smiled.

Michael graduated from St. Thomas Aquinas in the spring of 1968. There were a whole lot of Irish eyes smiling that day. All four clans saw Michael as their standard bearer, as he prepared to enter a world that none of them could even imagine. All the suffering and hard work of the generations before him was about to bear fruit. One of their own was about to go away to college on a full scholarship. Their genes had produced an intelligent, handsome young man who had risen to the top, both in academics and athletics. He wasn't going to just any college but to the ultimate destination: Notre Dame, home of the Fighting Irish. This was their boy...and he was Irish...and he was Catholic!

CHAPTER SIXTEEN

Margaret Mary O'Toole was Patrick and Kathleen's second child. She was known as an Irish twin, having been born barely ten months after Michael. She had her mother's unruly red hair, green eyes, and ghastly white skin, covered with thousands of freckles. She also possessed the proverbial map of Ireland on her round face with its distinctive round eyes and toothy smile.

Unlike Michael, who was tall and square shouldered, she was short, plump and round shouldered. While Michael had been smiling and gregarious since he was a baby, Margaret Mary tended to be quiet, and carried a serious countenance. When something funny happened, Michael would throw his head back and laugh, while she would just grin and nod a couple times.

For a variety of reasons, Michael could have been a tough act to follow in school, but for the fact that Margaret Mary idolized her big brother. When she started each grade at Sts. John and James, the nuns always gave her a warm welcome just because she was Michael's sister. She excelled in all her subjects in school, especially mathematics, and eventually the nuns asked Kathleen if it would be okay if they promoted her from third to fifth grade. She proudly agreed, and from fifth grade on Margaret Mary was in the same classroom as Michael, which only enhanced their status as "twins".

Patrick doted on his oldest daughter, recognizing that for all intent and purposes she was a mini-Kathleen. He especially got a kick out of how even as a little girl, she would furrow her brow, stick her bottom lip out and put her hands on her hips just like her mother, when she was displeased with something or someone. He would laugh until his sides hurt, and his eyes were watering, when describing her petulant nature to friends.

On the other hand, Margaret Mary and her mother Kathleen were often at odds with each other over any one of a thousand things, both small and large. Their running battles became routine background noise in the O'Toole home, not much different than if someone had left a radio playing all day. It went something like this.

"Margaret Mary, would you please set the table for dinner."

"Why doesn't everyone just set their own place?"

"That's not the way it works."

"We should change the rules then so one person doesn't get overworked."

Or...

"Margaret Mary, run next door to the Wilson's and get some milk."

"Let's just drink Kool-Aid tonight."

"Milk is better for you."

"You can't get rickets from missing milk at one dinner."

Or...

"Margaret Mary, did you finish your homework?"

"I think homework is an infringement on my personal time."

"Maybe, but why don't you bring it to me when you're done."

"I'm afraid you're going to have to take my word that it's done."

And so it went, year after year after year. Given the same directions or chores, Michael always just answered, "Yes ma'am".

Margaret Mary did not really care for sports, but like everyone in their extended family, she loved watching Michael play, and learned the rules of the games through osmosis. She found more pleasure in creating a scientific journal detailing the number and variety of birds who used their feeder in the back yard, noting the time and duration of their visits. The Sisters gave Margaret Mary lots of extra reading in the summer months, but instead of the novels they gave

Michael, they gave her books on physics, astronomy and biology.

Throughout grade school Margaret Mary went to Mass and Communion every day before school. She was a devout little girl, and like Michael, entertained the possibility of a religious vocation, but from a much earlier age. Her mother, grandmother and the Sisters all encouraged her, and answered any questions she had about religious life. Margaret Mary loved the Sisters and relished any chance to join them in the convent, like stopping by to pick up reading material. The convent was so peaceful and quiet that she felt that she could read a book a day if she lived there.

The convent was nothing like home where she had four younger siblings running around and demanding her attention. Altogether there were eight of them in an eight-hundred and fifty square foot bungalow. The constantly running television in the living room and radio in the kitchen added to the chaos. Often she went into her mother's side of her parent's clothes closet with a flashlight and a book, and just sat on the floor, reading with the door shut.

When Margaret Mary started high school at St. Thomas Aquinas, she was known less by her name, and far more as "Michael's sister". She was fine with being in his shadow, as this suited her natural inclination to be out of the spotlight anyway. What she had to learn to be wary of, were girls at school who befriended her solely for the opportunity to get to know Michael. After she invited them to the house, they would totally ignore her in their efforts to flirt with him. Others initiated conversations with her, only to quickly start asking about Michael's likes, dislikes and where he hung out. Eventually she got a reputation for being standoffish, because her cynicism outweighed a desire for new friends.

The boys, on the other hand, were so intimidated by Michael's size and ferocity on the football field, that they kept a respectful distance from her, for fear that their normal testosterone-fueled behavior would land them in trouble. The few brave souls who approached her after a few beers at a party, or just did not know who her brother was, found out quickly that Margaret Mary O'Toole was the epitome of a good Irish Catholic girl. There was no way that any alcohol-induced attempt to kiss her or lay a hand anywhere on her person would be tolerated. Sister Mary Joseph's health class lectures at Sts. John and James remained deeply embedded in her psyche for years to come.

Sister Mary Joseph told them to kiss with a closed mouth and keep the boys hands from wandering to their private areas. This was followed by a detailed description of what life for a teen-age girl who got pregnant would be like. She had mastered the ability to look directly into the eyes of each girl as she spoke, thereby enhancing the chilling effects of her warnings.

All of these factors meant that Margaret Mary usually walked the halls of Aquinas by herself, whereas Michael usually had an entourage. She didn't mind because, without fanfare, Michael always made sure she was invited if he and his friends were going to a party, to the show or just hanging out. Margaret Mary knew they were all friendly to her because she was Michael O'Toole's sister, but she didn't care. Her big brother always made her feel safe and loved.

Margaret Mary excelled in high school because she loved her schoolwork. It was the most important part of her life, because it was what she did best. She became a National Merit Scholar like her big brother and had a number of academic scholarship opportunities to some very prestigious universities as she neared graduation. There was considerably less commotion and recognition surrounding Margaret Mary's impending graduation, than there was with Michael. She was the co-owner of the honor to be first in the family to go to college. Yet, she did not receive the same acclaim, since it was quietly presumed she would meet a nice, Irish Catholic boy at school, get married and start having kids before finishing college. She kept it to herself, but their expectations did not match the vision she had of her future.

Part VI

Private and Public Roads

CHAPTER SEVENTEEN

The relationship that siblings share is usually longer than any other in life. It's comforting to know there is another person out there who lived and experienced much of the same past. They even provide a sounding board for each other as they age, to check the veracity of their memories. Brothers and sisters strengthen that unique bond between them by looking back together and laughing at a comedic event or reflecting on the sadness of a tragedy from their shared lives. Michael and Margaret Mary grew as close as a brother and sister could be.

There were two events from their past, one private, and one public, that they brought up most as they got older. The first one was the private event, experienced only by members of their immediate and extended family. It was important because it had all the necessary ingredients to make those of Irish heritage, especially those of the shanty persuasion, laugh until their sides hurt. Those from other cultural, religious and ethnic groups tended to cringe in disgust after hearing the story, citing its crude nature and lack of reverence.

The public event began with unbridled celebration and ended with gut wrenching sorrow and despair. They watched as these same Irish Catholics family members reacted with vile outbursts of profanity, and frightening displays of anger. Those from other cultural, religious and ethnic groups merely cried and prayed.

The juxtaposition of these two events, and the dichotomy of

the reactions between the Irish and non-Irish, goes to the very heart of why Michael and Margaret Mary cherished each other and their shared history and heritage.

The private event occurred on Easter Sunday in 1960. Grandma Bridgey and Grandpa Jimmy O'Toole, always invited their eight children, their spouses and their grandchildren over for a big Easter dinner. The family gathered at their one thousand square foot home on Nashville Ave. in Dogtown for brunch after ten-thirty Mass at St. James the Greater. This was an annual event that was becoming a logistical nightmare, due to the arrival of additional grandchildren almost every year. There were forty-six people in all, with an additional four "on the way". Seating everyone required folding tables in the living room, dining room, bedrooms, basement and garage, which also housed the keg of Budweiser.

This year the crowd was getting a little cranky since they had now been fasting for well over twelve hours. When everyone was finally seated, and each table had its share of ham and potato salad, Bridgey began banging a spoon on a pot which signaled an announcement was coming. In a loud and clear voice she said, "We might as well skip grace. We were just praying an hour ago and that should cover us for a while, so dig in!"

"Amen!" they all called out while laughing and grabbing silverware.

"I'm going to bring everyone bread and water," Jimmy announced, "That way it won't be such a shock if any of you get locked up!"

"You should know," Bridgey muttered under her breath as she stomped around the kitchen. There was no air conditioning, and the heat in the kitchen was beginning to take a toll on her patience.

"Hey can somebody bring us a pitcher of beer in the living room?" yelled uncle Tim, who was not accustomed to waiting past noon for refreshment.

"We need one back here in the bedroom too!" hollered uncle

Sean, "and why is it so goddam hot in here anyway?"

"It's so hot because Jimmy painted the inside of the windows and now they won't open!" declared Bridgey, while wiping her forehead with a dishtowel.

"It's cooler in the basement," announced aunt Beatrice as she exited the stairwell and headed for the keg to fill a pitcher, "but the smell of a dead mouse and Lysol down there is killing my appetite."

"You look like you could stand to miss a meal or two anyway," said her brother Pat to a round of laughter.

After ten minutes or so, Bridgey spotted a few of the kids starting to leave their seats. It was time for her to announce the traditional directions she gave her grandchildren at most crowded holiday gatherings by yelling, "Go outside and play. There's too many of you to stay in here! For that matter why don't you all go play in the street and maybe we'll get lucky!"

That brought lots of hoots and laughter from all over the house, but unfortunately the gaiety was about to come to an abrupt end. Grandpa Jimmy had polished off twenty-two Budweisers the day before at McCorkles Tavern down the street. Then he came home and ate eight hard-boiled eggs before stumbling to bed. He was sitting at a table in the basement eating a ham sandwich and drinking his first beer when he felt the beginning of a telltale rumbling deep within his bowels. Quickly he stood up and started for the stairs, pushing a couple of the grandkids out of his way. "Make way, make way!" he boomed.,

His own eight children, having been raised with one bathroom, knew immediately the gravity of the situation upon hearing Jimmy's patented plea. He hurriedly made his way up the first eight steps to the landing where the door was propped open to the garage. As he turned to start the next eight steps to the kitchen, the whole house heard the unmistakable sound of the release of approximately fourteen hours of pent-up flatulence.

Having grown up in the house, the experienced uncle Patrick hollered from the basement, "Run for your lives!"

"Women and children first!" screamed uncle Tim from the living room.

As Jimmy cleared the top step into the kitchen, Bridgey began hitting him with a roll of French bread. Even though she had previously waved the need for prayer, Bridgey began timing her swings with calls to the Holy Family. "Jesus, Mary and Joseph Jimmy, it's Easter Sunday for Chrissake!"

Slowly, but efficiently, the mind-numbing odor began to make its way into every corner of the house, garage and basement. With napkins held to their faces, everyone was trying to push themselves away from their table and get out of the house as quickly as possible. To make matters worse, the babies began to scream and load their diapers due to being frightened by all the commotion.

As Jimmy raced to the bathroom still hollering, "Make way! Make way!" two of his pregnant daughters-in-law, stricken with the morning sickness, exited the bathroom just in time for Jimmy to enter and slam the door.

At this point the entire family began to realize the severity of their plight when they found that the overhead garage door was locked, probably to protect the keg, and the walkout door from the garage to the back yard was missing its handle. The front door offered the only hope of escape after a few pieces of furniture were hastily moved out of the way.

The exodus took on a decidedly more religious tone as family members cried out such phrases as 'Lord have mercy!' and 'May God have mercy on our souls!'.

Finally making his way from the basement, uncle Mike warned loud enough for all to hear, "You know this odor is known to cause birth defects and brain damage! If you don't believe me, just look at the poor souls who grew up in this house!"

"Shut up!" screamed a few of those poor souls in unison.

Eventually, there were about twenty members of the family milling around the front lawn, and about twenty more in the back yard, who had escaped by kicking the rear door open. A large contingent of the O'Toole clan began gathering around the keg, trying to calm their nerves.

A number of families, in their new Easter outfits from the nearby Methodist, Lutheran, and Baptist churches were making their way to and from their own services. All of them walked to the opposite side of the street upon witnessing the commotion, with some whispering to their children not to look over at the O'Tooles.

Uncle Liam, who by now was well into his second pitcher of beer, hollered across the street, "Someone may have died over here, you know. You could at least act concerned!"

"Liam, haven't we made enough of a spectacle for one day!" his wife Kathleen hissed at him through clenched teeth.

As things gradually calmed down, the O'Toole mothers were collecting their children and hustling them into the back yard. The O'Toole fathers were smoking and drinking in the garage when Grandpa Jimmy sheepishly made his way out of the house. A hush fell over the men for a moment as Jimmy poured himself a beer without speaking.

Finally, his eldest son Patrick said quietly, "Dad have you ever thought of going back to Belfast?"

"Now why the 'fook' would I want to do that?" snarled Jimmy.

"Well I'll bet you could just walk through the Prot neighborhoods farting, and most of the bastards would be jumping into the channel and swimming back to England to escape the smell."

Even decades later, the story always made family members and their Irish friends double over with laughter. As they grew up, Michael and Margaret Mary noticed their non-Irish friends would just stare at them with a perplexed expression on their faces upon hearing the story. Some of those friends, co-workers and neighbors would solemnly add that they felt a story about flatulence on the holiest day of the year in Christianity was irreverent. But for the Irish, the incongruence of the story, was exactly what made the legend of the Easter Fart so memorable.

CHAPTER EIGHTEEN

The important public event in Michael and Margaret Mary's childhood actually had two parts. The first was the election of John Fitzgerald Kennedy to be the first Irish Catholic President of the United States. For the rest of their lives, the two of them loved to relive the celebrations which followed President Kennedy's election. Everyone in their world in November of 1960 was jubilant, cheering, laughing and crying with joy. Everyone of drinking age, or close to it, was partying and buying drinks for friends and acquaintances. It was later said, that every Irish Catholic man, woman and child voted that day at least once, even some who had passed away.

Having been acquainted with their tumultuous and subservient Irish heritage by their grandparents, they knew on a visceral level how deeply important and emotional the election of an Irish Catholic president was to the Irish all over the world. But Kennedy's victory in a majority Protestant United States of America, was too much for their grandparents to even imagine. After all, just a few generations before in Ireland, being Catholic meant having food withheld from you and your children by a Protestant hierarchy.

It was always fun to go back and relive the pride, excitement and celebrations. Grandpa Jimmy and Grandma Bridgey had a three-day party at their house for anyone who walked through the door. They kept the doors open, and didn't care who drank what, or who passed out where, for three whole days. When the celebrating spilled out in the front yard, some of the neighbors who were less enamored with the results of the election would call the police, but when the patrolmen showed up, they generally stayed at the party for an hour or better themselves.

Grandma and Grandpa Finnegan had an equally wild party at the Shamrock for nearly a week after the election. Big John had worked nearly night and day in the wards before voting day, and Maureen had worked tirelessly on the phone banks, making sure that every St. Louis residence with a phone got a call from the Kennedy campaign. There were shamrocks and Irish flags everywhere you looked.

To a couple Irish kids in St Louis it was a joyous moment in history. Any trace of that victim mentality that their immigrant grandparents had brought with them from Ireland seemed to be gone. American Irish Catholics now had one of their own in the most powerful position in the entire world.

Three short years later, thirteen-year-old Michael and twelve-year-old Margaret Mary, would watch as the memory of all that jubilation turned into gut-wrenching sadness and vengeful anger. These same adults who they loved so dearly, flew into violent verbal and physical rage at the announcement of the assassination of their beloved President. They witnessed a side of their elders that they did not know existed. They were frightened by what they heard and saw, and years later remembered cowering in corners both at home and at their relative's homes, when the screaming and pain got to be too much to bear.

They saw their Grandpa Finnegan throw at least a dozen glasses one at a time against the inside walls of the Shamrock, screaming that he would never open the doors to his precious bar again. He kept ranting wildly how the fucking rich Prots always got their way. He painted in green letters two feet tall, on the brick wall of the bar along the sidewalk outside, the words 'CLOSED FOR FUNERAL'.

Grandma Maureen, normally dressed beautifully, with her hair perfectly coiffured, was almost unrecognizable. Her red hair was standing wildly as if it had not been combed in a week. Her eyes were red and puffy from the tears which seemed to be at the ready all the time, and she wore the same old pants and holy sweater for days on end. Gone were the expected special smiles and hugs for her precious grandchildren.

Michael and Margaret Mary remembered visiting Grandma and Grandpa O'Toole and seeing the two of them both blind drunk. Grandma Bridgey was curled up in bed, facing the wall, sobbing and sniffling with a whiskey bottle and water glass on the nightstand next to the bed. She wouldn't even roll over to talk to them.

Grandpa Jimmy was parked in his overstuffed chair in the living room with his own bottle and glass on the table next to him. At one point, he leaned down, and while shaking his finger at them, he screamed, "Now you know what these fookin' Prots are like. They're all fookin' murderers and thieves! Don't you kids EVER forget that!"

Patrick and Kathleen were trying to comfort their children as best they could, but Michael and Margaret Mary both remembered that their parents had a wide-eyed expression of disbelief or hopelessness for days on end.

When some of Kathleen's brothers or uncles stopped by the house, the kids would overhear them ranting how maybe they would quit responding to emergency calls, for police and firemen in the wealthy Prot neighborhoods.

"Let the rich fuckers fend for themselves. That'll teach 'em a lesson" their Uncle Brendan had said in a menacing voice.

Pounding the table, their Uncle Colin slurred, "I'm all for that. Why do we keep risking our necks for the bastards anyway? They just couldn't take one of us in a position to tell them what to do for once! Fuck 'em!"

The kids were shocked not only at the language, but that their mother allowed it without scolding the men. It seemed as if she knew this was not the time. She didn't even respond to their father when he screamed at her to turn the 'goddam' television off because he was tired of listening to the assassination bullshit. Normally Kathleen O'Toole never let anyone talk to her that way but this was different. These men were madder than she had ever seen, and they seemed constantly on the verge of exploding.

Years later, as adults, they would reminisce about all they had seen and heard as kids in November of 1963. The cold, hard reality of life had bulldozed its way into what previously had been a cheerful and carefree childhood. They got to see first-hand the raw emotions and angry determination of the ancient Irish, as described by Grandpa Jimmy, still flowed through their veins. They watched how the resilience and tenacity needed to survive the Famine, as described by Grandpa Finnegan, was still alive in their Irish genes.

In short, the assassination of President John Fitzgerald Kennedy, cemented the tribal bonds of Irish Catholics everywhere.

Part VII

Intersecting Roads

CHAPTER NINETEEN

Ignatius Mahoney was born in August of 1950 to a mother of unknown heritage and an alcoholic Irish father named Hank Mahoney. His parents did him no favor naming him after St. Ignatius, since the moment he got to first grade at Sts. John and James School, he was tagged forever after as Iggy.

Iggy's mom died in a car accident when he was just two. Hank was drunk, fell asleep at the wheel and hit a tree. Thankfully, Iggy had been with a sitter at home. Hank lost his license, and never drove or drew a sober breath again. He took the bus or caught rides to work at the Anheuser Busch brewery in south St. Louis. A neighbor lady watched Iggy during the day until he started school. Hank managed to make it home at some point every night in time to feed Iggy dinner before he passed out.

The Mahoneys also lived in Ferguson on a short street off busy Paul Ave named St Louis Ave, in the third small frame house on the right. It was a two-minute car ride or a ten-minute bike ride west of the O'Tooles' house on Highmont. The trip from Highmont to St louis Ave took you through an older neighborhood of mostly brick homes, before going under two railroad trestles.

One rail line ran east-west and the other ran north-south before they met and ran side by side behind Iggy's house. Hardly an hour passed without a train rumbling by on one of the lines. Sandwiched between the two rail lines was the Universal Match factory. The factory ran twenty-four hours a day, providing constant noise for its neighbors on St Louis Ave from tractor trailers, whistles and loud speakers.

Hank forgot to register Iggy for kindergarten, so his first day of school was in first grade at Sts. John and James. He was not as well prepared as the other kids, and eventually found himself in the Group Three classroom. There was not a great deal of concern for a child's self-esteem in the Catholic or public-school system in the late fifties, and therefore most used the tracking system. Group One was for the smart kids, Group Two was for the average kids and Group Three was for kids like Iggy.

The nuns would say that if you worked hard you could move from the Group Three class to the Group Two class. Group Two were told that they could work their way into Group One. Neither of these promotions were accomplished very often because it meant someone had to move down a Group to make way for the promoted student. That would cause the proverbial "wailing and gnashing of teeth" from the demoted student's parents. In short, your Group placement was usually permanent.

Along with his inauspicious academic start, Iggy had an equally tough time on the playground. Some of the other kids would taunt him that 'when God was handing out ugly, Iggy went back for seconds and thirds'. He was a few inches shorter than average, and he was skinny as a rail. To make matters worse, his permanent two front teeth were broken off at an angle. In the summer, when almost all the boys got crew-cuts, Iggy's head showed four or five white scars where no hair would grow. When the hair started growing back in, Iggy always looked like he just got out of bed regardless of what time of day it was. The hair around the scars grew out in all directions like an unruly mop.

Iggy was basically raising himself. His father got home around five in the evening, staggering down the street from drinking all day at the brewery. After eating a sandwich and taking a shower, Hank would stumble up the hillside in the back yard to the tracks, and then head west towards downtown Ferguson. He knew that the less time he was on the public streets, the less chance there was to be picked up for public drunkenness.

When he got to the South Florissant trestle he would slide down the rocky embankment to the sidewalk, and only have another block to walk to his home away from home, the Subway Bar. The Subway was hidden in the basement under Gasen's Drug Store, so it almost never got a police visit, since any fighting or arguments were muffled by being underground. This was an alcoholic's dream bar, and rightfully held the unofficial record for more purple noses on its barstools than at any other drinking establishment in Ferguson.

In short, the Subway was a dive. Parents all told their children to stay away from the place, as the potential to get run over by the patrons was certainly higher than at any other location in the city. Nevertheless, it was fun, in the absence of other diversions, to watch the men leave the dark basement in a drunken stupor and emerge into the bright sunlight, stumbling around the lot looking for their cars. It was not quite as fun, if your father was one of the stumblers of course.

Almost all the kids at Sts. John and James got to know Iggy over the years, not personally, but by reputation. It was not unusual to hear the echoes of one of the nun's screaming, 'IGNATIUS SIT DOWN AND BE QUIET!' Also, if you left your classroom to go to the bathroom, or to take something to the office, there was a fifty-fifty chance you would see Iggy seated at a desk in the hall outside his classroom, or in the principal's office. Margaret Mary, who always tried to be a good girl, was always a little apprehensive around Iggy when she saw him in the hall or at the office, because he was always in some sort of trouble. Nevertheless, Iggy always smiled and greeted her cheerfully. This made her nervous, because she was unaware of the reason for Iggy's congeniality.

He smiled at her, because her big brother Michael was the sole person to befriend Iggy at school. Michael had taken Iggy under his wing on the playground at the beginning of third grade. It happened on the playground because Michael was in the Group One class, and of course Iggy was in the Group Three class, so that was the only place where they could have met each other during the day. Margaret Mary was unaware of their alliance, because the boys and girls were on separate playgrounds. This was how the Church was able to save the children from whatever sinfulness might arise by the genders playing together.

Michael was usually one of the captains who picked other boys for his team at recess for whatever sport was in season. He made it a point to pick the guys first, who were usually picked last. The boys with the thick glasses, the smallest ones or just the guys who couldn't walk and chew gum at the same time, made their way on to Michael's team.

In Iggy's case, Michael watched how mercilessly some of the other boys picked on him because of his appearance and his erratic behavior, which also made him a target of the nuns. Until Michael reached out and asked him to play, Iggy had always stayed off by himself on the playground. He was unsure if Michael was sincere at first, but after he regularly got picked first or second for a couple weeks, he felt his status both on and off the playground changing. Getting regularly picked first by Michael O'Toole was a guarantee of getting some respect from the other boys at school. It turned out Iggy was actually a good athlete, so they became a formidable duo on the ball fields. Iggy's courage was especially impressive as he appeared absolutely fearless when it came to facing fast balls or tacklers.

All the boys in school wanted to be near Michael both at school and afterwards, because of his size, his smarts and his athleticism, but none more so than Iggy. Iggy secretly revered Michael, who may have been the first person in his life to show him any kindness whatsoever.

Iggy's problems at school started first thing every morning

because of clothing issues. The girls' uniform was a white shirt, navy blue jumper and tie, and black and white saddle shoes. The boys' uniform was a white shirt, navy blue tie and pants, and black dress shoes. No exceptions. The nuns wanted everyone to look exactly the same and they were always on high alert for even the smallest attempt at individuality raising its ugly head. These breaks in uniformity could lead to the sin of arrogance, in a system that demanded humility above all else.

Iggy would show up for school wearing whatever he could find at home. He might have a blue shirt and no tie, or a collarless shirt with a red tie. On the days he had the right shirt and tie, the white shirt might have the same big jelly stain on it for a week. If he tore a hole in the seat of his pants, it might have a piece of grey duct tape over the hole to hide his underwear for a month. But nothing drove the nuns crazier than when he showed up to school wearing high top black sneakers.

Monday, it might be Sister Batista lecturing him on wearing proper shoes, then Tuesday it would be Sister Agnes lecturing him on not washing his jelly stained shirt. For his part, Iggy would stand there smiling his crooked smile, while being humiliated in front of the class. His smile was never interpreted correctly as being good-natured, but instead as a sign of unholy arrogance. Then he would be sent to the office used clothing locker to change the offending apparel. The time away from class meant that he would miss key facts needed to do his school work correctly, thereby guaranteeing him a 'life sentence' in Group Three. The repeated calls and notes to Iggy's father about his uniform problems went unanswered for the first two years of school since he was barely ever at home to answer the phone, and Iggy was too scared to give him a note from the nuns.

Early in third grade, one of the young nuns who got Iggy and the rest of Group Three, took it upon herself to visit Iggy's house on a Saturday morning. All of Sister Juniata's questions were answered when, after banging on the door for a few minutes, Hank Mahoney angrily yanked open the door in his briefs. They had never met before and Hank assumed she was there begging for money.

"Good morning Mr Mahoney! I just wanted to stop by and..."

Before she could finish, he loudly announced, "I don't have any fucking money so get your skinny ass off my porch."

After he slammed the door, Sister Juniata meekly walked away, realizing that clothing choices were the least of Iggy's problems.

Monday morning before class started she quietly sent Iggy to the office, where the principal, Sister Ellen, directed his attention to a small table behind her desk. There was a neatly pressed white shirt, navy pants, and tie from Ferguson Department Store. Underneath the table was a new pair of black dress shoes from Seymour's shoe store. She told him that he should get to school a few minutes early each day so that he would have time to change in one of the bathroom stalls down the hall. At the end of each school day, he was to change back into his own clothes before heading home. Sister Ellen told him that if the shoes got too small to let her know. Then she did something completely out of character for a strict disciplinarian such as herself. She knelt down in front of Iggy, kissed him on his forehead and hugged him for about five long seconds before sending him on his way. Iggy never forgot that morning, or the kindness of the Sisters of Saint Joseph.

By the time Michael, Margaret Mary and Iggy were all in the sixth grade, Iggy was at the O'Tooles almost daily. Patrick dubbed him Michael's skinny shadow, since he was a head shorter and almost fifty pounds lighter than Michael. For his part, Iggy tried to always stay in good graces at the O'Tooles by keeping quiet and answering all questions directed his way with respectful 'yes sirs' and 'no ma'ams'. Patrick had gone to the Subway to talk to Hank and see if it was alright that Iggy was spending a lot of time at their house. Hank told Patrick that if Iggy caused any problems, just whack him on the back of his head to straighten him out. Patrick told Kathleen in bed that night that he would have liked to whack Iggy's old man in the back of the head, but he was afraid Hank would take it out on Iggy. They both agreed he was better off at their house than at his own.

If Patrick raised his voice to holler at one of the kids, Iggy would jump up and run out the door, even though it wasn't directed at him. He was naturally fidgety, which always got him in trouble at school. It seemed he was always in motion, as if he was standing or sitting on a bunch of ball bearings. If he ate dinner with the O'Tooles, he was in constant motion at the table, and a couple of times, after a bad day, Patrick would slip and yell at him to sit still. Iggy would jump up, run out the back door in the blink of an eye and start swinging on the swing set. Kathleen would slowly push herself back from the table and walk very slowly outside. Once she got Iggy to stop swinging, she would crouch down and talk quietly to him, hug him, and then walk him back inside to the table.

The withering, disdainful look she would give Patrick as she sat back down, had the effect of making him very quiet for the rest of the evening. The kids all thought it was amazing how a short, one-hundred and thirty-pound woman could make a six-foot, two-hundred-pound construction worker cower with just a look. They laughed as they got older that her glare had the same effect as a clean right upper cut on their father.

As time wore on, Iggy ate almost all his supper meals with the O'Tooles, and even slept over a few nights a week during the summer months, and on weekends during the school year. If Michael was busy, or at practice, he liked to follow Kathleen around the house, and help her as she did all the household chores. He seemed to be coming out of his shell, as the two of them would chat almost non-stop while folding laundry or setting the table. Even with six kids of her own to deal with, she never seemed to be bothered by Iggy hanging around. She would just patiently listen to all his stories and comments of his day, while only interjecting an endless series of "uh-huhs".

One rainy Saturday in the summer after sixth grade, Michael

was gone to a friend's house for a party, leaving Iggy at the house all day. He was doing his usual chatter and helping Kathleen with her chores, when Patrick made what he erroneously felt was a humorous comment to his wife, telling her to 'be careful not to step on her new puppy'. A couple of minutes later, Kathleen asked Iggy to go watch TV for a while, so she could talk to Patrick, who she motioned to their bedroom, where they held their private talks.

The two of them were unaware that Margaret Mary was sitting on the floor of their closet, curled up with a book and a flashlight. It had become her private retreat, especially on rainy days, since the possibility of privacy in an eight hundred square foot house with eight people living there was nearly impossible. Kathleen was well aware of Margaret Mary's occasional use of the closet as a reading room, but was so angry at Patrick, that she forgot to check the closet.

"What the hell do you think you're doing?" she spit at Patrick through clenched teeth.

"What do you..." he started, before she cut him off.

"How DARE you call that little boy an animal. Isn't it bad enough he's being raised like one? The child has never had a mother to talk to! Did you ever think of that? Of course not. Why don't you think before you open that dumb mick mouth of yours," she added as she poked him in the chest repeatedly with her right forefinger.

Patrick just stood there and took the rebuke quietly. As a pipefitter crew foreman, he was used to barking orders and commanding the respect of as many as twenty rowdy men every day. But at the moment, he was standing in front of his wife with his shoulders slumped and his eyes downcast, like a wayward child.

Margaret Mary watched it all in amazement through a one-inch opening while holding her breath. She never heard her Kathleen, or anyone else for that matter, talk to her father that way. Her mother's face was beet red, her green eyes were blazing and her red hair was standing out from her head, giving her a frightening and commanding sense of power in that little room. In as quick a flash as she had lashed out, Kathleen turned, opened the bedroom door and walked out. Margaret Mary's heart was pounding as her father sauntered out of the room a few minutes later.

For some reason, Margaret Mary's eleven-year-old eyes began to well up. It would be years before she could put to words all the nuances of married adult behavior she just witnessed, and the dramatic lesson she just learned. She had witnessed the ferocity of her mother's protectiveness of her children. By the same token, her mother had protected her husband's status as the head of the house, by not making him look weak in front of his children. Her father had wisely realized he was in the wrong, kept quiet, and took the tongue lashing, while no doubt appreciating her discretion. She learned you can have a lion's heart in a small soft body, and soft heart in a large muscled body. She learned that having a successful relationship and marriage isn't about winners and losers, but mutual respect.

Later that summer, in 1962, Michael, Margaret Mary and Iggy's relationship was about to change forever. It wasn't unusual for Iggy to show up at school when they were younger with a split lip or a black eye. If anyone asked him what happened, Iggy would just grin with that cocky, crooked smile of his and say, 'You should see the other guy!' The other kids would just laugh and walk away, thinking to themselves that they were glad they didn't live in Iggy's world. The adults in his life hoped that his injuries were just a result of roughhousing with other boys, but secretly worried they came from his father. Iggy always seemed to be smiling, which had the effect of calming their worst fears.

CHAPTER TWENTY

When you turned on to Iggy's street, the first house on the right, on the corner of Paul and St. Louis Ave, was inhabited by an old lady who was the grandmother of the two teen age boys who lived in the second house on the right. The boys who lived next door to the Mahoneys were about five years older than Iggy, and were Eddie and Mitch Cantrell. Their fathers were brothers who had purchased the first two lots on St. Louis Ave right after they got home from the war and built their houses side by side. They were both small bungalows on slabs w/o basements like Iggy's house. The Cantrell brothers were ironworkers who died in a construction accident around 1957, leaving enough life insurance to pay off the houses, so the boys and their mothers would have a place to live.

Claudia and Rosalie Cantrell were the boys' mothers, and they were sisters. Slowly but surely, after the accident, the ladies began to spend more and more time drowning their sorrows at Monterey's Tavern, a block west on the corner of Paul and South Florissant Road. Eventually Claudia and Rosalie got their husbands' elderly mother to live in one house with the boys, and they lived in the corner house. The arrangement was to protect the boys from the knowledge that their mothers grew fond of bringing home a variety of the bar's patrons late at night for conversation and companionship. The older Mrs. Cantrell was willing to go along with the arrangement because it got her out of a rat-infested tenement in the city's north side.

In 1960, when the boys were about fifteen, their mothers announced that they were taking a vacation to Las Vegas with a couple of gentlemen they had met at Monterey's. The ladies left in one of the gentleman's station wagon and never wrote, called, or came back. Within a year, Eddie and Mitch had quit school and coaxed their grandmother into living in the corner house alone, leaving them in the house next to Iggy's.

Slowly but surely the driveways and the front yards of the two Cantrell houses filled with pieces of automobiles and motorcycles. The boys had a natural mechanical predisposition. Unfortunately, they were much more proficient at taking things apart than they were at putting things back together, which made for quite a mess. Nevertheless, they parlayed their talents into a fairly lucrative parts business for those Ferguson residents seeking a reduced rate on the price of used parts. Customers who stopped by looking for, say a starter for a fifty-six Ford, would be told that if they left a phone number, the boys would call if they found one. Sure enough, usually within a couple days, the customer would get a call. It was rumored that the parts were stolen, but that was only true some of the time, and the person that was coincidentally missing a starter for a fifty-six Ford, always lived at least twenty miles away.

It was also rumored that Eddie and Mitch had each done some time in juvenile detention facilities, which was true. They were never gone long because their grandmother was aware how her utilities and groceries were being paid. She was always quick to get a lawyer, pay their bail, and bring them home.

Like most of the kids in Ferguson, Michael and Margaret Mary were told to never go anywhere near those two houses next to Iggy's. On the regular occasions that Patrick would be dropping Iggy off at home, he never failed to mention to his kids that Eddie and Mitch were the most likely candidates in Ferguson to wind up in the state penitentiary in Jefferson City. For their part, Eddie and Mitch always just smiled and waved from their chairs on their front porch when the O'Tooles drove up with Iggy.

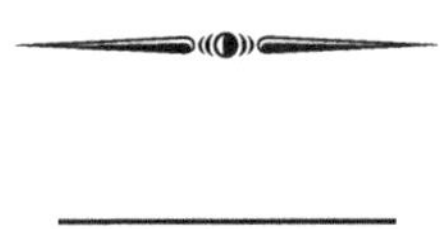

One exceptionally hot Saturday, in August of 1962, Eddie and Mitch were sitting on their front porch, trying to stay cool at about eight in the morning. Neither they, nor most of their neighbors, had air conditioning. Even their two big mongrel dogs, that they kept on long chains in the front yards to protect their inventory, were lying on their sides in the shade, perfectly still. Since everyone's windows were open all summer, there were few neighborhood secrets.

Around nine that morning, the boys heard Hank Mahoney cursing and swearing, then some loud commotion and the sound of a couple glasses or plates breaking. Unfortunately for Iggy, this was not an unusual occurrence when Hank woke up hung over. About fifteen minutes later they heard the back screen on the Mahoney's house slam shut, and spotted Hank stumbling up the steep grade to the tracks to head down to the Subway Bar. Most of the time during the commotion next door, Iggy would come flying out the front door, and run over to hide out at Eddie and Mitch's place until Hank left or passed out again. The boys would pour Iggy some milk and cereal for breakfast, or make him a sandwich for school, or on Saturday let him watch cartoons.

About fifteen minutes later, Mitch stood up, and while gazing over at Iggy's he said, "Somethings wrong Eddie."

"I know what you mean. We should at least have heard the little guy's cartoons on by now," Eddie added.

"Let's knock and see if he's ok," suggested Mitch.

"Go ahead," Eddie answered.

After knocking a few times, Mitch tried to look in a couple of windows when the old couple across the street yelled at him to get away from the house. Their reputation as thieves kept the unofficial neighborhood watch on high alert, even though their area of expertise was in the auto industry. They knew if they went in the house, one of the neighbors would call the police, and they weren't even a hundred percent sure if Iggy was there. They had seen Patrick drop Iggy off the night before, but what if he had snuck out the back when they weren't looking before Hank woke up? They were both on probation and didn't want the police involved at all.

"What do you think we should do Eddie?" asked Mitch as he walked back to the porch. "If these assholes around here see us go in the house we are going to jail."

"Well we can't just do nothing," answered Eddie. "The little guy might be hurt. How about if I ride over to the O'Toole's house where Iggy hangs out. I can ask if he's there, and if he's not, maybe their old man will come back and check the house. He won't care if they call the police on him. I heard half his wife's family are cops."

"Sounds good Eddie. I'll watch the house in case he comes out or comes home. But hurry up. I got a bad feeling," said Mitch.

Eddie jumped on his motorcycle and took off at top speed, racing under both trestles, making a quick right on Ferguson Ave, left on Hartnett and right on Highmont in about two minutes. His heart was racing as he got off the bike and started walking towards the O'Toole's door, where he heard the cartoons blaring. Eddie knew Patrick didn't like him and his brother by the looks he shot at them when he dropped Iggy off, but he took a deep breath and knocked anyway.

"Who is it?" Patrick bellowed from the kitchen.

"One of the Cantrell's," answered Margaret Mary from her bedroom window down the hall. Being the only girl, she had her own room. She had been intrigued by the sound of the motorcycle shutting off in front of the house and looked out. Michael, being the oldest, slept in the basement by himself, and was unaware of Eddie's arrival.

By now there were eight eyes looking through the screen door at Eddie. He looked like some strange creature to the four youngest O'Tooles, with his slicked back hair and a pack of cigarettes rolled up in his dirty shirtsleeve.

"All of you get away from the door," hollered Patrick as he got up from the table, sending Sean, Billy, Bobby and Kevin running for their previous stations on the couch. "What the hell do you want?" he barked at Eddie as he pushed the screen door open.

Backing down the steps, Eddie spoke quickly, saying, "I'm sorry to bother you but we're afraid something might be wrong with Iggy."

"What's that supposed to mean?" asked Patrick as he stepped off the porch towards Eddie in a menacing manner.

"There was a lot of noise over there about a half hour ago. Then his old man left. Iggy usually comes over, but he's not answering the door. There's no sound over there. No cartoons, you know? We're worried somethings wrong," Eddie spit out quickly while backing up.

Patrick, seeing genuine concern on the boy's face, stopped and said, "I'll follow you over." Then he jumped on the small concrete porch and yelled through the screen, "Kathleen, this kid thinks Iggy might be hurt. I'm taking the car!"

Kathleen came running from their bedroom pulling her shorts up, just in time to see the wagon backing out of the driveway. "Oh my God, did he say Iggy's hurt?" she asked wheeling around.

"He said maybe, mom," answered Margaret Mary.

Eddie and Patrick ran the stop signs at all the intersections amid a chorus of angry horns. Eddie pulled in the front yard at their house and Patrick pulled in the driveway at Iggy's. After banging on the front door loudly and calling Iggy's name a few times, he threw caution to the wind and kicked the locked door open, breaking the woodwork on the latch side of the jamb. Upon entering, he looked about wildly, until he saw Iggy in the hallway laying on the floor face down in a pool of blood.

Outside, the whole neighborhood heard him screaming, "NO, NO, NO! FUCK, FUCK! WHAT DID HE DO TO YOU! AW IGGY, IGGY, GODDAMMIT!"

Seconds later, as some of the neighbors watched from their porches, Patrick came running out the front door with Iggy's bloody, lifeless body in his arms. Screaming at the Cantrells, who were now in Iggy's front yard, "ONE OF YOU DRIVE MY CAR AND ONE OF YOU GO GET MY WIFE AND TELL HER TO MEET ME AT THE HOSPITAL! HURRY! HURRY!"

While cradling Iggy in his arms like a baby, Patrick one handed the passenger door, while Mitch started the engine. As Mitch sped away west on Paul Ave, Eddie retraced his path in the opposite direction at top speed back to the O'Tooles'.

"Drive as fast as you can, and don't stop at the lights kid!" screamed Patrick at the shaking Mitch. "GODDAMMIT! WHO COULD DO THIS TO A CHILD!"

Mitch stole a quick look at Iggy as they sped north on South Florissant Road. His head was covered in blood, some of it bright red and some dried and dark. Blood was running from a gash over Iggy's right eye, and also from his nose, mouth and ears. Mitch didn't look again. He couldn't. He turned west on Dunn Rd. and floored it. Just a minute or two away now.

For his part, Patrick had seen his share of injured and dying men in the war and it looked to him like Iggy was bleeding out. If he didn't get blood soon he would die for sure. "Dear God, help this child," he prayed aloud. "Blessed Virgin, Mother of God, save this boy. Sweet Jesus help him please!" he continued as the tears began to well up. How was he going to tell Kathleen? She had come to love Iggy like one of her own.

Mitch made a right on Graham Rd and a quick left into the emergency entrance of Christian Hospital. The second he slammed on the brakes, Patrick threw open the wagon's door and ran like a madman towards the emergency doors, screaming at the top of his lungs for help.

Fifteen minutes later, Kathleen pulled up with their next-door neighbor, Bob Wilson, and right behind them on his motorcycle was Eddie. Due to the comings and goings of uniformed policemen and firemen and ambulance drivers, Mitch and Eddie elected to stay outside after Mitch parked the O'Tooles' car in the visitor lot and pocketed the keys. They sat down in a shaded, grassy area about a hundred yards from the emergency entrance, lit the first of dozens of cigarettes, and waited for news.

Kathleen spotted Patrick right away staring into a curtained cubicle. As she stepped next to him, she saw two doctors and three nurses working on Iggy. When one of the nurses stepped away for a second, she caught her first glimpse of Iggy's bloodied face and torso, and her hand immediately covered her mouth to stifle a scream. Slowly she made her way to the head of the gurney, where she gingerly reached out to stroke Iggy's blood-soaked hair. Then ever so slowly she bent and kissed his forehead. As she gradually raised her head back up, Patrick could see her eyes were closed and there were tears streaming down her cheeks.

When she opened her eyes, she asked whoever would answer, "Is he going to be alright?"

"We are having trouble stabilizing his breathing and blood pressure," answered one of the doctors curtly. The medical team assumed that Patrick and Kathleen were Iggy's parents, so naturally, they were more than a little skeptical when Patrick told them was that he didn't know what happened to Iggy.

"But is he going to be ok?" Kathleen whispered again while staring at Iggy's lifeless little body.

"We are doing everything we can. Now why don't you step outside and give us a little more room please," abruptly answered one of the nurses, as other medical personnel were darting in and out of the cubicle with full and empty IV bags.

But Kathleen didn't move and when her eyes met Patrick's across the cubicle, he could see that her sorrow fading and her anger rising. Finally, she asked him threw tightly clenched teeth, "Who did this Patrick? Who could do this to a little boy? Did those Cantrell boys have something to do with this?"

Patrick's eyes were welling up as he watched his wife slowly stroke Iggy's bloody hair. He felt helpless and he hated that feeling more than anything else in the world. "No Kathleen. It was Hank. It was his father. His own goddam father." With that his voice broke and he turned away.

A new doctor appeared in the spot that Patrick vacated, and then he walked slowly towards Kathleen. Very gently he touched her arm, and then quietly asked her to step outside with him so that they could talk. When they reached Patrick, he guided the two of them into an unused curtained cubicle.

"I am Dr. Thomas Carlson. I am the head of the Emergency Department here at Christian Hospital. First, can you give me Iggy's full name?" he asked as he pulled up a clipboard from under his left arm, and a pen out of his shirt pocket.

"His name is Ignatius Mahoney," answered Patrick, "But I don't know his middle name."

"Are either of you Iggy's biological parent?" asked the doctor while writing.

"No, but we are all he has right now," answered Kathleen.

"What are your names?" he asked.

"Patrick and Kathleen O'Toole," she told him.

"Do you have an address or a phone number for either of Iggy's parents?" asked the doctor.

"His mother is dead and his father is a drunk. He's not home. They don't have a phone. They live on St. Louis Ave. in Ferguson, three doors down from Paul on the right, but I don't know the house number. His father did this to him. I found him unconscious on the floor of the house. A kid in the neighborhood was worried about him and came to get me," Patrick told him.

"Iggy's at our house a lot. He goes to school with two of our kids. They're in the same grade," added Kathleen. Can I please go back in there with him now? He needs someone to hold his hand.... dear God," she asked as her voice broke.

"I guess that would be okay. Normally we only allow immediate family but this is an unusual situation," he replied. "Also, the police have been called and are on their way," said Dr. Carlson, "and I'm sure they are going to have a lot of questions as well."

After starting to walk away, Kathleen turned and asked the doctor, "He is going to be alright, isn't he?"

"The truth is, I'm not sure," answered Dr. Carlson, "We are going to have to take him upstairs and operate to find out what is going on. He is not breathing very well, and he has a large bruise on his chest, so he may have a collapsed lung. Also, we suspect internal bleeding because we can't keep his pressure up."

"Jesus Christ," swore Patrick under his breath.

"Dear Lord," whispered Kathleen.

"We are going to do everything we can, I promise," Dr. Carlson said quietly.

"Everybody out of the way!" barked an older nurse as she made way for the gurney carrying Iggy. When they turned to look, Kathleen gasped as she saw the tube down Iggy's throat to help him breathe, and the multiple IV bags hanging over him.

"Can one of you start on some paperwork for me?" asked a wide-eyed young woman holding a clipboard. She had a Florissant cop standing next to her because the hospital called them when it appeared a child had been abused.

"You do it Patrick. I'm not leaving him," Kathleen stated as she hurried to catch up to the gurney.

"I'll need you to answer some questions for me too sir," the cop said politely.

"Sure," said Patrick. Then he turned quickly and yelled, "Kathleen I'll be up soon."

After doing the obligatory paperwork as well as he could, Patrick gave the young administrator his name, address and phone number, and told her he would pay for everything if need be. Turning his attention to the young police officer, Patrick asked him what he needed to know.

"Well, I got most of the info I needed while listening to you answer the hospital's questions, but I was wondering if we could step back into one of the curtained areas for a moment?" asked the officer. By now they had been joined by an older cop wearing sergeant's stripes, who quickly looked over the information they had so far. Afterwards the sergeant excused himself and picked up a phone at a nearby desk.

When the older cop returned, he told Patrick, "I heard you say this happened in Ferguson, so technically the Ferguson police should be talking to you. But they're heading to the boy's house first and asked if we could finish up here with you."

"What do you want to know?" Patrick asked, looking from one officer to the next.

"You stated that you thought it was the boy's father, Hank Mahoney, who beat the boy," the sergeant said, "but you didn't actually witness the beating, is that right?"

"That's correct."

"What makes you think it was his father?"

"Because we've seen marks on Iggy before, but nothing like this. And he's a worthless drunk."

"Also, we were wondering if all the blood on your arms and shirt is the boy's?" the sergeant asked.

"It is," Patrick replied, looking down for the first time at the mess covering him.

"I need to get a couple pictures of you with your shirt on. Then we need you to take it off and wash your arms and hands so we can see them better and get a couple more pictures," he asked politely.

"No problem," Patrick answered.

After spending so much time around all his cop in-laws, the Fitzgeralds, he knew these two were just doing their job by making sure he didn't have any scratches, cuts or other marks on his hands, arms or chest. Afterwards they kept the shirt, gave him one of those blue scrub tops, and let him go upstairs.

As Patrick was about to leave, the sergeant asked if he knew where they could find Iggy's father, and he told them no. In the elevator, Patrick thought to himself that he knew exactly where Hank was, but he wanted a couple minutes with the piece of shit before the police locked him up. First, he needed to see Kathleen.

Upstairs, in the surgical waiting area, Patrick and Kathleen were waiting for over an hour with the tension and dread building by the minute. They had hardly spoken to each other while Iggy was in surgery, choosing instead to pray silently.

Patrick felt his anger growing by the minute as he pictured Hank Mahoney on a barstool in the Subway Bar. He hoped that he could get to Hank before the Ferguson police picked him up.

Finally, a doctor dressed from head to toe in surgical scrubs came through the double swinging doors. He did not know the details of how Iggy was injured, only that his last name was Mahoney. After calling the name Mahoney, he expected to see one or two distraught parents stand and walk towards him. Instead, a tall stone-faced man in a blue scrub top, and a short, disheveled woman with unkempt red hair stood up. He intuitively felt that he was not seeing fear or grief in the faces of these two, but barely contained anger.

Hoping to diffuse whatever emotional outburst that looked imminent, he stuck his hand out towards Patrick and calmly stated, "Hello, my name is Dr. Hogan. Are you Iggy's parents?"

"No, but we are all he has right now. We're Patrick and Kathleen O'Toole." answered Patrick tersely.

"Doctor Hogan, how is he? How is Iggy? Is he going to be alright?" Kathleen shot back in rapid succession, fear starting to replace the anger on her face.

"Yes, I believe he is going to be alright," smiled the surgeon, "but he has some very serious injuries, and he is going to need a couple of days in intensive care so we can keep an eye on him. Thankfully, we were able to find where he was bleeding quickly and get it stopped. Also, he had a collapsed lung which we needed to inflate. His blood pressure and breathing are both stable now."

"Thank God," gasped Kathleen, her face finally softening as she crossed herself.

"Thank you, thank you, thank you!" Patrick called out, while reaching for, and then pumping, the surgeons hand quickly with both of his.

"Your welcome, but I have to tell you, this little guy is a fighter.

Most kids with severe injuries like this wouldn't even have made it to surgery, much less survive," he replied. After answering all their questions, Dr. Hogan turned and disappeared behind the swinging doors where he came from.

Kathleen turned immediately to Patrick and stated firmly, "I am not leaving Iggy alone for one minute. I'm going to stay with him until he comes home."

"I know sweetheart," Patrick whispered as he wrapped her up in his big arms and held her tightly. A few seconds later, he felt her body start to tremble and go limp, as she started to cry with her head buried in his chest to muffle her sobbing. "Let it all out," he whispered into her head of wild red hair. Slowly she regained her composure, until finally Patrick looked at her and said gently, "I'll bring you some clothes and stuff later, but if you don't mind I need to take care of something first. Okay?"

After wiping her face on his scrub shirt and blowing her nose in a tissue a nice lady walked up and handed her, she replied, "Sure, sure, and let Bob Wilson know that he can go on home. Also, tell him to tell Margaret Mary to call our moms to come over, and stay with the kids."

"Will do. See you later," he answered. After giving her a kiss on the forehead and one more hug, Patrick turned and headed for the elevator.

One of the recovery nurses came out a few minutes later to escort Kathleen back to see Iggy. As she followed the nurse, she knew, without asking, that Hank Mahoney was about to experience first-hand what he had done to his son. Her only regret was not being there to watch.

CHAPTER TWENTY-ONE

When Patrick looked around the emergency room waiting area, he spotted his neighbor Bob Wilson, sitting quietly reading a magazine. Bob hopped up right away and asked if Iggy was going to be alright.

"It looks like he's going to make it, thank God," Patrick answered, "but he's going to be in intensive care for a while. He had some internal bleeding and a collapsed lung."

"I spotted those Cantrell boys outside a while ago and asked them what had happened. I can't believe a man could do that to a child. It's just hard to imagine," Bob muttered, shaking his head.

"It's unthinkable, Bob. Listen Kathleen is going to stay here, so you can head home now if you want. I have a couple things to take care of, so could you ask Margaret Mary to call both of her grandmas to come over when you get back?"

"Sure, sure I will. I called Harriet, and she's been over at your place keeping an eye on things," answered Bob. "Hey listen, those two Cantrell boys are outside in the far end of the parking lot. Said they would keep an eye on your car until you came out. I know they have a reputation, but they seem like nice kids, really. Polite even. They said they kind of look out for Iggy. They look kind of sick though, about all this, and they are talking tough like someone needs to teach Hank a lesson. You might want to talk to them before you leave."

"You bet. Thanks for everything, Bob," smiled Patrick.

"Anytime, you know that," Bob told him as they shook hands.

As Patrick walked into the sunshine, he shielded his eyes and scanned the lot for the Cantrells. He saw them in the distance, leaning against his station wagon, smoking cigarettes, and trying to look tough. When they saw him walking towards them, they both dropped their cigarettes as if a parent had spotted them smoking and stood straight up. They were both a little wide-eyed and scared as he approached, even with their slick hair, rolled up shirt sleeves, and black boots. It struck Patrick at that moment, that they were only boys themselves, after all, at just sixteen or seventeen years old. Before today, he only thought of them as criminals. As he got closer, they looked even younger and smaller. He stuck his big hand out to each of them and shook them formally.

"I want to thank each of you for what you did today. Your quick thinking and actions saved Iggy's life, literally. The doctors said they got him just in time," Patrick informed them in a solemn voice.

Both of them looked nervously at Patrick, then each other, then at the ground, while shuffling their feet and jamming their hands in their pockets. They had not been praised for anything in so long they didn't know what to say or do. Quietly they each mumbled a thank you.

"So, Iggy's going to be okay Mr. O'Toole?" Mitch asked.

"He looked really bad," added Eddie.

"He's going to make it fellas, but he will be in intensive care for a few days so they can watch him real close," answered Patrick. "He was either punched or kicked real hard in the chest, and so he had a collapsed lung and internal bleeding."

As if on cue, the boys both turned away from Patrick as their eyes welled up.

"Shit," said Eddie.

"We try to look out for him, but..." Mitch trailed off.

"That old man of his is no good..." added Eddie.

Patrick walked up behind them and gently put a hand on each

of their shoulders while they hurriedly wiped their eyes with their shirtsleeves. "Listen to me now, both of you. You should be very proud of yourselves. I know I am proud of you."

"We make him breakfast and lunch sometimes when he ain't got any food in the house," said Mitch.

"We even let him stay over if his old man is really juiced and wound up. He must have caught the little guy sleeping or something," added Eddie.

"Wait until his asshole father comes home tonight." Mitch said, finally turning around to face Patrick.

"Yeah, we're going to beat the shit out of him, Mr. O'Toole," added Eddie.

"You're not going to do any such thing fellas," cautioned Patrick. "You two need to stay away from him and that house. You have to promise me that." After they nodded slowly, he added quietly, "I'll take care of Hank. Don't worry about that. Now go on home. And thanks again fellas," he added, while shaking their hands one last time.

With that, Patrick hopped in the station wagon and started it up. As he pulled away, he saw Mitch and Eddie getting on their motorcycle. He sped up to beat the stoplight on Graham Rd. so that they could not follow him. It was time to find Iggy's father.

He knew exactly where he was going and what he was going to do. He had kept a respectable and calm demeanor at the hospital, but as he drove he could feel his repressed anger building. The image of Iggy laying on the floor in a pool of blood was all he could think of at the moment. The rage he was beginning to feel was what Irish men were both capable of and plagued by. This was the rage that could protect your family and get you thrown in prison. This was a rage that had no fear of consequences, and at the moment, it was focused entirely on Hank Mahoney.

Patrick stopped the car at the stairs leading down to the Subway Bar. There was no need for a parking spot because this would not take long. After yanking the door open at the bottom of the stairs, he took one step inside and hesitated a few seconds for his eyes to adjust to the dark barroom.

Six steps away sat Hank Mahoney on a barstool, facing away from the bar and towards Patrick. There were two men standing in front of him, laughing and nodding, as was the bartender, standing nearby on the other side of the bar. Patrick strode quickly towards the group, pushing the two men to the side, causing them to spill their beers and curse loudly. He reached for Hank's hair with his left hand and yanked him off the stool in one motion. Hank wailed at the sudden pain and dropped his glass causing it to shatter.

"You know why I don't have my own shirt on you fuckin' asshole? Because it was covered in your son's blood!" Patrick screamed at the top of his lungs. He continued to pull Hank to the center of the barroom now screaming to everyone, "This fuckin' prick almost killed his own son this morning!"

At that moment, Patrick pulled Hank towards him with his left hand and hit him with a ferocious right that splattered his nose across his face, sending blood flying through the air. The next punch was an uppercut as Hank started to fall forward, catching him under the chin. The sound of Hank's jaw breaking and his bottom teeth slamming against his top teeth made such a sickening sound, that the other dozen or so patrons all groaned loudly in unison.

The man Patrick had pushed to his left now came towards him drawing his right arm drawn back. As Hank crumpled to the floor, Patrick wheeled left and punched him as hard as he could in the middle of his chest, knocking the wind and the fight out of him, as he fell backward gasping for air. Then the man he had pushed to the right jumped on his back, trying to choke him by wrapping an arm around his neck. His Marine training kicked in, and in one motion, Patrick dropped to one knee and reached over his shoulder to pull the man over his head. After he landed, Patrick swung a hard right to the man's face that broke his cheekbone and caused him to scream wildly. No one else seemed willing to come to Hank's aid. They were backing up against the outside walls of the bar, looking dumbfounded at what they had just witnessed.

As Hank was getting up on his hands and knees, Patrick kicked him as hard as he could in the face, causing the onlookers to groan again. Not finished yet, he pulled Hank to his feet, pummeling his torso, and screaming, "Let's see how you like collapsed lungs you cocksucker!"

All of this happened in less than a minute. The bartender, Art Donovan, a six-foot four-inch two-hundred and fifty-pounds mountain of a man was coming out from behind the bar with an axe handle in his hand, yelling at the top of his lungs, "Stop, Patrick! Enough! Stop! You'll kill him!"

Rage cannot hear or think. It is an all-consuming animal-like ferocity. It is a force unto itself, and takes over a man's entire being. As Hank fell backwards, lifeless, to the barroom floor, Patrick was starting for him once more, when Art swung the axe handle with a short quick motion that popped the back of Patrick's head. He stumbled forward, instantly blacking out from the well-placed blow. It was not the first time Art had used his weapon of choice.

Art knew most of the construction workers in the area, both from the bar, and because he had worked as an ironworker for ten years after the war, until he fell and broke his back. Patrick had taken up a bunch of collections from the pipefitters while he was laid up, helping him keep the lights on and food on the table for his wife and four kids. It was time to return the favor. For starters, he had probably just kept Patrick from committing murder.

Art went right into his drill sergeant mode and began ordering the remaining patrons to help with what needed to be done, before some unknown do-gooder came in and called the police. He told three young pipefitters standing in the corner to drag Patrick to his car. "One of you can drive him home. The other two can follow and bring the driver back. Don't say shit to nobody. Now hurry up!"

To the two men who had tried to help Hank he yelled, "Get off the floor and get your piece-of- shit buddy out of here. And hurry up goddammit!" As they began to drag the unconscious Hank towards the door, he directed a couple young carpenters to help. "And one more thing, don't take him to Christian Hospital. That's too close. Take him into the city to DePaul. They won't ask so many questions. I don't know you two very well, but you will keep your fuckin' mouths shut if you know what's good for you. You hear me?" They just groaned and nodded as they carried Hank out.

As he grabbed a mop and bucket of water on wheels to mop up the blood on the floor, Art bellowed even louder to the four or five patrons still left, "Not a word to nobody, you hear? Not even your wives! A couple of you start sweeping up this broken glass. Shit! Shit! This is bad...Beer is on the house for the next hour fellas!" he hollered in an attempt to buy their silence, if the cops showed up.

CHAPTER TWENTY-TWO

Kathleen had ordered that both grandmas be called because she was afraid that six kids was too much for just one of them. She was aware, of course, that between the two of them they had raised fourteen children, but they were much older now.

Grandma O'Toole, Bridgey, was sixty-two. She was doing pretty well health-wise, except that like so many immigrants who had experienced hunger early in life, she had a lifelong addiction to eating. She was probably more than twice the weight she had been on her wedding day. The hair around her face was perpetually stuck to her forehead and cheeks with sweat, and her jeweled eyeglasses always seemed to have dried sweat streaks on the lenses. Generally, she wore large shapeless dresses covered in loud prints, low-heeled sensible shoes, and nylons rolled down to just above her knees which showed whenever she sat down.

Upon getting the call from Margaret Mary, she went into high gear, brushing her graying but auburn-tinted hair, and as usual, applying too much of her signature bright red lipstick. She grabbed a fresh carton of Newports, along with a fifth of vermouth and a fifth of Jim Beam. In case her visit ran into the evening, she would not have to do without her precious Manhattans.

After shouting a series of orders at Jimmy on her way out the door, Bridgey backed the Chevy out of the drive and began the journey from Dogtown to Ferguson. She needed to hurry, because at twenty miles per hour, the thirty-minute ride would take about an hour if you stayed off the highway.

Grandma Finnegan, Maureen, reacted swiftly as well, yelling at the semi-conscious Big John to pull the Buick around to the front of the house from the alley. She was sixty-four now, and had managed to keep her weight down, largely by keeping busy with a variety of civic and church organizations. She tried to both dress, and wear her dyed-brown hair, in a style that resembled Jackie Kennedy. She also tried to wear the same jewelry, shoes and handbags as the First Lady. It all cost quite a bit, but Big John didn't mind since the kids were all gone, and it made the love of his life smile. She kissed him on the front porch, and then tip-toed down the stone steps in front of their big brick home in the Central West End.

As she pulled the shiny Buick from the curb, she couldn't help but feel excited about the chance to care for her grandchildren without their parents around. She worried all the time that they were growing up without enough emphasis being put on manners and proper speech. She didn't consider herself to be snooty, but she was their only grandparent who did not speak with a heavy Irish brogue. By driving twenty miles per hour, and staying off the highway, she expected to make the thirty-minute trip in about an hour.

When Harriet Wilson told Margaret Mary and Michael that Iggy was going to be alright, they were visibly relieved. They were not sure exactly what was happening, but knew Iggy was badly hurt. Immediately after, Michael ran out the door to baseball practice down the street at Forestwood Park. When Harriet told Margaret Mary to call her grandmothers to come over and watch them, she predictably put up a fight. She was, after all, eleven now, and therefore more than capable of running the household in her parents' absence.

"What do we need them for anyway?" she piped.

We don't know how long your parents will be at the hospital, and I have plans this evening," replied Harriet quietly, being aware of Margaret Mary's tempestuous nature.

"They are both very old, can't keep up with the little ones very well, or find anything in the fridge when it's time to eat," answered the little girl with her arms crossed. Truth be told, Margaret Mary did not like Grandma Maureen correcting her English, which she felt was completely unnecessary, considering she spoke perfectly already. She also didn't care for the way Grandma Bridgey gently swatted her behind when she was given an order that she questioned.

Harriet was doing everything she could to keep from laughing, while encouraging Margaret Mary to make the calls. "Well this is a direct order from your mother, and I think with your help they can probably do a decent job. Without you here, I would be worried though," she said.

"That's for sure," shot back the little girl. "After I call them I'm going to make sandwiches for the little ones. They haven't eaten since breakfast, and I know they're hungry."

"Sounds like a good plan young lady. Would you like some help with the sandwiches?" she asked politely.

"I can handle it by myself, Mrs. Wilson," she answered, while walking away to find her mother's telephone and address book.

Harriet was secretly glad that there were reinforcements on the way. The last five hours at the O'Tooles had weighed heavily on her sensibilities, with the four younger boys wrestling and shouting, the radio and television blaring constantly, and Margaret Mary walking right behind her talking incessantly.

Right on schedule, around two-o'clock, after everyone finished their sandwiches, Harriet heard a car horn blowing repeatedly, followed by a loud female voice yelling in an Irish brogue, "Get out of the driveway, you little ragamuffins before I run over all of you!" When she looked out, there was Grandma Bridgey steering her Chevy into the driveway, with a cigarette dangling from her smiling red lips. The effort was a partial success, with two wheels on the pavement and two wheels a couple feet onto the lawn.

Not more than a few minutes later, with the kids all standing at the driver's door of the Chevy chatting at the same time, there was another car coming up the street with the horn beeping. When Harriet looked, and the kids turned, they saw a long white Buick with a white-gloved driver waving at them. Grandma Maureen pulled the car over to the left side of the street, in front of the O'Toole manse, pointing the wrong way, with two tires a couple feet onto the grass.

After all the greetings were done, and the chaos had dwindled considerably, the two Irish women hugged each other and exchanged pleasantries. After the kids were out of earshot, they began a hushed conversation of their own.

"I'm so glad Kathleen had them call, aren't you?" asked Maureen, while slipping her white gloves off.

"Absolutely, I don't like the idea of that Lutheran women staying with my grandkids," whispered Bridgey.

"I guess she could ask the bunch on the other side of them to watch the kids. They're Catholic, but they're dagos. I don't know which is worse," replied Maureen.

"Well they're safe now!" grinned Bridgey, grabbing Maureen's hand as they walked slowly across the lawn to the front porch, with the five grandkids jumping around them. They were both as close to heaven as they could ever hope to be on earth, with this opportunity to stay overnight. While the two older women may have begun their lives in the separate Irish camps of 'lace curtains' and 'shanties', they were in complete harmony in their love for their grandchildren.

After sending Harriet back to her Lutheran hovel, they began to ask Margaret Mary questions. Both grandmas knew if you wanted to get answers you went straight to the little girl who they laughingly referred to as 'the boss'. Both ladies loved and relished Margaret Mary's spirit and inherent nature to take charge.

"So, what happened to Iggy?" asked Grandma Maureen

seriously as they sat down at the kitchen table.

"Iggy got hurt really bad is all I know," answered Margaret Mary. "Dad took him to the hospital, and Mr. Wilson took Mom."

"Where are his parents, child?" asked Grandma O'Toole.

"His mother is dead, and his dad is a drunk I heard Mom say," she replied, adding, "Iggy stays here a lot grandma."

About this time, Michael walked in and took his grandmother's attention from his sister, as so often happened when he entered a room. After bending to kiss each of them, he asked if they heard anything else from the hospital.

"Not yet Michael. Hopefully soon. Now could you please turn that damn television down before I unplug it?" commanded Grandma Bridgey.

"Sure, grandma," he said.

"Now what would we all like for supper tonight?" asked Grandma Maureen loudly, as all six kids swarmed their grandmothers offering suggestions and advice and school stories all at the same time.

"Alright, alright!" boomed Grandma Bridgey after a few minutes. "Now it's time for you all to go out and play in the traffic."

"GRANDMA!" they hollered, making sad faces and feigning hurt feelings.

About an hour later, around three-o'clock, the old women were bustling around the kitchen, there was a sharp knock on the front screen door. A few seconds later, after Margaret Mary had called for them, Bridgey and Maureen were looking through the screen into the obviously distraught face of one of the young men who had driven Patrick home. After asking them to come out on the porch, he quickly and quietly explained the circumstances, adding that he needed to move Bridgey's car so they could back the family station wagon into the driveway. They all agreed it was best to back it as far as possible into the driveway, which extended to the rear of the house. That way when they pulled Patrick out of the back end, where he was laying, they could carry him in the back door with little chance of anyone seeing.

The young man who knocked on the door, and then moved Bridgey's Chevy into the street, was Kevin Dolan. His brother Brendan, who was driving the O'Toole's station wagon, began to back it down the drive. Their buddy, Tommy Callahan, parked his vehicle in the street and began to walk over to the house to help carry Patrick. All three were well versed in the procedure from hauling their drunken fathers in the house a hundred times over the years. They also knew to keep a low profile during the proceedings, to keep the nosy neighbors in the dark.

The two old women also had a lifetime of experience in getting their husbands in the house quietly when they were brought home either drunk or beat up, from a one kind of altercation or another. Speed and silence were paramount, so they quickly rounded up the six grandkids, and herded them into the house while the wagon was backing down the drive. While shaking her finger at them, Grandma O'Toole admonished them to be completely quiet, stay in the living room, and not ask any questions. Grandma Finnegan hurriedly closed and locked the front door behind them, then moved swiftly to open the back door, and hold the screen door, so the three men could carry Patrick in as quickly as possible.

The kids were understandably wide-eyed and worried at the abrupt change in the mood and behavior of their grandmothers. They were also getting an important lesson, learned early in many Irish families, in the art of damage control. It was an art learned through observation and osmosis, rather than by verbal instruction.

"Oh, dear Lord," said Maureen in a hoarse whisper as the men struggled to get through the doorway.

The Dolan brothers were on either side of Patrick, who was on his back, with their arms locked under him at his neck and waist. Tommy Callahan came in last holding his legs, grunting, "Where do you want him?"

"Down the hall, in the back bedroom on the right boys," whispered Bridgey.

"I'll get an ice bag going," said Maureen.

About that time, Bridgey spotted the ever-curious Margaret Mary peeking around the corner from the dining room into the kitchen. "What did I tell you little girl!" she hissed through clenched teeth.

As her head disappeared, Michael's appeared at the other doorway from the living room to the kitchen, watching the three men carry his father down the hall. "Is dad okay?" he asked Maureen who was headed that way with a towel full of ice.

"He's going to be fine, Michael. Now please be a good boy and keep your brothers and sister in the living room. Get going! Now!" she added impatiently.

"Is dad drunk?" asked Margaret Mary, whose head had reappeared in the dining room doorway.

"Of course not child! He just fell and hit his head! Now what did I tell you?" barked Grandma Bridgey, stepping angrily towards her.

Finally, the three men laid Patrick on his bed and stepped back. As Maureen slipped the ice between his head and the pillow, Bridgey stepped in and closed the door.

"Jesus, Mary and Joseph," whispered Bridgey as she walked over and touched her son's face.

"Thank you for bringing him home, boys," Said Maureen as she shook each of their hands earnestly. "Come by the Shamrock any time for a drink on the house, you hear?"

"That's okay ma'am," said Kevin.

"No problem," added Brendan.

"We should go," added Tommy, who was on probation for an altercation of his own and was having visions of police cars rolling up at any minute.

After filling in a few more details for the old women, the men left by the back door one at a time, so as not to attract too much attention, and slowly made their way across the street to Tommy's car. They didn't go anywhere near the Subway Bar for months.

Without speaking, Maureen and Bridgey began a well-practiced routine of putting one of their comatose men to bed and doctoring his injuries. Boots off, bloody, dirty clothing off, more ice and towels brought in, and then of course the long vigil, anxiously hoping for a relatively quick regaining of consciousness. They both knew of men who did not wake up or woke up with vision, speech or motion defects. Their rosaries came out immediately.

About the same time that Patrick was put into bed, Hank Mahoney's two buddies were dropping him off at the emergency room at De Paul Hospital in north St. Louis. Hank was still unconscious, with a broken nose, cheekbone, jaw, and eight ribs. The two men concocted a tale of being jumped by a gang of black men in Fairgrounds Park, not too far from the hospital in the City. That would put the St. Louis City cops in charge of the investigation. For the time being anyway, they were going to heed the warning and instructions of Art Donovan, the barkeep of the Subway Bar, and keep their mouths shut about what really happened. Without any fanfare, the two of them took off without giving anyone their names.

When the various police departments started talking to each other, their investigation would eventually bring them to the O'Toole's front porch in Ferguson. Neighbors on Iggy's street told the Ferguson cops that the man who kicked in the door, and carried Iggy out of the house, was the same man who brought him home a few times every week. There was a carpenter down the block who told them he had seen Patrick on jobsites and thought the guy's name was O'Toole.

Another old neighbor with a purple whiskey nose, told them that Hank almost lived at the Subway, and that his wife was dead. The police went over to the Cantrell house and questioned them after they got back from the hospital but were met with silence. They knew Iggy was safe, and they were hoping that their new friend, Patrick O'Toole, was beating the shit out of Hank Mahoney. They felt no incentive to help the cops and perhaps get Patrick in trouble. When the Ferguson police were done at the Mahoney residence, and with the neighbors, they had lunch, and then decided to call the Florissant police to see what they had learned from their interview with Patrick.

The Florissant police told the Ferguson police, that Patrick had already left the hospital when they called to see if he was still there. When the Ferguson police finally made their way to the Subway, they found the bar oddly quiet and deserted for a Saturday afternoon. When they asked the bartender where everyone was, he just murmured that business had been slow, which they knew was a lie, because one of them had noticed a dozen cars outside the place just a couple hours before. Both of them noticed the squeaky-clean floor in front of the middle of the bar, and that the rest of the floor had its usual dirty, sticky haze. Art said someone had dropped a pitcher and he had mopped up.

By seven-o'clock Saturday evening, there were two young, uniformed Ferguson policemen standing on the front porch of the O'Toole's house on Highmont. When they pulled up, there were dozens of kids playing kickball in the street or hide and seek in and around the houses and bushes. All of them had stopped to witness what was going on at the O'Toole's. Some ran home to tell their parents of this exciting development in the usually boring Forestwood subdivision. This was of course free entertainment for the struggling young families who one by one started to come out on their porches to watch.

Many of the kids were crowding around the patrol car, or trying to inch nearer to the officers, to try to hear what was being said. The O'Toole kids had been kept indoors, and when the police car showed up, they were sent to their respective bedrooms. Their worldly grandmothers knew to expect this visit and didn't want them hearing the upcoming conversation.

These two young officers had no way of knowing that Bridgey had been questioned by the police dozens of times over the years about Jimmy's affairs and whereabouts. She had never revealed a single piece of useful information and had become quite accomplished at obstructing injustice.

The young officers also had no way of knowing that Maureen's father, and some brothers, sons and nephews were police officers. They were unaware that she had spent the last sixty years listening to the men in her world discuss interrogation techniques, and what mistakes criminals always make to incriminate themselves. In short, the two young police officers were about to engage a formidable duo and would have little success.

"Hello officers, may we help you?" Maureen called to them as she approached the screen door, wearing her best Jackie Kennedy smile.

"Yes ma'am, we are looking for a Patrick O'Toole," answered the first officer.

"Well, I'm Patrick's mother-in-law, Maureen Finnegan, and this lady to my left is his mother, Bridgey O'Toole," she replied, with a wide gesture towards Bridgey, who was also smiling as if she had just won the big pot at bingo. "Maybe the two of you know my husband, Big John Finnegan?" she added, successfully avoiding the officer's question, and letting them know of her political connections.

"Stepping out on the porch with her best imitation of an unsteady old lady, Bridgey peered closely through the bottom half of her sweat-streaked glasses at the name tag of the red-headed officer in front, who had been doing the talking. "Are you by any chance related to Katie Conley in St James the Greater parish?" she asked.

"Yes ma'am, that's my mother, but I..." started Officer Conley politely.

"Well, young man, don't you look grand in your uniform!

Doesn't he look grand, Maureen?" Bridgey asked as she turned towards Maureen. Both of them were still smiling from ear to ear.

By now Maureen was also doing her own best impression of a spindly old lady, as she stepped gingerly onto the front porch, while reaching towards the second officer for help that she did not need. "You're a fine-looking boy to be sure Officer Conley," she piped in agreement with Bridgey.

"Thank you both, really, but..." started Officer Conley.

"Would either of you like something to drink?" asked Bridgey with a big smile. "It's hot and you both look like you could use a cold beer!"

"Look, is Patrick O'Toole here or not ladies?" the second officer interrupted sharply.

"I don't care for your tone, young man," shot back Maureen, in her most indignant voice.

"And what be God, is your name?" quipped Bridgey, now leaning towards the second officer's name tag, while feigning far worse eyesight than she actually had.

"My name is Officer Frank Patelli, ma'am," answered the swarthy dark-haired young officer in his official tone.

"I see. Pastarelli. Hmm," mumbled Maureen.

"It's PATELLI ma'am," corrected the officer.

"Did he say *Pray-for-telli* Maureen?" asked Bridgey. "Who is Telley?" she added, while turning towards Maureen with her hand behind her ear. It seemed a recently acquired deafness had been added to her eyesight issues and her new-found mobility problems.

"It's P-A-T-E-L-L-I," he spelled loudly, as his exasperation grew.

"There is no need to scream at two old ladies now, is there Officer Portadelli?" scolded Maureen, while looking over her glasses and acting her best 'disappointed mother' role.

"You don't see Officer Conley behaving so disrespectfully, now do you?" asked Bridgey while raising her painted-on eyebrows.

With that, the frustrated and demoralized Officer Patelli turned on his heel and walked quickly back to the squad car.

"Those I-Tal-Yuns are such an excitable bunch, aren't they Bridgey?" asked Maureen.

Officer Conley smiled grimly through tight lips at the two old ladies grinning back at him on the porch. Resignation was setting in as he realized they still had not answered the original question about whether Patrick was home. He also knew they never would. He had seen this type of act played out many times by his Irish relatives and neighbors.

First, Officer Patelli was the only one of the four people on the porch who did not know who Big John Finnegan was. Every Irish man and woman in St Louis knew, or knew of, the legendary St. Louis power broker. Maureen bringing up his name was a "shot across the bow" as the saying goes. Pushing her too hard, or upsetting her, could very well make a young Irish cop's career ambitions hit a dead end before they even had a chance to get started.

Second, Officer Conley's father had been a St. Louis City police officer and detective for twenty-five years before he passed away. His dad had come up in the department under two lieutenants named Fitzgerald, both of who were now St. Louis City police captains. His dad had always loved the Fitzgeralds because they always stood behind their officers. He also talked for years of how he had been able to drink free beer at the Shamrock Bar, owned by Big John Finnegan, who had married into the Fitzgerald clan. Young Officer Conley's excellent police intuition, and budding detective skills, told him that this old lady in front of him was, therefore, the sister of two St. Louis City police captains, and the mother of two St. Louis City police lieutenants.

Third, the fact that Bridgey had mentioned that she knew his mother gave the young officer even greater cause for concern. It meant that if things didn't go the way old Mrs. O'Toole wanted them to go, every wagging female Irish tongue in Dogtown would know about it by the time the noon Mass let out at St James the Greater tomorrow morning. His mother would be mortified, and there was no way he was going to risk that.

Finally, even if Patrick O'Toole was in the house, it was going to take a dozen well-armed elite cops and a bulldozer to get by these two. Discretion was definitely going to be the better part of valor in this scenario. He would merely tell his sergeant that they had not found Patrick O'Toole at the house on Highmont, which was true. He would explain all the ramifications to his Italian partner over coffee later.

"Ladies, if you see Patrick, would you ask him to come by the station for me?" asked Officer Conley.

"Absolutely!" smiled Maureen.

"Isn't he a fine young man, Maureen," stated Bridgey, loud enough for him to hear as he walked away.

"Indeed, he is! May the road rise up to meet you Officer Conley!" she shouted after him while waving.

Even if nothing else was accomplished, Officer Conley knew he had garnered a good report card for his mother's benefit tomorrow morning at Mass.

CHAPTER TWENTY-THREE

In the days that followed, Kathleen never left Iggy's side. She caressed him, kissed him, and talked to him continuously, so that he would know he was not alone. She saved her tears for visits to the restroom. While he was in surgery, she begged the Blessed Virgin, mother to mother, on her knees in the chapel at the hospital, to do everything she could to save his life. She also made a promise to Jesus that if Iggy survived, she would take him home and protect him as fiercely as one of her own. When she finished her prayerful pleading, a chill raced up her spine, which she took as proof that she had been heard.

Early the next day, around 9:00 Sunday morning, she made two phone calls. The first was to her mother Maureen, and the second was to her beloved father, Big John Finnegan. Jesus and Mary had done their part from heaven, now it was time for people on earth to do their part for this little boy.

After Maureen assured her that she would get all the children to Mass, Kathleen wanted to make certain that her mother would personally call her brother Michael Fitzgerald, who was a captain on the St Louis police force, and her sons, Kathleen's brothers, Colin and Brendan, who were lieutenants on the force. Kathleen and Maureen had spoken briefly the night before about Patrick's condition, and what he had done. They both agreed he was probably going to need some family help to stay out of jail.

As it turned out, Maureen had already made those calls on her own late Saturday night. When she made the follow-up calls Sunday morning, she was assured that witnesses were already not being interviewed and evidence was already not being collected. Michael,

Colin and Brendan had used their influence to ask their colleagues in Ferguson and Florissant to look the other way.

Big John was getting dressed for 10:00 Mass when the phone rang. "How is the little boy doing, Katie," he asked right away, using the pet name for his daughter that he had used since she was a toddler, and that only he was allowed to use.

"He's going to live, but it's going to take a long time for him to heal. He looks terrible daddy," she answered in a quivering voice. Then without hesitation, "Dad, I want to adopt Iggy as soon as possible." Suddenly her voice had taken on a demanding tone that Big John was all too familiar with. He could visualize the tight lips, the growing freckles, and wide eyes.

"Well certainly darlin'. I will definitely look into it tomorrow when City Hall opens, but these things take time..." he started.

"NO, dad. I want to bring him home from the hospital. I don't want to wait for lawyers and court dates. And I definitely DON'T want him going with some social worker to some unfamiliar house or INSTITUTION!" she exclaimed, unsuccessfully trying to keep her voice down.

"Listen to me now Katie, these things are complicated..."

"THIS ISN'T COMPLICATED DA! THIS LITTLE BOY'S FATHER ALMOST BEAT HIM TO DEATH. HIS WHOLE WORLD IS UPSIDE DOWN!" she yelled into the receiver. Then, after a few quiet moments, in a trembling voice that was breaking her father's heart, she whispered hoarsely, "Oh daddy who could do such a thing?"

Big John listened as his precious Katie let out, mournful, sobbing groans from deep within a mother's soul. He wished with all his might that he could take her in his arms and make everything okay, like when she was a little girl. He covered the mouthpiece as he started to speak, feeling a lump in his throat, and needing to wipe away his tears. A man needed to be strong, so that his children would feel safe and secure, but he had an unusually large soft spot for his only daughter.

"Daddy?" she asked after a thirty second silence. She heard him clear his throat, then silence again. "Dad say something."

In a gentle, and unusually quiet tone, he answered, "I'll take care of everything sweetheart. By the time Iggy's ready, the hospital will have everything it needs to let you take him home. Okay then?"

"Thank you," she answered. "I love you daddy," she added, her voice breaking again.

"I love you too. No more tears now darlin," he whispered. Then all she heard was a faint sniffle and him clearing his throat before he hung up. Like most fathers, he knew that twenty sons together couldn't pull on your heartstrings the way one daughter could.

All during Mass his mind was spinning in a hundred directions as he plotted how he was going to get the necessary papers from the St. Louis County government center, to Christian Hospital. His power base was in St. Louis City Hall. If this was a Catholic hospital run by nuns, it would have been a cake walk. He had found jobs at one time or another for the siblings of half the Irish nuns in the city and county. This was going to be a lot more difficult than the usual 'favors'.

After Mass, he steered his big Caddy through the streets to the Shamrock and parked in the alley behind the bar. Here he could have complete privacy on a Sunday, to make calls without worrying about being overheard, and to receive visitors without prying eyes in the neighborhood seeing who was coming and going. He began to run down in his mind, all the older immigrants for who he had gotten civil service and construction jobs. Many of them had children and grandchildren all over the city and county, who had pursued the American dream, gotten a college education, and were now working in respected professions.

Liam Gallagher, who was still mopping floors at St. Louis City Hall, was always bragging about his oldest daughter, who had left the convent and was running the foster care program in the county's Social Services Division. She should be a big help in navigating him through the necessary caverns at the County Government Center, which was located in the City of Clayton, adjoining the western border St. Louis City.

Jimmy Flaherty had retired after thirty years of raking leaves and cutting grass for the City Parks Department, and still stopped by the Shamrock occasionally. He never let the conversation go on too long, before it became necessary to mention that his middle boy, Sean, was a big-shot lawyer at the County Courthouse, which adjoined the Government Center. He was now a partner in one of the county's silk-stocking law firms.

Pat McDonough had fallen six stories off a scaffold while laying brick twenty years ago. Big John had seen to it that his widow, Maggie, got a good job in the civil courts building in downtown St. Louis, to make sure her six kids had a roof over their heads. Since then, he had heard that she had moved to the county to be closer to her grandchildren, transferred to the civil courts in Clayton, and had continued to move up until she was now the top administrator for the civil courts in the county. She was a master at quietly getting cases on or off the court docket in her building, and trading favors with her counterparts in criminal, traffic and family court. She had saved any number of careers for politicians, business agents and even priests who had their DWI charges disappear.

Steadily, Big John worked the phones in the back room of the Shamrock, with the aid of a bottle of bourbon and a few long cigars. His sixty-six-year old brain was working in a precise and calculating manner, remembering names, their relations and an endless number of favors owed and delivered.

Finally, around six-o'clock Sunday night he made his last two calls. The first was to Eddie Kiley, who was the state representative for the area that took in Ferguson and Florissant in north St. Louis County. The second was to Tommy Flanagan, who was now a circuit court judge from north county. Both had come to Big John with hat in hand when they decided to run for their respective offices.

Five days later, on Friday morning, when it was time for Iggy to leave the hospital, Kathleen was in the office of the head administrator for Christian Hospital. She was showing him, and the hospital's social services director, and a police lieutenant for the

Florissant Police Department, a stack of signed, stamped and notarized forms and paperwork. The paperwork showed that Patrick and Kathleen O'Toole were now the legal guardians, and would soon be the adoptive parents, of one Ignatius Mahoney, a minor. One of the papers was signed by Iggy's father, and relinquished his parental rights. Two St. Louis City homicide detectives and two uniformed officers had gotten that signature at two-o'clock in the morning, in Hank Mahoney's hospital room at DePaul Hospital a couple nights before.

Grinning from ear-to-ear, Kathleen wheeled a patched up but smiling Iggy out the front door of the hospital, where Big John's long, shiny, black Cadillac was waiting. "Are we all ready?" boomed Big John, as he rolled his portly form out of the front seat.

"Absolutely, dad!" Kathleen called out to him cheerfully.

"I'll second that!" called Iggy.

After getting Iggy situated in the back seat, and closing the door, Kathleen turned, wrapped her arms around her father, and pressed her head against his chest for ten seconds. Big John gently patted his daughter's back not saying a word. Finally, she leaned back and looked up at her hero through misty eyes.

"Enough of this now!" he bellowed. Clearing his throat, he turned abruptly and called out, "Let's go home!"

"What is that on the windshield?" asked Iggy.

Big John hadn't noticed until then that a young Florissant cop had left a parking ticket when he went in to use the restroom. He had been in a well-marked 'no parking' zone for about an hour. Quickly he reached out and grabbed the ticket and stuffed it in his front shirt pocket.

"Do you think you can get the ticket fixed dad?" asked Kathleen very seriously from the backseat. When he looked in the rear-view mirror, he saw a huge grin on her face.

"Don't be a smartass Kathleen," grumbled Big John as he started the Caddy.

At this point, Patrick couldn't help but lean out his window in the front seat and laugh with abandon. It was a good day for the O'Tooles, the Finnegans, the Fitzgeralds, the O'Keefes and of course, Ignatius Mahoney.

Iggy thrived in the coming years at the O'Tooles'. He also started to do much better in school, although he was still stuck in the Group Three class. Kathleen badgered the nuns at Sts. John and James for a year, until they finally relented and moved Iggy to Group Two for eighth grade.

Iggy loved having clean, pressed navy pants and white shirt ready for him every morning. It was no longer necessary to sneak in and out of the principal's office to change clothes every day. It felt so good to be part of a real family for the first time in his life. He quickly and willingly grew accustomed to the flow of life at the O'Toole's, doing his chores and homework without even being asked.

Night time had been a little rocky at first, with Iggy waking up shaking and crying from nightmares. Kathleen would always come in quickly to soothe him back to sleep, but it worried her that he always claimed to not remember what the dreams were about. Finally, six months after he came to live with them, she figured it out while he and Kathleen were drying dishes and putting them up.

Iggy purposely waited until they were alone and blurted out, "Can my dad ever come back and take me away?"

Kathleen stopped what she was doing, took Iggy by the hand, and sat down in a kitchen chair so she could look directly into his eyes. "Absolutely not, sweetheart. Remember, once we adopted you, legally you became one of our children. He cannot take you anymore than he could take Michael or Margaret Mary," she assured him, in as soothing a voice as she could muster.

"But what if he just jumped out from behind a tree, or something, and just grabbed me? Could you find me?" Iggy asked quietly, revealing the source of his nightmares.

"He is NOT going to do that, Iggy, I promise," she answered assertively.

"Are you sure? I mean how can you be sure?" he asked quietly.

"I am one-hundred percent sure," she said firmly, while squeezing both his hands. Then in the next breath, "Patrick, come in here please," she called out towards the back door where he was playing catch with the kids.

"What is it?" he asked, looking through the screen door.

"Just come in and sit down next to me please," she told him firmly.

When he was settled, Kathleen turned to look at Patrick with pleading misty eyes, while still holding on to Iggy's hands. Quietly, she told him, "Iggy wants to know if he is safe. He wants to know if his father can sneak up, grab him, and take him away."

At first his brow furrowed, his eyes widened, as he glanced at Iggy, then back at his wife. The first feeling that had washed over him was anger, that the animal that beat his son still had a frightening hold over the boy. But with another look at Kathleen's wide stare, and noticing how gently she was handling the situation, the sixth sense of a loving married couple let him know what she needed from him, and it was definitely not a loud angry response.

"Come here," said Patrick quietly while extending his big calloused hands. As Iggy turned towards him, he laid those hands firmly on the boy's shoulders, giving them a gentle squeeze. Looking directly into Iggy's eyes he quietly and deliberately said, "First, I know for a fact that your father is a thousand miles away from here. Second, I promise you that I will never, ever, ever let anyone hurt you again. You are my son now, and I would jump in front of a train to protect you. I would fight ten men if need be to keep you safe. So, you can stop worrying about that right now and forever, because it's not going to happen. Okay?"

"Okay," Iggy replied with a flash of his crooked grin. Immediately, Patrick could feel, and Kathleen could see, the tension leave Iggy's being.

"Now go on outside and play," said Patrick as he began to stand.

As the screen door slammed behind Iggy, Kathleen circled her arms around her husband and squeezed him with every bit of strength she had. "God, I love you, Patrick," she whispered.

"Honey, that boy could not have found a better mother than you anywhere. I mean that," he replied.

Grandpa Jimmy O'Toole's assurance was the reason they were so sure that Hank was never coming back. One of Bridgey's nieces had joined the order of nuns who founded and ran De Paul hospital. Sister Mary Joseph was a registered nurse in the orthopedic ward. Bridgey had called her and asked if she would let them know when Hank was due to be discharged, so that they could surprise him by arranging a ride, since he didn't drive. The good sister was glad to oblige and told her aunt what a sweet gesture that was. On the big day, Sister Mary Joseph told Hank that a friend called to say that he would be picked up in front of the hospital, at the southbound bus stop on Kingshighway.

About five minutes after Hank sat down at the bus stop in front of the hospital, a long black Lincoln pulled up in front of him. The door swung open, and a short bow-legged older man got out, walked over to Hank and sat next to him. The older gentleman showed him a pistol and then explained to Hank, in a thick Irish brogue, that 'if he didn't get into the car quietly, his brains were going to be splattered all over the fookin' sidewalk.

Hank quietly got into the backseat of the Lincoln with the older gentleman. They drove him to a cornfield in the bottom land near the Missouri River, in west St Louis county. Hank was told to kneel in the dirt and open his mouth. The older gentleman then stuck the barrel of his empty pistol in Hank's mouth and said, "Good bye ass-hole," and pulled the trigger. After the hammer clicked, and Hank shit his pants, he was told that if he ever showed his face in St. Louis again, the next time the chamber would be loaded.

Iggy graduated from Sts. John and James grade school with Michael and Margaret Mary. He had been one of the O'Tooles now for almost two years, and he relished being part of a family. Patrick and Kathleen were mom and dad, Big John and Jimmy were grandpa, and Maureen and Bridgey were grandma. He referred to the six other O'Toole children as his brothers and sister, and they called him their brother. He had always looked up to Michael and was never far from his side. He was protective of Margaret Mary, as if she needed looking after, and the two of them became close confidants.

Patrick and Kathleen's siblings provided him with twenty something aunts and uncles and legions of cousins. Of course, they all knew Iggy's story, and readily accepted him into the family right away without any fanfare. He had never even received a birthday card before, and now got a stack of them every year. Kathleen knew from her cleaning, that he kept all of them under his bed in neat rubber banded stacks. When no one was around, he took them out and read them again. The O'Tooles made Iggy feel loved, grounded and protected.

In high school, Iggy was unable to keep up academically with Michael and Margaret Mary. He was usually enrolled in different classes than they were, certainly not in the advanced pre-college courses, but he always worked hard and kept a strong "C" average.

Iggy had never played any organized sports growing up, but always envied the attention Michael got, especially from the girls, for his athletic prowess. In the summer before his senior year of high school, Iggy announced he was going out for the varsity football team. Patrick and Kathleen tentatively gave him their blessing, but secretly worried about his safety, and how he would take it when he got cut. After all, by this time, he was only about five-foot-eight and one-hundred and sixty pounds soaking wet and had no experience. To make up for lost time, he began going to the school weight room every day with Michael, and downing protein shakes like water.

To everyone's surprise, Iggy turned out to be the fastest kid going out for the team. During wind sprints, head coach Charles Hastings could hardly believe his eyes or his stopwatch. He was all-state caliber fast, and of course speed is the one thing you can't teach. The speed made him a natural for wide receiver, but he couldn't catch very well. They tried him at defensive back, but it became clear that Iggy's lack of experience was going to cost the team a lot of touchdowns. Nevertheless, the coaching staff couldn't help but admire his courage and aggressiveness during blocking and tackling drills.

But Coach Hastings noticed an interesting thing when the team split up for intra-squad scrimmages at the end of practice. Iggy always lobbied, even begged the coaching staff to let him play blocking back in front of Michael, his all state running back. The St. Thomas Aquinas offense basically consisted of three plays: Michael left, Michael right and Michael up the middle. He knew the story how the two of them had become brothers, and after a relentless daily campaign from Iggy, the coach finally gave in and gave Iggy his wish, knowing full well he was too small for the position.

It didn't take more than a few snaps though, to realize that Iggy would sacrifice life and limb to keep anyone from laying a hand on Michael. Another observation was that with his speed, he got to the holes much faster than the starting fullback, who weighed in at 210 pounds. This meant Michael didn't need to hesitate for the holes to open. On sweeps outside, they had always had a problem with Michael over-running his big slow-footed blocking back, but Iggy's speed got him to his outside blocking position in half the time, allowing the plays to develop much faster. Since the imposing Michael never had to break stride, it was taking multiple tacklers to bring him down.

In addition, it looked like Iggy could make up for his lack of size with ferocious hits on would-be tacklers. It didn't matter who they were or how many there were, he threw himself at them like a missile. He didn't seem to be afraid of anything, and quickly popped up after each play. Compared to his childhood, football was a walk in the park for Iggy.

After a couple days of this, Coach Hastings got the other coaches together after practice and asked them what they thought about Iggy playing blocking back. To a man, they agreed that this new setup was bringing huge rewards. The coaches also noticed that there seemed to be a kind of intangible communication between the brothers. Michael seemed to be able to read Iggy's blocks almost before he made them, making the two of them a dominant force, even against the starting defense.

By the time the summer practice sessions ended, Iggy was not only on the team, but slotted to be the starting blocking back. When Iggy ran into the house on Highmont that night, he was literally bouncing up and down telling Patrick and Kathleen the news. Kathleen was hugging him and bouncing up and down with him, while Patrick shot a sideways quizzical look at his all-state running back son. Michael nodded lightly to affirm the news was true, while smiling ear-to-ear.

"Can you believe it, dad?" shouted Iggy as he broke free from his mom.

"I'm speechless!" declared his dad loudly, as he slapped Iggy on the back, "Congratulations!"

"What the heck is going on?" Margaret Mary asked while coming down the short hallway from her bedroom to the living room.

Two of the four younger boys came running in from the back yard, and two entered the hallway from the bedroom the four boys shared. "What is it, what happened?" they all wanted to know.

"I not only made the team, but I'm starting at blocking back in front of Michael!" shouted Iggy over everyone, as they hugged him and slapped his back.

After a few more minutes, the pragmatic Margaret Mary announced, "Let's all go to Ponticello's for pizza and celebrate!"

When the cheering calmed a bit, Patrick said, "Alright, alright, it is a special occasion, but no one orders soda, just water. It costs too much and we can have soda when we get home."

"And no cheese bread either!" Kathleen added, "I'll make some to have with the soda when we get back."

As everyone started to head for the front door, Patrick stopped Iggy, stuck out his hand and said the words that every young man longs to hear from his father, "I am very proud of you son."

Iggy shook his hand and looked back at his dad through suddenly misty eyes and half-whispered, "Thanks, dad."

CHAPTER TWENTY-FOUR

In the first couple games of the season, Michael and Iggy looked like an insurmountable machine. Iggy could take out multiple defenders by throwing his body at them, and Michael would use his long legs, muscle and agility to run around or over whoever was left. It was a beautiful thing to watch.

Margaret Mary went to all the games, and cheered her brothers on, even though she felt football was an 'uncivilized, Neanderthal form of entertainment'. Casually she would glance up at her father's face after a big play and see the kind of pride she felt fathers only held for sons. She didn't feel slighted or jealous though, because her analytical, scientific approach to life, recognized it merely as an unchangeable difference in the way the two genders interacted. Patrick showed her a guiding tenderness during quiet moments together that Michael never received, but made her feel like the most special girl on the planet.

Kathleen came to the games but didn't ever understand all the rules, partially because she sat next to her daughter most of the time. The two of them chatted on a wide range of subjects that had nothing to do with football. Margaret Mary found the differences between her mother and father, and gender differences in general, to be both humorous, and possibly worthy of some sort of academic study.

She also relished watching her two grandfathers, who stood together against the fence surrounding the field, away from the crowds in the stands. The two old Irish immigrants watched every minute of every game as they had for years. It was 1967, and Grandpa Finnegan, Big John, was seventy-one now. He used a walker to get around at home, but just a cane in public. All his weight had taken its toll on his knees over the years. Grandpa O'Toole, Jimmy, was sixty-seven now, and used a cane at home but not in public.

The two of them had a few reasons for being away from everyone. First, the steps in the bleachers were difficult to navigate. But before mobility was an issue, their distance afforded them the ability to drink bottles of beer from their cooler, which they wrapped in brown bags so no one would suspect they had alcohol on school property. Finally, their cursing referees and continual slander of any and all opposing players who were either not white or white but not Irish, was deemed unacceptable for young ears.

Michael had become for them the epitome of everything they had worked so hard for in America. Physically he held a commanding presence at six-foot-two and two-hundred and ten pounds of muscle. He had broad shoulders, a square jaw and sparkling, blue, smiling Irish eyes. He was St. Thomas Aquinas' scholar athlete, and a National Merit Scholar who would soon be offered a full scholarship to what they considered to be the finest university in the country, the holy ground called Notre Dame. Michael was going to carry the football for the Fighting Irish, to be sure, but more importantly, he was going to carry all the hopes and dreams of his immigrant grandparents. No one was going to tell this beautiful boy that 'no Irish need apply'.

The two old men loved to watch their grandson run down the field with those bright white letters on his back screaming 'O'Toole'. They were especially delighted when Michael ran over a player on the other team who was black, or had an Italian, German or Polish name on his back. This was why they couldn't sit in the stands. After the games, the two of them would sit on the tailgate of Jimmy's old truck with a bottle of Bushmills, a fresh case of beer and long cigars. They would talk and laugh about all the players with names like Pirelli or Kleinschmidt who got carried off the field after trying to tackle Michael. The conversation was always pretty much the same.

"It would take four or five of those greasy fookin' dagos to bring him down," Jimmy would exclaim in a semi-drunken boast.

"I bet that big dumb pollock shit in his pants when Michael ran him over!" Big John would holler back with slurred speech.

Nearby, Grandma Finnegan exclaimed, "Jesus, Mary and Joseph, can't you behave just for a little while. Those boys' folks are somewhere in the parking lot. What if they hear you? We'll have a brawl on our hands".

"Well it is true, Maureen," giggled Bridgey quietly.

"That kraut lineman, the one the newspaper bragged would be Michael's match, was unconscious when they carried him off the field!" laughed Jimmy loudly.

"Did you see the way that nigger linebacker ran away from Michael!" boomed Big John.

"DAD PLEASE! You can't talk like that around the children!" Kathleen hissed at her father, clearly not pleased with the example he was setting.

The quality of their example for their grandchildren was always diminished proportionately by the amount of alcohol consumed. Yet it always seemed that their interest in treating them to free lessons in history, philosophy and sociology increased proportionately.

Later that season, on a cool Friday night in October, Aquinas was playing their cross-town rivals from Mercy High School in University City. Michael and Iggy were having a great game, with Michael already over a hundred yards early in the third quarter, and Aquinas up by twenty-one points. At the end of a fifteen-yard gain, four Mercy defenders were pulling Michael down when the referee blew the play dead. Just as Michael relaxed, Mercy's safety ran up full speed and speared him in the chest, knocking him onto his back with a late hit. Immediately everyone in the stands gasped and groaned at the flagrant foul, but there was no flag thrown.

Iggy saw the whole thing as he was picking himself off the

ground back near the line of scrimmage. As the five Mercy players were celebrating above Michael, Iggy's blue jersey was flashing towards them at full speed. They didn't see him coming, but everyone in the stands watched, and heard the sickening crunch, as Iggy hurled himself at the unsuspecting group.

In an instant Iggy was on his feet, but as each Mercy player stood up, he would head butt, shove or throw them back to the ground. Iggy looked like he was possessed, until more of the Mercy players realized what was happening, grabbed him, and started pummeling him. What ensued was an all-out brawl as both sidelines emptied, and the teams started pushing and shoving each other.

When the coaches and referees finally restored some order, and the players started receding, there was Iggy straddling his beloved Michael who was still on the ground trying to catch his breath and collect his wits. He had his helmet in his hand and was swinging it wildly at any Mercy player who came too close, while screaming obscenities at the at the top of his lungs. Finally, while the Aquinas players talked Iggy down from his raging rant, everyone saw the head referee making a clear motion with his right arm towards the Aquinas sideline, as he formally threw Iggy out of the game. Coach Hastings was clearly animated as well as he made his case to the official about the late hit that started everything.

When Patrick spotted Iggy standing over Michael swinging his helmet, he hurriedly ran down to the fence, hopped over and started running towards the melee. By the time he got to Iggy, the Aquinas assistant coach, Father Montgomery, was grabbing him by the arm to drag him towards the sideline.

"I've got him Father," said Patrick as he grabbed Iggy's other arm, "I'll take care of it."

"Well hurry up and get him out of here!" yelled the priest. "What an embarrassment for the entire school!"

"Absolutely, Father," Patrick shot back with his most serious tone and facial expression. "We can't put up with this kind of behavior!"

Everyone in the stands watched as Patrick grabbed Iggy roughly and started marching him towards the fence, where Grandpa

O'Toole and Grandpa Finnegan were standing. From a distance, it looked like an angry father pulling his son off the field while dishing out some harsh words of discipline.

As Patrick got Iggy out of earshot of the other players, he leaned in close to him and whispered hoarsely, "Way to go Iggy! Those fuckin' cheap shot artists deserved what you gave 'em! I am so proud of you right now, sticking up for Michael like that! Now don't smile. It has to look like I'm really pissed."

Later that night, back at the O'Toole's house on Highmont, both grandfathers were shaking Iggy's hand, slapping him on the back, and smiling from ear-to-ear.

"That was a great hit you put on those fookin' assholes, boy," said Grandpa O'Toole, while gently swaying in a boozy haze.

"Bunch of fookin' pricks, they were," added Grandpa Finnegan flashing his tobacco stained teeth.

"For Chrissake! Would the two of you PLEASE watch the language!" hollered Kathleen from the kitchen.

"You're a fine lad, Iggy," said Grandpa O'Toole.

"The heart of a lion, he has!" quipped Grandpa Finnegan.

"The courage of one for sure!"

"A true Irishman!"

"A fighter to the core!"

"Always stand up for family, boy!"

"And other Irishmen!"

And so it went, into the wee hours of the night, with the younger children watching and listening. The women clucked their tongues and shook their heads in a fake display of disapproval for the benefit of the children, while also secretly admiring what Iggy had done. Michael happily sat on the couch letting Iggy reap all the praise for once. He told everyone he was fine, with just a large bruise on his chest.

Margaret Mary stayed in her room, listening to all that was going on, and analyzing the interaction between her family members. Nothing went unnoticed by her. She absorbed what was said, and unsaid; what was shown to the outside world, and what was only seen by family.

As she listened to the drunken ramblings of her two old immigrant grandfathers, she knew they were coming to the end of the road physically, but they were leaving a legacy of family and friends who they had helped get a foothold in America. Now some their children and grandchildren were pursuing the American dream by going to college and becoming respected professionals.

The Irish community's tribal bonds ran deep and wide in St. Louis, and were serving them all very well.

CHAPTER TWENTY-FIVE

As high school graduation neared for Michael, Margaret Mary and Iggy in the Spring of 1968, all of them were busy making plans for the future. Patrick had been assured by the union that Iggy could start his apprenticeship as a pipefitter right after graduation. He couldn't wait. Margaret Mary had earned a full scholarship to St. Louis University, which was run by the Jesuits. She was told that her propensity for argument would be admired by them. Michael had signed his scholarship papers with Notre Dame, and picked his courses for the fall. His presence was sought at no less than a dozen graduation parties, and each of the hosts was well aware that an invitation to Iggy and Margaret Mary must be included.

After the football season ended, Iggy and Margaret Mary noticed that Michael seemed to want more time alone, and they attributed that to the constant hoopla he was surrounded with during the season. Then at dinner one night, he announced that he didn't want to play basketball or baseball during senior year, even though he had lettered in both sports in each of the three previous years. Patrick said it was a good idea, so that he wouldn't get injured and lose his football scholarship.

During quiet moments, Margaret Mary asked him time again if everything was alright, and he always gave her that big winning smile, and told her she worried too much. Others noticed that they saw Iggy around town without Michael for the first time since the two of them were just little guys at Sts. John and James. Iggy kept telling everyone that Michael had a lot of preparation to do before leaving, and that he wanted to spend as much time as possible with the rest of the family. Kathleen was worried that he was isolating.

She wasn't buying the excuse that he was nervous about leaving, because he had always been so confident and self-assured like his father.

Iggy and Margaret Mary were both worried about the change in their beloved Michael and spoke to each other about it often. He seemed to be living in another world in his head, leaving his natural, gregarious nature behind. Even more disturbing, was that their health-conscious, straight arrow Michael had started drinking. He just had a few beers at parties over the winter, but by springtime was getting drunk every weekend. He didn't get drunk at parties, preferring to drink alone in a park, listening to the radio in his old Chevy, while staring into space.

Margaret Mary prayed for him every day, and Iggy made it his job to be around to drive him home, so he wouldn't get a DWI and lose his scholarship. Often they had their hands full trying to sneak Michael into his basement bedroom without their parents seeing him drunk.

Finally, in the last couple weeks of July, he seemed to come out of his funk. He knew football practice started August 1st at Notre Dame, and he knew he had to get ready for the grueling two-a-day practices in the summer heat. Iggy and Margaret Mary heaved a huge sigh of relief every time they saw him running in the neighborhood or hear him say he was heading to the gym. Finally, the big day arrived, and Patrick loaded up the station wagon with Michael's belongings on a sunny Saturday in late July. It was time to head to the hallowed ground known as Notre Dame. Kathleen was staying home with the rest of the kids. She had already said what she needed to say that morning as she helped him pack his things in boxes. They were in the basement, and she was working with misty eyes.

"I'm very proud of you Michael," she whispered to him while holding his face in her hands like she did when he was little.

"I know mom," he smiled.

"I love you Michael," she whispered.

"I know you do," he answered quietly, "I love you too."

"Let me have your hands," she said, holding hers out to take them. With that she bowed her head and started to pray, "Blessed Mother, you know what it's like to let your son go out into the world. Please take care of my son, Michael, in Jesus' name, Amen."

When Michael came upstairs, he hugged his younger siblings, except for his Irish twin, who was strangely absent. He quietly made his way down the short hall to her bedroom, where he knocked lightly and opened the door a crack. "Can I come in?" he asked. He heard a quiet 'yes' and then sniffling. When he stepped in the room, he saw Margaret Mary curled up in her pajamas on her unmade bed, facing the wall away from the door.

"Aren't you going to say goodbye Maggie?" he asked gently as he sat down on the edge of the bed. Only one person on earth got away with calling her Maggie, and only when no one else was around. It was their little secret. She made everyone else call her by her formal full name, Margaret Mary.

"I don't want to say it, Michael," she whispered without turning around. He knew if she had been crying, she would never turn to face him, because he would see her blotchy red skin and running nose. She hated crying. She thought it was weak.

"No hug either?" he asked quietly.

Again, she shook her head without turning. He smiled as he looked at her disheveled red hair. It always seemed a perfect match to her personality.

"I'll be home for Thanksgiving," he said, trying to offer something positive.

Margaret Mary raised her arm and waved a weak goodbye without turning around, then dropped her arm again. The pain of losing her 'twin' was almost unbearable. They had done everything together their whole lives. His absence was going to leave a huge void. Michael always made her feel safe, and he knew how to make her laugh, when no one else could figure out how to pierce her serious nature. Now he was leaving.

"I love you, Michael," she said, trying to swallow the lump in her throat.

"I love you too, Maggie," he smiled.

When Michael stepped onto the front porch, his dad was already waving him over and pleading, "Let's Go!"

Iggy, always his shadow, was sitting in the back seat directly behind the front passenger seat looking out the window at him and smiling. As they pulled out the drive, and started down the street, many of their long-time neighbors were out on their front porches waving good-bye. This was a little village that took pride in Michael's accomplishments. They watched him grow up from a baby. They watched out for his safety when the kids were playing in the street. They had let Kathleen know if they spotted him around Ferguson with the "wrong crowd". They had yelled at him to get out of trees and off roofs when he was trying to retrieve an errant ball.

They had purchased hundreds of candy bars and other goodies from him to help raise money for sports uniforms and equipment. They had given him small gifts for First Communion, Confirmation and eighteen birthdays. They watched him learn to ride his first two-wheel bike while shouting encouragement. They all saw his name in the paper every year for getting straight A's and congratulated him. In the last few years they followed all his remarkable athletic feats chronicled in the local papers.

A little piece of each of them was in that station wagon with Michael as it disappeared down the block.

Part VIII

Rough Roads

CHAPTER TWENTY-SIX

Michael called and said he was getting a ride from school with another student from St. Louis on Thanksgiving Day, and that he should be home by two in the afternoon. Everyone was eager to see him after his four-month absence and hear about Notre Dame. Iggy and Margaret Mary's leader, Patrick and Kathleen's baby boy, the pride of Ferguson, was coming home for Thanksgiving dinner. The house on Highmont was buzzing with excitement. The smells of turkey, dressing and pie wafted about as Kathleen and the grandmas bustled about the small kitchen. Patrick and the grandpas hollered at the football game on television, and at the kids to settle down.

Sure enough, just before two o'clock, Michael walked through the front door, and announced, "Hello everybody!"

As though a switch had been flipped, the whole house became quiet. The television was turned off, the kids quit wrestling, and the women ran into the living room to see what had happened. All of them stood staring and disbelieving what their eyes were seeing. Michael looked disheveled. His normally close-cropped hair was long and uncombed, and it looked as though he had not shaved for a week. His clothing was wrinkled, frayed and dirty. He had a can of beer in one hand and a small cooler in the other.

With slightly slurred speech, he then announced, "I have a surprise for all of you!" He then turned to open the storm door behind him and waved in a young woman whose clothing and hair were as unsightly as Michael's. She was clearly shy and uncomfortable, barely raising her gaze off the floor. Then, with a smile and some flair he called out too loudly, "Everyone, this is Janet! She is my wife and we are expecting a baby in the spring!"

Michael was clearly drunk, and now the girl looked terrified. The silence following the announcement was almost unbearable, and the uneasiness in the air was palpable. Always in charge of the situation at hand, Margaret Mary jumped out of her chair with her hand outstretched, and said cheerfully, "Hello Janet, my name is Margaret Mary. I'm Michael's sister. Can I take your coat?"

After a quick handshake, Janet started to take her coat off and said, "Thank you."

"Please come in and sit down, sweetheart. I'm Michael's mother, Kathleen," she smiled, as she took the girls arm and led her to the chair Margaret Mary had just left.

Michael sat the cooler down next to the television, immediately to his right. As he surveyed the room, he felt his father to his left in his favorite chair, and saw both of his grandfathers sitting side-by-side on the couch at the far end of the room. Due to poor hearing and eyesight, both of them looked perplexed. Michael just smiled and waved at them.

"What the hell is going on?" asked Grandpa O'Toole, who refused to wear his hearing aid.

"This is Michael's wife, Jimmy," Grandma O'Toole called out from her post next to Grandma Finnegan, standing in the opening from the dining room to the living room.

"Are you kidding?" asked Grandpa Finnegan loudly.

"Where did you get married, Michael?" asked Grandma Finnegan.

This was the loaded question that everyone in the room was thinking. The answer would tell them if the girl was Catholic and if the wedding had been performed by a priest. If she wasn't Catholic, there would be immediate questions about the child being raised Catholic. If they had not been married by a priest, the marriage was invalid, and the young couple would be living in sin.

"We were married at the courthouse grandma. The priests wanted us to jump through a bunch of hoops," slurred Michael after taking a swig of his beer.

"HOOPS?" she shot back.

"Dear God," added Grandma O'Toole.

Quiet until that moment, Patrick got to his feet and tersely asked, "Can I see you outside Michael?"

"Sure," was the boozy reply.

After the two of them were on the back patio, and the door closed, Patrick spoke through clenched teeth. "What the fuck is going on here? Is this some kind of sick joke?"

Swaying slightly from side to side, all Michael could muster was, "No sir."

"You show up with a wife and a baby on the way with no warning; no notice at all; not even a phone call? Is this any way to treat your family? And that poor girl, Jesus Christ Michael. And to top it off you come in here shit-faced?" Then after a brief silence, while Patrick tried to collect himself, he asked more quietly, "Is she Catholic?"

"No sir."

"I cannot believe what I am seeing and hearing," Patrick said as he turned away from Michael and stared out into the yard. "Why don't you go stand in a hot shower for a while and try to sober up. And while you're at it, wash that filthy hair and shave. You look like hell."

"Alright," was all Michael could muster as he turned to go back in the house. Patrick had never spoken to him like this, but he knew he deserved it. He was already dreading the thought of being here without the protection of his boozy cloud.

Patrick went back inside and asked the grandparents to go to one of their other children's homes to eat. They said they understood and began to get their things together to leave. In one of his very few gentle moments, Jimmy whispered to his son, "Take a deep breath, boy. You look like you could explode."

Then in another rare moment, Big John put his arm around Patrick, and quietly said, "It's going to be alright, boy. You'll see."

After the grandparents left, Patrick told the four younger children to go downstairs, play pool, and stay there until he told them to come up. He could hear the shower running down the hall in their only bathroom. Kathleen and Margaret Mary, to their credit, had taken Janet into the kitchen and were chatting away, while they began to make arrangements for the food to be served a lot later than they had planned. Patrick sent Iggy downstairs to find Michael some clean clothes. He would have liked to have done the same for Janet, but he didn't want to embarrass her by insinuating she looked dirty and unkempt.

Over the next few hours around the dining room table, the story of what happened in the four months since Michael left, came out. He and Janet slowly wound their way through the whole mess in short bursts, and tears, a little bit at a time. To their credit, Patrick and Kathleen held their shocked and angry disbelief in check. As the booze wore off, it was clear that Michael was becoming more and more embarrassed. He knew how badly he had hurt his parents. He was the golden boy who never got anything but praise from both of them, and now this. Janet added some details but could not have known how fast and how far Michael had fallen.

Michael had been cut from the freshman squad before school even started for being late to several practices, and eventually missing a couple altogether. When he was told to pack his things and leave, he wasn't sure how much of his scholarship was based on football, and how much was based on academics, but he knew that he was going to be short on tuition.

It didn't matter, because by the time classes started in September his nightly drinking made it impossible to get up for his classes. Before the first week was up, he dropped all his classes, and started working as a bouncer in a bar near campus where he got exactly what he didn't need, free drinks. This is when Janet entered the picture.

Janet was waiting tables full time at the bar, and the two of them began talking a lot during their shifts. Eventually Michael started walking her to the apartment that she shared with two other girls.

He was still staying in his dorm room, because no one told him he had to leave. One thing led to another, and in late October she told Michael she thought she might be pregnant. A trip to the free clinic confirmed it. When they went to Janet's parents to tell them the big news, they told her to pack whatever she had left at the house and leave. They still had four kids at home, and Michael would say later they were living in squalor.

The mood lightened a bit when Margaret Mary blurted to her parents, "You two are going to be grandparents, and I'm going to be an aunt."

Patrick and Kathleen figured Michael came by his drinking problem naturally because of Patrick's escapades with the Irish curse. They secretly hoped that the drinking would be short term, and that its effects just caught him by surprise. They still didn't know about his drinking episodes the previous summer.

None of them were particularly happy with the situation, but Patrick and Kathleen left the table for about five minutes, and when they came back, they told the young couple they had a plan. Kathleen told them they could use Michael's bedroom downstairs, if they wanted. It was a far cry from the dreams she had of him coming home from Notre Dame with a law degree and buying a big home in West County.

Patrick told Michael he could call the pipefitter's union hall in the morning to see if they couldn't place him somewhere on a temporary work permit. This was equally hard to swallow since he often sang Michael's praises to his co-workers.

Finally, Kathleen told Janet that she would call Big John in the morning and see if he would pull a few strings to get her a clerical job at City Hall, or the County Government Center. He was officially retired, having turned the Shamrock over to Kathleen's oldest brother, John Jr, but unofficially he still wielded considerable power because of the number of people and families that owed him favors.

Michael and Janet thanked them profusely. They knew they had few prospects and no money when they arrived, so this was a huge relief. Like most parents, Patrick and Kathleen knew they couldn't let their terrible disappointment at this turn of events cause them to turn their backs on Michael.

Patrick told Michael that they expected him to give up the drinking, since they saw it as the primary cause for his failures. Kathleen and Margaret Mary stood to give Janet long, warm hugs which prompted her to start crying. She was amazed at how quickly this family had welcomed her into their home when her own parents had thrown her out.

Within a couple weeks, Michael's work permit came through and he was now a new pipefitter. The permits were handed out in these situations to member's relatives, to circumvent the traditional apprenticeship program, which was now watched closely by the federal government to insure fair minority hiring. Iggy couldn't have been happier. Patrick had managed to get him in the union apprenticeship program the previous June, and now the two brothers were reunited by occupation.

Big John came through, of course, and arranged for Janet to replace a recent retiree who had a clerical job at City Hall. She was going to start after the first of the year. The baby was due in May, and the job would allow her to sit at a desk and stay off her feet as the pregnancy progressed. All that was needed now was for Michael to stay sober.

For a few months, Patrick and Iggy drove Michael to work and back home since he and Janet did not have a car. Janet was taking the bus to downtown St. Louis from the Ferguson bus loop, where their next-door neighbor Bob Wilson dropped her every morning on his way to work. Finally, in March, Michael bought a decent car, on time, from one of his father's friends at work. Both he and Janet were so happy to have some personal freedom again, to go shopping, or to the movies whenever they felt like it.

It seemed that all the planning and work to get the young couple started on the right foot was paying off, until a couple months before the baby was due. Michael got paid on Friday every week and had been faithfully going to the bank and then straight home. This Friday, with everyone waiting and worrying and praying at home, he stopped at a bar, spent most of his check there, and then topped off the night by wrecking the new car and getting a DWI around midnight. In the ensuing week, they learned he had also been hiding the fact that he was coming to work late or not at all.

It was at this point that his parents realized he must have THE GENE. He had inherited it from Patrick, who had quit drinking on the never-talked-about Saturday morning years before, when he woke up on their front lawn, and Kathleen gave him the ultimatum.

In a culture that prides itself on drinking too much; in a culture where virtually everyone in the family drinks to excess at gatherings; in a culture where everyone laughs uproariously at the exploits of their drunken friends and relatives; you really had to work at being ostracized for drinking. Michael had accomplished this rare distinction.

There isn't much worse in a blue collar Irish family than for a man to be such a booze hound that he cannot support himself and his family. No matter how much you drink, you absolutely, positively must get up and go to work every morning. It took a hundred years for the 'No Irish Need Apply' signs to completely disappear. It took strong, hard Irish men like Jimmy O'Toole and Big John Finnegan, their whole lives to gain enough prestige and power to be able to put their own people to work.

They had fought long and hard to bring the Irish in America out of a life of poverty. They were making sure there would never be another Great Famine. In America, unlike Ireland, a man who wanted to work, could work. There was no king or aristocracy that held all the land and the purse strings. Through their skill in politics, and their determination to establish labor unions, the Irish in America had been able to shape their future and control their destiny.

Having a job meant gaining self-respect and the respect of others. A job meant your wife and kids have a roof over their heads, food on the table and shoes on their feet. Having a job meant your kids didn't have to quit school, when they are ten or twelve years-old, to work the farm or in some god-forsaken factory. In America, you could work hard so your kids could stay in school and have a better life than their parents. They could even go to college, but it all started with getting up every day and going to work.

In mid-June Janet gave birth to a beautiful baby girl that they named Nora. Janet had to quit work a few weeks before the birth because of the swelling in her feet and legs. The plan was that she would stay home and take care of the baby. This of course meant that their little family's well-being was solely on Michael's shoulders.

Patrick had preached to Michael about his responsibilities and got him to agree to go to Alcoholics Anonymous meetings. Finally, Patrick got him a job about a hundred miles from home at a new power plant being built in Eastern Missouri. The plan was that since Michael had no car, he would be dependent on the other fitters for transportation, both to the plant from St. Louis early on Monday mornings, and during the week, while they all stayed together at a cheap motel. Patrick told a couple of the men Michael was riding with, about the situation, and they promised to keep an eye on him.

Every Friday night after work, Michael and three other men would ride together back to St. Louis without stopping, and with their paychecks intact. Everything seemed to be going according to plan. Michael was not drinking, and he and Janet were saving for a place of their own. In September of 1969, Janet announced that she was pregnant again. Michael convinced everyone at that point that he needed to stay at the plant on most weekends to work overtime with a second baby coming. He had been sober almost six months, and this seemed like a thoughtful decision to be able to take better care of his young family. The other fitters told Patrick that if Michael was working seven days a week, and ten hours a day, he would never have enough energy to walk the eight miles to the nearest tavern.

Michael told Janet on the phone in early December that he would come home for a couple weekends around Christmas and New Year. No one at home had seen him in three months, but the other fitters assured Patrick that he was going to work every day. They had been coming by the house on Highmont with Michael's paycheck every Friday night. Two Fridays before Christmas, they told Patrick that Michael had kept his check to buy Christmas presents. When the other men returned to the plant Monday morning, Michael was nowhere to be found. One of them called Kathleen and gave her the news.

Christmas came and went without any word from Michael. Janet was so distraught that she barely got out of bed for a week. Patrick and Kathleen's mood went from disbelief to fear, then shock, and finally anger. Over the next few months, when relatives, people at church, or people in the neighborhood asked how he was doing, Patrick would shrug and walk away. Kathleen would tear up and be unable to answer at all. Margaret Mary and Iggy were dumbfounded as well.

Michael had gone from family standard bearer to worthless shit-bum in a little over a year. Eventually, everyone just quit speaking his name. It was just too unbelievable and painful.

Janet gave birth to their second baby girl in May of 1970 and named her Maura. At Kathleen's urging, Janet agreed to have both of the girls baptized at Sts. John and James. By her own admission, Janet had little formal religious training, but said she liked being part of a family when they prayed, and when they went to church on Sunday. She told them she wanted to eventually convert to Catholicism.

The next time anyone saw Michael was seven months after Maura's birth, on Christmas Eve of 1970. He had been gone, without a word, for just over a year. He showed up at the house on Highmont about eight o'clock in the evening, just as everyone was settling down to exchange gifts. When he opened the front door to let himself in, he was dirty, unkempt and so drunk he could barely stand or speak.

Patrick jumped up immediately, grabbed him, then literally threw him off the front porch onto the front lawn. He then half-dragged, and half-walked Michael back to the old car he had parked partially on the front lawn. Everyone inside, and for that matter half the neighborhood could hear Patrick cursing and screaming at Michael. “I don’t want to see your drunken ass here again until you get your shit together! YOU HEAR ME! AND DON’T COME AROUND FOR MONEY EITHER YOU FUCKING BUM! NOW GET THE HELL OUT OF HERE!” Patrick screamed as he slammed the car door with all his might. There were many pairs of eyes at the O’Toole picture window. There were a lot more at the neighbors’ windows as well. No one had ever seen Patrick like this.

Iggy and Margaret Mary ran down the street hoping to catch Michael at the stop sign at the corner of Forestwood Dr, but he was going too fast. Kathleen ran down the hall to her bedroom and slammed the door, sobbing. Janet looked like a deer in the head-lights, with Nora on her lap, and Maura next to her in her punkin’ seat. The other four kids just sat and stared, angrily realizing that their big brother had just ruined another Christmas.

The next day, everyone was so somber that it seemed they were mourning a death rather than celebrating the birth of their Savior. But, in a way, they were grieving. Their talented and handsome son, brother, husband and father was gone. No one knew for how long, or if it would be forever.

CHAPTER TWENTY-SEVEN

Margaret Mary graduated from St. Louis University magna cum laude, with a double major in philosophy and theology in the spring of 1972. She had also acquired a teaching certificate so that she could fulfill her lifelong dream to teach in the Catholic school system. She could have made twice as much money over time in the public-school system, but her heart was in Catholic education. Also, she hadn't stopped entertaining the possibility of becoming a nun, and she felt the daily proximity to them would help her discern what her future should be.

No one approaching the status of a Prince Charming had appeared during her four years in college, and even if he had, she was more adept at shunning admirers than attempting small talk. Also, although she had not confided her feelings to another soul, she had decided long ago not to participate in the sexual revolution.

In the fall of 1972, Margaret Mary started her first job at Epiphany parish in south St. Louis, as a third-grade teacher. She saved her money, and within a couple years, she was able to put a down payment on a fixer-upper a few blocks from school. Half of the men in the family were in the building trades, so fixing up the house was being done for the cost of materials, sandwiches and beer. The other half of the family were in law enforcement and fire protection, so they made sure she was the safest single woman in all of St. Louis, without her knowledge, of course.

It took a couple of years, but eventually she got the place just the way she wanted. There were lots of kids in the neighborhood from Epiphany, and they all knew they could stop by for a little tutoring from Ms. O'Toole between four and five in the afternoon.

Daily Mass was no longer a requirement, but Margaret Mary rarely missed a day. She wanted above all else to keep Michael's safety on God's list of things to do every day. She missed him terribly and worked hard not to let worry keep her from living a full life, but it was difficult.

By now it had been over four years since anyone had seen Michael on that Christmas eve of 1970. Iggy and Margaret Mary talked about him often and admitted to each other that they both cruised areas where the homeless gathered, hoping to spot him. They also left his picture at the two main shelters downtown. The truth was that he could have been anywhere in the country. Patrick did not want Michael's name mentioned, but Margaret Mary and Kathleen talked of him often, and regularly had a good cry together when Patrick was not around.

Janet had converted to Catholicism and started work again at City Hall. She saved her money while living with the O'Tooles, and eventually moved into a place of her own with Maura and Nora, a couple blocks away on Bayview Dr. The family had given her their blessing to get her marriage to Michael legally annulled, so that she would be free to marry again. By the summer of 1975, Nora was six and Maura was five. They were happy and beautiful little girls with a huge extended family watching over them and their mother.

Then on a cold Saturday night in January of 1976, Margaret Mary's phone rang about ten pm. She jumped up from the couch, half-asleep, with a feeling of dread due to the late hour of the call. She made the lady on the other end repeat what she was saying three times because all her brain would let her hear, was the name Michael.

Sensing she may have woken Margaret Mary, the lady on the phone slowed down and tried again, asking, "Are you Margaret Mary O'Toole?"

Finally, after clearing her throat, Margaret Mary said quietly, "Yes, I am." Immediately she felt her chest tighten and her pulse quicken.

"My name is Angela Parker. I am the overnight intake nurse at Malcolm Bliss Psychiatric Hospital. Do you know a man by the name of Michael O'Toole?" she asked.

"Yes ma'am, my brother," she answered, feeling a wave of nausea starting.

"The police brought him in about an hour ago. He's unconscious, but we got your name and number from his wallet. We were wondering if perhaps you could come down and make certain that this is your brother. Sometimes the homeless find wallets that don't belong to them," the nurse explained.

"Yes, of course," said Margaret Mary quickly, "I'm only ten minutes away. I'll get dressed and be right there."

"Thank God," she whispered as she hung up the phone. Her mind was reeling. She felt elation at the news that Michael was alive, but at the same time fearful of the fact that he was unconscious. She was running from room to room getting her keys, shoes and coat together, wondering what was so wrong that the police took him to the state mental hospital, instead of a regular emergency room.

Margaret Mary jumped in her VW Beetle and roared off down the street and made a right on Arsenal St. She told herself she needed to commune with God to slow her heartrate. She prayed the Our Father and Hail Mary over and over until that familiar peace began to descend upon her. While sitting at the light, waiting to cross Hampton Ave, she closed her eyes and asked God to protect her beloved Michael, as she had done every night before bed for more than five years now. Another five minutes and the foreboding structure called Malcolm Bliss Hospital appeared on her right.

The guard at the gate had her name on his list, so he directed her to look for a door with an amber light over it, on the right side of the massive structure. She parked in a visitor space in the deserted lot, ran towards the door, and rang the buzzer over the sign.

She was shaking as much from fear as from the cold. A tall male orderly dressed in white asked for identification, and then led her down a maze of dimly lit hallways. All the offices and rooms were dark, and she already knew she would never be able to find her way out. Her stomach was flipping as though she was on a carnival ride, in anticipation of whatever awaited her.

The stoic orderly stopped in front of an office, opened the door, turned on the light and motioned her inside. "Dr. Goldstein said to tell you he will be here as soon as possible, but it may be a while, so make yourself comfortable."

"Do you know where my brother, Michael O'Toole is? I mean do you know what condition he is in?" she asked.

"No ma'am, I'm sorry, you will have to wait for the doctor," he answered.

The office was dimly lit by two dusty table lamps and had the unmistakable smell of old musty books. There were plenty of them, lining two walls on cheap bookcases with bowed shelves. The shelves also held stacks of papers and file folders. The desk was in even more disarray, piled high with manila folders, and used paper coffee cups. In the front was a small nameplate that read 'Dr. Morris Goldstein'.

Being very neat and organized herself, the unkempt state of the office inspired little confidence in Dr. Goldstein already. Also, if this was Michael, she was not looking forward to telling the family that he was being cared for by a Jewish doctor. As the minutes ticked away towards midnight, her head began to pound, and her stomach began to hurt. Once again, she closed her eyes and began to pray.

After what seemed an eternity, she heard someone shuffling down the corridor. A short, bespectacled man in his late fifties, or early sixties walked in, smiled, and stuck out his hand. His hair looked somewhat like the hair on the picture of Albert Einstein in her classroom. His clothes looked like he had been sleeping in them for days. "I'm very, very sorry for your wait. It must be terrible to be waiting like this, but it could not be helped. I'm Morris Goldstein," he announced with a weak handshake, unlike the men in her family, who took pleasure in making you wince while shaking your hand.

"I'm Margaret Mary O'Toole," she replied. "A nurse on the phone said you may have my brother here and I want to see him." Her demeanor was brusque, as she wanted to convey that she was not some delicate girl, but a capable woman who was to be taken seriously.

Looking over the top of his dirty lenses at her, the doctor said, "Okay then, but first we need to talk." With that he moved slowly to pull his desk chair out in front of the desk, across from the chair she had been using. As he sat down he motioned for her to do the same. "Please, sit Miss O'Toole. The gentleman that arrived here this afternoon might have stolen your brother's wallet, and there was no picture ID."

"This afternoon! The lady on the phone told me he had been here an hour! What's going on here? Why would you wait?"

"Let me explain," the doctor said quietly, while looking directly at her eyes. "The man we have here was found in Carondelet Park by a man walking his dog late last night, just over twenty-four hours ago. He called the police, who thought the man they found was dead. But when the paramedics arrived, they found a pulse. Sometimes when it's this cold, the pulse slows so much it is hard to detect. They transported him to City Hospital, where they did a thorough exam while trying to bring his body temperature up. Luckily, they found no signs of foul play."

"So, he's alright, then?"

"Physically yes, but the ER doctor ran blood tests and found a dangerously high blood alcohol level of .25, but no drugs and no track marks on his arms."

"I don't even know what track marks are!" Margaret Mary interjected loudly, becoming increasingly anxious about the outcome of this story. "And you still have not said why I wasn't called earlier."

"Very well. I'm getting there. Track marks are needle marks on drug abusers' arms," Dr. Goldstein told her. "So, the ER staff was having a problem with the gentleman, because when he woke periodically through the night, and into this morning, he should have been sobering up, but instead he was talking incoherently. Then he started to become rather violent, and he is very large and muscular, so they finally gave him a shot to put him to sleep. They determined that the outbursts had a mental cause, because of the absence of drugs, and therefore made the decision to send him here about noon."

"Dear God," she murmured, folding her arms across her abdomen and rocking forward and back with her head down. At this point she wasn't sure if she wanted it to be Michael or not.

"The alcohol has long worn off, but his behavior is still erratic. He doesn't seem to hear us or see us when he comes to, and without sedation he is uncontrollable. When we went through his clothing we found a small leather wallet with your name and phone number. But we have found in the past, it is best to try and wait for the patient to wake up before we make phone calls. We have scared people to death, by bringing them down here, and then finding out the wallet was stolen or lost, and it's not their loved one. You told the nurse who called you that your brother has been missing and could be homeless, which is why the decision was made to ask you to come down."

"Michael disappeared five years ago. He abandoned his wife and daughters. For some reason, he started drinking too much and just lost all control of his life," said Margaret Mary, while still rocking gently. "Can I please see him now?"

"In a moment," he said, reaching into his pants pocket, "do you recognize this?" In the palm of his hand was a gold crucifix sitting atop a bundle of distinctive bright green glass beads. It was a rosary.

A pitiful high-pitched yelp escaped from Margaret Mary's lips as she covered her mouth with one hand, and slowly reached for the rosary with the other. Tears streamed down her face as she put the crucifix to her lips and kissed it gently. Very quietly, between sobs, she told Dr. Goldstein, "Its Michael's rosary. Our grandparents gave us each one for our Confirmation. They had a jeweler put a St. Patrick's medal above the cross on each one. The medals were from Ireland. The rosaries were blessed by Pope John XXIII in Rome."

Dr. Goldstein reached for a box of tissues and handed them to

Margaret Mary. He waited and watched as she dabbed her eyes with her left hand, and crossed herself with the right, which was clutching the rosary. She kissed the crucifix again, wrapped it in a tissue and put it in her purse. "This rosary has some very real emotional meaning for you."

"It means that Michael never lost his faith," she whispered.

Having been raised in an Orthodox Jewish home by his German immigrant parents, he was very familiar with the importance of religious ritual, and therefore knew to treat what he just witnessed with respect and dignity. "Alright then, why don't we take a walk now," he said as he stood, extending his hand, in the genteel manner in which a gentleman would help a lady from her chair.

As they proceeded down a long corridor, Dr. Goldstein explained to her that even if Michael's eyes open, he would not be able to see or hear her, because of the medication. "Another thing," he added as they neared a well-lit area behind large double doors, "We had to restrain him so that he would not harm himself or others. It is very difficult for loved ones to see, but it is necessary. Do you understand?"

"Yes," she answered nodding, as they paused just outside the doors.

"Also, his clothing was so filthy and ragged, that we disposed of them. All he has covering him is a sheet, because when the medication wears off, he is so agitated that we can't even get a gown or scrubs on him. Okay? Are you ready?" he asked as he reached for the door handle.

"Yes," she whispered, with eyes closed.

As they entered the large room, the doctor led her to a bank of individual spaces that were curtained off. As he pulled the curtain open, Margaret Mary stepped in and gazed unbelieving at her barely recognizable big brother. His hair and beard were long, matted and filthy. The unseeing eyes were open, staring out of deep dark sockets, but they were definitely Michael's. She stood silently next to the examination table with her arms folded across her chest, taking in a scene that belonged in a horror movie. His wrists and ankles had leather restraints on them.

Margaret Mary bent down and peered intently, at the small triangle of freckles on the right side of his neck that she had kidded him about when they were kids. The sight of it made her begin to cry again. "It's him," she whispered, as she stood up straight. "My God, Michael, what have you done to yourself." Slowly she turned toward the curtain behind her, and began to make a mournful whimper, as she crossed herself and prayed out loud, "Dear God, please take the demon away that is killing my brother." With that, her shoulders began to shake, she dropped her chin to her chest, and began sobbing loudly.

Very lightly, she felt the hand of Dr. Goldstein on her shoulder. In a calm quiet voice, he started, "I am so sorry Ms. O'Toole. But keep in mind, he is alive and breathing on his own. He seems to have had what we call a psychotic break, or mental breakdown. Rest assured, I am going to do everything in my power to bring your brother back. But, it's going to take some time."

Still facing the curtain, head down and eyes closed, she nodded. After a minute, she turned to Dr. Goldstein, began wiping her eyes and said, "Michael has an enormous extended family, and when they hear the news, their first instinct will be to come down here hoping to help. I'm talking dozens of them. I don't want them seeing him like this, but I have to tell them he's alive. Hiding this from my parents, my brothers, my grandparents, and his wife and daughters is unthinkable."

"Well, first of all, until I find out what is going on here, I would not want anyone interacting with him, because I don't know who or what is the trigger. Second, they can't get in the hospital without me writing up a clearance for each one individually. So, you can honestly tell them that they will have to wait," Dr. Goldstein told her with authority.

CHAPTER TWENTY-EIGHT

Over the next few months, Margaret Mary went every Tuesday after school to speak with Dr. Goldstein at the hospital before he went home for the day. On Tuesday evenings, she dutifully called her parents, grandparents, Janet and of course Iggy, to tell them any news, and if she had seen Michael through the one-way glass. As St. Patrick's Day approached, she knew she would be bombarded with questions by everyone in the family who stopped by the Shamrock, which is where they traditionally gathered. Also, this was to be the first St. Pat's day at the Shamrock without Big John, who had passed away the previous year at age seventy-nine. For both of these unhappy reasons, she considered not attending, but Kathleen finally convinced her to come.

The evening of St Patrick's day, as she made her rounds, she noticed Grandpa O'Toole waving her over to his favorite booth where he was holding court with a few of his old cronies. Jimmy was seventy-six now, barely mobile, and he had a question of his own about Michael. Through his slurred speech, he asked, "Little girl, I want to know when you're going to get rid of Michael's fookin' Jew doctor?"

"How dare you Grandpa!" she shot back. Then, jumping to her feet, "You've never even met the man! Dr. Goldstein happens to be a very kind man, and more importantly, he probably saved your grandson's life!"

With that, she stormed out the front door of the tavern. No one ever spoke to her grandfather that way. Jimmy just sat there with his mouth open, surprised and speechless. As she stepped outside, Margaret Mary knew she had been disrespectful, but for once she didn't care. She was not about to let anyone defame that sweet man, after all he had done. Patrick had heard his daughter from the next booth and watched as she stomped away. He had to laugh to himself, because it was like watching her mother when they met some twenty-seven years ago, right here in the Shamrock.

The apple hadn't fallen too far from the tree as the saying goes. His baby girl had lightning bolts shooting out of those green eyes, and wild strands of unruly red hair popping up all over her head when she got mad, just like her mother. He had to laugh too, at the fact that no man, and only a couple women, ever got away with talking to Jimmy O'Toole like that. "It's genetic, dad," he grinned as he passed Jimmy and patted his shoulder on his way out the door to calm his only daughter. He found her pacing and fuming on the sidewalk outside.

"Don't start on me, dad," she snapped.

"I'm not..."

"I'm sick of that!"

"I know..."

"Their old-world prejudice...Like I won't do what's best for Michael!"

"You're in a tough situation, aren't you sweetheart?" coaxed Patrick.

"You have no idea. None of you do." she told him, softening a little.

"No, we don't. All I know is that there is no one in the world I would rather have watching out for Michael's best interests than you." Quickly she turned away from him, arms folded across her chest. Just like her mother he thought. He dared to smile since she couldn't see him. He walked up behind, wrapped his big arms around her, and whispered into her red mop, "I love you sweet-heart. So does your grandpa. He's had a few too many and is sitting in there right now regretting what he said. How about we go back inside and give everyone a chance to make up?"

"Alright," she said, wiping her eyes and patting her hair down before turning around.

As they approached the booth, Grandpa Jimmy jumped up and raised his hands in mock surrender. "I'm sorry little girl. I know you love the boy. I know you'll see that they take good care of him. Why you're so smart, with a college degree and all..."

"I'm sorry too, grandpa," Margaret Mary offered.

Patrick walked past them as they hugged, thinking that now he had seen everything. His father, the mighty Jimmy O'Toole, saying he was sorry. Only a red-headed granddaughter could make that happen.

As summer arrived, Margaret Mary began to hear about, and see, small incremental improvements in Michael. At first when she watched him through the glass he was sitting, slack-jawed and staring blankly from a wheel chair. Over time she noticed him sitting up straighter, moving his lips as if he was talking to himself, and rubbing his hands together as if drying them. Dr. Goldstein said these were all good signs, showing he was coming out of his personal darkness. She still was not allowed to enter the room where he sat though.

The doctor also brought him down carefully from his alcoholic state, with medication to ease the withdrawal process. Gradually the medication was removed, and since there were no side effects, he then prescribed three hot showers, and a full massage every day in an effort to build his sensory perception. Finally, he tried music therapy in the hope that certain songs or notes might trigger his brain to want to communicate. By mid-summer, Michael was walking on his own, staring blankly most of the time. He still had not spoken a word.

One Tuesday in late August, as Margaret Mary stared through the one-way glass, she almost jumped in the air when she noticed that Michael was clearly focusing on his surroundings. That horrible blank stare seemed to be gone. He was back! She wanted more than anything to rush in and hug him, but of course the door was locked, and Dr. Goldstein was not about to allow that just yet. She couldn't wait to get home and tell everyone the good news. There had been so little of it for so long.

Once a week visits were not going to be enough anymore, so the next day she watched with Dr. Goldstein, as Michael strolled around the big common area, seeming to want to interact with others, but hanging back. He still wasn't speaking as far as she could tell. She told the doctor she wanted to touch him and talk to him in the worst way. It had been almost six years now, but unfortunately he didn't think that was a good idea yet.

"Michael has come a long way," he explained to Margaret Mary later in his office. "But I don't want to jeopardize his progress by shocking him too early with visitors. I need to talk to him and establish a close relationship over time, to try to find the root cause of his breakdown. There has to be a whole lot more going on inside Michael than just a penchant for alcohol. Alcohol abuse wasn't the cause of his break. I believe it was a symptom of something else, and an effort to self-medicate."

"That is a huge disappointment, but it does make sense," agreed Margaret Mary.

"Remember what I told you that first night, let's remain optimistic, since he is alive and improving. His caregivers think he may be on the verge of speaking. I see more patients than I want to think about, that never make it back after they have had a similar breakdown. The last thing we should do now is rush him," said Dr. Goldstein.

"Alright," replied Margaret Mary, "you know best."

"I will keep you informed. Give me your number, and get a message recorder, and I will try to give you an update regularly between your visits as he and I get to know each other."

Over the next couple months, Dr. Goldstein prodded Michael gently, but regularly, to speak. Near the end of October, his diligence paid off. Michael finally spoke to him. Margaret Mary was almost delirious when she heard the news on her recorder. She couldn't wait to call everyone in the family and spread the great news. When that was accomplished, she left Dr. Goldstein a message, asking when she could talk to Michael. The return message was brief and disappointing. He didn't think it was time yet.

All of Margaret Mary's extended family thought they should be able to start seeing Michael, and they were not shy about telling her as much. Most felt that the love and support of family was what he needed most. Iggy went on a rant for ten minutes one night at her house. Caught between the doctor and her family was making her more and more anxious, and angry at both sides.

She finally got a chance to sit down with Dr. Goldstein in mid-November. She told him of the frustration and anger building in her family. "Did you tell him I'm here and that I love him like I asked? Did you tell him he's got a hundred family members praying for him daily? Can't I at least talk to him on the phone? What is he saying?"

"I tell him everything you tell me to say to him, but the truth is that he has told me he doesn't want to see anyone or talk to anyone yet. He said he isn't up to it and he will let you know when the time is right."

"You have got to be kidding. I don't believe it," she said incredulously. "After all this time! And all the worrying!" Margaret Mary felt deeply hurt at first, and then she could feel her anger building.

"He did ask me to give you this," said Dr. Goldstein as he handed her an envelope across his desk.

She opened the envelope quickly and pulled out a single sheet of paper with Michael's unmistakable cursive handwriting on one side. It said:

Maggie,

Please don't be angry with me. I love you and I miss you. I'm not myself yet, and I don't want to jeopardize my progress. When it's time, you will be the first. The doc says you have been coming by every week for almost a year.

I am so very sorry for all this. Would you please tell Mom, Dad, grandparents, our brothers, Janet and the girls, how very sorry I am, and that I love them all.

Michael

As she dabbed her eyes, Margaret Mary sat back in her chair, across from Dr. Goldstein. She looked defeated, and merely shrugged. "Okay then," was all she could muster.

"Be patient. It's going to be alright, Ms. O'Toole," the doctor assured her.

"Just call me Maggie, doc. You and Michael are the only ones with permission to call me that. As much time as we spend together, I think it's time to dispense with the formalities," she offered, without sitting up.

"Alright. Well why don't you call me Morris then."

"Fair enough," she countered.

They both stood up and shook hands like two conspirators who just struck a deal.

There was no way Margaret Mary was going to tell everyone that Michael didn't want to see them. She was just going to lie and say it was the good doctor's orders. They were all elated that Michael had finally spoken, so she would just let them live off that good news for the time being. When she got home, she opened her Bible to the story of the 'Prodigal Son'. She prayed to Jesus every day that he would make sure their story would have just as happy an ending.

By the end of the year, Margaret Mary knew that Michael and Dr. Goldstein were having productive conversations daily, but she was not told their content. He had asked for his rosary though, which she took as a very positive sign. She continued to protect her family by hiding the fact that Michael did not want to see anyone yet. She just kept telling them the doctor said he was just too fragile, which was also not true. The burden of lying was starting to get to her, but Dr. Goldstein just kept telling her they were making great progress, and to be patient.

When she went to Confession, she didn't even try to enumerate all her lies because it would have been overwhelming. She just soothed her conscience by telling herself that the lies were for the greater good.

CHAPTER TWENTY-NINE

On the Saturday a week before Easter in 1977, Margaret Mary's phone rang at eight in the morning. It was Dr. Goldstein asking if she could come to the hospital right away because he wanted to show her something. The fact that he had sounded a bit excited, which was very unusual for the good doctor, had her heart pounding. All he would say is that he would have a pass at the front gate.

She had planned to plant a bunch of annual flowers in the front yard that morning. The neighborhood was still largely German, and they kept their homes so nice that she always wanted her house to appear as nice as the others. Grandpa O'Toole called them "dour-krauts" because of their relatively humorless demeanor. He thought that the play on the word "sauer-kraut" was uproariously funny every time he said it. She gave him a pass on his poor manners since it was a huge improvement over "fookin' Looterans" which is what he used to call them, just as loud as he pleased, when he could still defend himself.

Recently, Grandma O'Toole pulled her aside and in a conspiratorial tone asked about Michael and if she still felt it was wise to have a Jew doctor taking care of him. "Margaret Mary, you know they don't believe in Jesus, so they are not going to heaven. They don't even have souls for god's sake!" she croaked hoarsely.

"Are you sure about that grandma?" she asked with mock respect.

"Absolutely, child. Michael needs an Irish Catholic doctor. They are the only ones with enough smarts and the proper training to care for us. Even Jesus left his Jew family so that he could become a

Catholic. Only then was he able to heal the sick!"

Margaret Mary took it in stride this time around since she was getting thicker skin. The family had all gotten a good laugh the last time Grandpa O'Toole was in the hospital. Grandma O'Toole had run off a series of doctors for any number of infractions, like having a name that ended in an 'i' or having brown skin.

Then there was the time she went to the dentist near their home for the sole reason that his last name was Mahoney. Halfway through the cleaning, he let it slip that he was from Northern Ireland and was actually an Episcopalian. She left immediately with only her top teeth cleaned and vowed never to pay for the cleaning. When one of the grandkids heard her tell the story, he said, "What's the big deal grandma? We are all Christians."

Quickly she grabbed his ear and told him in no uncertain terms, "We are NOT Christians young man. WE are CATHOLICS, and don't you ever forget it." Margaret Mary loved her grandparents, but their worldview could be a bit narrow at times.

Many members of the extended family wanted to know if Michael was going to Mass, since it was a mortal sin to miss if you were well enough to go. They also asked if they had a priest on staff to hear his confession regularly, so that his sins were forgiven, in case he died while he was there. That way he could get into heaven more quickly.

Margaret Mary had decided that she would expand her web of deceit and tell them all that there was a priest on staff to hear confessions, say Mass and give Michael Holy Communion. She rationalized her lies by telling herself that she was bringing peace of mind to their worrisome nature. As she paced back and forth in a public waiting area at the hospital, a smile crept across her face as she remembered a Reader's Digest article she read recently on Freud and analysis. Freud told a colleague at one point, not to try analysis on the Irish. He said they were 'impervious' to its benefits, meaning they were unaffected by the process. She would have to ask Dr. Golden about that sometime.

After a half hour, an older, short, black orderly walked in and called out, “Margaret Mary O’Toole?” She followed him down the shiny hallway like she had done so many times before. They stopped at the elevators, then took one up to the third floor, to Michael’s patient ward. He motioned her into the room where she had watched Michael through the one-way glass without his knowledge. She had started to hate coming here, especially the mournful cries of the afflicted. They gave her chills. She hated that Michael was still here. How could he get better here? Where was the Michael she grew up with? What were his demons?

Praying quietly in one of the big overstuffed chairs always helped, while she waited for Dr. Goldstein. The prayers made her feel stronger and more resilient. She hoped Michael still prayed his rosary. She spent many of her lunch periods in church on her knees praying for him. Her father, Patrick, had taken to inviting their pastor over for supper, during which he was always asked for a special prayer for Michael. It showed how much respect he had for the priests’ special connection to God.

She remembered when they were younger, that her dad would always go to the rectory, right before they left for a long weekend, to get a special dispensation to eat meat on the road if they were unable to find fish on Friday. Eating meat on Friday was a sin. The pastor always made him promise to make every effort to find fish, before he would grant the dispensation. It always made quite an impression on them that their father, who was an imposing man, a construction foreman who ordered a dozen rough men around every day, humbled himself to a priest in these instances, and asked his permission.

“Good morning, Maggie,” said a familiar voice, pulling her out of her prayerful, meditative state of mind.

“Good morning, Morris,” she replied, getting out of the chair. She was always surprised by the fact that they were about the same height when they spoke to each other. "You snuck up on me," she added.

"Soft soled shoes today. Supposed to be a day off, but I came in to do paperwork. No phones ringing and so forth."

"I thought Jews went to church on Saturday," she asked, raising her eyebrows in mock disapproval.

"Well, first of all, it's called temple or synagogue, not church," he smiled. "Second, I go to temple on Friday night. Also, I was raised in an Orthodox home but I'm a Reform Jew now, and even if I did miss, we play a little loose with some of the traditional rules."

"I stand corrected," she smiled.

"I hope I didn't alarm you this morning," he said.

"Well, it was a bit unsettling to get a call to come down on a Saturday, but you said it wasn't an emergency. I was praying just now to try and relax," she answered, with the butterflies starting to return.

"You being a devout Catholic is going to be an immense help to me," he told her, in a more serious tone, while gesturing for her to sit. "I asked Michael some time ago to try to journal his feelings and life experiences, in the hope that we might get to the root of his problem. I must admit, there is a certain number of references, concerning Catholicism, that I really don't understand. Being Jewish, it's hard for me to have the kind of deep understanding I believe I'm going to need to help Michael fully. I guess I'm asking for your help to gain insights and interpret some of religious symbols and references in his journal."

"What do you mean by interpret?" she countered quizzically. "You act like it's in code, or something."

"No, not at all. He just gave me this notebook to read yesterday morning and walked out. I was so happy to get such a lengthy, detailed communication from him, that I read the whole thing last night in one sitting. This is a huge breakthrough, but before I discuss it with him I want to be clear, not just about the facts, but the subtle nuances. I want to know not just what he said, but what he didn't say. Also, as a sibling so close in age, you can act as a kind of arbiter of the accuracy of his memory. We can't forget that his brain did a major shut-down here for an extended period of time."

"Does Michael know you are showing this to me?" she asked.

"Yes. I went to him this morning. We are both early risers, so I started to ask him some questions that I had. He just said to 'ask Maggie to read it and answer your questions'. He also said to tell you not to tell anyone about what you read."

"Morris, I don't like the sound of this. Just how serious is it?" she asked quietly.

"I'm not going to lie to you Maggie, some of it is hard to read."

"Now you are really scaring me," she said, as another thousand butterflies took flight in her stomach.

"There is no reason to be frightened. Michael is safe. Truthfully, I think that writing his story down and handing it over to us has taken a heavy load off his shoulders. He is usually very abrupt with his answers and gives me the impression he wants to run and hide, but today he actually seemed more relaxed and cordial than I've ever seen him."

"That's really nice to hear, Morris," she smiled.

"Maggie, here are the two legal pads he wrote on," he said as he fumbled in his briefcase.

"Holy cow, how many pages are there?" she asked.

"Fifty or so, I think," he answered. "And one more thing. I want you to promise me you won't read this until you are at home, okay?"

"Sure, I guess so." He had read her mind. She couldn't wait. Finally, some answers.

"Here is my card with my home phone if you have any questions. I would like you to call right away when you are done though. I want to get your reaction before you have a chance to think too much, if that's okay?" he asked.

"Sure, I guess," she murmured.

As Margaret Mary made her way to her VW across the parking lot, the legal pads under her arm seemed to weigh a hundred pounds. As she steered her way home, the dread coming over her was replacing any thought of flower planting today.

She parked in front of her bungalow and walked slowly up the steps, so preoccupied that she didn't even hear the twelve-year-old girl next door say 'hello'. The normally cheerful Ms. O'Toole just unlocked her front door and disappeared.

Inside, Margaret Mary kicked off her shoes, closed the blinds and then uncharacteristically, so early in the day, poured a tall water glass full of wine. As she curled her legs under herself on the couch, and sat the wine glass down, she glanced at Michael's handwriting on the top page. It made her smile until she read what he had printed in bold letters across the top of the first page, 'MAGGIE, PLEASE DON'T TELL ANYONE'.

CHAPTER THIRTY

MICHAEL'S STORY:

When I was twelve years old, at the start of seventh grade, I was chosen to be the lead altar boy by a new priest at Sts. John and James named Father James O'Malley. He told me I could call him Fr Jim, and he gave me little gifts for all the extra work I did. Sometimes, it was a special holy card that brought the holder extra indulgences, and other times it might be a candy bar. I began to really like Fr. Jim. He was young, friendly and kind, unlike our gruff old pastor, Fr. Donovan, who always made me feel nervous about making a mistake. When I was a new altar boy, in fifth grade, I missed catching a host with the gold plate. It had gotten stuck on an old man's lips, and I pulled the plate away too soon, and the host fell to the ground when he tried to maneuver it into his mouth with his tongue. I heard the parishioners gasp as Fr. Donovan crossed himself and bent over to pick up the host. He then slowly walked over to the altar and set the host down. He glared at me all the way back to the Communion rail, so I knew I was in big trouble. I was shaking after Mass in the sacristy as Fr. Donovan told me how my mistake had allowed the Body of Christ to be dropped on a dirty floor. No matter how many times I said I was sorry, he said that I probably shouldn't be an altar boy. He finally bent down towards me and started poking my chest with his finger and telling me a hundred

Our Fathers and a Hundred Hail Mary's were in order to remain an altar boy.

As Margaret Mary poured her second glass of wine, she was remembering back that if Michael was twelve, it was 1962. She could also see the faces of crabby old Fr. Donovan and the young, personable Fr. O'Malley. She also remembered asking her parents if she could serve Mass, and them laughing at the prospect of a girl being an altar boy. After reading about Fr. Donovan, she was glad she couldn't be a server.

Anyway, you can see why I was so happy to get a new priest. Also, dad was gone during the week for the better part of a year working at a power plant out of town. When he was home on the weekends, he was busy catching up around the house, so it was nice to have a grown man to talk with about the Cardinals and other sports stuff. Sometimes during the week after six-thirty Mass, he would invite me to the rectory for breakfast. Mom said it was okay, and it was great not having to walk all the way home when I was so hungry. Remember we couldn't eat before receiving Communion. The sisters told us that our throats and stomachs had to be completely clean to receive Jesus' body. After we had breakfast, Fr Jim would let me hang around until school started at eight-thirty. It was great not having to run all the way home and back on these mornings. I had a great time eating pancakes and talking to Fr. Jim about sports, and after a while I began to think of him as a friend. I even started telling him my confession face-to-face instead of waiting in line on Saturday afternoon in church. Before I knew him, I was afraid the priests would know who I was in the dark confessional by my voice. I was so comfortable with Fr. Jim that I would ask him to hear my confession after breakfast, and we would go to his room in the rectory. He always said I could come talk to him anytime. One day in February in seventh grade, school was called off because of a big snow, but

I made it to church anyway to serve six-thirty Mass. Fr. Jim told me how proud of me he was for making the extra effort. I was busting with pride. I just knew Jesus had heard one of his consecrated, holy priests compliment me. After Mass, we trudged over to the rectory for breakfast, and then up to his room on the second floor. I thought maybe I was going to get a candy bar. When we were in his office, he sat behind his desk and I sat in a guest chair on the other side of the desk. I was already feeling as high as a kite when Fr. Jim put his elbows on his desk and leaned towards me and smiled. He told me quietly, 'Michael, I think you have what it takes to be a priest'. I couldn't believe my ears! The first thing I thought was wait until mom, dad, and all the grandparents hear what Fr. Jim said! I knew they were going to be so proud of me! Then his face got a serious look on it, and in a softer voice, he asked me to come around the desk to him. He asked me to come closer, and then he put his hands on my shoulders. I remember we were eye-to-eye with him seated and me standing. Quietly he told me there was one thing that bothered him. He said he wondered if I was being completely truthful with him in confession. He said that to become a priest, you had to confess ALL your sins. I went from being as proud as I have ever been, to feeling confused and light-headed. I would never lie to a priest. The sisters told us it would be like lying to Jesus himself. I started to sweat, while desperately trying to remember what I had forgotten. I told Fr. Jim that whatever it was, I didn't leave it out on purpose, and that I wanted my soul to be free from sin. He said that he had been praying that I would be truthful because it was so important for priests to never lie. I told him I would never lie to him. He was looking me right in the eyes, when he took one hand and poked me with his finger right below my belt buckle. Then he whispered, 'does your penis get hard at night when you crawl into bed?'

Margaret Mary dropped the tablet as she felt the wave of nausea and flash of heat encompass her. Beads of sweat formed on her upper lip and forehead, and she felt like she was going to faint. Slowly she lay down on the couch and stared at the ceiling, waiting for her body to return to normal. For ten minutes, she laid on her back, until the sweating and hyper-ventilating finally slowed down. More than anything, she hoped that she was wrong about what was coming in Michael's story. Finally, with shaking hands, she picked the tablet off the floor and continued reading.

> *I was so embarrassed that I couldn't speak and just stared at the floor. I couldn't figure out how he knew about that. I knew that Jesus gave priests special powers that normal men did not have. If they could change the bread and wine into the body and blood of Jesus, maybe they could see into your soul. I was starting to feel kind of dizzy, but finally I nodded 'yes'. Then he asked me if I touched it, and I nodded 'yes' again. That's when he pulled my chin up and told me that touching it was a grave sin called masturbation. He asked if I had heard of this sin and I said 'no'. He said that the sisters didn't talk about this sin because women didn't know about it. Fr. Jim told me that only ordained priests knew how to control the urge to touch it. He said only special boys who are called by God, are taught how to avoid the grave sin of masturbation. He said he would teach me if I promised to never tell another soul, and I said 'yes'. He whispered that that there is a liquid stored in the testicles that the devil puts there to make your penis hard. He said the devil is tempting us to touch it, but you must avoid the sin of masturbation to remain holy. Then he said he could help and began to slowly unbuckle my belt and pull my zipper down before sliding my pants and underwear to the floor.*

When she laid the tablet down, Margaret Mary heard herself making that awful high-pitched sound she made that first night at the hospital, like a wounded animal. It was coming from deep within her, from a dark place of fear and pain. She fell to her knees on the floor and bent forward until her forehead was touching the carpet. In her mind, all she could hear was, 'this cannot be.... this cannot be.... this cannot be....' when the voice of the twelve-year-old girl next door jolted her back to reality.

"Are you okay, Ms. O'Toole? Do you want me to get my mom?" she was asking with her face pressed to the screen door.

"I'm fine, Amy. I just stubbed my toe. Go on home now. I'm fine."

"Are you sure?"

"Yes honey, everything's okay."

After the little girl left, Margaret Mary felt her breakfast coming up, and ran to the bathroom just in time. When she returned, she had a couple cold wash cloths for her head and wrists. One by one she closed the windows and doors and pulled the shades. Only then did she reluctantly pick up the tablet.

Fr. Jim said I was lucky there was no pubic hair yet because it would be much harder not to masturbate when it came in. He told me to close my eyes, then he put one hand on my shoulder and with the other, started to touch my penis and testicles very gently. It got hard right away and within five or ten seconds, I felt something shooting out, and thought I was peeing, but I couldn't stop it. It was a feeling I never had before. Then my knees buckled and I started to fall. Fr. Jim caught me, held me in his arms, and stroked the back of my head. He kept whispering that everything was going to be okay, and that he would take care of me. After a minute, he leaned me away from him, pulled my underwear and pants up, zipped them and buckled the belt. He asked if it felt good to get the devil's liquid out of my body, and I nodded 'yes'. He said it feels wonderful to be pure again, doesn't it? And I nodded 'yes'. Fr. Jim hugged me and said 'God bless you Michael. Remember, masturbation is a grave sin, and from now on when the urge to touch yourself becomes too strong, tell me during your confession. We will get rid of the devil's liquid, and keep you pure, until you can resist the temptation on your own'.

With tears streaming, Margaret Mary needed a break to think. She walked unsteadily to her bedroom and flopped across her bed face down. The thing that made this so hard to fathom was, how could a man of God could do such a thing to a child? For that matter, how could anyone do something so horrible to a child? The sisters said that a priest was Jesus' representative on earth. Talking to a priest was like talking to Jesus. Jesus had told Peter that 'whatever he bound on earth was bound in heaven, and whatever he loosed on earth was loosed in heaven'. He gave Peter that power, and Peter handed that power to others down through the ages by the laying of hands on those chosen to be priests.

She couldn't make sense of it. She loved Michael deeply, but had the alcohol and the breakdown damaged him in some way? Morris said that his mind was intact. Did he believe Michael was telling the truth? Why hadn't Michael said something before now? She wished she could talk to Michael face-to-face. She wanted to call Morris but he said to finish reading first. She lay still, in prayer for a half hour, before aimlessly walking from room to room, straightening up and moving things around. Finally, she felt strong enough to pick up the tablet again and began to read.

Afterwards, I walked home in the snow deep in thought. I wanted to tell someone what had happened so much but knew I couldn't. I felt so proud to be considered for the priesthood, and yet, felt like I had done something wrong. But Fr. Jim was my friend. He was a priest. He would never commit a sin with me, so it had to be okay. Mom and dad had never said a word about sex. What little I knew was from overhearing older boys talking and laughing at the park. During the winter and spring, I went to Fr. Jim's office in the rectory a few times a week. Since he first touched me, all I could think about was when I would see him the next time. It seemed like a switch was turned on, and I couldn't turn it off. I felt like I was addicted to something, but I didn't know what it was. It was a horrible sin to touch yourself, and I only had one way to get relief. I asked Fr. Jim if it was normal to be getting these urges so often, and he told me the devil works extra hard to get the soul of a future priest.

Margaret Mary threw the tablet across the room. Her mind was bouncing in a hundred different directions. This was so sick. There were too many details for the story to be made up. What would be the point? Dear God Michael, what you must have gone through! I wish you could have told someone. How did you hold it together for so long? How could the same hand that touched the Body of Christ, touch a child like this? She remembered Sister Angela telling them the story of Jesus saying, 'let the little children come to me'. Dropping to her knees, she looked to the heavens and called out, "How could you let this happen, Lord! I don't understand!" Her sobbing was relentless for ten straight minutes. Finally, after washing her face, she returned to the couch, tablet in hand.

I was thirteen that summer when Fr. Jim started coming over to the house once a week for dinner when dad was working out of town. Mom loved his company and was thrilled that he had taken such an interest in me. Dad said he was glad Fr. Jim was around to keep an eye on things. When he asked if it was alright if I went on a weekend trip with him, they were actually beaming with pride. Fr. Jim told them it would be like a retreat, at a friend's cabin in the woods, and that I could meditate and pray about God's calling to be a priest. We all knew there was no greater honor for an Irish Catholic family than to have a son become a priest. Unfortunately, there was no praying on the trip. This was the first time he had me start touching him. I was so shocked when he began to undress that I turned around. Fr. Jim laughed and said if I wanted to be a priest, I needed to learn how to help others stay pure and free from sin. I felt special and ashamed at the same time. I felt like running away and compelled to stay at the same time. I felt like I was watching a movie of someone else doing these things, but it was me. Starting that first night we both laid together under the covers without any clothes on. I can't even write down all of what happened. It's just too humiliating and embarrassing. Before we left, he must have sensed my nervousness, so he sat me down and told me we were doing God's will, and not to tell anyone because only those chosen for the priesthood knew about this. Then he made me swear before God to keep our secret.

Margaret Mary could hardly see the page anymore. She felt like someone was tearing her heart out of her chest. GOD'S WILL? She remembered her parent's pride at Fr. Jim's interest in Michael, and she remembered feeling jealous of his special treatment. If mom and dad ever found out that they had been sending him off with a monster, it would kill them. Would they ever be able to believe this? She knew her grandparents would never believe it. Michael had been the family hero, the perfect child, the pride of Sts. John and James and Ferguson. It was no wonder Michael broke down, she thought. He was trying to hide with everyone's eyes on him.

As she walked to the bathroom for more tissues, she felt her anger building. Her precious faith was being assaulted. Where was your protection of children Jesus? Where was Michael's guardian angel he was promised? Where was the Blessed Virgin when this young boy was being molested repeatedly by an animal posing as a man of God?

During eighth grade, Fr. Jim would come over regularly for dinner, help mom with the dishes, and then sit on the patio with dad and have a couple beers. After I went downstairs to get ready for bed, he would come down to purify me, as he called it. There were more trips, and even sleepovers at the rectory. He was constantly pressuring me to do things with him that I don't want to talk about and would like to forget about. He kept calling it God's will. I turned fourteen in the middle of the school year, and as I went through puberty, I got bigger and stronger. I was almost as tall as him, and my voice changed by the end of eighth grade. At this point, Fr. Jim seemed to have less and less interest in me. I was never sure how I felt. I would feel relieved that he wasn't around as much, and the next day I would miss him. I didn't tell anyone, but this was when I first started having this odd sensation that I was two people in one body. I got lots of praise but felt depressed. I would look at girls with a normal physical attraction but felt like I was damaged in some way and they would know. The worst fear I had was that someone would find out what I had been doing, and think I was queer. I became obsessed to the point that I started waking up at night, in the middle of a nightmare, where everyone at school and church found out. Everyone was calling me fag and homo, and then dad kicked me out of the house. I would be soaking wet from sweat when I woke up.

Margaret Mary felt like she was on an emotional roller coaster, wanting to hug Michael and tell him she loved him one minute, and feeling genuine rage coupled with thoughts of revenge the next. How did he endure this? How can I help? Can anyone ever get over this? Wouldn't it be nice to run into Fr. Jim at the market some day?

As I went through high school, I found myself obsessing about sin. My sins were piling up, and I did not see any way out. I felt the weight of hundreds of sins on my shoulders. Even worse, I could not bring myself to go to Confession. The family still talked about me becoming a priest, but I knew that was impossible now. Staring at girls' bodies and wondering what sex would be like with them meant I wasn't a homo, but every time I did that, I committed another sin of lust. I was consumed with impure thoughts and seemed to be unable to make them stop running through my head. At times, I thought I was going to go crazy. There was no way I could get into heaven now. I was doomed to an eternity in Hell.

Margaret Mary was getting more and more angry. She wanted to scream, 'You are not crazy Michael! You are not going to hell! Everyone loves you and wants you to come home, no questions asked! God, how she wished she could tell him hold him and tell him that right now! Margaret Mary was beginning to see what happened. She was also seeing what a horrible weight the Church could put on a child. The tears had finally stopped, and now her rational, can-do mind was starting to take over. What would Michael need? They just wouldn't tell anyone about this, so that he would be comfortable enough to come home. No one needed to know anyway.

I must say that sports, and in particular football, really helped me cope. I felt in control on the football field. I enjoyed running full speed into defenders. It felt good to be physically exhausted, because it helped me sleep through the night. When not playing a sport in high school, I would run miles and miles to wear myself out. It worked very well for a long time. Being a part of the different teams, did a lot to keep my mind occupied. When I got to senior year, I was hardly ever thinking of Fr. Jim anymore. I was so busy with sports and school and applying to college, that my internal life seemed to be doing better than it had in a long time. Everyone wanted to celebrate as we neared graduation. That was when I first tried alcohol. I liked it way too much for some reason. Then I decided to rest, and not play basketball and baseball. Unfortunately, that just gave me more time to drink. By the summer of 1968 the drinking actually started uncovering a dark hole in the past that I had tried to bury. I would sit alone and drink and ruminate, but never about happy stuff. Passing out became the goal. Now, there were officially two Michael's: the successful public Michael that everyone else saw; and the sinful Michael that lived in my head, where I could see all the things I had done with Fr. Jim again and again.

Margaret Mary felt like she had just finished a marathon. She was exhausted from all the pain and emotion. It was dark outside, and when she finally looked it was eight-o'clock Saturday night. She was sitting on the floor, head down, surrounded by a dozen wadded Kleenex tissues. She had just read about the systematic destruction of her big brother's psyche. A monster had dismantled her beloved brother and threw him in the gutter. Michael had taken such loving care of her all those years growing up, and now it was going to be her turn to take care of him.

An Irish Catholic priest had done this to him. She didn't know if she could ever say that out loud. Her faith and beliefs were teetering on the edge of a cliff. Her whole life to this point had revolved around the Church. She taught at Catholic school, coached CYC girls teams, volunteered for Catholic Charities, and even worked bingo on Friday nights. The worst part was that she felt the reverence and trust for Catholic priests, was gone forever.

She had trusted them without question, sought their counsel on life's most difficult and personal issues. She had hung on every word that came out of their mouths during the Sunday homilies. Suddenly, it all seemed so silly, childish and ridiculous. Like Michael, she had always done what she was told without questioning. They called this having a strong faith in the Church. To become a nun, you must take vows of poverty, chastity and obedience. She could only guarantee them two of the three now.

CHAPTER THIRTY-ONE

After finishing Michael's story, Margaret Mary called Dr. Goldstein. It was too late to get together, and they agreed they wanted to meet in person, so they made plans to meet Sunday morning. Margaret Mary did not want to talk in a restaurant or someplace where they could be overheard, so they decided on Forest Park. It was the first Sunday in April, and the weather was supposed to be nice, so they agreed to meet at noon at the statue of St. Louis in front of the Art Museum. Dr. Goldstein said he would bring coffee, and she was to bring a blanket so they could sit on Art Hill.

"Hello Maggie," Dr. Goldstein grinned, as he approached her on the blanket.

"Hello, Morris," she replied.

For a few moments, the two of them just sipped their coffee, and watched the golfers walking in front of them, with the sparkling reflection pool as a backdrop a couple of hundred yards away at the bottom of the hill. Margaret Mary had not been able to sleep, so she was wearing dark glasses to cover her red swollen eyes, and a ball cap over her unwashed hair. They both seemed to want the other to start the conversation.

"Well, today is the first time I ever missed Mass intentionally," she finally mumbled. "Another big sin for the O'Tooles."

"Seems to be a pre-occupation with sin in your family," the doctor added quietly.

"Trust me, it's not just our family, Morris. By the way I don't know of a single Irishman named Morris."

"And I know of no Jews named Patrick," he smiled back at her.

"Different tribes, to be sure," she added.

"That's kind of the reason I wanted to talk to you before I spoke to Michael."

"I need to hug my brother, Morris. I didn't sleep a wink last night," she offered, with a tear streaming slowly rolling down her cheek.

"That will be up to him now, but I will ask him tomorrow. Are you up to answering a few questions for me?" he asked gently, pulling a small notepad from his front shirt pocket.

"Sure. I've got a few of my own," she shot back.

"For starters, do you remember this priest, Father O'Malley?"

"Of course, he was at the house quite a bit back then, like Michael said."

"Did you think it was odd for him to be at the house so much, or showing so much interest in Michael?"

"Not at all. As a matter of fact, it was kind of a feather in our cap to have a priest as a family friend. Women would sort of brag to the neighbors that Father so and so was over last night," she explained. "It was a big deal for him to say the prayer before meals and bless the house and stuff like that. My parents were absolutely giddy about O'Malley acting as a mentor to Michael. They were proud to have a son considering the priesthood."

"I think I told you I grew up in an Orthodox home, so I am very familiar with religious rituals and rules. We have more than our share. Also, Catholics do not have a monopoly on shame and guilt. We sort of wrote the book on those two, so I am sensitive to some of Michael's issues here," Dr. Goldstein added in a thoughtful manner.

"Well I'm glad for that anyway. People make fun of us. Like when we cross ourselves before prayer. It gets old. It's just ignorance, really," Margaret Mary told him.

"Exactly, and that's why I need to clear up a few things for myself, so I don't inadvertently disparage Michael's beliefs out of ignorance."

"That's fine. Go ahead."

"I just feel that's there is more going on with Michael, than I am used to seeing. I've treated a lot of childhood sexual abuse victims as adult patients. They are traumatized to be sure, so most block out the memory as a survival technique, so they can function normally out in society. It takes a great deal of therapy, and building of trust, before they will remember, and admit to being abused.

"Men in particular keep it secret because of society's misguided notion that male victims grow up to be abusers. While this is true in a very small percentage of cases, the vast majority actually become hyper-vigilant in protecting their own children, and children in general. There are often telltale signs we look for when counseling a potential abuse victim, and then it becomes a matter of coaching an admission from them.

"But in your brother's case, he had a complete psychotic break. After getting the alcohol out of his system, during the first month or so, he tended to ramble incoherently to himself. There seemed to be some recurring words or themes that I could make out as I watched him day after day. He was going to hell; God would never forgive him; and a kind of endless chant, that one of the Catholic orderlies thought was the 'Hail Mary' and 'Our Father' prayers. I would sedate him sometimes just to break this endless chant, so he could rest.

"As you know it was months before he spoke, and then only in short phrases and answers. I tried and tried to get him to open up and speak of his family and childhood, but it was like hitting a wall. I wanted him to journal his thoughts, but it was always very ho-hum stuff. Then, kind of 'out of the blue', he hands me these two tablets, and walks away without explanation. This was a huge breakthrough, and I was really excited. Later in the day I sought him out because I couldn't wait to talk to him and ask questions, but he just bluntly told me to 'ask Maggie' and walked away. So here we are," concluded Dr. Goldstein with a deep breath.

"Yep. Here we are," Margaret Mary answered wistfully. "So, what would you like to know?"

"For starters, what is the significance of Holy Communion?"

"Holy Communion is one of the Church's seven sacraments. As a child, you make your First Confession, which is another sacrament, so that your soul is clean before your First Holy Communion. You also do not eat right before Mass so that your body is clean as well. Then, during the Mass, the priest blesses the bread and wine, by making the sign of the cross over them. This changes the bread and wine into the actual body and blood of Jesus Christ."

"You mean metaphorically, of course," interrupted Dr. Goldstein.

"No sir. Catholics believe in transubstantiation, which means the bread and wine are actually transformed."

"Seriously?"

"Absolutely. This is a central tenet of the Catholic Church. This is what makes the priest so special in our eyes."

"I'm sorry, Maggie. I'm not trying to be irreverent. It's just that it seems so ..."

"It's an actual re-creation of the Last Supper. The words are taken literally. If I'm not mistaken, Jews have a few laws that are taken literally from Scripture concerning dress, diet and work on the Sabbath, that may seem a bit odd to an outsider as well."

"You're right, I'm sorry. I just...well...Let's begin again," said Dr. Goldstein. "How does Confession work?"

"You are supposed to examine your conscience and make a list of all your sins. Sins are things you may have said, done or thought, that would do harm to yourself, to others or to God. On Saturday afternoon you go to church and tell your sins to the priest. Both of you are in darkened cubicles, side by side with a dark screen between, so that he can't see you. He will give you a penance, which is almost always the reciting of an assigned number of 'Our Fathers' and 'Hail Marys'.

"If you are truly penitent, sorry for your sins, they are forgiven. In essence, the priest has the power to take away your sins. There are mortal sins, which are the worst, and venial sins. You can't go to Communion if you have a mortal sin on your soul. You really shouldn't receive Communion even if you only have venial sins, if it has been over a year since you last Confession."

"How does the priest know if you are sincere?" asked Dr. Morris.

"He doesn't, but God does. The priest is God's direct representative on earth, so lying to him is like lying to God. That's serious business," answered Margaret Mary.

"So, do you think Michael was saying a penance over and over in his delirium?"

"That's what it sounds like to me."

"So, your priests, are very powerful figures. If they can change the nature of bread and wine and forgive sins in God's place, they have god-like power. You need them to get in to heaven. Does that sound right?"

"That's right. The priests' power comes from the scriptural passage where Jesus tells Peter 'You are the rock upon which I will build my church. Whatever you bind on earth is bound in heaven, and whatever you loose on earth is loosed in heaven'. That made Peter the first ordained priest, and he gave his power to the other disciples by laying his hands on them, and repeating Jesus' words. That chain of power has been continuous to the priests of today."

Dr. Goldstein noticed that, little by little, as she answered his questions, she was going from her usual animated voice pattern, to more of a monotone sound. He saw she was staring straight ahead, instead of at him, and he could see tears trickling down her cheek from under the sunglasses again. It seemed like her answers were causing sort of a melancholy change in her demeanor. "I see," was all he said, giving her a chance to regroup.

Softly, she began, "Our parents, grandparents and the nuns all told us that priests were higher than mere humans. They said priests were our link to God. They said they gave us our path to heaven." Then becoming a little more animated, "They said we could go to a priest with any problem and he would help us, and he could be trusted to keep our secrets. They said we should always obey the priests and do whatever they said." Then, turning to face him, and getting louder, "Do you think my mother and father would let one of their beloved children spend that much time with a mere MORTAL? Or go on weekend trips and sleepovers with ANY other adult? There is NO FUCKING WAY MORRIS!" she shouted at him, causing a few passers-by to look over at them.

"No, I do not," he answered gently.

Lowering her voice and speaking through clenched teeth, she added, "They trusted this man with their son because he was supposed to be Jesus' representative. If my father, my uncles, my brothers, my cousins or God help us all, my grandfathers, knew what this monster was doing to Michael..." Then, with her nose and eyes running freely, and her voice quivering, she literally spat out, "They would have cut his balls off and let him bleed to death."

A wide-eyed Dr. Goldstein leaned back to regain his composure. He had just witnessed a startling metamorphosis of this pretty young woman. He watched a devout and devoted Catholic grade school teacher change before his eyes, into the visage of someone so consumed by rage, that she could contemplate murder. He was also startled by the fact that he had never seen this type of language and level of anger from a female. Her face was nearly purple, and it seemed a thousand red hairs were poking from under her cap like they had been charged with electricity.

This was indeed a different "tribe" as she had said earlier. Margaret Mary was staring out at the reflection pool again, so he decided to sit quietly until she was ready to speak.

After a few minutes, she blurted, "Anything else you want to know Morris?"

"As a matter of fact, ..."

"Make it quick!"

"I need to know how to help Michael forgive himself. Normally I ask a member of the clergy from the patient's denomination for help, but clearly that is out of the question here. It is essential to recovery, and frankly I'm not sure what to do," Dr. Goldstein stated plainly.

Margaret Mary let her head sink slowly between her knees which she had drawn to her chest with her arms. "Dear God, neither do I," she whispered.

Part IX

The Road Back

CHAPTER THIRTY-TWO

Dr. Goldstein called Margaret Mary on the first Friday of June 1977, to say Michael was ready to see her in person. It was seven and one-half years after Michael first disappeared, seventeen months after he was found comatose in Carondelet Park and two months after she read his story.

Visiting day was normally on Sunday in the communal area of the hospital but they agreed it might be better for this first visit to be private. She was finally going to see Michael on her regular Tuesday night visit in Dr Goldstein's office. When the day arrived, she was so nervous she could barely concentrate to teach, and gave her class a lot of study time. In the days leading up to the visit, she prayed for serenity, strength and patience. The waiting was unbearable.

On Tuesday evening, with her heart racing, she walked from the parking lot to the same side door of the hospital she went through that first night. Once again, an orderly escorted her down the shiny hallways toward Dr. Goldstein's office. He was trying to make small talk, but she didn't hear a word. When they arrived, she took a deep breath, grabbed the door knob and pushed the door open.

Dr. Goldstein was behind his desk grinning, and Michael was in the same chair she always sat in for their visits. As he stood with a sheepish grin, Margaret Mary took two steps, and almost dove into his chest. With her voice breaking she whispered hoarsely, "Oh Michael...finally...thank God...oh my...oh my...it's you...."

Still hugging her tightly, he playfully replied, "Well, who were you expecting Maggie?"

After breathing deeply a few times, she leaned back, took his face in her hands, pulled him down to her and kissed his forehead.

Still holding on she looked right in his eyes and whispered, "I've missed you so much."

"I've missed you too. I'm so sorry about all this Maggie."

Letting go of his face, she quickly hugged him again with all her might. Then, trying to speak through heaving gulps of air, she told him, "There is no need for that. Please don't say that. You're alive. You're here in my arms. That's all I care about. That's all anybody is going to care about."

After a minute or two, they separated and looked each other up and down. Without a word they just kept grinning and wiping away tears. Dr. Goldstein handed them his ever-ready box of tissues across the desk and sat back down.

"How are you feeling. You're so thin. Are they feeding you enough?" she asked, slipping in to her take charge mode.

"I'm feeling good Maggie. Really. Please don't worry," he told her quietly, slipping into his protective big brother role. "You look beautiful."

God, how she had missed that deep comforting voice. He had always made her feel so safe. He could always pick her right up with those compliments. At this moment she felt like she was whole again. "Oh, Michael..." she whispered, her quivering lip, giving in to a real shoulder shaking cry.

"Please don't cry," he told her while putting his arms around her again.

Slowly, they separated, as Margaret Mary regained her composure. Again, they looked at each other, a bit unsure where to begin. "First thing everyone asks when they see me is 'How is Michael? Everyone misses you terribly, especially mom and dad."

"I've missed them too. Here, let's sit down," as he motioned to the second chair. "The doc here, says you have been coming at least once a week all this time..."

"You would do the same for me, you know it," Margaret Mary broke in, before another apology. "Everyone sends their love."

"How are the boys and Iggy," he asked.

"Kevin just got done with college. Sean, Billy and Robert have all found good jobs since graduating from college. Iggy is Iggy," she grinned, "He's a journeyman pipe fitter now. He seems happy. None of them is married yet. I think Iggy misses you the most. He told me he feels like he's missing an arm, you too were so close. He used to drive around aimlessly for hours hoping to spot you."

"Oh man, that makes me feel terrible," he said, shaking his head.

"Michael, please don't. That's the past. You think Iggy cares about that! You know as well as I do, that he would step in front of a train for you. You should have seen him when I said we were going to talk today! Smiling that goofy grin of his."

The thought of Iggy's smile, made Michael smile, then he added, "Now the big question. Janet, Nora and Maura. God, I hope they're alright. They all deserved much better than I gave them. I can't believe..." he trailed off, for the first time lowering his eyes and looking dejected.

"The girls are doing great in school. They're so pretty. Getting taller by the day. They seem very happy Michael," she added, trying to pick up his mood change.

"And Janet?" he asked, finally raising his eyes to look at her again.

"Well, I wish it was different, Michael, but Dr. Goldstein said it was alright to...well...so what happened..."

"Maggie, just say it. No more secrets. Secrets almost killed me."

"Okay. Janet got an annulment," she said, barely louder than a whisper, searching his face. "She remarried a couple years ago... He seems like a great guy...Michael I am so sorry to have to tell you this..."

Looking directly at her now, he broke in, "No need for you to be sorry. I left without a word. What else could I expect? Is he good to the girls?"

She nodded 'yes' and then grinned, "With dad, your brothers and grandpa breathing down his neck, what do you think? And mom has the Fitzgerald cronies driving patrol cars by their house about every ten minutes, you know that."

They both laughed at the thought of the clan watching the

poor guy so close. "Some things will never change, I guess. It feels so good to laugh with you again, Maggie." Then in a more serious tone, "It's alright. One thing I've learned from Dr. Goldstein," he said, gesturing to the observant doctor, "is not to shut out the past. No matter how painful it is, you have to face it and move on."

"Sounds like a great plan," Margaret Mary agreed.

"Look, Maggie, I don't want the whole world to know what happened, but I do want mom and dad to read it in my handwriting. They're going to have trouble believing this about a priest, so it's best if they see it came right from me. Let mom and dad decide whether to tell Grandma and Grandpa O'Toole and Grandma Finnegan. They know them best. You know how they are. They're old, and mom and dad may decide it's better not to upset them. Ask mom and dad if they want to tell the boys, or have you do it, or...they need to know what happened to me. No more secrets," Michael added in a firm tone.

"What about Iggy?" she asked, both understanding that Iggy was a special case. She wondered to herself if Michael would want to tell him personally.

"Let Iggy read it after mom and dad. I'm sorry, but I just can't talk about it yet, you know, like out loud."

"I understand. They will too. I'm just so very, very happy that you had the courage to get it out. It's the only way we could ever get you back," she told him, tearing up once again.

Dr Goldstein interrupted, "Michael and I discussed that if they are agreeable, we would like to invite your mom and dad to come in for a meeting, to ask either of us any questions they may have. I know they will need a chance to digest all of this for a while, but make sure they know they are welcome to visit."

"Do you want them to come one at a time or together," she asked.

"Either way," replied the doctor.

"I think they should be invited together. My dad will need the extra push from mom," added Margaret Mary, remembering how much influence she could exert over her father when she wanted.

Then turning to Michael, "They can't wait to see you."

"I want to see them too, but I'm a nervous wreck about what everyone will think of me. The doc says I have no control over what people think, and that all I can do is tell the truth, and let the chips fall where they may," Michael said calmly. "Still it's going to be really hard facing them, especially dad."

Dr. Goldstein chimed in, "We will face them together, Michael. They will surely see that this was not your fault. You were a child obeying someone who you were afraid to say no to. He abused his power over you, and your parents will see that immediately."

"Absolutely. They love you more than life, Michael, you know that," Margaret Mary added.

"I kept telling Dr. Goldstein that I feel guilty about the fact that I kept going back to O'Malley. One day he asked me if this had happened to one of my younger brothers, or cousins, would I blame the child? That's really when the light bulb went off. I turned a corner in forgiving myself that day," Michael said with confidence in his voice.

"No one is going to blame you, Michael, trust me," she replied.

"Thanks Maggie," Michael replied after letting out a huge breath.

"Morris, is there a timetable on when he can come home?" Margaret Mary asked.

"Not yet," he answered.

"I want to see how these visits go, first," added Michael.

"Sounds like a great plan," grinned his little sister before standing up to give him one more long hug, this time without tears.

CHAPTER THIRTY-THREE

On the way home from the hospital, Margaret Mary decided to go directly to her parent's home on Highmont. She knew it would be a sleepless night if she just went home. She would worry all night about giving them Michael's story. It was about seven o'clock when she pulled up and stared at the little house while her blood pressure slowed.

She knew this was going to change their whole family forever. What happened to Michael was going to strike at the very core of their beliefs, just as it had done to her. She dreaded going in, but it had to be done. They needed to know the cause of Michael's breakdown. That was the question her parents asked over and over. They were waiting for her to call, so they were surprised when she came in the front door.

They were ecstatic that she had come by for a face-to-face talk. Patrick still had on his work boots, jeans and a dirty t-shirt because he didn't want to miss her call if he was in the shower. Kathleen was at the kitchen table folding laundry like she had almost every night as long as Margaret Mary could remember. The wonderful smell of fried chicken, Patrick's favorite, was still wafting through the house.

When the three of them were finally seated at the kitchen table, she told her parents how good Michael looked and sounded. They looked like children on Christmas morning when she told them they could visit Michael whenever they wished. Then, she inhaled a deep breath, and took the two tablets out of her bag.

"What have you got there, sweetheart?" Patrick asked.

"Maybe it's a list of clothes and toiletries Michael's going to need when he comes home," Kathleen wondered aloud.

"No, I'm afraid it's way more serious than that. Michael wrote down everything that happened to him that caused his breakdown, and landed him in the hospital," Margaret Mary told them.

"Well we knew something went terribly wrong. That's why we kept asking if you knew anything," Kathleen told her.

"Let me see those," Patrick said, reaching across the table.

"In a minute. I just want you both to know how hard it is for Michael to share this with anyone. He kept this secret bottled up so long it almost killed him. He just asked that you both read it all, and not just parts of it," she told them. "It's not going to be easy."

"Well why don't you just tell us, then, and get to the point," Patrick shot back.

"Really, what's with all the suspense. You're scaring me," Kathleen said quietly.

"I'm sorry, really, but you just have to read what Michael wrote," she told them gently. Then the one thing she did not want to happen, started. Her lips began to quiver, and then she started sobbing.

"Jesus, what is it that's so upsetting?" Patrick said as he handed her a napkin.

"Now I'm worried," whispered Kathleen. This was proof positive that the content of those tablets was going to be very hard to deal with.

"You look so tired, sweetheart. You've been carrying the load for all of us for too long. Why don't you go home and get a good night's sleep," Patrick told her.

"That sounds good, dad. Maybe I will just do that and give you two some space," she agreed. Call me if you want to talk. Otherwise I will come by tomorrow after school around four o'clock to get the tablets. Michael wants Iggy to read them too. One more thing. Michael said it's up to you if you want to tell the boys or the grandparents about everything, but he doesn't want anyone else to know. Okay?" Margaret Mary said, scanning their anxious faces.

The next day, she stopped by the house as planned. She thought she could hear muffled construction type noise as she walked up to the porch. When she looked in the screen door, she saw her mother sitting at the kitchen table with her head down on her arms.

"Mom, are you okay?" she asked as her mother lifted her head to reveal two red swollen eyes from crying.

"What do you think?" she answered curtly.

"What's all the noise downstairs?" Margaret Mary asked.

"That's your father destroying the two bedrooms and the bathroom downstairs. He announced it all had to go. He's been down there all day," Kathleen said slowly.

"Why don't you go down there and stop him?"

"He needs this. He needs to let it out. It's better here at home."

"Well, if you won't go down and stop him then I will," Margaret Mary said as she strode towards the basement door.

Quickly, Kathleen jumped up and blocked her daughter's path to the door. "You're not going anywhere, so either sit down or take the tablets and go."

"Mom! What's going on?"

"For men like your father, Sadness turns into anger. Instead of tears it comes out as rage. It's not pretty."

"Well why don't you go down and talk to him, or comfort him?" she asked, getting louder. "What if he destroys the whole house?"

"He built it for Michael, Janet and the girls. If he wants to destroy it, that's his business, not yours," getting louder herself.

"This is ridiculous! He might hurt himself!" Margaret Mary cried out as she started around her mother.

Kathleen grabbed her daughter by the arm and jerked her roughly away from the door. "You aren't going anywhere, little girl! I will not let you see him like this!" she hissed, so Patrick wouldn't hear.

They heard an animal like yell, and then the sound of a sledge hammer pounding against a wall.

"He...we...feel we are to blame...for Michael..." Kathleen choked out the words over the sound of the pounding in the basement.

"Mom, please!"

By this time, Kathleen had her back against the basement door. "There is no goddam way I'm going to let you see him like this, so just pick up those fucking tablets and leave. We'll be fine."

Margaret Mary could not believe the angry determination in her mother's face. She had never heard her talk that way. It frightened her. Slowly she backed up, picked up the tablets and walked towards the front door. When she got there, she turned and walked slowly back to her mother, put her arms out, and pulled the two of them together in a sobbing embrace.

As she drove away, she thought about what must be going on in her parent's minds. The guilt alone would be traumatic. But she believed her mother when she said they would be fine. This was no time to talk about their visit with Michael, so she just left one of Dr. Goldstein's cards on the kitchen table. Now it was time to see Iggy. He lived in an apartment in Florissant, about fifteen minutes north of her parents' home. She had called the night before to tell him she was coming by. It was about six o'clock Wednesday evening when she arrived, so she knew he would be home from work. "Jesus, Mary and Joseph," she whispered to herself, "dad took the day off to destroy the house. What is Iggy going to do?"

As she got out of her VW in the apartment parking lot, she spotted Iggy getting out of his pickup truck, with a beer in one hand, three more dangling from a six-pack ring and his lunch box under his arm. "Well, well, so what's the big news you couldn't share on the phone?" he smiled.

"Give me one of those beers, and I'll tell you!" she shot back.

Once pleasantries were exchanged inside, Margaret Mary told Iggy the serious nature of what she was going to leave him to read. She told him Michael only wanted the two of them, and their parents, to read his story. She also impressed upon him Michael's concern about others learning of its contents. She finished by saying he could get to see Michael soon, and gave him Dr. Goldstein's number.

"I can't wait to see him, Margaret Mary," he grinned. "But I am a little scared about what might be on these pages."

"I know. Take your time and call me when you're done. We can talk. You can ask me questions. It's not easy to read, Iggy."

"Gotcha," Iggy replied.

He didn't realize it yet, but Iggy was about to be the fourth person to have his life turned upside down by Michael's story. Later that night, near midnight, Iggy called to say he was finished reading. Everything else he tried to say was interrupted by the onset of sobs, and the lump in his throat. Much of the time all she heard was sniffling and deep breaths. After about ten minutes, she quietly told Iggy she was going back to bed, and he should try to get some sleep also.

But of course both of them lay awake all night, their thoughts bouncing between happy childhood memories, and what their beloved Michael had endured. Both wanted desperately to help but had no idea how to go about it. Iggy called in sick to work the next day for the first time ever. He was shaken to his core and careening from wild anger to paralyzing sadness. He never imagined one could stare at a ceiling so long or be unable to stop crying.

Part X

Road Warriors

CHAPTER THIRTY-FOUR

Iggy was waiting for Margaret Mary in front of her house when she got home from work on Thursday. After they got inside, they hugged, cried, ranted and cried some more. Both wondered how it had all taken place under their noses without either one noticing anything. They agreed Michael had done a remarkable job covering up his horrible secret, and that Father O'Malley had to have been some kind of monster. They also commiserated on what this whole revelation had done to their faith, and how their blind trust in priests had been demolished.

Margaret Mary told Iggy what she had seen going on at their parents' house the night before. They talked at great length about the guilt they must be feeling, to have turned your child over to a monster. They reminisced about what Patrick and Kathleen had done to protect Iggy, and raise him as one of their own. Their parents were people who were passionate about protecting children. Now this.

After dinner, they decided to call their parents and see if they could all get together Saturday morning, around ten, and talk about who to tell, and how much they should be told. It was going to be a fine line between not hiding things from loved ones, and yet protecting Michael's privacy. The conversation turned towards reminiscing about their grandparents, and how hard they had worked to provide a better life for their children and grandchildren. Now this.

Grandpa Finnegan would have been eighty-one now. Grandma Finnegan was seventy-nine, Grandpa O'Toole was seventy-seven, and Grandma O'Toole was seventy-six. How would this affect their health and their steadfast belief in their beloved Catholic Church.

Was it worth telling them at all? Patrick and Kathleen were fifty-four and fifty-two respectively, and they were going to have some big decisions to make concerning their parents, and their four younger boys.

Sean, Billy, Bobby and Kevin ranged in age now from twenty-two to twenty-five and were all still single. It had to be impressed upon them that their big brother needed their support, and that they had to be trusted to keep this within the family for his sake. Neither Margaret Mary nor Iggy envied their parents' position in the middle of this. They agreed though, after discussing all their worries, that they needed to remain upbeat and optimistic about Michael's return, for everyone's sake.

When Margaret Mary drove down Highmont Saturday morning, she spotted a huge pile of construction debris in front of her parents' home. Well, she thought, at least that seems to be over with. When she went inside, Kathleen was folding laundry on the kitchen table.

"Isn't Kevin the only one still living here? Why are you always folding laundry, mom?" Margaret Mary told her mother in an exasperated tone.

"Your brothers like to bring their laundry over to save money. I don't mind. I can do it in my sleep," she answered.

"They can save money, and do it here themselves, you know!"

"I know. I know. You sound like your father."

"Speaking of the devil, where is dad?" Margaret Mary asked, while purposely avoiding the subject of the pile of junk in the front yard.

"He's out back with your grandfather and Iggy," Kathleen told her.

"It's just ten o'clock now. How long have they been out there?" she asked her mother, who just disappeared down the hall without answering.

When Margaret Mary looked out the back screen, she saw the

three of them had moved the patio table to the back of the yard, under the tree. They were all leaning forward, with their elbows on the table, talking very quietly and seriously. As she walked towards them, she called out, "Hey what's going on, I thought we were all going to meet at ten-o'clock?" She felt they all looked a little sheepish when they turned towards her.

"Great minds doing great things, little girl!" Grandpa O'Toole called out through a toothless grin. The walker he hated was next to him.

"Hi Margaret Mary," said Iggy quietly.

"Your mother and I already discussed what we were going to do about Michael coming home, and what we were going to tell everyone. So, there is really no need for the big pow-wow."

"It looks like you're having a big pow-wow to me," she answered curtly.

"Not at all. Your grandfather was here early this morning to supervise the garden planting, and Iggy got here just a little before you. We're just talking union stuff, like what jobs are coming out of the ground, and things like that. Nothing you are interested in," Patrick told her, while barely looking up. "Why don't you go see if you can help your mother?"

Normally, Margaret Mary would have pitched a fit about being excluded like this, but something inside told her that now was not the time. She hated the way her father had been dismissive towards her, but seeing his hands bandaged with blood-stained gauze, she decided that maybe he would not be in the mood for a healthy dose of her opinion on the matter. Reluctantly, she turned and walked back toward the house.

Back in the house, she watched the three of them from the kitchen window. The smiles were gone, and her grandfather was regularly pounding the table as he leaned forward to make an angry point. Her father kept holding up his bandaged hands to quiet him. Her brother, Iggy, was listening intently, while periodically leaning forward and poking the table top with his right forefinger for emphasis. She knew they had lied to her about the topic of their conversation by watching their passionate body language now. She knew they had to be talking about Michael, but she would never guess in a million years the exact nature of their discussion.

"This is fookin' unbelievable! A man of God! If I would have known I would have strangled the cocksucker meself! I swear it!" Jimmy ranted.

"Dad! The neighbors!" cautioned Patrick.

"The Prots would jump all over this in the old country. They were always spreading rumors about our priests being homos because they wore dresses and didn't marry!" Jimmy told them.

"Dad! Calm down!" begged Patrick.

"Calm down my ass, boy! By the looks of those hands and the pile of shite in front of the house, you're in no position to tell anyone to calm down."

"Dad, I encouraged the boy to go with this animal. I told him it was an HONOR for Chrissake! Don't you think I'm upset too! A FUCKING PRIEST DAD! I feel so guilty!" Patrick hissed.

Iggy was watching the wild eyes and beet red faces of the two men he most admired in the entire world. This is going to tear everyone apart with guilt and shame if we don't get a handle on this, he thought to himself.

"I say we find this 'fooker' and I let you watch while I choke the life out of him with me bare hands. It would be like choking the devil himself!" Jimmy hissed back.

"Don't think for a moment I haven't thought of doing it myself," Patrick added. "This whole thing makes me sick to my stomach. What I hate the most is feeling so helpless. This fuckin' asshole fucked up my beautiful boy's life, and now he's walking around somewhere free as a bird."

To this point, Iggy had hardly said a word. He just listened as the two of them tried to come to terms with their pain and anger.

He loved them both, and they loved him, but they had all adored Michael. It was as though their star had been ripped from the sky by a sick animal, and they wanted him punished without mercy.

There was a break in the ranting for half a minute, while the two older men caught their breath. Then without warning, in a businesslike monotone, Iggy said, "If you can find him, I'll kill him."

You could have heard a pin drop as Jimmy and Patrick turned to look at Iggy. He was stone-faced. His eyes calmly went from one to the other, showing no emotion.

"Iggy, don't talk that way. Would you want to spend your life in prison for Chrissake! You're a young man with your whole life ahead of you," said Patrick. "Your grandpa here was just blowing off steam."

"I would do it, boy. I've got one foot in the grave already, but your dad's right you've got your whole life. This isn't 1920 you know, where the cops might look the other way in a situation like this. Fookin' radio and television tell everything to everybody," Jimmy croaked. He was thinking back on how Kathleen's grandfather had known of his ordeal in Forest Park with the Russians, but kept it to himself.

"I'll bet the Fitzgerald's could find this prick. They wouldn't have to know who killed him. I think they would feel like us, you know, good riddance," said Iggy.

"That may be true, Iggy, but there are no secrets between cops. One slip to one reporter and Michael would be on the front page. There is no fucking way I'm taking that chance. He's been through enough. The least we can do at this point is protect him," Patrick told him.

"I agree, boy," added Jimmy. "The Prot newspapers would have a field day with this. The headline would be 'Homo Priest and Altar Boy'. That's all we need."

"If this got out about Michael, and anything happened to O'Malley, the cops and reporters would be on the front porch," reasoned Patrick.

"All I'm saying is that if you can find him, I'll kill him. No one but us would ever know," Iggy repeated, in an unsettling businesslike tone.

"I'd like to watch," Patrick said under his breath, without looking up.

"I'd pay to watch," Jimmy added quietly.

A few uncomfortable minutes passed without anyone saying a word. Each of them was considering Michael's ruined life, and the possibility of such drastic revenge. Even considering the act brought silent embarrassment and a giddy sense of righteousness at the same time.

Finally, Iggy said in a matter-of-fact tone, "You know I bet the archdiocese would know where O'Malley is. It's only been fourteen years." As he got up from his chair to leave, he didn't notice the meaningful sideways glance that Jimmy and Patrick gave to each other. "I'll see you all later."

As Iggy walked away, Patrick casually leaned back in his chair and said, "Dad, do you remember mom's cousin Eileen? Does she still say the rosary at St. James every morning before Mass?"

"She does. They also speak on the phone about once a month."

"She never married, did she?"

"She did not."

Waiting a few seconds for that to sink in, Patrick asked, "Does she still work at the bishop's residence, cleaning and cooking?"

"She does. She's had the job for forty years. She's on her second bishop." Then in a flat tone, Jimmy leaned forward and added, "I know where you're headed here boy. This is no small thing. First of all, your mom would have to be the one to ask her. That means I would have to tell her about Michael. She's not going to ask Eileen for a favor without knowing why. You know how she is. The second problem, is that the two of them bathe in holy water, if you know what I mean. We'd be askin' both of 'em to commit a grave sin."

"Alright. I guess it is a long shot. Anyway, he might already be dead," Patrick told him.

"I would at least like to know that the 'fooker' isn't walking around smiling, I'll tell you that," answered Jimmy.

The conversation had made the feeling of helplessness start to subside for both Patrick and Jimmy. There was a reason why the Irish liked the old adage, "Don't get mad, get even". For men who saw their purpose in life being to protect and provide for their families, doing nothing in a situation like this, was nearly impossible. The gene pool that brought them to this moment was full of fighters and survivors, not those who reflect on tragedy, and accept it.

As for Iggy, he laid down on his couch that evening, remembering that he literally owed his life and everything he had accomplished, to the O'Tooles. They had protected him and nurtured him when his own father had left him for dead. They had fed him, clothed him, and put a roof over his head, without asking for anything in return.

As Iggy started to doze, he could see in his mind's eye, as clear as if he were watching a movie, the first day that Michael O'Toole picked him to be on his team on the playground at Sts. John and James. They became friends that day, and ever since, he valued Michael O'Toole's friendship more than anything on earth.

CHAPTER THIRTY-FIVE

An hour later, Jimmy was back home, standing on the landing leading from the garage to the kitchen, trying to catch his breath. Steps were his enemy these days, but they had lived in the house in Dogtown so long, they couldn't even imagine living anywhere else. Bridgey was at the stove frying steak and potatoes for dinner. Finally, she turned and looked at him quizzically.

"You alright, old man?"

"Yes, but I have something to ask you."

"Ask away."

"You know your spinster cousin, Eileen?"

"Yes, and you calling her spinster is why she doesn't like you."

"Do you still pray the rosary with her?"

"I do. I did this morning."

"Does she still work at the Bishop's residence?"

"She does. For over 40 years now."

"Could you ask her a favor?"

"Like what?"

"Finding the whereabouts of a priest that used to be at Sts. John and James thirteen or fourteen years ago. His name is Father James O'Malley."

"I'm sure she could. The Bishop thinks the world of her, I know."

"Bridgey, she needs to find out without the Bishop knowing."

"That changes things. Why is that Jimmy?"

"I'd rather not say. Can't you just ask her?"

"She'll want to know why all the secrecy. She could lose her job! By the way, isn't O'Malley the name of the priest that took such an interest in Michael? Didn't he talk to him about becoming a priest and all? They went on little trips together." As she finished she felt her stomach flutter. "Jimmy, does this have something to do with Michael?"

Jimmy was looking at the floor now, trying to figure a way out of this. When he finally looked up, those crystal blue eyes she had fallen in love with fifty-six years ago were welling up. This was a first. "Bridgey, could you just ask her?" he whispered.

Slowly, she walked across the kitchen to where he was standing and wrapped her arms around him. This was her white knight, her protector and the father of their eight children. This was the incredible man she had watched walk out of the house every work day at five in the morning, to wait at the bus stop in thunderstorms, blizzards, and blistering heat to provide for all of them.

Then she began to feel the shudders deep within his old frail body as he desperately tried not to cry out loud. His head was buried in her bosom, and his arms were at his sides.

"Jimmy, let it out for God's sake. What is it? It's okay. It's okay. Tell me."

Seated at the table a few minutes later, holding hands, Bridgey asked Jimmy again if it had something to do with Michael.

"Yes, Bridgey, but I don't think I can say it out loud."

"Please Jimmy, just try."

"This f-f-f-fookin' priest," he stammered, "he made Michael do things."

"What things?"

"Sex things," he whispered quietly.

Bridgey stared at Jimmy for what seemed an eternity. Jimmy wouldn't make eye contact.

"A priest could never do such a thing," Bridgey whispered, "it's like Jesus himself hurting a child. It can't be...it's impossible Jimmy..."

"It's true. Patrick and Kathleen read it in Michael's own hand. The shame of it almost killed him. The doctor and Margaret Mary have talked to him about it. They believe him."

Slowly Bridgey got up and walked over to the sink to stare out the window at the crucifix atop of St. James the Greater church steeple. Poised high above the neighborhood, the sight of if had provided her with endless hours of comfort and security over the years as she cooked and washed dishes. If what Jimmy said was true, then what else was... if the priesthood was...Michael would have no reason to...Patrick would never...

The last thing she remembered was her knees shaking, before they gave way. Slowly she sank to the floor, holding onto the edge of the sink.

Jimmy hurried to her side and caught her just as she started falling to her right. Not a word passed her lips, or a tear left her eye, as Jimmy helped her fall gently on her side. What scared him the most was the dark stare, and her mouth hanging open. After all they had been through, he had never seen Bridgey falter like this. It scared him when she didn't respond to him right away. He called her name and kissed her cheek to no avail. Finally, a cold wet towel on her forehead seemed to bring her around whispering over and over, "Not a priest...not a priest...not a priest..."

The next Saturday morning, Bridgey took her place next to Eileen in the second pew from the front. The two ladies looked quite a bit alike, as their mothers had been sisters, but at seventy years old, Eileen was a bit younger than Bridgey. Eileen was a rather large woman, with a round, pink cherubic face and blue eyes. Like Bridgey, her hair was usually stuck to her forehead from perspiration. The ladies prided themselves as being daily communicants, and looked forward to joining the other fifteen or twenty ladies to say the rosary on Saturday mornings before eight o'clock Mass. Saying the rosary brought them peace. They spoke to each other often after Mass about the calm that the Blessed Virgin brought for their efforts.

Bridgey did not feel peaceful today. All the 'Hail Marys', 'Our

Fathers' and 'Glory Bes' in the world weren't going to fix that. She just didn't know if she could get Eileen to do her bidding without telling her about Michael. She had promised Jimmy to ask Eileen for this favor, but it wasn't going to be easy.

"Eileen, do you have a moment?" she asked on the church steps after Mass.

"I do. What is it Bridgey?" she smiled. The two had been close for many years, and often shared memories of their mothers back in Ireland when they were growing up.

"I was wondering if it would be possible to find out the whereabouts of a priest who used to be at Sts. John and James about fourteen years ago?" asked Bridgey innocently.

"I'm sure I could find out from the Bishop. What was his name?" asked Eileen.

"His name was Father James O'Malley. One of the kids wanted to send him a note," she added, trying to act nonchalant. She wasn't sure, but she thought she saw Eileen's eyes widen just a bit at the mention of the name.

"I seem to remember the name," Eileen answered, "I'll see what I can do."

Truth be told, Eileen's brain started to spin. As a domestic housemaid, her presence was often disregarded as though she were invisible. This meant that sometimes she overheard parts of conversations she probably was not supposed to hear. She had been at the Bishop's residence so long, cleaning and serving, that she had become somewhat of a fixture. The Bishop needn't have worried though, as she knew it was a sin to repeat anything she heard.

Through the years, she had heard O'Malley's name mentioned in hushed conversations a number of times. She surmised that he had some sort of a problem, maybe drinking, and therefore, had been moved around quite a bit.

When Bridgey turned to chat with a couple of other ladies from the rosary group, she started to remember a horrible letter on the Bishop's desk she read five years or so ago. She knew it was a sin to snoop, so she confessed it, and swore to never repeat what she read to anyone. Now, here was her favorite cousin Bridgey, asking about the same priest mentioned in the letter. Eileen was feeling anxious now as Bridgey turned around to face her again.

"Eileen, I know this is a lot to ask, but do you think you could find out where Father O'Malley is without asking the Bishop, or anyone else for that matter?" she asked. Bridgey knew that she was asking Eileen to commit a sin by going through files and records without permission. This was a lot to ask of her pious cousin.

"I don't know Bridgey. If one of the children wants to get a note to him, they could send it to the bishop's residence, with a request to forward it to Father O'Malley. Why does it have to be a secret like this?"

"If I knew, I would tell you. I would. Never mind, Eileen. I shouldn't have even asked such a thing. It was wrong of me." Jimmy was just going to have to find another way. This isn't right, Bridgey thought to herself.

Eileen knew by the look on Bridgey's face that it had pained her to ask. They had known each other since they were little girls. This was so out of character for her. Why was the secrecy so important? "No apology needed," she said quietly.

"Fair enough. Thank you, Eileen. Again, I'm sorry to have asked. Take care."

The cousins hugged and went their separate ways.

While Eileen walked home she thought about that letter she had seen on the Bishop's desk. The same sinking feeling overtook her as the day she first read it. It had been a recommendation from some psychiatrist with a German name, to remove O'Malley from the priesthood, and to keep him away from children. The letter had described O'Malley as having an uncontrollable urge to fondle, and have sexual relations with, pre-pubescent boys. She remembered that sentence clearly because it had taken her breath away.

She felt at the time, that the charges could never be true of a priest, because they held the power of Jesus Christ himself, entrusted to them through St. Peter. Priests were in a realm between God and man she thought, and there was no way that hands that touched the sacred Body of Christ could ever touch a boy in such a way. She remembered thinking, at that time, what a challenging job the Bishop must have, dealing with crackpot Protestant accusations like this. As a young girl growing up in Ireland, she remembered the adults talking about how the Prots were always making accusations against their priests. The most popular accusation being how priests and nuns had secret babies and put them in orphanages.

When she finally got home and sat down, she started to ponder a conversation she had overheard a few months before. She often went to her older sister Maeve's home for dinner on Friday night. Maeve had married one of the Flynn's who were in the bricklayers' union. Maeve's husband, Hugh, had died in a construction accident a few years before, so her kids stopped by for dinner occasionally to keep their mom company. Eileen's nephew, Timothy, a bricklayer like his father, was in the kitchen talking to his mother that night, while Eileen set the table in the dining room.

He was telling his mother that he had seen Michael O'Toole in a lounge at the mental hospital on Arsenal Street. Timothy said they were on a scaffold outside repairing some loose brick and spotted him through a window.

"Do you mean your cousin, Michael, the scholar athlete at St. Thomas Aquinas?"

"That's the one. He was curled up on a couch in a bathrobe."

"Not the one who got the scholarship to Notre Dame?" asked Maeve.

"That's the one. I didn't knock on the window because I didn't want to embarrass him, but it was him alright," answered Timothy.

"Jesus, Mary, and Joseph," Maeve had said, while crossing herself, "that tall, good looking boy, with brains to boot. He was the family darlin'."

"I know, but didn't you hear he walked out on his wife and kids years ago?" asked Timothy.

"I suppose I did now that you mention it." Maeve recalled. "What a shame."

Eileen had not given any more thought to the conversation she overheard months ago until now. She knew Michael had left his family. His being in the mental hospital had been news, though. Why hadn't Bridgey mentioned Michael being in the hospital? She may have been embarrassed, but they had been so close over the years. Bridgey loved that boy more than life itself. She had been so proud of his scholarship to Notre Dame. Then she quit talking about him at all.

Eileen's mind was starting to race. She was still bothered about Bridgey asking for Father O'Malley's whereabouts. Then there was that letter accusing O'Malley of the most horrendous of sins. What if the letter were true? She wished now that she had never read it. O'Malley had been at Sts. John and James where Michael went to school. Then there was Michael's unbelievable fall from what he had been, to winding up in a mental hospital. What if O'Malley hurt Michael? She could barely stand the thought of it. A priest would have had to be taken over by the devil himself to do such a thing.

Eileen's head was hurting now. She walked slowly to the medicine chest for aspirin. After swallowing two she prayed while looking in the mirror. "Dear God, give me strength and courage. Guide me Lord. Show me what you want me to do. Blessed Virgin you have always been by my side. Have I been placed in the middle of something for a reason? I don't think Bridgey would ever ask me to sin, unless it was for a very good reason."

Eileen laid down as she often did after praying for help and guidance. Not always, but some of the time she awoke with a sense of confidence and direction. Today was one of those days. She awoke with the conviction that she needed to get some answers to her questions.

It took her a few days to get up her nerve and find the right time to go through the Bishop's files. She had worked for Bishop Shaughnessy for over twenty years now, starting in 1956. She worked for Bishop Murphy for twenty years before that, starting in 1936, a year after she arrived from Ireland. Bishop Shaughnessy had been born, raised, and went to the seminary in Ireland, so the two of them always had a lot to talk about. She had been at the Bishop's residence now for over forty years. She loved her job and really had no thoughts of retiring.

After all this time, Eileen had unlimited access to all the rooms in the mansion, both to clean, and to bring the Bishop and his guests snacks and drinks. She knew that the Bishop's assistant, Monsignor Dolan, unlocked the Bishop's massive office, pulled the curtains, and put the day's schedule on his huge mahogany desk every morning. Eileen followed him into the office to dust and empty the trash while the Monsignor methodically unlocked all the drawers in the desk, and each of the twenty or more file cabinets against the wall. He usually left with a smile and a nod to Eileen and hurried out to say eight a.m. Mass at the Cathedral across the street.

Eileen always went to the six-thirty Mass during the week, so that she could get a jump on her duties. After the Monsignor left, she would go to the kitchen to make the Bishop's coffee, which she would place on his desk with a roll, before nine a.m. Then he would come down from personal residence upstairs to start his day. It was the same routine every day.

On the Wednesday morning following her talk with Bridgey, she said a continuous stream of Hail Marys to calm herself. This was going to be the day. Her hands were shaking as she dusted the file cabinets and waited for Monsignor Dolan to leave. The day before, she found the cabinet labelled 'Transferred and Inactive Archdiocesan Personnel'. The second and third drawers were labelled for clergy only.

As she pulled the first drawer open, she became nauseous at the thought of committing a willful sin. She pushed on, through the second, and then the third drawer, looking through the section with the O's, which was quite large. Whispering an Our Father she gingerly plucked the file for one *Father James O'Malley*. As she slid the drawer closed, she slipped the large file under her arm, under her sweater, and buttoned it up. She always wore a sweater, even in the summer in the old residence, because it was always so chilly in there. Today she was sweating profusely.

Quickly, she walked out of the office to the lockers in the back hall by the kitchen, opened her locker, and dropped the file in her shopping bag. Knowing she could never work with the file in her locker, she told the cook to tell the Monsignor she was sick and left for the day.

Eileen was still sweating as she waited for her bus out on Lindell Blvd., even with the sweater off. The cook had mentioned that she did not look well, and she definitely felt sick. What she would read that day in the file was not going to help her feel any better.

Four hours later, around noon, Eileen's young neighbor from upstairs, Mary McCarthy, was pounding on her door. "Are you alright Eileen? Eileen, please answer the door!" she was calling out. For the last half hour, she had heard her poor old neighbor sobbing and crying louder and louder. When she heard Eileen retching as she threw up the rest of her breakfast, Mary came down to check on her.

Finally, she used Eileen's spare key to let herself in. She had a baby on her hip and one in tow as she called Eileen's name again. When she spotted her, the old woman was on her knees, with her head in one hand, a rosary in the other, in front of the toilet.

"Eileen, you're scaring me to death. Are you alright? What's wrong?"

"I'm fine child. Just help me up. I think the poison is gone."

"Poison?"

"Something I ate."

"But I heard you crying?"

"From the stomach pain, is all. No need to worry. I think it's over."

After thanking her young neighbor, Eileen went back to her overstuffed chair where she had been reading. She laid a cold rag across her eyes and forehead and began to silently pray. What she was seeing in the file was more upsetting than anything she could have ever imagined, before that day.

CHAPTER THIRTY-SIX

It was all there in the file. Every lurid detail in the life of a monster who called himself a priest. Father James O'Malley was an Irish immigrant, who had been sent to the St. Louis Archdiocese in 1957 at the age of twenty-seven, from the Chicago Archdiocese. The Bishop in Chicago had written only of a need for a 'fresh start' for this bright, enthusiastic, young priest. The 'fresh start' clause was a sign that Fr. O'Malley had gotten himself in some sort of trouble.

The letter went on to say that he had been accused of some inappropriate behavior and had tearfully asked for forgiveness. 'Inappropriate behavior' was language used to convey that the indiscretion was of a sexual nature. The age of the priest and his recent ordination would lead St. Louis Bishop Patrick Shaughnessy to believe that the indiscretion was with a female, possibly a parishioner. Celibacy was very difficult for young men, and hopefully he had learned a valuable lesson.

The Bishop went on to say that he felt that Fr. O'Malley's personality and energy would make him a great asset to the St. Louis Archdiocese. Since Bishop Shaughnessy was a firm believer in the power of confession, forgiveness and prayer to change lives and souls, he welcomed the young priest with a hearty handshake, before assigning him to St. Cronan's parish in the Forest Park East neighborhood. In the event of another "indiscretion" he knew that the largely Irish parishioners could be counted on to keep quiet.

Bishop Shaughnessy wrote to the old pastor at St Cronan's, that the young priest was looking for a "fresh start". The pastor, Fr. John McGuire, was also familiar with the euphemism, and knew that Fr.

O'Malley had gotten himself in some sort of trouble. After meeting the affable young priest, with his quick smile and handsome features, he even quietly wondered if the young man had been seduced. Fr. McGuire was going to keep an eye on him and keep him on a straight path.

Fr. McGuire, like Fr. O'Malley and Bishop Shaughnessy, was also an Irish immigrant. He had been ordained in Dublin, and his call to the priesthood had come a bit later than most. He had spent a couple of years after secondary school making a living as a boxer, among other things. He had won his share of bouts, but his mother had convinced him that the call he was hearing to be a priest would bring him far greater rewards in the long run. His mother had been right. He was able to help countless people in need of direction in their lives, and he wouldn't change his decision for the world. Fr. McGuire loved being a priest. He was a short, stocky, no-nonsense kind of guy, with a few telltale scars on his face from his early years. He was sixty years old now, and felt it was time to get some help from some young legs.

The Catholic Church in America in the late nineteenth century and well into the twentieth century, was growing in leaps and bounds. Then after World War II, especially in the big cities, there were new parishes springing up everywhere to accommodate all the returning GI's and their young families.

During this period, the priesthood in America was populated by an inordinate number of Irish priests. There were a few reasons for this phenomenon. First, the Republic of Ireland was nearly one hundred percent Catholic. Second, there were few career opportunities for young men in a largely agricultural economy. This contributed to Ireland's seminaries being full of bright young priests. Finally, unlike America, Ireland had a finite number of parishes to send new priests.

Often the men who were sculpting and steering the growth of the American Catholic Church were Irish bishops. They often turned to their homeland for the manpower they needed to run all of these new parishes, in cities like New York, Boston, Philadelphia, Chicago and St. Louis. Like Irish cops, Irish building tradesmen and Irish politicians, the Irish clergy in America stuck together. This was the formula that had served them all well, not just to survive, but to thrive. Irish tribal bonds ran deep in America.

Fr. McGuire had always felt that celibacy was much more than just a "difficult challenge" like it was described in the seminary. He had never broken his vows, but he could see how a good looking young priest could be tempted, especially after being secluded in the seminary for years. He thought he could be an excellent mentor and role model for young Fr. O'Malley.

Fr. McGuire set about introducing his new assistant to the parish staff, the nuns and the parishioners. He assigned the young man several responsibilities, which he cheerfully accepted. Fr. O'Malley turned out to be a natural at working with the primary age school children, getting them ready for their First Confession, First Communion and Confirmation. He put the children at ease with his quick wit, smile and willingness to take as long as necessary to allay their fears, especially concerning Confession. This made Fr. McGuire very happy, since his gruff nature and impatient manner was never conducive to getting the kids to relax.

Seven-year-olds are understandably nervous about going into a dark closet to confess their sins, especially since it was always difficult to remember them. Nevertheless, they knew they needed to cleanse their souls if they were going to be able to make their First Communion. Fr. Jim, as he instructed the youngsters to call him, had gentle manner with the children made the whole process much easier for everyone. The nuns and the parents were delighted with his effect on the kids. When Fr. Jim was coming to the classrooms to instruct the children, the sisters would have them all sitting up straight, with their hands folded on their desks. Father's arrival was a big event.

Sometimes, boys in fifth through eighth grades, who had been especially good that week, would be picked to accompany Fr. Jim back to church to straighten the missals, and hang up the freshly laundered cassocks they wore as altar boys. It was an honor, and it was nice to get out of class for a while, especially when the weather turned warm and sunny in the spring.

About a year after Fr. O'Malley came to St. Cronan's, Fr. McGuire was looking all over the rectory for the watch his mother had given him when he left Ireland. Finally, he figured he must have left it by the sink in the sacristy, when he washed his hands and arms before Mass early that morning. He was glad that the kids were back in class after lunch and recess, so that he could make a quick trip across the playground to the back door of the church.

But what he saw when he opened the door to the sacristy stopped him dead in his tracks. Fr. O'Malley was seated in a chair fondling a young boy about twelve-years old, who had his pants and underwear around his ankles.

The old pastor yelled so loud that the boy fell over backwards. "What the hell is going on here, O'Malley!"

The wide-eyed young priest began to stammer, "I was just...he said he had a pain...I thought..."

"Shut up and get out of my way!" McGuire hissed at him, causing O'Malley to back up against a wall. Then, turning to the boy on the floor, he spoke in as soothing and gentle a voice as he could muster. "Don't be frightened, boy. You've done nothing wrong. Let me help you up. Pull up your trousers, and tuck in your shirt. Alright, now go on back to your class. One more thing, I want you to keep quiet about this until I have a chance to talk to you, okay?" Immediately, the boy nodded and ran out the door.

McGuire could barely control the rage he felt building. He took two steps and back-handed O'Malley with his right hand to the right side of his face. O'Malley fell to his left to one knee and started to say "Wait, I can explain..." when McGuire yanked him to his feet with his left hand and hit O'Malley with a solid right fist that broke the younger man's jaw on his left side. He fell to the floor whimpering and crying. His right eye was swelling shut, and his nose was bleeding.

"Get up you piece of shit!" McGuire told him in a scary, quiet tone. When O'Malley didn't move, McGuire pulled him to his feet, and pushed him against the wall, without releasing the front of O'Malley's jacket. McGuire put his face two inches from O'Malley's, staring at him with wild, violent eyes.

"Listen to me, you perverted son-of-a-bitch, you have one hour before school lets out, to pack and get off my parish property. If I ever see you again, I'll beat you until your own mother wouldn't recognize you! Do you understand me?" Then, after O'Malley nodded, McGuire told him, "Go straight to Shaughnessy's office. He'll be expecting you."

Then, without warning, the old priest delivered a sharp blow, with everything he had just under the younger priest's rib cage. It knocked the air out of his lungs and he dropped to the floor, gasping for air.

As McGuire stormed out of the sacristy, all he could think of was the fear in that little boy's eyes. Fear of a priest! A priest that MOLESTED him! In God's house, no less! He could feel his eyes tearing up as he marched across the playground to talk to the boy. Maybe I should wait and have his parent's present. I don't want to frighten him anymore. 'Dear Lord help me' he prayed.

What Fr. McGuire didn't realize was that there were five more young boys that had been 'lucky' enough to be picked for 'special duty' with Fr. O'Malley the year before he left St. Cronan's.

When Fr. McGuire reached the rectory, he sent the secretary home for the day so she wouldn't get a look at O'Malley. Then he closed the window and door to his office before calling Bishop Shaughnessy. He bluntly told the Bishop's secretary that he needed to speak to him right away and he didn't give a shit if he was in a meeting with the pope.

"For goodness sakes, John, what is so important?" asked the Bishop, a minute later.

For the next few minutes he heard the expletive-laced gravelly brogue of the old pastor as he ranted loudly and clearly about what he had just witnessed. He then literally screamed into the phone, "Is this why the son-of-a-bitch needed a fresh start? So he could molest more children? He shouldn't be a priest! He should be hanging by his nuts from a tall tree! What do I say to this poor boy's parents? And what if he did this to more of these boys?"

"John! For God's sake calm down! I'll take care of this. Tell the parent's how sorry we all are. Tell them O'Malley will never have the chance to do this again. Ask them not to tell anyone. We don't need the whole parish catching wind of this. Surely, they don't want the world to know what happened to their boy. Why he'd be teased unmercifully. If they are still angry, and talking of going to the police, you send them to me, alright?" Shaughnessy told him with military-like precision.

"Fine!" barked Fr. McGuire. As he hung up, he had the nagging thought that the Bishop had not been nearly so outraged as he thought he would be. He thought that maybe his cool demeanor may have been a reason why he was the Bishop, but still, this was an innocent child. It never crossed his mind that the Bishop handled more "indiscretions"', and "inappropriate behavior" than he could ever imagine.

After getting off the phone, Shaughnessy snapped at his assistant, Monsignor Flaherty, "Now I know why Chicago dumped O'Malley on me! I need another one of these characters like I need a hole in my head!"

'What's the problem, sir?" asked Flaherty.

"McGuire at St. Cronan's caught O'Malley groping a twelve-year-old boy in the sacristy. What the hell is the matter with these men?" he answered, dropping his head and putting his hands on either side of his face. Both men knew they had at least five more "fresh starts" working out there in the archdiocesen parishes.

Finally, Shaughnessy raised his head and told Flaherty, "O'Malley is on his way, and when he gets here I want you to put him in the old custodian's quarters in the basement. Let him stew down there for a while until I can figure out our next move."

About eight o'clock that night, Bishop Shaughnessy took up a regal pose behind his desk and told Monsignor Flaherty to bring O'Malley up to him. He wasn't prepared for what walked through the door, but the sight did not make him feel even an ounce of sympathy. O'Malley had dried blood down the front of his shirt, and tissues dangling both nostrils. His right eye was deep purple and swollen shut. The left side of his face was swollen up nearly the size of a football, and he was trying to hold a towel full of ice on it.

"Did you know that kindly old Fr. McGuire used to be a professional boxer in the old country?" the Bishop asked sarcastically.

"I did not sir," he mumbled through his swollen jaws. At that moment, he started to feel a little dizzy, and began to sit in the chair across from the Bishop's desk.

"Don't you dare sit down young man," the Bishop scolded.

Not sensing there was any room for explanation or excuses, O'Malley got down on his knees, then lay face down in front of the desk. Clearly, he had been in this position before and knew the routine. After some quiet sobbing he said, "Will you hear my confession sir?"

"Indeed, I will, young man," the Bishop answered in a purposely pompous voice.

"Bless me Father, for I have sinned. My last confession was a week ago. Today I touched a boy in an inappropriate way. For this I am deeply sorry, and it will never, ever happen again."

As he stared down at the seemingly penitent priest before him, the Bishop was tempted to ask if he had done this to any other boys at St. Cronan's. Experience taught him that he probably had. He also wanted to know if he had done this same disgusting thing in Chicago. Truthfully, though, he didn't want to know the answer to either question. The Bishop told O'Malley that he was going to send him to a retreat in rural Missouri, run by an order of priests called the Servants of the Paraclete, who work with troubled priests. The hope was that they could fix him so he wouldn't do this to children anymore. This would be his Penance.

As the Bishop made his way around the desk, he ordered O'Malley to kneel. He then extended his hand so that the penitent priest would kiss his ring as a sign of respect and humility. "I hope that you pray night and day for this demon to be removed from your being, young man. Stay on your knees and pray the rosary out loud, so that you may be forgiven."

As O'Malley tearfully began the rosary, Bishop Shaughnessy returned to his chair and immediately began to plan for what he needed to do if the parents of this boy threatened to go to the police. Theses sick bastards put me in a horrible position, over and over he mused. His least favorite duty as bishop was meeting with the parents of the molested children. He would tell them since the priest had confessed, this whole situation was now covered under the seal of the confessional, and that if they told anyone, they could be excommunicated. He would then remind them, that excommunication meant they could never receive the Sacraments again, jeopardizing their salvation.

The victim and the parents were then told they would get a couple thousand dollars for counseling, if they agreed to sign a pledge of secrecy. The amount was fluid, according to how angry they were and how affluent they were. Often the victim's father was out of the picture due to death or desertion, and this sum of money was a huge benefit to the single mother. The routine had been working perfectly for decades.

CHAPTER THIRTY-SEVEN

The records that Eileen took from the Bishop's file cabinet told a remarkably similar story over and over throughout the tumultuous career of Father James O'Malley. He served in one parish after another throughout the Archdiocese, in gradually longer periods of time, followed by months of absence for "personal reasons". The end of each assignment was always accompanied by a letter from the pastor stating that Fr. O'Malley was 'overly fond' of children, or that it would be best if his next assignment was one where he would be in the 'company of adults only'. Some of the records had letters with explicit details, while others indicated the pastor had phoned the Bishop, who wrote down an account of the conversation. Some of the files were a result of the Bishop's direct contact with an angry parent.

On one occasion, the Bishop wrote about the father of one of O'Malley's victims who lived in a parish in Jefferson County, on St. Louis County's southern border. The man's brother lived in a parish in St. Charles County, on St. Louis County's western border. He found out from his brother that O'Malley had molested a boy there five years before, and the parents had been assured it would never happen again. They too had been paid for their silence.

The man, named Richard Sullivan, was so angry, and slightly inebriated, that he went to the Bishop's residence, beat on the front door and screamed, until the police arrived. Bishop Shaughnessy, always the politician, asked the police to let him go, and invited the man and the police inside. Then, with the policeman in the hall for protection, the Bishop reminded the man that the "incident" was under the seal of the confessional, and that he risked excommunication, and salvation, by revealing the details to anyone.

When Mr. Sullivan told him where he could stick his salvation, the good Bishop then played hardball and asked if he wanted their whole parish to know about this. He told him that the poor boy would be tortured by his classmates for being perceived as a homosexual. The Bishop then told him that if the story got in the papers, all their friends and relatives would also know. Finally, Mr. Sullivan said he just wanted to make sure that this animal never did anything like this to another child.

Bishop Shaughnessy told him that he was just as angry and horrified about what Fr. O'Malley had done, and that he could promise Mr. Sullivan that this would never happen again. He then offered Mr. Sullivan, who had the hands and clothing of a mechanic, two thousand dollars for his son's counseling, if he agreed to sign a nondisclosure statement. Mr. Sullivan accepted the check and walked out the door. The formula to protect the church from scandal had worked again.

Eileen had forced herself to read on, hoping that eventually there would be an end to the story that showed her beloved Bishop Shaughnessy would finally do the right thing and send this animal to jail, or at the very least, get him removed from the priesthood. Unfortunately, the heart wrenching stories continued. She was also praying that she wouldn't see Michael's name in the file. Jesus, Mary and Joseph, she prayed, what would she tell Bridgey if she found him in this horrible man's file.

She didn't see Michael's name, but her suspicions were aroused once again when she saw that O'Malley had spent two years at Sts. John and James in Ferguson. That was Patrick and Kathleen's parish, where Michael had gone to school. O'Malley had been there from 1962-1964. She knew Michael would have been twelve in 1962 because she wrote down all the children's birthdates, and always sent them cards on their birthdays. It seemed that the boys he molested were always around that age.

The letter in the file from the pastor at Sts. John and James was dated September of 1964, asking to have O'Malley removed from the parish. In it he described the repeated requests by the principal to have O'Malley banned from school property. Her nuns insisted he was spending far too much time in the boy's bathrooms. The pastor also described how O'Malley repeatedly ignored his instructions not to have any boys in the rectory.

The file showed that O'Malley had been sent to a half dozen parishes and three mental health facilities between 1957 and 1974. There were also several documented requests to other bishops, in other diocese, to take O'Malley off his hands. All of those were rejected, some mentioning that they already had their share of "problems". Finally, in early 1975 a frustrated Bishop Shaughnessy sent him to the Paraclete Fathers in New Mexico with a letter asking them to keep him indefinitely. Shortly after, there was a letter sent to the Vatican, asking to have Father James O'Malley defrocked, meaning he would no longer be a priest. Bishop Shaughnessy no longer wanted to be responsible for him.

The reply from the Vatican reminded the Bishop that priests were ordained for life and encouraged him to be creative in finding a suitable ministry for Fr. O'Malley. The letter then urged the Bishop to pray for guidance, asking the Lord for whatever level of compassion and forgiveness was needed to help Fr. O'Malley

In early 1976, the Paraclete Fathers sent O'Malley back to St. Louis. The letter from them said that after a year in treatment, the head psychiatrist said he had little success with the patient's sociopathic urge to be with young boys. The recommendation was that he be under close supervision at all times, and under no circumstances was he to ever have access to children.

The file showed that Bishop Shaughnessy then decided to make Father O'Malley a chaplain for a few of the religious orders of nuns in St. Louis. Each of them had facilities where they cared for their own sisters who were elderly or had become chronically ill. This posed a problem with transporting O'Malley from one facility to another, since the Bishop had taken away his license to drive and forbade him from going anywhere without an escort.

In the end, the decision was made to have Father James O'Malley be the permanent on-site chaplain at the St Cecilia Home for the aged in west St. Louis County. It was an enormous facility that cared for elderly lay people and those from various religious orders. He arrived there in October of 1976. Sister Mary Angelica, who ran the facility, was told that O'Malley was never to leave the premises without an escort, and never to be left alone with children.

By the time Eileen closed the file that evening, it was nearly eight o'clock. After her first dose of reading had caused her such physical trauma, she decided to read the file in small increments, which took a long time. She felt her beloved Bishop was complicit in putting all of these children in danger, and this struck a nerve deep down in her faithful Catholic soul. The same soul that had never even considered questioning a member of the clergy, now began to doubt the character of those she had once held in such high esteem. This was the root cause of her pounding head and nausea. There was nothing so innocent and deserving of protection as a child of God, yet it appeared the Bishop valued the avoidance of scandal, over their safety and security.

Eileen went and stood under a hot shower until the heat ran out, subconsciously feeling that maybe it would wash away this feeling that she was dirty, for even having read O'Malley's file. Lying in bed that night, wide-eyed and shaky, she thought she may have to claim illness again in the morning, after returning the file. She did not see how she could face Bishop Shaughnessy. It was going to be very difficult not to ask him how he could have continued to place children in harm's way year after year.

It turned out to be the most restless night of her life. Why hadn't

O'Malley been turned over to the police and put in jail? How many little boys had he molested who never told anyone? He can't really be a priest anymore if the devil has taken over his soul, can he? Isn't this exactly how the devil would work to destroy the faith of God's people, and doubt the Holy Mother Church? Hadn't the devil taken on many forms, even trying to tempt Jesus himself when he was praying and fasting in the desert?

Finally, around midnight, Eileen got up and sat at the kitchen table and prayed for the Holy Spirit to come upon her and give her guidance. She closed her eyes, folded her hands and lowered her head to rest upon them. After a while, she lapsed into an uncomfortable sleep for nearly an hour. She awoke with a memory from when she was a little girl, of five or six-years-old in Ireland.

She was hiding in the straw in the barn to surprise her father when he walked in with another man. She overheard them talking about a man who had molested a little girl. She didn't know what "molested" meant at the time, but their tone conveyed that it was a terrible thing. The other man told her father that they found that man floating in an eddy in the river nearby. Both men agreed it was no great loss.

After returning to bed, Eileen was still unable to turn off her thoughts, so she knelt next to her bed as she had done as a child. She had always sought help and strength in the most trying times from the Blessed Virgin. The Mother of God had helped her throughout her life to fight temptation and find answers. Slowly and solemnly she began to say her rosary, one bead at a time, one precious Hail Mary at a time.

It started as a tingling in her spine, and then became a warm sensation throughout her being. It ended with thousands of goose bumps covering her from head to toe, as a small voice inside quoted a sentence from the mouth of Jesus. *"It would be better for you if a millstone were hung around your neck and you were thrown into the sea, than for you to cause one of these little ones to stumble."*

CHAPTER THIRTY-EIGHT

A few days after Eileen returned the file, Bridgey received an anonymous letter in the mail. All that was enclosed was a slip of paper with the words St. Cecelia's Home for the Aged printed neatly. The next morning that slip of paper was underneath Jimmy's coffee cup. That evening when Patrick got home from work, Kathleen told him to call his father. After talking to his father, Patrick called Iggy to say that the three of them were going to meet in the back yard on Highmont again on Saturday morning. It had been two weeks since their last meeting. Bridgey and Eileen were never mentioned.

A few days before, on Tuesday evening, Patrick and Kathleen had been able to see Michael in the hospital. All three of them had been unnecessarily anxious. Patrick and Kathleen only wanted one thing, which was to see Michael alive and well. Everything else paled by comparison. All Michael wanted was unconditional love. He got all he could handle and more. It was an hour filled with tears, hugs, laughter and a whole bunch of stories about Michael's daughters, Nora and Maura. All three felt immense relief after the meeting.

On Saturday morning, when Patrick, Jimmy and Iggy were seated around the patio table out under the tree, Jimmy asked how the visit went with Michael.

"It went perfect dad. It was like he was returned to us from the "other side". It was our old Michael, you know, clear-eyed and smiling," Patrick answered. "I mean he's pale from being inside, and too thin, but the doc said the medicine can hurt your appetite."

"Oh, dear Lord, wait 'till his grandmothers hear that. They'll be cookin' night and day," Jimmy grinned. "How did Kathleen do?"

"Lots of tears. She never took her hands off him. It's been brutal for her. A mother always sees her son as her little boy. She thought we might have lost him forever. On the way home, all she kept saying, was how he was still as sweet as before."

"Did you talk about this fuckin' priest at all?" asked Iggy.

"No, the doc told us to just keep it light. As far as I'm concerned, I don't care if we ever talk about him. I sure don't want Michael to ever know we went looking for the fucker, that's for sure. The last thing we need is him having some kind of setback," Patrick cautioned.

"I agree," said Iggy.

"Me too," added Jimmy.

"So, dad, where is he?" asked Patrick.

"St. Cecelia's Home for the Aged in West County. I called out there asking regular questions like 'does someone come in to say Mass?' and they told me that they have an in-house chaplain by the name of Father James O'Malley," Jimmy told them.

"I'm glad he's still in town," muttered Patrick, "but it's going to be hard not to go for a visit, I'll tell you that."

"So, Iggy, you've had some time to think this over. I don't blame you one bit if you've changed your mind. This is no small thing. No matter how much you plan, something can always go wrong. Trust me, I know. It's a huge risk for you," Jimmy warned.

"I agree Iggy. It's easy to say things in anger that you regret later. When you first learn about something like this, you can get so fucking mad that you can't see straight or think straight," Patrick told him.

"I appreciate that, but I want you both to know, I owe my life to Michael. He's been standing up for me, and protecting me, since we were little kids. His friendship is the reason I'm sitting here today. He's the reason the Cantrells went to get you when I was bleeding to death. He's the reason you adopted me. This is a no-brainer, believe me. I have not had one moment of doubt since we talked two weeks ago," Iggy assured them.

"Well, alright then. But remember there will never be any hard feelings if you want out," Patrick told him, in a very solemn tone, "okay?"

As Iggy nodded, he thought to himself, that even if he did back out, these two would find some way to go after the man responsible for ruining Michael's life. "To me this is like putting a rabid dog down. Nobody will shed a tear for this animal. I bet if the truth be told, there are a whole busload of his victims out there."

"I was thinking the same thing, Iggy," Jimmy agreed.

"I don't think there is any doubt about it," Patrick added.

"I wonder how we could find out?" asked Iggy.

"Let's do one thing at a time," Patrick told him, "first there is a couple of guys you need to talk to. They both have a little experience, or expertise in this kind of thing, I guess you could say. When your grandpa leaves, I'll give you their names, and how to get in touch with them," Patrick said.

"Can you trust them to be quiet?" asked Jimmy. "Are they Irish?"

"Yeah dad. I've known them both for many years."

"Alright, then, I'll be on my way. Good luck, boy. I'll be praying for you," Jimmy told Iggy, as he grabbed his walker and slowly made his way to the house.

"Why did you send Grandpa off?" Iggy asked.

"The less each person knows the better Iggy. Anyway, the first guy I want you to talk to is our 'special' business agent down at the hall. Do you know Billy Boyle?" asked Patrick.

"I've heard the name but I've never met him or seen him at a union meeting."

"He's not that kind of business agent. He's in charge of special projects. His father was named Martin, and he was a close friend of Brian Reilly, our old business manager. Brian and Martin were friends in the old country. They got into some kind of trouble over there and decided to come to America. Martin helped Brian build the pipe fitters union to what it is today."

"Is Martin that old-timer whose nickname was Boom Boom?" asked Iggy.

"That's the one. He got the name because after he spoke to a scab contractor who refused to use union fitters, his job sites coincidentally blew up at night," Patrick grinned.

"Gotcha," Iggy grinned back, "who is the other guy you want me to see?"

"The other guy is Sean Doherty. He's a fitter. I've worked with him quite a bit. He's a good welder. His father was Fat Bob Doherty, who was a business agent for the Brewery Workers Union here in town. He probably weighed three hundred and fifty pounds. Good guy, and a lot of fun. Anyway, his boy Sean was in special ops in Viet Nam. He was one of these guys they would drop behind enemy lines in the jungle at night for search and destroy missions. They would live off the land and were never to use their pistol except in case of emergency. He was a decorated war hero, but it took him a while when he got back to, you know, calm down a little.

"One night after he got back, three assholes in a bar picked a fight with him, and he damn near killed two of them. He did a couple years in the pen in Jeff City, and when he got out, the brewery wouldn't take him back with the felony and all. I knew Fat Bob from grade school at St James, and he asked me to get Sean on as a fitter. He's a nice guy, but quiet. Doesn't talk much."

"Alright, so when do I meet these two?" asked Iggy.

"First, Iggy, remember that they have no idea what we're up to, and you need to keep it that way. Believe me, they don't want to know. I'll tell them what you need, they will give you the info, and you go on your way. If you ever see either one again, just walk on by like you never met. Okay?" Patrick asked.

"No problem," Iggy answered as he stood up to leave.

"Alright, I'll call you in a couple days," Patrick said as he walked him to the gate.

After Iggy left, Patrick went back in the house to find Jimmy drinking a beer at the kitchen table. "I thought you would be gone by now. Nine a.m. is kind of early for Budweiser, isn't it?" Patrick chided.

"It's nine in the evening in Ireland, boy. I'm still on Dublin time where drinking is concerned. Anyway, a weary traveler needs nourishment."

"How can you be weary at nine a.m.?"

"The weariness piles up, boy. It's not the time of day anymore, it's the years."

"Oh, I see."

"Look Patrick, Kathleen just left and I want to talk while we have a moment."

"What is it dad?" Patrick asked as he poured a cup of coffee and sat down.

"We have to be very careful with this. There may be a weak moment or two in bed at night when you will want to tell Kathleen. You must be a hundred per-cent tight-lipped on this. If you let something slip to one person, it could mean prison for all of us. You especially need to remember who your in-laws are. There are probably a couple dozen Fitzgeralds and Finnegans who are cops by now. I know they're family but a cop is a cop. When this is done, we don't want to wake up the next morning and see ten cops standing on the front porch," Jimmy told him in a quiet, earnest voice.

"I know dad. I've thought of that too."

"A long time ago when you were a little guy, the cops would be standing on the porch asking your mom loads of 'fookin' questions, about where I was and when I got home, or who were my friends. She could always answer honestly that she didn't know a thing, because she didn't. Cops are damn good at spotting a lie. They're tricky. All she had to do was tell the truth, because she didn't know anything."

"That's true," answered Patrick.

"Anyway, you're doing the right thing not telling me who Iggy is going to talk to. It's also smart not to tell Iggy how we know where this fooker is. The less everyone knows, the harder it is for the cops to put a story together. The last thing, is that when the three of us are around the family, there can be no whispering to each other. If this gets in the papers, there will be a ton of loose talk and guessing, about who did it. We don't want anyone to think they saw us plotting secretively, you know?"

"That's a good point, dad."

"They might wonder, but they'll never know. They won't ask either, because really, they won't want to know. The cops might dig around and find out that Michael and this priest had a history of some kind. They might think they have motive, but like we were saying before, there's probably a busload of families with the same motive."

"I agree. You're a little smarter than you look."

"Don't be a smartass boy," Jimmy told him as he finished his beer, grabbed the walker and got up to leave.

Patrick let Billy Boyle know that Iggy was coming by for advice, and that he could be trusted. Billy knew Iggy had been elected sergeant-at-arms recently, which meant he has to keep order at the meetings. Iggy had a reputation at the hall for being fearless both on and off the job. Whether he was tossing a drunk out of the hall or swinging in a boson's chair a hundred feet off the ground, Iggy never backed away. Billy Boyle respected a man like that, because he had the same reputation.

Billy was sixty-five years old now and kind of a relic from a bygone era. When Brian Reilly was building the union, he needed men like Billy, and his father Martin, to take care of the dirty work that needed to be done and keep their mouths shut. Eventually, Brian made Billy a 'special' business agent, who didn't need to be elected. Brian thought so much of him, that before he died, he made sure Billy could stay on the payroll as long as he wanted.

Billy had few day-to-day responsibilities any more, but he still rolled his three hundred pounds out of his black Cadillac at the union hall every morning. He never married, and really had nowhere else to go. Billy had a red, pock-marked face and a large purple nose. Both looked like they could explode at any minute because of his starched white collar and tie, straining at what used to be a neck. After visiting his office, others joked that it seemed he had his water glass full of Bushmill's surgically attached to his hand.

Iggy saw Billy waiting for him on the bench where they were to meet, because Billy was always afraid somebody would put a bug in his office. "Thanks for seeing me Mr. Boyle," Iggy said respectfully, with his hand outstretched.

"That's quite alright young man. Any son of Patrick O'Toole is always welcome. By the way, is your crabby old Grandpa Jimmy still kicking?" he smiled.

"He's a little slower these days, but sharp as a tack," Iggy smiled back.

"That was one little mick you didn't want to fuck with back in the day," Billy added, while sipping from his water glass.

"That's what I hear," Iggy answered.

"Did they ever find that shit-bum brother of yours? The whole world at his feet, scholarship to Notre Dame, and he pisses it away."

"They did. He had some problems, that's for sure," Iggy said, biting his tongue.

"Well, what can I do for you?"

Iggy started to tell Billy that he needed advice on how to get into a large hospital type of facility, without being noticed, to perform a small task which would take about ten minutes. He told him that the task might be a little dirty, but he needed to get out and drive off unnoticed. Iggy also told Billy he had been to the facility the day before, acting like he was visiting a patient. For the next fifteen minutes, Billy asked Iggy a variety of questions, trying to get a mental picture of the setting.

Iggy told him how the facility sat a hundred yards from a very busy road, and that there was a long drive through the wooded grounds, up to the front door. He described how there was a circle drive to drop passengers, and a parking area to the left a few hundred yards away. Iggy told him how there were two long wings off the main building, and that there were a few doctor and chaplain parking spots on each side of the circle drive. He told him the employee parking was off to the right.

Without mentioning the name of the facility, Iggy described the busy entry foyer, with people moving in all directions, and the information desk. He described how the place was squeaky clean, with shiny terrazzo floors, high ceilings and bright fluorescent lights. He told Billy he knew exactly where he was going, and how long it would take to get in and out.

Billy began to go over the particulars, like a banker going over a loan application, asking more questions and delivering observations. Calmly and professionally, he took a step by step approach to instruct Iggy on what he needed to do.

"First things first Iggy. If that's a permanent limp it has to go on the big day, one way or another. It's like a spotlight on you."

"My hip freezes up sometimes. It's an old football injury. I can get a shot or something," Iggy answered.

"Well don't forget. Nobody misses a limp," added Billy.

"Got it."

"The busy streets are to your advantage. Easy to blend in when you leave. The long drive on the wooded grounds is not good because you stick out and there is only one lane in and one out. If its blocked you're screwed. It's none of my business what you are up to, but using a gun indoors is no good. The sound can wake the dead. You want to wear a workman's uniform in grey or brown. You will be seen, but you won't be noticed.

"Don't be carrying flowers or a wrapped present because every woman in the building will be staring at you. If you are going to a patient room, call that morning to make sure they haven't moved who you are going to visit. If you get there and you find out they've moved him, turn around and go home. Every person you ask for a room number will remember you.

"Driving a van is better than a truck because it's harder to see the driver's face. If you are in a no parking zone, leave the flashers on so security knows you are coming back right away. A car is okay but it's more likely to attract some gung-ho security guard's attention, because they figure it's a patient visitor. Don't park where you can be blocked in. Don't leave the keys in the ignition so some asshole can steal it.

"If you're going in a patient room, take a small wedge so you can block the door. A place like that won't have locks on the door. By the way wear sunglasses so nobody can see that goofy eye of yours. Wear soft sole shoes so you don't make noise on the terrazzo, and don't wear bright orange socks or some shit like that. No jewelry. Women pay attention to that stuff. Walk at a regular pace, with no eye contact and no smiling."

Iggy thanked Billy for his time, shook his hand and walked away, grinning at the thought that he probably just got a crash course on a list of details that it took Billy a lifetime to collect. He would tell Patrick later that it was like listening to a surgeon describe an operation.

A couple days later, Patrick called and said he set up a meet with Sean Doherty for the next day. He was working at the power plant at Washington University. Sean said they could talk on a bench on the north side of the quadrangle at lunchtime.

When Iggy approached Sean, he was munching a sandwich and staring into space. He looked like a coal miner, covered in black soot from head to toe. Sean was trim, with "popeye" forearms, a flat top haircut and a "fu man chu" mustache. He looked like the last guy on campus that you should pick a fight with. Iggy stuck out his hand

and asked, "Are you Sean?"

"I am. You must be Iggy. Fellow fitter huh? You don't want my filthy mitts touching you," he smiled. "Sit. We're crawling around in these fucking tunnels underneath this place. It's a mess." Sean took a beer out of his cooler, and offered Iggy one, but he declined. Then he took a cigarette out of his shirt pocket, lit it and inhaled deeply. "So. To the point. Patrick says you need a little professional advice. You got twenty minutes. What's up?"

Iggy went through a general description of the facility, and how he was going to a particular patient's room, and that the patient would be seated. Iggy knew this, because Jimmy had gone to the home, acting like he was going to visit O'Malley, to get his room number. He also found out he was confined to a wheel chair in his room most of the day, due to a mild stroke a few months back. That was a big break, since Iggy wouldn't have to lure him to a private spot. He told Sean that he had gotten great advice already on getting in and out without being noticed. "Sean, this is hard to ask, but Patrick said you were in special ops in Viet Nam. He said you had some specialized training that you might be able to share. I was never in the military."

"I see," said Sean as he opened his second beer, and flipped his cigarette on the ground. "Say no more. My guess is that you want to quickly dispose of this individual with the least possible chance of getting caught. Well unfortunately, you came to the right place. I'd rather be an expert at something like horticulture or geology, but things didn't go that way. You should see my lawn and landscaping though, it's beautiful."

"I'm sorry. If you would rather not, I understand," Iggy told him quietly.

"No, it's okay. It doesn't bother me much anymore...talking about that stuff...thinking about it...I owe Patrick big time. When I got out of jail, I couldn't buy a job, and he took care of me. No lecture. No bullshit. Just show up and work. Because of this job, I got a beautiful wife, two kids and a nice house. Things are good," Sean told him. Then he abruptly stopped talking, downed his beer, and stared ahead for a minute, while lighting another cigarette.

Iggy was starting to feel a little uncomfortable. He didn't know this man at all, and here he was asking him for tips on killing someone. He was thinking of leaving when Sean cleared his throat, turned and looked right at Iggy. "This must be awfully important to Patrick. He thinks the world of you. He said I could trust you. I only hope you thought about what you're doing. This is no small thing. It can mess with your head if you're not prepared for it."

When Iggy nodded, Sean began to talk in the same business-like tone that Billy Boyle had used, while staring ahead. "You said you had a plan to get in unnoticed. Have a wedge or something to keep the door to the room closed so no one can walk in and surprise you. Guns are out of course. Even with a silencer, you never know if the bullet will pass through the target and then go through a wall.

"Don't touch the door when you enter. You can push it with your elbow or hip because hospitals doors don't have handles. Strangulation takes too long and it can be too loud if they start kicking and knocking shit over. You have to use a knife. Use a new thin, five-inch fillet knife. Some people can't handle killing with a knife because it's too up close and personal, but it's the only way if you want to make it out clean. You have to stand behind the target. You said he would be seated.

"Take your take your left arm and wrap it around his head at eye level and pull the head back hard. At the same time, you make one pass across his throat from ear to ear with the knife. If you don't have the left arm high enough you'll cut your own arm. Do it really quick so he can't get his hands in the way. You must pull the knife hard back towards yourself. If you don't you may not get the arteries and the son-of-a-bitch will get up and start fighting. Then you're fucked. Especially if he can still yell. Take both arms away immediately, otherwise he will grab his throat and then grab you with bloody hands. He'll be limp in ten seconds and bleed out completely in sixty. Watch that he doesn't fall out of the chair and make a bunch of noise. If you need to, grab the hair on the back of his head. There won't be blood there.

"There's so much blood that it can run under the door in a couple minutes because a hospital won't have carpet. Ideally, do it as far from the door as possible. You're going to have blood on the knife hand and right arm or shirt sleeve. Ideally, you put on two loose fitting rubber gloves that extend to the elbow before cutting him so they catch any blood, and you can get them off quickly.

"Bring a bag and take everything with you...the knife, the gloves, any prop you brought in. Don't forget the wedge. If you don't think you're going to have time to put gloves on, have a long sleeve shirt you can take off and put in the bag. You can bring a clean matching shirt with you. Now, very important, don't step in the blood. If you do you're fucked. Have a cloth in your back pocket to use to open the door to get out. Don't drop it.

"If you get there and he's not in the room, just leave and come back another day. You start asking where he is, and the whole place will know you're there. If he's in bed, just get close, pull the knife quickly and slice him hard with a backhand motion from your left to right.

"When you leave the room, walk slowly with your chin up. Don't make eye contact, but don't look away from anyone. If I were you, I would drive about five minutes, pull over, strip and change clothes. You'll have blood on you somewhere so change everything, even shoes, socks and underwear. Put all the clothes in the bag. Then I would have another place down the road five minutes, already picked out, to dump the bag. Don't dump where you stop to change. You'll be there too long and someone may start watching.

"Getting rid of that bag is the key to not getting caught at that point. Quicker the better in case you get pulled over or get in an accident. This is when you are most at risk. Don't use a dumpster behind a building where some guy smoking will see you. Use a dumpster in plain view in a busy lot. Nobody will notice you that way. I wouldn't drive on empty or country roads. You'll stick out like a sore thumb. Stay in heavy traffic. That should do it."

"I can't thank you enough, Sean. I wish we could have met under different circumstances," Iggy told him quietly.

"We still haven't met," Sean shot back as he stood, lit a cigarette, picked up his cooler and started to walk away. Turning back to Iggy he said, "One more thing. You walked up today with a slight limp. No matter what it takes, on the big day that has to go."

Iggy sat there, trying to breathe normally again. He could hardly believe what he had just been told in the last ten minutes. Sean sounded almost robotic, he thought. Man, oh, man. That is one guy you don't want mad at you. Iggy mused. As he made the long walk back to his car, Iggy mused how remarkable it was that Patrick and Billy, and now Patrick and Sean, all trusted each other without question. There seemed to be no doubt about their loyalty to each other. Now they were trusting him.

CHAPTER THIRTY-NINE

Patrick and Iggy had talked at great length about not involving anyone unless it was absolutely necessary, and they could be trusted completely. But he was going to need help with the next step. The premise he was going to use to enter the facility, was to act as a package delivery driver. So, the first thing on the agenda was getting a plain white van.

They couldn't rent anything because that would require paperwork and ID. They just needed the van for a half day, but they also didn't want to borrow the vehicle from a friend and get them involved in this without their permission.

Sitting at a breakfast counter one Saturday morning in late June, a smile crept across Iggy's face as the perfect solution came to him. Who could get use of a vehicle without strings attached, put plates on it, and be trusted to keep their mouths shut, no matter what the police threw at them? Who else but his old neighbors, Eddie and Mitch Cantrell. As the saying goes, those two wouldn't say shit if they had a mouth full of it.

The last time he saw them was a few years back when he drove by his old house. The two of them had been seated on their thrones on their front porch, surveying the ever-present piles of used auto parts in the front yard. He decided to head over to their house right after breakfast. The cousins were sitting in exactly the same places that they were three years before. It was nine a.m. and both of them were already drinking beer and smoking their ever-present cigarettes. They were both smiling from ear-to-ear as he walked up.

"Well, well, look what the river washed up!" Mitch called out.

"He must want money, he looks serious," added Eddie.

'No, just couldn't stay away from my two favorite people in the whole world," Iggy grinned.

"Whoa, hold it right there. He does want money!" chided Mitch.

Two of Ferguson's most nefarious characters were leaning back in their old recliners, like they didn't have a care in the world, thought Iggy. Even with their long greasy hair, dirty hands and ripped jeans, Iggy had nothing but warm feelings for the two men who had protected him as a little guy. They had undoubtedly saved his life on that horrible morning fifteen years ago.

"I'm missing my new Cadillac and the police told me to check with the Cantrells," Iggy smiled, as he poked fun at them.

"You've come to the right place, sir. Come on in. If we can't find your car we sure as hell can find one just like it!" Eddie proclaimed proudly. Iggy started up the steps and walked inside with the two of them asking him questions at the same time. The interior looked like it hadn't been vacuumed or dusted since their grandma died five years before. There were beer cans and dirty dishes everywhere.

"Good to see you guys!" Iggy told them.

"Same here little buddy!" added Mitch.

"To what do we owe this pleasure," asked Eddie.

The three of them reminisced for a while at the kitchen table before Iggy told them why he was there. He told them he needed a white panel van without side or rear windows, for a day. He also told them it had to have working plates that weren't out of date. Whereas most people would be skeptical of such a request, and ask a dozen questions, the Cantrell's were just the opposite. They had been taking requests for auto parts from people for years, and never asked a client a single question. Likewise, their clients knew not to ask any questions of their own.

For your average working stiff, the thought of getting caught doing something illegal and going to jail scared them to death. For guys like the Cantrell cousins, skirting the law was a fun adventure. Cloak and dagger schemes provided them with thrills and excitement that made life interesting.

When Iggy was finished, Eddie and Mitch looked at each other and smiled.

"We just happen to have what you're looking for in the barn at the farm," said Mitch.

"It's been missing for a year, so nobody is looking for it, if you know what I mean," added Eddie smiling.

"Do you think I could rent it for a day?" asked Iggy.

"C'mon little buddy. No way we would charge you!" Mitch told him.

"Yeah! You're like the little brother we never wanted," laughed Eddie.

"Well thanks, I think," laughed Iggy. "Is it clean enough not to draw attention, and good tires?"

"Oh yeah," the two chimed in unison.

"The last request is that it absolutely, positively, has to start every time, and run like a top. This is a situation where calling Triple A is not going to be an option, if you know what I mean. If it won't start or it quits running, I'm fucked big time."

"No problem Iggy. We'll go over it with a fine tooth comb," Eddie laughed.

"If you want, we could follow you just in case?" added Mitch.

"No, no. This is a one man show," Iggy answered.

"Give us a week or so, okay?"

"Absolutely. I don't want you rushing," Iggy told them. "Listen I really appreciate this you guys."

After they walked and talked down memory lane for a few more minutes, they shook hands, and Iggy went on his way. He laughed to himself how eager they were to help even though they hadn't seen each other for three years. There was something about boyhood friends that bonded you in a different way than men you met as an adult, he mused. Boyhood friends knew where you came from, what mistakes you made, and were always happy to see you. The Cantrells probably also felt some affinity for Iggy, since they too had sort of raised themselves.

The farm was a relatively new development. They didn't know

until their grandma passed away that she owned twenty acres near De Soto, about a hundred miles south of St. Louis. The lawyer said she left it to them, free and clear. Mitch and Eddie had immediately seen the value in having a place like this to hide "misplaced" vehicles until a new owner could be found. Also, the barn meant they didn't have to rent garage space when they needed to dismantle one of their new acquisitions.

The two of them had been in and out of juvenile hall and then the county jail any number of times, for a variety of petty crimes, but nothing too big yet. The last thing Iggy needed to tell these two would be to keep their mouths shut.

True to their word, the Cantrells called a week later and said the van was ready. They said it had a new battery, tires, points, plugs and starter. They told him the plates were legit, registered to them, so he didn't have to worry about being pulled over. They used the van to move things like fenders and bumpers, that were large, and needed to be out of sight.

Iggy had settled on a Wednesday in mid-July for the big day. He didn't want the Cantrells nosy neighbors watching him changing vehicles, so he asked them if they could leave the van by eight in the morning, at Northwest Plaza near post F-12. He told them since it was such a busy lot, he wouldn't be noticed switching vehicles. Northwest Plaza was a huge shopping center, along Lindbergh Blvd. on the way from Iggy's apartment to St. Cecelia. It was only ten minutes down I-70 from the Cantrell's place in Ferguson. He told them he would call later that afternoon after he returned the van to the parking lot, so they could pick it up.

Iggy made the trip to St. Cecelia's a few times to get a feel for the distance and traffic. He went to Sears at Northwest Plaza and bought two dark brown workman's long sleeve shirts, a pair of pants and a hat that resembled a UPS uniform. In addition, he purchased a low-rise pair of work shoes with soft soles, a pair of sunglasses, a fillet knife and a big loose-fitting pair of rubber gloves. Back at home, he washed the clothing several times to make it look well-worn and scuffed the new shoes.

For some reason, he wasn't nervous as the day got closer. Like they decided, Jimmy and Patrick did not know what day he was going to St. Cecelia's. Iggy planned to call in sick Wednesday but work the rest of the week. Then, two nights before the big day, it hit him what he was about to do, and he was up and down all night. Tuesday at work he looked like hell, which would help his claim of being sick on Wednesday.

Tuesday night he couldn't even lay down, so he just paced, watched television and played solitaire. He tried to focus on what this animal, O'Malley, had done to ruin Michael's life. Many times, over the last month, he had wished that the fucker's death was going to take longer and be more painful.

When he got anxious thinking about what he was going to do, he reminded himself that if he backed out, either Patrick or Jimmy would do it. Whether Jimmy cared about going to jail or not, he would definitely get caught shuffling in the walker. That left Patrick, and he couldn't stomach the thought of his dad possibly going to jail. He knew he could do it, and that he was the right choice, but it was still a really long night.

Throughout the night Iggy had make-believe conversations with Michael. He asked him why he didn't tell someone back then. He told him how sorry he was that he had to bear this horror alone. He assured Michael that even though he was shaky and thin now, he would soon be his old self, and that it was time to let someone take care of him for a change. We can't act like this didn't happen, or ask for a do-over, like when we were kids Michael, but we can send this fucking animal to hell where he belongs.

Wednesday morning, Iggy took his usual shower but didn't use after shave, like Billy told him, so there would be no tell-tale signs of him coming or going. He didn't feel like it, but he ate a decent breakfast of toast and cereal, like Sean suggested so he wouldn't get light headed.

Iggy wasn't as immersed in Catholicism as the rest of the O'Tooles because of his first twelve years with his dad. They had never gone to Mass, and he only went regularly after he was adopted. He did have twelve solid years of Catholic school under his belt, though, so he felt Catholic even if he only went to Mass now for weddings and funerals. He did have daily conversations with God in the shower, and this morning was no different.

"Dear Lord, I don't know how you let the devil take the form of a priest, but it has surely screwed up my family, and probably many other families as well. I know there are reasons for everything, but this one is hard to take. It's like the nuns and priests fed us a huge line of crap all those years, and now it's hard to know what to believe. I'm about to kill someone, but I do not believe it's murder. This animal got under your radar somehow, and now he's going to get exactly what he deserves.

"How could you let my brother Michael, one of your finest creations, become a victim of this guy? How could anyone take this loving, caring and cheerful boy and trash his soul? He almost died, Lord! Michael was like an eagle soaring over the rest of us, and this animal coaxed him out of the sky, ripped his wings off and left him to flounder.

"Dear Lord, the worst part is that this evil thing posed as one of your holy men. We were taught these men lived in a realm higher than mere humans. Michael was a wide-eyed innocent, following what he thought YOU were telling him to do, through a man YOU anointed. This evil thing grabbed a sensitive, innocent child, lied to him, used him, and pitched him over a cliff. Some evil thing did this to my brother Michael, and today, that evil thing is going to die. Amen."

After getting out of the shower, Iggy got dressed in his new clothes, put the cloth in his right rear pants pocket, the wedge in his right front shirt pocket, sunglasses in his left front shirt pocket and wallet in his left rear pants pocket. The knife, extra shirt and gloves were put in a large brown shopping bag that he folded neatly to look like a package he could put under his arm. Finally, he added a clipboard with a piece of paper attached like an invoice to help him look the part. Then he sat down to watch the clock.

Iggy left his apartment in Florissant at 7:30 and made his way to Lindbergh, where he headed south towards Northwest Plaza. Because it was rush hour he got there just after eight and made his way towards the F-12 post. Eddie and Mitch had done their part, so after he got in, he found the key in the ashtray. He drove the van south on Lindbergh to Manchester Rd. and headed east about five minutes to his destination at St. Cecelia's. It was almost 8:45.

As Iggy drove slowly down the entry drive, he saw the circle drive was busy with visitors and employees being dropped off at the main entrance, just like when he made the trial runs. He rolled past the entrance to the left and stopped just shy of the handicap and doctor spaces that were perpendicular to the building and put his flashers on. He left the driver's door unlocked, put the key in his right front pants pocket, grabbed the package and clipboard and stepped out. With his hat and sunglasses, he concealed his personal features.

Walking at an even pace, he went in the main entrance and headed left down the west wing. An older female volunteer was on the phone at the main desk, with two ladies waiting for her to finish. No one seemed to notice him as he continued down a hundred feet or so to Room 128 on his right, where Jimmy told him O'Malley now lived. The nameplate next to the door said *Father James O'Malley, Chaplain*.

Without knocking, Iggy pushed the door open with his hip and peered inside. Immediately on the right was a hospital type bed, then an open space before the wall with the window. In front of the window, O'Malley was seated in his wheel chair, looking at the television mounted on the wall on the left. "Father O'Malley?" Iggy asked.

"That's me young man," he answered.

"I've got a package for you," Iggy told him nonchalantly. As he let the door close, He acted like he dropped his pen and put the wedge under the door. "I'll need you to sign," Iggy added, as he walked towards O'Malley and casually dropped the "package" on the bed to his right out of O'Malley's reach.

"Sure, sure," O'Malley told him, smiling. "Does it say who it's from?"

"I'll look," Iggy told him.

As he handed the clipboard to O'Malley, he mentioned what a nice view he had, and moved behind the chair, as though he was gazing outside. While O'Malley was clicking the pen that wouldn't write, and squinting at the fake invoice, Iggy pulled the gloves and knife from the "package". "It says the package is from Michael O'Toole," Iggy said as he deftly reached from behind the old man with his left hand to grab the clipboard and pen, tossing both on the bed to his left.

"Michael O'Toole?" O'Malley murmured quietly.

Iggy wasted no time. He quickly wrapped his left arm around O'Malley's head and pulled it back, while reaching around front with his right hand at the same time to slice his exposed throat. Immediately Iggy pulled both arms away and watched as O'Malley grabbed for his throat with both hands. From behind, Iggy heard O'Malley make some sucking noises trying to breathe, right before he slumped forward. It was over in seconds, just like Sean said.

Once Iggy was sure that he wasn't going to fall out of the chair, he wiped the knife on O'Malley's shirt, then dropped it in the bag on the bed, followed by the gloves. He inspected the arms of the shirt he had on, and determined they were clean, so he put the extra shirt back in the bag. Gently he rolled the bag up again and tucked it under his left arm. After picking up the clipboard and pen, Iggy stepped around the chair and stared at what he viewed as nothing more than a dead animal.

"Burn in hell, motherfucker," Iggy whispered, to the lifeless body of the former Father James O'Malley. Blood was starting to drip on the floor, so Iggy yanked the bedspread off the bed and let it drop to the floor as a makeshift dam. Quickly he turned, walked to the door, listened for a moment, put the wedge back in his shirt pocket and pulled the cloth from his pants pocket to open the door.

He pulled the door open a couple inches, looked out and then stepped into the busy hallway. Casually he walked out the front door and turned right towards the van. It didn't seem like anyone had even noticed him. He opened the van, started it and made a left down the long driveway towards Manchester Rd. Looking at the clock, Iggy noticed he had only been on the grounds fifteen minutes. He had been operating in an almost robotic mode and hadn't even had time to even feel nervous. Suddenly he felt his breathing and his pulse start to speed up as the adrenaline finally kicked in. Looking in his rearview mirror, he saw no signs of excitement, just routine coming and going.

After turning on Lindbergh, he headed to the busy Schnuck's Grocery lot at Clayton Rd. where he parked and stripped like Sean had told him. After putting on a pair of shorts, tee shirt and tennis shoes, Iggy drove down Lindbergh again towards Northwest Plaza. Little by little, he felt his pulse and breathing slow down. He had previously picked out a dumpster that was in plain view at a gas station, and pulled in to throw away his bag. He drove back to Northwest Plaza, parked the van near F-12, and put the key in the ash tray. It was 9:45. He had been gone less than an hour and forty-five minutes.

Iggy called the Cantrells from a pay phone, drove home, and

collapsed into bed. He had only slept a couple of hours over the last two nights, so he fell asleep almost immediately. He didn't wake up until almost ten that night. After a shower, and making his lunch, he went back to sleep until the alarm went off at five a.m. It felt just like any other Thursday morning as he pulled on to the construction site just before eight a.m.

Part XI

Further Up the Road

CHAPTER FORTY

Nothing showed up on television Wednesday night about the killing. It was Thursday morning before the newspaper mentioned the murder.

St. Cecelia's surely did not want the publicity, and the police would always prefer to do their preliminary investigating without scrutiny from the press and television cameras. They initially thought the killer might be someone working or living in the facility and put the place on lockdown until they completed a thorough search and interviewed a number of residents and employees.

The head administrator of St Cecelia's called the archdiocese right away, because O'Malley was technically still under their supervision, and they would be responsible to notify next of kin. The detectives found it very odd though, when the auxiliary bishop from the archdiocese showed up, and seemed more concerned about keeping the murder out of the press, than finding out who did it and why. Those are the questions the victim's relatives and friends always ask first.

The murder of a priest is front page news, and the police knew it was just a matter of time until someone leaked the story, so they wanted to have some answers ready when the time came. All day Wednesday they searched the facility and grounds, and interviewed as many people as possible, but they were coming up empty. The St. Louis Post-Dispatch hit the streets at five a.m. Thursday morning with a headline halfway down the front page that read, *Local Priest Found Murdered in Nursing Home.* Sure enough, by eight o'clock Thursday morning, the trucks from the local television stations were parked in front of the main entrance.

Billy Boyle arrived every morning at the pipe fitters complex at seven a.m. The security guards at the entrance were always retired city cops, usually Irish, who always smiled when they saw the black Caddy pull up. They made their living on opposite sides of the legal line, but their heritage and age gave them a feeling of comradery. The smiles were also a result of Billy dropping off a cold twelve pack on hot days or a fifth of Bushmills on chilly days at the guard shack.

Billy went inside his office that Thursday, set out his coffee, sandwich and newspaper as always, when he spied the headline. He sat down, picked up the paper with both hands, and began to read how the disabled chaplain of St. Cecelia's Home for the Aged, was found in his room at one p.m. on Wednesday, after he didn't show up for lunch. It went on to say how the police had questioned the staff and some residents but had no suspects and no clues.

A crooked grin made its way across Billy's plump, ruddy face as he remembered his conversation with Iggy weeks before about getting in and out of just such a place. Quietly, he mumbled to himself, "Well I'll be goddam. A priest. What the fuck did this character do to piss off the O'Tooles? Well, if you followed your orders, they shouldn't find you, Iggy my boy."

At just about the same time, Sean Doherty opened his paper at his favorite Denny's Restaurant where he stopped every morning before work. After ordering, the same headline caught his eye. He brought the paper closer to his face and began reading about the murder until finally under his breath he said, "Sonofabitch, he did it." As Sean read further, he saw that the police had not released the method of killing. He thought to himself that they must not want to freak the whole city out. A sliced throat is messy, and it's usually planned and personal.

Two days later, on Saturday morning, after saying the rosary and going to Mass, Bridgey, Eileen and four other old ladies were sitting around a table at the coffee shop on Tamm Avenue, down the street from St. James the Greater.

"Good Lord, did you hear about the priest getting murdered out at St. Cecelia's Home!" exclaimed Maeve O'Connor in between sips of tea.

"What a horrible thing to do! To a man of God, no less!" added Rosie Walsh.

"I hope they find the animal, and hang him," blurted Kate Mullanphy, while crossing herself.

"Jesus, Mary and Joseph, what's the world coming to?" asked Maggie Joye.

"I surely don't know," said Bridgey, while shaking her head and spooning sugar.

"Nor do I," agreed Eileen, "nor do I."

Bridgey and Eileen didn't even look at each other. They had never spoken of the matter since Bridgey asked Eileen for the whereabouts of O'Malley, and they never would. Neither would shed a tear for the deceased priest, nor feel any guilt about their part in his demise. They had made their peace with it. Deep down they knew what would happen to O'Malley, whether they helped or not.

Both ladies knew how the Irish men in their lives had persevered for generations, to feed and protect their families. They noticed how the men would be talking quietly in a corner until a woman entered the room, then go silent. In the coming weeks, there might be an explosion at a job site, or an Italian gangster would be arrested, or a Polish candidate might get picked up for solicitation a week before an election.

The women were protected, because they could usually claim ignorance. But they learned from watching their mothers and aunts that sometimes it was necessary for them to do more than look the other way. Hundreds of years under British rule in Ireland, and decades of second-class citizenship in America taught all of them some extremely important lessons. Survival depended on everyone sticking together, and sometimes survival is messy.

That same Saturday morning, there was another discussion of the priest's murder going on in a guard shack at McDonnell-Douglas Aerospace. Bobby and Tommy Callahan were brothers and both were recently retired after thirty years as St. Louis City police officers. Bobby was coming on at eight a.m. to take over for Tommy, who worked the midnight shift. The brothers, now in their fifties, were identical twins, and had been Golden Gloves boxers in their youth. They were broad-shouldered, square-jawed, red heads back then. Now they were a little stooped, with gray hair and beet red faces. They were both confirmed bachelors, who still spoke with a heavy brogue, even after all these many years.

During their police careers, they had been asked on more than a few occasions to 'tune-up' uncooperative suspects, because of their "pugilistic proficiency", as their lieutenant once described it. A 'tune-up' was when a cop punched a prisoner or suspect in a part of the body that wouldn't show easily. The suspect may also have been asked to hold a magazine or phone book on his head before getting whacked with a night stick. The idea was to get the prisoner to become more cooperative, or to help him remember some forgotten details, or just to follow the law in the future.

Tune-ups were performed in the back of paddy wagons or in basement holding cells to eliminate unnecessary interference. They proved to be an effective deterrent to crime, by helping prisoners decide to either reform or move from St. Louis altogether.

"Did you read the story about that dead priest Bobby?" Tommy asked.

"I did indeed. And didn't we tune-up that prick a few years ago?" Bobby asked.

"Indeed, we did. At the request of our esteemed captain, Brendan Finnegan, if memory serves," Tommy answered.

"That's right. Captain Finnegan had the 'fooker' locked in a paddy wagon in the alley behind the precinct house, I believe," said Bobby.

"And wasn't Captain Finnegan very clear, that a regular tune-up wouldn't be quite enough for the likes of Mr. O'Malley?" asked Tommy.

"Clear as a bell. I see you remember he told us not to call him 'Father' as well," agreed Bobby.

"No way you could refer to a man who fondled little boys, 'Father' to be sure. I remember enjoying that tune-up far more than any other," Tommy recalled.

"I would have to agree. I did too," added Bobby.

"Didn't we dump the 'fooker' in the alley behind the Bishop's residence?" asked Tommy.

"That's correct. Quite a sight he was by then. The Captain called it an early Christmas present for the Bishop," grinned Bobby.

The brothers, who fancied themselves lace curtain Irish, liked to speak with clarity, and were always dressed in neatly pressed uniforms. Usually, only one brother would do the tune-up. He would take great care to ceremoniously hand the other brother his hat, belt, shirt and undershirt beforehand, while the perpetrator watched. He would then tell the individual that they did this so as not to get his blood on their clothing. Oftentimes, this alone was enough to get the desired information from the individual.

On the night in question concerning O'Malley, the esteemed Captain Brendan Finnegan gave a direct order, for both Callahan's to take turns with the tune-up, and to take their time. Captain Finnegan was the older brother of Kathleen O'Toole, which made him Michael's uncle. At the time, he knew nothing about Michael's history with O'Malley.

"I would bet the farm that Mr. O'Malley fondled the wrong little boy, and now that little boy is all grown up," Tommy mused.

"Indeed, Tommy. Mr. O'Malley won't be fondling little boys anymore, to be sure," agreed Bobby.

"I'd wager he's fondling the devil's cock, as we speak," added Tommy.

"Let's hope he has the devil's cock up his arse," said Bobby.

"His will be done," Tommy said as he bowed his head slightly.

"Amen, my brother," Bobby said, as he bowed his head as well.

"Will you be coming to our sister Mary's house this weekend?" asked Tommy.

"Indeed. I wouldn't miss one of Mary's home cooked meals for the world," answered Bobby.

Cops were more apt to view priests as human than the average Catholic, because they were the ones who found them in a variety of indelicate situations. In cities like St. Louis, with a high percentage of Irish Catholics in the population, Irish Catholic cops would take the Irish Catholic priest to the Irish Catholic Captain, who took him to the Irish Catholic Bishop, who promised to "take care of the situation".

No one in this chain of command was going to let newspapers, and their Protestant owners, use the opportunity to smear their beloved Catholic Church. If a priest was caught with his pants down, or drunk and disorderly, there was no need for the entire world to know. If the Bishop said he would take care of the problem, that's all they needed to hear. After all, a Bishop would never lie.

What the Callahan brothers did not know that night was that this was the third time O'Malley had been brought to Captain Finnegan. Once, he was found with a boy in a public restroom in Jefferson County, and another time a parishioner had filed a complaint with the St Charles County Sherriff's office after his son was molested. Cops from the surrounding area brought O'Malley to Finnegan because the Catholic Diocesan offices were in his precinct, and he was known to have a personal relationship with Bishop Shaughnessy. On both occasions, he had personally delivered O'Malley to the Bishop, and had been assured both times that it would never happen again.

Since it had happened again, Captain Finnegan enlisted the help of the Callahan brothers, to send a much stronger message to the Bishop. This was a much different issue than a priest getting caught with a prostitute or being found face down in a gutter after binge drinking. Child molestation disgusted him. It was a crime he couldn't tolerate, and he assumed that the Bishop felt the same way. He expected the Bishop to make sure O'Malley was locked up somewhere away from kids, but instead he just moved the animal to a parish farther away, where he would molest more kids.

In December of 1974, the day after the Callahans pushed the unconscious and barely recognizable O'Malley out of the paddy wagon in the alley behind the Bishop's residence, Captain Brendan Finnegan made a formal face-to-face visit to Bishop Patrick Shaughnessy. He marched into the Bishop's office, in an official manner, with his hat under his left arm, wearing his formal blue uniform, complete with Captain stripes and a chest covered in medals.

As the Bishop stood to greet him with a smile and a handshake, the Captain raised his right hand as a stop sign, and then put his right forefinger over his lips in the same manner one does to make a child stop talking. The Bishop's brow furrowed, and as he put his hands on his desk and leaned forward to object to the disrespectful gestures, the Captain firmly told him with exaggerated enunciation, "SIT DOWN!"

"I beg your pardon!" the bishop replied, hardly believing his ears.

"How about this, SIT THE FUCK DOWN!" the captain replied, even more forcefully.

Seeing the Captain's fierce eyes, beet red face and clenched jaw, the Bishop realized that at this moment, his best option was to sit down. The Captain laid his hat down, put his hands on the desk, and leaned forward, getting his face within a foot of the Bishop's. Slowly and deliberately, he delivered an ultimatum to him. "If I ever see, or even hear, that this rotten cocksucker O'Malley is anywhere near my city ever again, I am going to personally put a bullet in this sick motherfucker's head! Do you understand me?"

The trembling, wide eyed Bishop started to speak when the Captain put his finger over his lips again, picked up his hat, turned on his heel in a formal manner and walked out of the office. The first of January 1975, Father James O'Malley was sent to New Mexico to the Paraclete Fathers for treatment.

CHAPTER FORTY-ONE

In the months following Fr. O'Malley's untimely demise, detectives from the St. Louis County Special Task Force took over the case from the local municipality, where the murder took place. They had taken great care to interview all the staff and residents, who were anywhere near the front entrance or O'Malley's room. They had only one small lead from the seventy-eight-year-old lady who volunteered at the front desk. Clara had seen a delivery man in a dark brown uniform like UPS, come in about the right time. He did not stop at the front desk like most delivery drivers do for directions.

She had been distracted answering the phones, and did not see him leave, but she thought he had a hitch in his gait. After questioning, the younger men realized she was speaking of a slight limp. The detectives thought this was probably their man, because UPS records showed that none of their trucks were at the nursing home at the time of the murder.

They did not think it was a deranged resident or staff member, because the murder was too quick, clean and well-planned. They reasoned instead that this was a professional murder, for revenge or perhaps to silence the priest, although neither motive seemed very plausible. The only way they could research their theory was to interview O'Malley's superiors, close friends and relatives.

They soon discovered that he had no relatives in America, and no one at the nursing home had seen him get a single visitor in the nine months he lived there. The staff said that even after his small stroke a couple months before, they never saw him get a visitor. The stroke had only affected mobility in one leg, so he had been able to resume his chaplain duties rather quickly, with the help of a wheel chair.

When the detectives approached the archdiocese about looking at his file, they were met with resistance. The spokesperson said at first that they didn't let anyone see personnel files. When the detectives said that was ridiculous, since he was dead, they were referred to the lawyer for the archdiocese. They were incredulous, since one would expect the archdiocese to bend over backward to help find the killer of one of their own. When they questioned the lawyer about this, he went into a long explanation about the Seal of Confession, and how only the Bishop could view the file.

All the avoidance and excuses made the detectives angry enough to finally get a judge to grant a search warrant for the file. The archdiocesan lawyer then had a number of restrictions put on the warrant. The file could not be removed from the bishop's residence, only the two detectives could see it, and then only with a priest present.

What the detectives read over the course of that day made their skin crawl. Father James O'Malley had been a serial child molester who was clearly protected and enabled by his boss, Bishop Patrick Shaughnessy, for twenty years. After five or six hours they returned to their car and just sat for a while, staring out the windshield without saying a word.

Detective Grundhauser, who was German Lutheran, finally said, "I can't believe what I just read. Why wasn't this guy turned over to law enforcement years ago?"

Detective Santini, who was an Italian Catholic, answered, "It's a little complicated by the fact that if the guy confessed his sins to the Bishop, he is then bound by the Seal of the Confessional, not to tell anyone what he was told. The whole idea is to offer the compassion and forgiveness of Jesus," Santini told his partner in a robotic matter, as if he was reading from a grade school catechism book.

"Are you shitting me? I mean after a dozen times, don't you think that the magic seal could be broken for Chrissake?" yelled Grundhauser. "I mean what about the safety of the kids?"

"I don't know what to say. I'm in shock," said Santini quietly, still staring straight ahead.

"The worst part is that the kids' names were redacted from the file! That robot priest they had watching us said it was to PROTECT THEM! I almost lost it on that one. Now we can't even track any of them down to see if they thought about killing this creep! I don't believe this!" Grundhauser said while shaking his head.

"This makes me embarrassed to be a Catholic. Really, it's one thing for the sick fuck to molest kids, but who could keep sending him back out there to do it again and again? Unbelievable," added Santini.

"Truthfully, I've got two boys at home, and I applaud whoever killed this fucker. I mean it," said Grundhauser.

"I agree, but we have a job to do. Maybe the cops here in the city know something about this guy. At least we should be able to go after the Bishop for aiding and abetting," Santini shot back.

"Are you kidding me? The Irish control things down here. They're thick as thieves. You think they're going to go after an Irish Bishop and an Irish priest? SHIT! You're dreaming!" Grundhauser ranted in disgust.

"Well I made a note of all the parishes where he was placed. Maybe if we nose around, we can get a lead on someone who popped off about this guy," Santini offered.

"Come on! Get real! They sent him all over the place, farther and farther away as time went on for almost twenty years! We're talking access to thousands of kids." Grundhauser scoffed. "Anyway, by the look of things somebody hired a pro to kill him. He could be in Jamaica by now. All we have is a faceless delivery man with a slight limp, which he may not even have anymore."

"You're right. Why should we care who did it anyway?" mused Santini. "It's bad enough when some old alcoholic uncle does this to a kid. Hell, every cop in the house lines up for tune-up duty. Then if he gets convicted, half the time the guards in prison look the other way, while the prisoners beat him to death. I just can't wrap my mind around a priest doing this."

There was no mention of Captain Finnegan bringing O'Malley to the Bishop three times. It had now been nearly three years since his last visit, when he delivered the ultimatum. Captain Finnegan was thankful and relieved, when he saw that O'Malley was dead. He had always beat himself up for his part in setting O'Malley free to molest again. The thought of it kept him up far too many nights seeking solace in a bottle of whiskey. Each time, the Bishop convinced him that the son-of-a-bitch would be locked away in some monastery. At the time he just could not conceive that a man of God would lie to him, and then let this fucker off to do it again.

Brendan had no clue that O'Malley was the reason for his nephew Michael losing his scholarship, leaving his wife and kids and nearly dying homeless and broken on the street. Brendan Finnegan had never married. He told everyone he was married to the job, because he loved being a policeman. He and his little sister Kathleen had always been close, and she asked him to be Michael's godfather. Brendan doted on him while he was growing up and made nearly all of Michael's high school football games.

A year after the killing, Brendan was at Kathleen and Patrick's house for a cook out. After everyone had gone home or to bed, Brendan and Kathleen sat up talking and reminiscing about their childhood. During a short break in the conversation, Brendan asked for the first time if she knew why Michael had the breakdown, and tearfully, she confided to her big brother what happened between Michael and O'Malley. She told him that O'Malley was the priest who was killed in the nursing home, and she was glad he was dead. Big brother Brendan gave her a long hug and told her how sorry he was.

The next day, at police headquarters, Captain Brendan Finnegan handed in his badge, filed his papers for his pension, and retired without warning or giving a reason. Everyone at his old precinct thought it odd that he left the job he loved so abruptly, but he told them he just had enough. He was never seen at the precinct house again. Over the next year, he came to family functions less and less, and eventually quit coming all together. Within two years of retiring, he was found dead in his home among dozens of empty whiskey bottles. There was no food in the fridge. Brendan Finnegan, brother, uncle and captain...just had enough.

At the beginning of December in 1977, the O'Tooles got word that Michael would be home for Christmas, and that he was going to stay home for good. Patrick, Kathleen, Iggy, Margaret Mary and eventually his younger brothers had been visiting on Tuesday evenings and Sundays for a few months. He had put on weight and was looking more like his old self. Most importantly, he was wearing that famous smile of his almost all the time. Margaret Mary kidded him by calling it the smile that made the girls at CYC dances swoon.

It had been about five months since O'Malley was killed, but Michael knew nothing about it, since he was sequestered in the hospital without access to a newspaper.

The plan was for Michael to stay with Margaret Mary for a while. Patrick told him that he had inquired at the union hall, and he could go back to work as a fitter whenever he wanted. Iggy gave him the use of his new Camaro, saying he would be fine driving his old pickup for a while. The truth was that Iggy bought the car just so Michael would have wheels when he got out. Kathleen was over the moon about having her whole brood home for Christmas.

Christmas Day was a glorious event at the house on Highmont. There were relatives dropping by day and night, giving envelopes full of cash to Patrick, for Michael. Grandma Bridgey had twisted the arms of every uncle, aunt and cousin within a hundred miles to help Michael get back on his feet. There was no alcohol served that Christmas, or ever again in the house on Highmont. Grandma Bridgey, and Grandma Maureen sat on either side of Michael on the couch, with their shoulders and hips against him, and each keeping a hand on his knee for hours. It was as though they thought he might float away if they moved.

Grandpa Jimmy bellowed that Michael was the safest man on earth. He said with all that padding around him he could survive a direct hit of a meteor from space. It was a good-natured jab directed at the size of the two ladies for sure, but it also was a declaration of how much they all wanted to protect him. Grandma Bridgey shot back with lightning speed, that Grandpa Jimmy wouldn't know a meteor if it hit him in the arse.

Grandpa Jimmy sat on a hard kitchen chair in front of Michael for a couple hours with their knees touching. He told him a host of jokes he had been saving up, making Michael laugh until his sides hurt. The two of them had traded jokes since Michael was a little boy. Humor was the place where they had always bonded.

Little by little over the years, most of the extended family would learn the reason for Michael's breakdown. They didn't get all the details, just enough to satisfy their curiosity. There's always a few booze hounds that talk too much, but for the most part, they kept that knowledge to themselves. There was an unspoken sense that they would all try to do their part to protect him now, since they were unable to protect him back then.

CHAPTER FORTY-TWO

The news of Michael's homecoming began to travel along the tavern to tavern circuit, with much speculation on where he had been and why. It was news because he had been so well known, due to his appearing in the papers for his athletic prowess. People always wondered why he never played for Notre Dame, came home, and then seemed to disappear. It's human nature to wonder and speculate, and there were literally hundreds of O'Toole's, O'Keefe's, Finnegan's and Fitzgerald's out there to ask.

For the most part, the extended family knew very little, and tried their best to deflect the questions, by shrugging and claiming ignorance, which was mostly true. Often they were told he had been molested, but the part about it being a priest was not shared with anyone. At this point in time, the thought that a priest could do such a thing was inconceivable.

In the months after O'Malley was murdered, detectives Grundhauser and Santini received a dozen or so calls, mostly anonymous, from men claiming that he had molested them when they were eleven, twelve and thirteen years-old. There were also a number of calls from women who either suspected, or knew, that their brothers or sons had been molested by O'Malley. The worst ones were the tearful accounts from the women whose sons and brothers had committed suicide, died of an overdose, or drank themselves to death as a result. Some of the callers said they were glad

O'Malley was dead, and some said they wished they had done it themselves.

Neither of the detectives had their heart in finding O'Malley's killer, as they felt it was good riddance, yet the stories surrounding this animal kept coming their way. The callers would be asked what parish the victim lived in, and what years the abuse took place. The dates always matched up perfectly with their notes from O'Malley's file concerning his assignments in the diocese. By the end of 1977, they had pretty much shelved the case. As they suspected in the beginning, there was no telling how many victims there were, and the number of potential suspects increased exponentially when you considered the number of friends and family members of the victims.

In February of 1978 they got a tip from the Clayton police. They had picked up a drug dealer who claimed to know who killed the priest in the nursing home. He was looking to make a deal to get his sentence reduced. Reluctantly, Santini and Grundhauser went to Clayton to interview him. The dealer, Freddy Banks, was best friends since childhood with a pipe fitter by the name of Sean Doherty.

He said Sean's son had been killed by a hit and run driver six months before, and Sean's life literally unraveled. His wife blamed him for the tragedy, because he wasn't watching the boy close enough while she was gone. She left with their other son, and Sean began to drink himself into a stupor every day. In one of his blackout binges, he told Freddy that another pipe fitter, a guy by the name of Iggy, had done the killing. When they asked where Sean lived, Freddy said he left town two months before, and he did not know where he went.

Good police work got them the full name of Iggy Mahoney from some fitters they knew. They got his address from the white pages and set about seeing if he was a victim or had ties to one of O'Malley's victims. Speaking to Iggy's friends, neighbors, and the patrons of several bars where Iggy hung out, they found that he grew up in Ferguson, attended Sts. John and James grade school and St. Thomas Aquinas High School.

Grundhauser had an aunt and uncle who had lived in in Sts.

John and James parish for decades, and they told him the story of Iggy being adopted by the O'Tooles. They also told him the sad story of how Michael O'Toole had been such a rising star and wound up in the mental hospital on Arsenal Street. The detectives' notes from his file, showed that O'Malley had been at their parish from 1962 to 1964. DMV records showed that Iggy and Michael would have been twelve to fourteen years-old at that time.

The detectives decided to stake out Iggy's apartment, just to get a look at him, and see if he came close to the description that the receptionist had given. Iggy got back to his apartment about 4:30 every evening. When he got out of his truck and started towards his building, he was walking with a noticeable limp. Santini and Grundhauser turned and looked at each other and grinned. He was also short and thin.

Iggy's hip made his limp much worse if he had been sitting for a long time, or if the weather was cold. This night, in late February, it was twenty-five degrees outside, and he had just driven forty-five minutes from work. Iggy had met Billy Boyle and Sean Doherty in warm weather after he had been walking a while already, so his limp wasn't so noticeable. They had both warned him, but the problem was that Iggy never gave his limp any thought at all.

The next day, the detectives hit some bars around Ferguson asking a lot of questions. They interviewed some friends of Grundhauser's aunt and uncle who lived near the O'Tooles in the Forestwood subdivision. It was clear that the rumor mill thought that Michael's problems may have been due to being molested, but nobody seemed to have a clue who had done it. The detectives went back to County Police headquarters in Clayton, and after running everything by their boss, they got the okay to pick Iggy up for questioning the next day.

When Iggy came out for work the next morning, the two detectives identified themselves, handcuffed him, and put him in the backseat of their car. They told him they would explain when they got to Clayton. Before he got in the car, Iggy gave his neighbor the O'Toole's home phone number, and told him to let them know what was happening. Kathleen called the construction trailer at Patrick's jobsite, told them it was an emergency, and that Patrick should call home immediately. The power of Irish geography was about to kick into high gear.

Patrick called his mother, Bridgey, and asked her to call her younger sister, Mary Margaret. Bridgey got Mary Margaret her first job in America as a maid in one of mansions in the central west end over fifty years before. Jimmy had gotten Mary Margaret's husband, Danny Feherty, a job as a hod carrier for the bricklayers when they got married. Danny and Mary Margaret had seven smart, courteous children, and the oldest was named Timothy.

Timothy got a scholarship to St. Louis University, went on to law school and graduated at the top of his class. He had an exceptionally sharp mind for legal details and was a gifted orator. In Timothy's world, they did not call it the gift of gab. He was one of the most sought-after criminal defense attorneys in the Midwest, because he rarely lost a case. Timothy Feherty wore Armani suits, silk ties and generally travelled about town in a chauffeured limousine. He was a brash, red-faced barrister with an unruly head of wavy silver hair. He was loved for his charitable nature, and his jovial manner. Timothy's parents were very proud of him.

Like any good Irish Catholic boy, when his mother called, he always stopped what he was doing and spoke with her. Right away, he knew something was wrong by her shaky voice. "Patrick and Kathleen's boy Iggy has been picked up and they don't know why. Bridgey is beside herself. She loves that boy. He's your second cousin for God's sake..."

"Mom, it's going to be alright, I promise. Did they say where they were taking him, or what they picked him up for?"

"He's going to Clayton, near your office. They don't know why they grabbed him. Dear Lord Timothy, can you get away?"

"I'm leaving right now, mom. Call aunt Bridgey and tell her it will be okay."

As he pulled on his suit coat, Timothy told his secretary to cancel his appointments and send the car around. They only had to go six blocks, but he knew the limo made a statement even before he entered a building. Timothy beat the detectives to the jailhouse because of morning rush traffic and set about winning over the cops at the front desk with his ribald jokes and laughter.

When the detectives pulled up to the jail entrance, the limo was in their way in front of the main doors, and the driver was reading the paper. After parking behind the limo, Grundhauser and Santini walked through the doors on each side of Iggy, who was still in cuffs. Even though they had never spoken, Iggy and Timothy recognized each other from weddings and funerals.

"Good morning Iggy!" Timothy bellowed, feigning more familiarity than there actually was.

"Morning Tim," Iggy said quietly, trying to process what he was seeing.

"Detectives, I'm here to represent Mr. Mahoney. If you don't have any objections, I would like a quick word with him before we proceed," Timothy told them while smiling warmly.

"I guess so," Santini mumbled, knowing full well that any chance of getting Iggy to incriminate himself just went out the window.

The detectives knew who Timothy Feherty was. Anyone who watched the evening news, would recognize his cheerful red face from the television interviews after getting one of his clients declared not guilty. But this didn't make sense. Why was a high-priced attorney like Feherty representing a gimpy construction worker who looked like he couldn't afford ten minutes of his time? Even more perplexing was how did Iggy Mahoney have enough clout to get Timothy Feherty to show up at a moment's notice?

Secure in an interview room, Timothy went right to work, the friendly charm gone for the moment. "Have you said anything to them?"

"No. Grandpa Jimmy always said don't speak if you get arrested."

"He's a smart man. Do you know why they picked you up?"

"No."

"Have they asked you any questions at all?"

"Yes. The one asked what parish I grew up in. He asked if I knew his aunt and uncle from Sts. John and James. He said he had friends in Forestwood."

"Did you say anything at all?"

"No. It seemed like they were letting me know, with the questions, that they knew all about me already."

"Alright, Wait here. Let's see what's going on." When Timothy stepped back into the hall to talk to the detectives, the cheerfulness was gone and he went on the offensive. "Gentlemen, could you please shed some light on why my client was brought here?"

They knew they had a loose connection tying Iggy to the murder, and now they knew Mr. Timothy Feherty was going to smell blood and cut that connection in two. "Do you remember that priest, O'Malley, that got murdered in that nursing home?" Santini asked him.

"Sure, I remember," Timothy answered.

"Well we started getting a lot of calls claiming the good father had molested them or their loved ones. He had been assigned to their parishes when they were kids. It seems he went after young boys, around twelve years-old."

"So, what does all this have to do with my client, Mr. Mahoney?"

"I'm getting there," barked Santini, already getting annoyed with the lawyer's attitude. "We thought that due to the nature of the murder, it may be a friend or family member of a victim, but there were a lot of victims. Then we got a tip from an informant that your client was the killer. We did some checking, and it turns out your client and his brother, Michael, were twelve to fourteen years old at the time O'Malley was at their parish. Then we found out that Michael had been hospitalized on Arsenal Street for nearly two years, and the rumor is that it was due to being molested."

"Is this an anonymous informant? Is he an eye witness of the crime?"

"Hang on, Mr. Feherty. There is an eye witness who described a man who entered the nursing home at the exact time of the murder. Her description matches your client, right down to his limp. Furthermore, your client called in sick on the day of the murder."

"First, does your informant have first person knowledge of the crime, or is this some desperate jailhouse snitch?" Timothy asked sharply.

"The informant was given this information by a man with first-hand knowledge, who is a pipe fitter, like your client."

"Where is this man?"

"We can't find him."

"Second, what exactly did your eyewitness say about the possible murderer?"

"She said she saw a short delivery man, with a thin build and a limp."

"So, she didn't see his face?"

"No."

Timothy Feherty was quite adept at interpreting body language, and these two detectives were clearly uncomfortable with the reliability of the evidence they had used to bring Iggy in for questioning. Without further ado, he went into his pompous "summation before the jury" mode for the detectives benefit.

"So, let me recap, and see if I have the facts straight. You have a dead priest who was at my client's parish fifteen years ago. You have a self-made theory for motive on why the priest was killed. My client's brother has been hospitalized as an adult, and you have a tavern rumor as to why he was there. My client and his brother happened to be twelve in 1962. You have a vague description of a delivery man, whose only crime was being in the nursing home.

"Now let's look at Mr. Mahoney, shall we. He has probably been accused by someone trying to get his sentence reduced, who got his information from someone you have never met, because he conveniently disappeared. As far as I can tell, his only crimes so far are calling in sick and walking with a limp. Also, I did not hear one word about any physical evidence at the scene. Did you just forget to mention it, or were you just saving it for later?"

"Look, we're just trying to do our job, Mr. Feherty. There's no reason to get cute. There's no jury to impress," Grundhauser remarked with a little anger attached.

"Just doing my job. Not trying to impress anyone," Timothy replied.

"I'm guessing your client won't be making a statement," Santini said sarcastically.

"You would have guessed correctly," Timothy grinned, his jovial nature returning.

After the detectives took the handcuffs off Iggy, he and Timothy walked outside to talk for a moment on the sidewalk. "So, what's going on? Why did they bring me in?" Iggy asked right away.

"Well, they wanted to question you about that priest who was killed in the nursing home a while back," Timothy told him matter-of-factly. "They said he was molesting children years ago and made a lot of enemies. Then they came up with some far-fetched theory about how you and Michael were at Sts. John and James when this O'Malley was there. Somebody gave them the idea that Michael's problems were related to being molested."

"But why would they think I did it?" Iggy asked.

"Because somebody told them you did it. It was a jailhouse snitch who claimed a pipe fitter told him it was you. But they can't find the guy."

"Holy shit," Iggy said quietly, hardly believing Sean would do that.

"Nothing to worry about. Even if he exists and they find him, he'll never admit to the cops to being part of some murder scheme. Anyway, they have absolutely no physical evidence. All they know is that a thin delivery man with a limp came in the nursing home. They also claim you took off work on the day in question," Timothy said.

To himself, Iggy was thanking Billy Boyle for suggesting he call the doctor and get a prescription the day in question. "Man, oh man, this is crazy, wild stuff."

"I wouldn't give it another thought Iggy. They're grasping at straws."

"I can't thank you enough Timothy. Just send me the bill."

"Happy to help. No way I charge family in a situation like this. Anyway, it looks like you already lost a day's pay. I know the old man used to have a fit if it rained and they couldn't lay brick. He'd have to sit home and not get paid. Listen, my office is just up the street, so I'm going to walk back to work. I'll have my driver take you home. What a great country, huh? Leave home in a cop car in cuffs and come back in a limo!"

"No shit. Thanks Timothy, that's really nice of you," Iggy grinned, while shaking his hand.

"Help yourself to the snacks and beer in the fridge, Iggy," Timothy smiled, as he walked away. He got a kick out of Iggy offering to pay, as it would probably be a whole week's paycheck for him. Anyway, Timothy knew if his mom and dad found out he charged Iggy, there would be hell to pay, he laughed to himself. Without aunt Bridgey having brought his mom to America and getting her a job, and without uncle Jimmy getting his dad in the bricklayer's union, I might not even be here. Hell, not just here, but living in grand style, he smiled.

Timothy had to admit, it seemed like the police had stumbled on to something though. He knew about Michael's issues, but not that it had been a priest. Jesus, no wonder it fucked him up he mused. That would fuck with anybody's head. If it was true that O'Malley molested Michael, he knew the O'Tooles were definitely capable of going after him. His dad told him stories about Uncle Jimmy that would curl your hair, and he heard about how Patrick had damn near killed Iggy's father.

Now here's Iggy getting accused of killing this fucking pervert. It wasn't unthinkable. All he knew, was that he didn't want to know. Ironically, Kathleen's family was steeped in the law and order business. Nowadays, the Finnegan's and Fitzgerald's had countless family members in the fire department, on the police force, working as public defenders, prosecutors, and of course, politicians.

As he sat down to eat lunch that day, at a fine restaurant, with white linen tablecloths and a hundred-dollar bottle of wine, Timothy Patrick Feherty couldn't help but smile at how well Irish tribal bonds had worked that day. It also made him think of his father's favorite joke that he shared with an attorney from another firm who joined Timothy at the table for lunch. When the time was right he asked his guest, 'Do you know why God created booze?' just like he asked other unsuspecting pawns a thousand times before. They always replied 'no' and then Timothy would burst out laughing that, 'it was to keep the Irish from taking over the whole fucking world!'

CHAPTER FORTY-THREE

In April of 1978, four months after he came home to live with Margaret Mary, Michael returned to work as a pipe fitter. He enjoyed the comradery of the other men, and there was the feeling of accomplishment associated with building something you could look back on at the end of the day.

He wanted very much to have some sort of relationship with his daughters, but he was aware they didn't know him at all, and it would take time. He was thankful that the rest of the family had kept up their relationship with Janet and the kids. As soon as possible, he started sending child support money to Janet, to try and catch up on what he owed them. Michael knew it would take more time than money to build any trust in his relationship with Janet.

Janet had married a nice guy by the name of Joe Redding, who turned out to be a great husband and father. Nora was nine and Maura was eight now. Joe and Janet also had two boys of their own who were now five and three, and they still lived in the Forestwood subdivision, on Bayview Dr, just a few blocks from the house on Highmont. Patrick and Kathleen could not have been happier that their granddaughters were so close. The girls attended Sts. John and James, just as their dad, aunt and uncles had done.

In late May, Nora was going to celebrate her Confirmation, and everyone agreed it would be a terrific opportunity for Michael to begin to get involved in the girls lives. Having the whole family around would help with the awkward silences that would normally accompany a reunion like this.

The Confirmation was to be held at the St Louis Cathedral for four parishes from north St. Louis County. The newly appointed

Cardinal Patrick Shaughnessy would be confirming all the children, on the last Friday in May at 7:00 p.m. His Eminence, the Cardinal, had overseen the diocese for over twenty years now, and had just celebrated his seventieth birthday. Formerly, the only people who knew of the Cardinal's role in enabling O'Malley's sick activities, were Detectives Santini and Grundhauser. Recently though, Jimmy and Bridgey O'Toole also found out about the instrumental part he had played in helping O'Malley molest Michael and many other children.

They got the information from Bridgey's cousin Eileen, just a few months before. Eileen was dying of cancer, and since she didn't have a husband or children, Bridgey moved in to help care for her near the end. It may have been the effect of the pain medication lowering her inhibitions, or just a need to unburden herself before she passed away, but one morning she told Bridgey everything she had seen in O'Malley's file.

She told Bridgey how then Bishop Shaughnessy, had repeatedly moved O'Malley from parish to parish for close to eighteen years, enabling him to molest more little boys everywhere he went. She told her this was the reason she had retired so abruptly from working at the Bishop's residence. After reading the file, Eileen said she couldn't even stand the sight of the man.

Bridgey went home and told Jimmy what Eileen told her. They both sat at the kitchen table wondering how their beloved Bishop, now promoted to Cardinal, could have been a part of something so evil. Jimmy asked if Eileen was out of her head with pain or drugs, and Bridgey told him that she was her normal self, speaking calmly and clearly.

On the big night, Nora wore a beautiful green dress which made her hair look even redder than it was. Her mom bought her new black patent leather shoes and put green ribbons in her hair. Her

Irish eyes were smiling. She was also excited to tell everyone that Bishop Shaughnessy had just been made a Cardinal, so she was going to be confirmed by a Cardinal!

There were going to be about thirty family members at the cathedral to see her confirmed. The rules said they were only allowed ten guests but everyone agreed that this was a big night not just for Nora, but for Michael as well. Margaret Mary had been asked to be her sponsor. She gave Nora the beautiful rosary that she had gotten on her Confirmation. Sometime in the future, she would find out that it was the exact same rosary as her father's. That would make the gift even more special, giving Nora and Michael a unique bond.

Grandma Maureen, Kathleen's eighty-year-old mother was there, announcing that this was the thirtieth Confirmation she had attended for her grandchildren. Maureen was still spry enough to walk down the long aisle of the Cathedral, but Bridgey, now seventy-seven, had to use a walker. Seventy-eight-year-old Jimmy was now relegated to a wheel chair for this type of event. The three of them sat near the front so they could see and hear clearly.

As the procession of children passed by the O'Toole clan on their way to the altar, where his Eminence Cardinal Patrick Shaughnessy awaited them, a half dozen hands reached out to pat the smiling Michael on his shoulders. A dozen more relatives turned to wink or nod at him. It was a sweet way to welcome Michael back into the fold once again. As the outpouring of love showered down on her oldest son, Kathleen quietly started to cry tears of joy from a few rows behind him. She bowed her head and thanked the Blessed Mother, who she had prayed to daily for her son's return. Patrick watched what was going on around Michael and felt he could not have been prouder of his family than he was at this very moment.

When the service was over, Cardinal Shaughnessy, in his new red hat, led the procession of newly confirmed Catholic boys and girls, and their sponsors, out the massive doors at the back of the Cathedral. There was a huge oak chair, like a throne, with red crushed velvet upholstery waiting for him outside, since he was no longer able to stand the length of time necessary to greet all the children and their families. There was definitely a regal aura around the Cardinal, as people bent to speak to him, congratulate him and kiss his ring.

The O'Toole's congregated at the bottom of the stone Cathedral steps, congratulating Nora, and telling Maura she would be up there next year. To one side Michael was shaking hands with Joe Redding, and giving Janet a quick hug, while Margaret Mary and Iggy looked on. Others were arguing over where they should go to eat, but most were just catching up on the precious details of each other's lives.

Grandma Bridgey and Grandpa Jimmy were among the last to exit the mammoth doorway, because of how slow they moved. Grandma Bridgey shuffled toward the Cardinal in her walker, with her rosary dangling from one hand. Grandpa Jimmy was next to her, slowly pushing the wheels of his chair.

As they approached the Cardinal's throne, Nora called out from the bottom of the steps, "Grandma, hurry up! We're waiting to take pictures!"

"I'll be there in just a moment, child!" Grandma Bridgey called back, raising her hand with her forefinger extended in the air.

Cardinal Shaughnessy leaned forward like he was about to get off his throne, but Bridgey pushed her walker in front of him, and stated in her most beautiful, lilting, Irish brogue, "Wasn't it a beautiful service, your Eminence?"

"It was indeed. I believe I hear the sound of my homeland in your voice young lady," the Cardinal smiled. He had worked hard to lose his own brogue years before.

"And don't you look grand in your new red hat!" Bridgey exclaimed, while smiling broadly. "I'll bet your mother and father are so proud, looking down on you from the heavens, as we speak."

"Thank you, darling. I'm sure they are, too," the Cardinal grinned.

"And with such a gorgeous evening. We're so blessed aren't we your Eminence?"

"God's gifts abound for his people," replied the Cardinal. "But if you don't mind, I need to get going because..."

Bridgey had pushed the walker forward enough so she could put her hand on the Cardinal's arm which was resting on the arm of the chair. Then she bent forward and did the same with her other hand on his other arm. This allowed her to put much more of her weight on his arms, both to hold herself steady and to hold him in place. She got her face so close to his, that he could smell the onion on her breath from dinner. She made eye contact with him, squinted slightly, and spoke to him quietly through slightly clenched yellow teeth.

"I must say just one more thing before you go. I'm concerned for your safety your Eminence. You know they never caught that ruthless priest killer. He's still out there, and for all we know, he's waiting for his chance to kill again. Rumor has it that the dead priest... now what was his name...hmmm...O'Malley...that's right...was a child molester. Maybe that's why he got his throat cut. But who knows what a murdering maniac like that is thinking? Nevertheless, it would probably be best if you slept with one eye open, though, if you know what I mean."

Those who were watching the exchange, saw the Cardinal's eyes pop wide open, and his head snap back against his throne. Those who weren't watching could not miss the wild, loud cackling laughter that came out of Jimmy's mouth. A hundred heads turned to see what the noise was all about.

Some saw Cardinal Shaughnessy, walking faster than he had in years, towards the entrance to the Cathedral. The young priest with him had to run to get ahead and hold the door for him. Others just saw an old lady shuffling behind a walker, and an old man pushing his wheel chair, slowly making their way to the handicap ramp. As they started down the ramp, they saw the old lady's face was flushed, and the old man was smiling from ear-to-ear.

By this time, the whole clan of O'Toole's, was making their way to the bottom of the ramp. When Grandpa Jimmy and Grandma Bridgey finally got to the bottom, Patrick's brother Liam called out, "Mom, what did you say to the Cardinal?"

His daughter Colleen blurted, "Grandma, he looked like he saw a ghost or something."

Patrick came over and added, "Mom for God's sake, it looked like you scared the hell out of the poor man." Then turning to his father, "And why would that be funny! The whole crowd heard you!"

"How about you all just mind your own 'fookin' business!" smiled Grandpa Jimmy.

"What kind of a way is that to talk on the Cathedral steps," Kathleen scolded as she got closer to hear what was going on. "In front of your grandchildren, too!"

Grandma Bridgey added, "Why don't you all go out there on Lindell Avenue, and play in the traffic? Maybe we'll get lucky!" That sent both Grandpa Jimmy and Grandma Bridgey into raucous laughter, tilting their heads back and holding their sides. This was the irreverent way that the two of them used to tell their large brood to go outside years ago, when it seemed there were too many kids, in too small a house, on too hot a day.

The thirty or so members of the family were looking at Jimmy and Bridgey, then at each other, trying to figure out what the hell was going on. At that moment, Jimmy O'Toole slowly rose out of the wheel chair, and turned towards Bridgey. Gently, he rolled her walker out of his way, and stepped so close to her that their stomachs were touching.

Slowly he put one of his crooked hands on each side of her face, looked in her eyes, and then loud enough for the whole family to hear, told her, "Bridgey O'Keefe, I love you with my whole heart and soul, and you're still the most beautiful woman I ever laid eyes on."

As Bridgey's bottom lip started to quiver, Jimmy slowly put his left hand in the small of her back and slid his right hand around the back of her neck and buried his fingers in her hair. He leaned towards her, and just as softly and tenderly as the very first time, fifty-six years before, on the altar at St. James the Greater, he kissed his bride.

Epilogue

May the Road Rise Up to Meet You

OCTOBER 18, 1994; 3:05 PM

After Margaret Mary got in her car, and turned the key, she sat for a moment and got one last look at the beautiful setting in front of her. It was no wonder Michael loved it here. Worthington College was a small liberal arts school, in rural Southern Illinois. He completed his PhD the year before and was now working as an assistant professor of psychology.

Michael's specialty, and the area in which he most gifted, was individual counseling. His time with Dr. Goldstein inspired him to become a compassionate and dedicated instructor, in a field he credited for saving his life. He went to school nights and weekends for eight years to get his Bachelor's and Master's degrees, before quitting his job as a pipe fitter, to study and research full time for his PhD.

Slowly, Margaret Mary made her way through this peaceful, idyllic college town, wishing she didn't have to leave. She was thinking back to when she visited Michael once a week in the hospital, when the only thing she wanted in the whole world, was for him to walk and speak again. These days she travelled an hour each way to visit him once a week in his third story office, at this beautiful institution he now called home. He had come so far, that sometimes even he felt the need to pinch himself to believe it was true. As Margaret Mary sped up the ramp to get on the highway and head home, she started to smile, then giggle, then laugh out loud again at what happened that morning.

When she entered the lobby of the administration building, around eleven, she said hello to the young blonde-haired blue-eyed male student at the desk, and signed in. "Is Professor O'Toole in his office," she asked politely as she had many times before.

"Well he may or may not be in his office, because I am no longer going to bother about his comings and goings," he said, raising his eyebrows and tapping the desk rapidly with his pen. He was clearly not happy about something Michael had done or failed to do.

She was taken aback, because the students here always seemed so courteous, clean-cut and helpful. She read his name tag, Chip Johnson, which was directly above the Ralph Lauren Polo emblem on his shirt. "Well Chip, I'm sorry you feel that way. I'm Professor O'Toole's sister. Can I ask what upset you?"

"Well, early this morning, around eight o'clock, a new black Cadillac pulled up out front in the no parking zone. A short thin man in a suit got out and walked in the front door. I said, 'excuse me, can I help you' and he just looked at me with this crooked eye and said, 'no thanks Chippy'. He really was sarcastic in the way he said it too!"

"Did he sign in?" Margaret Mary smiled, even though she had a pretty good idea who it was. Iggy had been elected to be a business agent for the pipe fitters, and they all drove black Cadillacs. The comment about his eye sealed the deal.

"As he was walking, or more correctly, limping past me, I told him he was in a no parking zone, and that he needed to move his car, then come back and sign in. Do you know what he said? 'Don't get your pretty underwear in a bunch junior, I'll be right back.' I could not believe how rude this man was," Chip huffed, as he folded his arms across his chest.

Margaret Mary was on the verge of laughing, so she turned away for a moment to collect herself. When she turned back she kept her hand over her mouth so Chip would not see how close she was to laughing. She was visualizing Iggy pissing this kid off. He couldn't stand people like this. Chip was everything that Iggy wasn't: a clean-cut, good looking college kid that followed the rules. "So, was he here for Professor O'Toole?"

"Oh yes. And a big part of my job is to have the staff sign in and out. That way we always know if a professor is available when a student stops by, or if someone like yourself walks in, we can tell you when he left and where he went. Anyway, Professor O'Toole and that nasty man came down the stairs ten minutes later. I asked the professor very politely, where he was going, and what time did he expect to return. Do you want to hear what that creepy little man said to me? He said, 'Hey junior, why don't you mind your own fookin business'."

As soon as he said it, Margaret Mary busted out laughing. She tried to compose herself, but it was no use. She was laughing so hard she needed a tissue off the desk to wipe her eyes. "I'm sorry Chip, I just couldn't..."

"Then Professor O'Toole starts laughing out loud, like he just heard the funniest joke in the world," Chip added, while looking at her wide-eyed.

"I'm really sorry for laughing, Chip I just think..." That was as far as she could get, and then the image of Michael and Iggy walking by this kid would hit her...How different their lives had been from his... what they had been through...poor Chip, in his polite, vanilla world, coming face to face with his polar opposite, Iggy, in his rough and tumble, never a dull moment world. She just couldn't stop laughing.

"I really don't see the humor!" Chip told her, a little louder.

Barely containing herself, she tried again, "You see, my grandfather used to say that to people all the time, and..." It was no use, she lost it again and laughed so loud that people were starting to stare.

"Well laugh if you like, but I don't appreciate being talked to like that!" barked Chip. "And I don't believe for a minute that anyone's grandfather would EVER use language like that. I mean what grandfather talks like that?" On that note Chip had enough and stormed right out the front door.

Margaret Mary made her way over to the elevator, and then to the third floor to see her big brother. Her visit with Michael turned out to be a laugh fest as they reminisced and told stories about the exploits of their numerous unique and irreverent relatives. In the end, they both agreed that Chip was due a formal apology, and a nice gift.

Margaret Mary stood at one point, and using her best upper crust voice imitation, said, “MY GOOD MAN, you’re in the stuffy world of academia now, and you had better start acting the part.”

“I agree emphatically, DAHLING!” Michael shot back with the same tone.

Back and forth it went for a couple of hours, with both of them offering up images of what it would be like if some of their more “colorful” relatives met Chip. They both agreed that compared to life with their tribe, Chip may just as well have come from another planet.

Margaret Mary added, “You know I asked our cousin Tim Feherty one time, what it was like to be in a palatial office with a bunch of Ivy Leaguers one minute, and then go back home to have dinner with the wild bunch. You know, with all those boozy bricklayer brothers of his telling dirty jokes, and farting at the dinner table. He said he feels like Jekyll and Hyde sometimes, but he wouldn’t trade his time with his family for all the money in the world.”

“No kidding. You know what dad said all the time, ‘get used to them, because you can pick your friends, but you can’t pick your relatives’,” Michael laughed.

On the highway, Margaret Mary rolled down the window of her car, felt the chilly air, and hung her wild red mane out the window for a moment before rolling it back up. She turned on her radio, and happily tuned in to her favorite station KSHE 95. She shivered, as immediately the words of her favorite song poured out of the speakers. It was Dylan’s voice, singing *Shelter From the Storm*. His poetry had spoken so clearly to her, and gave her such hope, when

Michael was laying in that hospital somewhere between life and death.

In a little hilltop village, they gambled for my clothes
I bargained for salvation, and they gave me a lethal dose
I offered up my innocence, and got repaid with scorn
"Come in," she said, "I'll give you, shelter from the storm"

Well I'm living in a foreign country, but I'm bound to cross the line
Beauty walks a razor's edge, someday I'll make it mine
If I could only turn back the clock, to when God and her were born
"Come in," she said, "I'll give you, shelter from the storm"

As the song ended, her face was wet with joy. She felt God's love deep within her being, in the place the sisters had called her soul.

She felt its buoyancy. She felt its bliss. She felt its warmth. She felt its kindness. She felt its security.

It was real. It was all she would ever need.

9 781977 207562